QUANTA CHRONICLES
BOOK III

EMERGENT

B.A. CRISP

NAPLES, FL   WASHINGTON, D.C   OXFORD, U.K.

Book III of the Quanta Chronicles Series

The characters and events in this book are fictitious. Any similarity to real persons, living or dead, is coincidental and not intended by the publisher.

2Portal Publishing

620 Herndon Parkway Suite 120A

Herndon, VA 20170

The publisher is not responsible for websites (or their content) that are not owned by the publisher.

Editors: Michael Waitz & Tyler Thorpe

Cover/interior by Ashley Ruggirello/www.cardboardmonet.com

2 Portal Publishing provides this author for speaking engagements. To learn more, please email: dcrisp@2portalpublishing.com

Library of Congress Cataloging—in—Publication Data

Crisp, BA

Emergent (book title): BA Crisp.—First Edition Series Book III Quanta Chronicles

ISBN 978-1-7343087-3-0 (paperback) 978-1-7343087-4-7 (e-book).

1. Supernatural—Sci Fiction.

2. Adventure—Fiction. 3. Coming of Age—Sci—Fiction. 4. Self-Realization —Fantasy

Fiction. LCCN: 2022923953

In Memory of Sgt. Linda Pierre
KIA
April 16, 2011
Forward Operating Base Gamberi,
Nangarhar Province, Afghanistan

ACKNOWLEDGMENTS

To Autumn V.
For strength, courage, and grace under fire. A warrior of
compassion, inspiration, and love

To Chef Greg & Monika
For your friendship, help, and inspiration

To Sharon, Steve, & Melissa
For shelter and peace post hurricane

For the beings who feel alone and forgotten on this remote
planet:
You're not. We're here.

"In the councils of government, we must guard against the acquisition of unwarranted influence, whether sought or unsought, by the military-industrial complex. The potential for the disastrous rise of misplaced power exists and will persist."
—Dwight D. Eisenhower

"All matter originates and exists only by virtue of a force... We must assume behind this force the existence of a conscious and intelligent Mind. This Mind is the matrix of all matter."—**Max Planck**

ABOUT THE AUTHOR

B.A. Crisp is a best-selling author. Mr. Mew, her covert ops cat, remains unimpressed. Crisp's portfolio includes working as an egregiously underpaid advisor for private contractors, nonprofits, and public sector agencies, providing research, strategic intelligence, and analysis on matters of national security and human rights. Notably, she also worked as a Psychiatric Assessment Specialist for a major metropolitan hospital. Crisp earned degrees from Ursuline College, graduating Summa cum Laude, and The George Washington University's Graduate School of Political Management, earning a valedictorian distinction. She attended the London School of Journalism and the University of Oxford, Exeter College. When she isn't working or writing, she hides out at defunct missile silos, adores her friends and family, waxes philosophic after too many dirty martinis, and explores the unknown with insatiable curiosity.

PROLOGUE

EYES ONLY

JOURNAL ENTRY #1:
DECEMBER 3, 1993

MY DEAREST CELESTRIAL,

If these words are read, we've failed, and the worlds I've known, irretrievable.

As part of a hybrid, human, and otherworldly collective, we are bound by ancient oaths and brought together on Earth to reign in multiple strands of chaos, to save an infinite number of lives both here and *beyond*.

I've lived predominately detached from every incarnation previously fitted around my consciousness, centuries of unique existences briefly led and extinguished through quick swipes of death. Typically, I have no memory of my former lives, but this time, it's eerily different. I recall them all. The line between my copious birth and death dates holds a myriad of interplanetary mothers and secrets within short but simple dashes. These memories, I pray, will sustain me throughout infinite inanimation —if this be my fate. But it's other important things I now struggle to remember. Like passwords and portals.

As I review my pasts, I realize how subtle the influences that shape every destiny, even ones like mine, which morph through multiple embodiments, and at times, questionable choices. Fragments of former incarnations rise like cinders through my awareness. Orphan. Foster child. Hybrid experiment. Celestrial. Human trafficking survivor. CIA case officer. Celestrial. Hybrid. Warrior. Mother. Valkyrie.

Me.

A mom.

In this life, my daughter's name is Hope. It's a first for me to be a mother in semi-human form. Hope is seven months old Earth time. We've never met.

Creating a human-hybrid child was not part of my objective and Hope isn't naturally made. In Earth year 1985, I was the adolescent victim of a fallopian egg heist when unacknowledged factions of the US government discovered I'm not entirely human and possessed of BOUO (Blood of Unknown Origin). A doctor stored some of my half-human *eggs* during experimental testing. In 1992, she inserted a Source Bearer's sperm into a surrogate. The child was later stolen and remains MIA.

My existence in this realm, like my daughter's, is forbidden and unexpected. My father, a Camaeliphim and Balancer for the Source, violated intergalactic protocol when he fell in love with my human mother. I was naturally-un-naturally conceived, which no one thought possible. My parents tried, unsuccessfully, to hide me in American foster care on this planet when they fled. I suppose they hoped I'd fall through bureaucratic cracks, get lost, and lead a normal *human* life. But the Ormian Council found me. It grudgingly opened a small rip in the universe to restore some of my memories. The Council is riding a sliver of probability that I might serve as a backup Balancer for my AWOL father.

Being hybrid unduly complicates both my cosmic and Earthly obligations. I never know who's telling the truth, wielding hidden agendas, or where, exactly, I belong. Consequently, I look human enough to pass on Earth and just hybrid enough that I must conceal highly specialized skills. Some humans consider me an "*angel*". This isn't *exactly* the case. Fortunately, most humans fail to recognize what stands before them. If they did, I think it would unduly '*freak them out*', provided I'm not covertly netted again for *further study*.

Only Silent Secreters—humans with clandestine cosmic clearances—are "read into" mysteries kept from the general population. Here's one: Sentience on this planet gives life to the Source—not the other way around. Without human *observers*, the Source scatters, and matter fails. Humans *feel, create,* and give credence to all "reality." It oozes through the energy produced in their biological containers. This energy, positive or negative, turns undefined *spooky action at a distance* into breathtaking or heartbreaking substance. *Us. Them.* And "*it.*"

Everything seen, heard, smelled, tasted, thought, or felt comes to life because humans give it existence by *just being.* Human consciousness is an antenna that drives frequencies and vibrations into thoughts, which turns energy into action that often manifests into matter. The Source is a loop wave of expression driven by communication and creativity; its energy considered neither *good* nor *bad* but transformative. It's the vibrations that can be lower (negative) or higher (positive). Hence me, the Balancer, much to everyone's (even my own) surprise and chagrin.

Here's another secret: Energy on this planet should be free. Organized opposition controls the limits of the human mind and its energy. While being human is a hugely precious gift—it's also a fleeting mirage, a phantasm of collapsible photons made manifest, one deeply and sometimes, I think, inhumanely controlled—by those with clearances so deep they make the Mariana Trench look like a kiddie pool.

What most humans don't realize is that away from Earth, seasons and time do not exist the way humans recognize such. Time is collectively agreed to by humans who give it a measurement to make sense of and organize this world—just like their religion and monetary systems. Most of these constructs—time, money, religion, politics, run on lower vibrations disguised as faith, beauty, Truth, or knowledge. This engineered stratagem is a contrivance to severely control human populations and perception, internal wealth, external existence, and to increase fear.

A concrete definition of consciousness is also beyond human comprehension. It appears as a hazy concept of semi-awareness, never fully grasped because it isn't found inside the human brain. It resides all around. Some of my kind feel it's *time* (pun intended) that humans are made privy to cosmic secrets and otherworldly visitors. Others disagree and find humans quite primitive, repulsive, and predictable, unready for such high-powered knowledge.

Secret number three is that humans have more power than they realize. Their complexity sparks trillions of invisible photonic tendrils to help Earth guard the gate to multiple worlds, including a parallel one I once knew and deeply miss. And the Source uses this energy in unison with neutrinos—a perfectly tuned choir, to keep the entire multiverse in harmony on a major filament of Superposition.

When those of my kindred, Camaeliphim, first learned about this planet, we helped other worldly beings tend Earth as a universal repository, a sort of seed bank, to guard diversity eons before what humans think of as, *The Beginning*. Improvements to this planet and its biological entities were made using epigenetics and other advanced technologies beyond human comprehension.

Earth, as humans call it, is our best experiment and our grandest failure. Humans aren't the enlightened stewards we expected. They notoriously and constantly disrupt cosmic balance. But this isn't entirely their fault. The human appetite for opportunism, its affinity for distraction, along with an almost insatiable desire for instant gratification, are helped along by subatomic particle bits known as Bezaliels.

Bezaliels comingle like schools of fish and hitch onto other dimensions in hyperspace, riding interdimensional currents. They jump off entangled strings of warped space for planetary visits when skittishly low vibrations attract them.

Bezaliels latch onto sentients as springboards to solidified evolution—a chance to take form—like a parasite. This enables insatiable spontaneous consumption and complete resource depletion of the human container. Sadly, Bezaliels recently broke the barrier of alternate reality—where things, highly strange things—now slip through parallel universes, into this four-dimensional world. This deeply confuses humans. But it makes hybrids and other non-terrestrials uneasy too.

The Astral Weavers, guardians of Ninmah's Portal, do their best to make repairs in the rips of space and shove things that shouldn't be here back where they belong. Ours is a thankless job. We have more than our share of work.

A race for continued existence drives my team deep into Earth's arteries, to find missing pieces of a code. The cryptograph we seek once belonged to a celestrial named Nikola Tesla. It was stolen from the US Pentagon and taken to the Cave of Seven Sleepers, allegedly near, or *under*, Jordan. The majority of humans on this planet are oblivious to this dire cosmic situation at the insistence of world leaders who remain at the mercy of the Ormian Council.

We could raise human vibration, I think, if we told humans

what was at stake—their lives and this planet—but earthly and Ormian factions believe cosmic disclosure only serves to set off massive human panic and/or breed rebellion. It is my opinion that their secrecy is more about control maintenance and retaining power structures than it is about preventing hysteria.

Most humans without a *need-to-know* are led to purchase worthless trinkets, texts, and useless potions to make them believe enlightenment is only a keystroke, pill, or conceit away. Still others, prodded through effectively placed propaganda, eschew alternate realities and otherworldly visitors as the stuff of conspiracy theorists and loonies. I struggle with whether to reveal our celestrial and interdimensional secrets. If I do, I risk being infinitely inanimated for treason. I think human blindness harms humans more than it helps them—but I'm certainly in the minority.

Here in the caverns under the Wadi Sura Plateau, I feel this planet's pain. It roams throughout dark chambers and slithers its way into rocky veins and mineral-hardened arteries. It occasionally spews gasps of disappointment. Sometimes I imagine the ground trembles with regret or purposely causes waves to rise in anger. These days, clouds bitterly cry, and trees wilt in sadness. Every sentient thing on this planet, humans aside, senses this retreat of connection—and on some level realizes that nothing will remain without intervention. How casually blind most humans are to this reticent despair. Again, not entirely their fault.

It won't be easy for my team to locate Tesla's lost file in such a sad underground labyrinth. But we need to find the code and throw Raga, the lead Bezaliel, into the Source Vortex. If this isn't enough, our quest includes finding a host of missing star seeds sold into slavery on the underground Tar market.

My eye necklace offers just enough light to write without disturbing my team, a collection of some of Earth's finest men and women, hybrids, and celestrials. In this case, technology does have advantages—yet I know even the best intentions are no match for random quantum fury.

Salima Heminzen,
    Exp. 001 Dr. Samantha Ryan Blake, Exobiologist
    Aka Princess Scathatch

ONE

SELECTED

TOMORROW IS the beginning of a deadly or delightful day, a sojourn of compromises or ultimatums, trust, or treachery, and hopefully, no corpses.

I put away my maps.

Kitsune, my soul guide, snuggles her soft fox fur against my legs before pouncing off to chase after a golden spiny mouse.

Tonight's shelter is a football-field-size cave, which contains over 5,000 paintings, some human-looking, some not, created more than twenty-thousand years ago. Scientists believe the red, white, and black pigment stenciled hands accompanying the paintings, "differ significantly in size, proportion, and morphology from human hands."

Dr. Kimathi, the archaeologist on our team, feels the use of these colors is an attempt by some unknown class of humans to summon mystical powers, perhaps protection, or esoteric knowledge. But I know better.

Many of the strange beasts were, she says, intentionally disfigured or purposely erased in prehistoric times. She doesn't know why. Always surrounded by humanoid-looking creatures, these drawings hold my attention due to their size and shape, having long tails and human-like legs. Even headless, they appear to spit out or swallow humans. Others are trapped in nets of gold. If it weren't for the tails, I'd think the strange creatures were Usta —but Usta, as far as I know, don't behead, or consume humans— vaporize them yes, but eat them, no.

"Just for your SA (situational awareness), we've got uninvited visitors coming over the ridge," Master Sergeant Hogan says when he slips into the cave.

"Who?" Reggie asks.

"Hell, if I know," Hogan says. He tosses a weapon to a nearby operator. "But they sure as shit don't look human."

"I told ya, mate," Dr. Monica says. "We shoulda' made camp at the Cave o' Swimmers instea'." She picks up her weapon and heads outside with our team of special forces. She's not wrong, I think. The Cave of Swimmers depicts serene beings with wings. It feels far more inviting and much less creepy.

Dust swirls and retreats along the plateau, a desolate section of the Sahara, close to the Libyan border. A multitude of hazy bobbing forms appears on otherworldly horseback, their bluish skin, red hair, and copper armbands coming into focus as they barrel toward us on iridescent silver mounts. "It's Lozen," I say. I wave and signal my team to stand down. I don't need to worry about the twenty Sherpas behind us, who not unexpectedly bow in reverence toward the Astral Weavers, having known of them for centuries through the oral stories of their people from as far away as Tibet.

"What the fuck is a Lozen?" Master Sergeant Hogan asks, M4 assault rifle laser pointed at my friend's cranial vault.

"She's an ally," I say. "That's her name. And I'd lower your weapon if I were you."

"She sure as shit don't look human," he says again, spitting a chunk of slimy tobacco juice at a nightjar nesting nearby, one that squawks in protest. "None of 'em look human. What the hell are they?"

"Beyond human," I say. "You might want to lower your—" And before I finish, Lozen kneels on Hogan's chest. His gun is at least ten yards away from his feet, while the tip of her tantalum spear teases pressure on a vulnerable, pulsing artery in his neck.

Stuck in the middle of this unexpected standoff with Reggie, between Lozen's unit, and my team, they raise weapons against one another, distrust permeating the air thicker than a sudden, unexpected sandstorm. If Lozen chooses, she can flash-broil Hogan into a lump of overcooked carcass and take down the rest of his unit too.

"Oh, sweet Jesus," Barbara interrupts, making the sign of the cross. She exits the cave entrance where she's been cooking dinner. She's armed with a large olive wood cooking spatula Nimbu gave her. "Put away your toys and come eat, there's plenty for everyone." She looks down at Lozen. "Get off that man!"

Without warning, a chilly gust of wind pushes its way through the camp, almost knocking Barbara off her feet. She squints and briefly gazes upward, a look of distress settling into scrunched forehead lines. She makes the sign of the cross and stands a little straighter, refusing, I think, to back down from the sudden wind or this impromptu standoff. When the wind abruptly subsides, Barbara slides a free finger through a loose orange-silver tendril of hair and slips it back behind her left ear.

Her eyes leave Lozen to scan the small crowd of warriors. "Drop 'em!" she yells, wildly waving her spoon like a conductor's baton and using a drill sergeant's voice—except she isn't one. She used to be my foster mom. Weapons lower. "That's better. Now, come get some stew." She waddles back to the cave, thighs banging together, muttering under her breath.

Reggie and I lift eyebrows in each other's direction.

"Does Barbara know about Astral Weavers?" I ask.

"If she does, she never told me," Reggie says.

"If she doesn't, she never flinched," I say, wondering where Miss Barbara, as we call her, summoned enough bravery to enter a potential bloody line of fire and then single-handedly abort a gunfight with a wooden spatula. Barbara's a self-described Christian woman, who prefers her Bible over battle. So, why she didn't take one look at the Astral Weavers, douse them with holy water, and run screaming, rosary in hand, all the way back to Cleveland?

Reggie looks broader than usual tonight under a comma of moonlight. His pewter-colored beard and black combat boots almost gleam. He smiles, shakes his head, and follows his wife. I've never seen such a tough hybrid go so soft when it comes to his 'this life' mate. It's as if every time he looks at Miss Barbara, he sees her for the first time. An intimidating hybrid by any other standard, Reggie may not be much for words, but he's exceptional at killing what needs to die, and his training garners a great deal of respect from the Delta and SAS operators we've plucked from elite units to accompany us on this mission.

Technically, these operators aren't working for Delta, Grey Fox, or SAS. Since the US and UK are not at war with anyone—or *thing*, on the Gilf Kabir Plateau, special ops are prohibited. The world's darkest intelligence agency, Komokuten, recruited these "trustables" as private contractors. This operational detachment team is *borrowed* from this world's Armed Forces. If our training for this mission didn't kill or severely wound them, they were provided "cosmic clearances" and redressed in uniforms void of identifying insignia. Hogan was at the top of his class.

By contrast, each Astral Weaver wears a copper armband wrapped around ostrich-egg-sized biceps and stuffed with cardinal feathers. Most are shirtless. Under the new moon, their arms reflect ancient charcoal-colored tattoos with symbols no sentient being outside their realm has ever been able to decipher. As cunning battle strategists, Astral Weavers guard the twelve gates to the Portals of Ninmah. They can traverse dimensions if hybrids like me open portals for them. And now, we meet again at another cave entrance, the Wadi Sura, otherwise known as the Cave of Beasts, with Lozen at the top of *her* class.

Lozen, who stands at least two feet taller than Master Sergeant Hogan, himself a crusty man in his mid-thirties and of respectable stature, un-straddles herself and offers Hogan a four-digit hand to help him to his feet. He refuses and looks away, embarrassed I think, that a *female* so stealthily relieved him of his weapon. "No thank you, ma'am," he says. He sullenly shuffles through sand to pick up his gun. "You *are* a ma'am, right?"

Lozen doesn't nod or shake her head. "I am what I am and can teach you what I know," she says, without a hint of swagger.

"Pfft, right. What are *you?*" he asks, circling her. "I read all the security briefings. I didn't see anything about seven-foot-tall blue creatures with chrome feathers poking out of their chests."

"That's because we didn't expect her," I say. "Lozen, meet Sergeant Hogan, Hogan meet Lieutenant Lozen, guardian to Ninmah's Portal."

"Ninmah's what? She's a *lieutenant?*" Hogan shakes his head in confusion, rubbing the butt of his gun against his neck. "In what dimension? I'll be damn. Never seen *anyone* do what you did a moment ago." He thrusts his hand out to shake Lozen's, who stares at him in bewilderment but doesn't offer hers. "Hell, I don't think I even saw you coming."

"What is this?" she asks me, staring at Hogan's open palm.

"A sign of respect," I say. "Humans call it a handshake. He's impressed with you."

"Hmm," she says, a hint of suspicion in her breath. Lozen scrutinizes Hogan from the top of his head to the foundation of his boots. She takes his hand and slaps it flat against her chest just under her neck, and plasters her large hand on his chest, but this time he doesn't topple over—he staggers two steps and recovers. "This is our..." But before the rest of the words escape her lips,

Hogan's leg sweeps Lozen. She falls with a thud, a look of complete shock on her face. "You are a human, no?" she asks, mentally scrambling, I think, to recover her dignity.

"I can teach you what *I* know," Hogan says, his voice loaded with lots of swagger and a sneering chuckle. He turns and orders his men into the cave for dinner.

Lozen narrows her eyes at Hogan, and I already know she might stand down now, but no way in Raga will she allow him the last word...or leg sweep. Twelve giant pale blue beings with long red hair don't even try to conceal their amusement. It is *I* who help Lozen up for the first time ever, trying to hold down a laugh that silently shakes my sides until it gushes up through my throat. "I'm shocked he got *you* off your feet."

I met the Astral Weavers almost seven years ago at Plum Hook Bay, back when I was a troubled Ohio teen. As a ward of the court, I was remanded into Reggie's care behind the gates of a nuclear reactor testing facility, known as NASA Plum Hook Bay, along with eleven additional and equally fucked-up kids from around the globe.

The Astral Weavers occasionally show up unannounced to ensure parallel realms remain unthreatened and, as needed, sew up tears and holes in the fabric of space so dimensions don't leak into one another. Lately, they've been working over-time. I didn't exactly *meet* the Astral Weavers either. I tripped over them in a cave when I was sixteen. I remember it well because it startled the piss out of me. Lozen's team sat in a cross-legged circle. Their palms faced heavenward, fingertips barely touching, balancing a pulsating metallic orb floating over their heads. I thought they were dead. Bennie said it was "extended hibernation," a trans-state to guard the sphere for the next Balancer, which was supposed to be my dad. He never showed.

"The human, Hogan," Lozen says. "Has potential...if prop-erly saddled." She purses her lips as her eyes follow him into the cave. "I'll check with my sister to see if she requires additional spousal accessories."

I wave my finger at her. "No absconding with humans to other realms. And especially no handing them off to sister Valkyries as spousal accessories."

"May I take some of this Hogan's parts? I'll leave most of him here."

"Absolutely not."

"Why do you work with humans?" Lozen asks, squinting toward our basecamp just inside the cave. Together, we watch a soldier spit tobacco on the ground. "They're terrifying and uncouth." She shivers. "This planet always makes me feel ill... there's bad energy."

"You haven't spent enough time here," I say. "I'm half human too, remember?"

"You're not like them," she says. "You might be worse." She smiles and winks at me.

In so many ways, Lozen is right. Despite my best effort, I've never quite fit in among purebred *Homo sapiens-sapiens*. I prefer to live a life of clandestine solitude on Earth among humans with high clearances. I *pass* for human above ground. Others aren't so fortunate. At least some factions of my government try to understand, even if narrowly, the hybrid part of me.

"We have much to discuss," Lozen says, holstering her tantalum spear. "The Intergalactic Council is surprised to learn you're *engaged* to Lord Luca Harrington. I'm deeply concerned you accepted his offer. He isn't exactly known for soul mating once you grant him the friendliness of your thighs."

"He's never socialized between my thighs," I say. What I don't say is what a kiss and connection Luca and I shared back in Oxford. It takes every atom of my Golden Blood to resist the overpowering primal human impulses I experience when it comes to that hybrid. I wish my amygdala and hormones could be artificially tweaked against such banal desires. I fear Luca uses my attraction to his advantage. I'm sadly convinced too, given his highly unique and illegal pedigree, Luca is incapable of love.

"Clever hybrid you," Lozen says. "A hunter always longs for what it can't catch."

"I didn't have much choice," I say, looking down at the blood-red diamond melded to my left ring finger, unsure as far as Luca is concerned, who trapped whom. I deny to Lozen the fact that I'd take Luca into my bed faster than a comet if I thought I could trust him.

A shock of brilliance skitters across my ring's facets. This ring, symbolizing my engagement to Lord Harrington, is conspicuous on my somewhat human-looking hand, even though I am nominally considered celestial nobility. This latter subject is one of heated debate on Earth and beyond. My Camaeliphim relatives claim that even a drop of human blood disqualifies my standing as an Ormian Princess. Frankly, I'm not the Princess type. I prefer swords to tiaras.

As Lozen and I stand in silence, I try to convince myself this impending royal union with Luca is a shorter passage to finding my daughter and throwing Raga into the Source Vortex, a job he insists is a sure death sentence without his help. So, here I am, the nearest thing to a Balancer this world has, but paling in comparison to my fully fledged Calmaeliphim father, who is not the least bit human. He was supposed to keep this planet balanced but disappeared in Viet Nam when I was three. Forces conspired. I was the next best choice, although not much of one, Reggie reminds me, because I'm part human. And I forgot the portal password.

Luca's inside the Cave of Beasts, about fifty yards away, showing the engineers on our team how the Tesla coil, the one he and I found at Port Meadow, works with my cube pendant. The coil and the pendant are to be combined with a silver sphere, one guarded back at NASA Plum Hook Bay, to create X Points, or portals to other worlds.

It doesn't go unnoticed that my life is not lining up in an orderly orbit, but instead, rains down on me like an asteroid shower. Reggie has reminded me a bazillion times that my throwing Raga into the Source Vortex is the only way to save this planet. I don't even know what a Source Vortex is, let alone where it's located—and to make matters even worse, I am bound to this stupid plan because I made an unbreakable agreement with *Not Who,* a cosmic "it" force that appeared to me as two "men in black" while I was trapped in a military hospital.

If this weren't bad enough, this unmet daughter of mine exists thanks to my mom's human sister, a woman so warped she isn't happy with an Earthly title of countess, but trafficks kids to Nephilim in some twisted desire to be named a minor celestial queen. My aunt, *aka* Dr. Evelyn Dennison, *aka* Countess of Teviot, got into the caves ahead of us near the Russian border, in a race to find Tesla's lost files.

This life is, without question, the most interesting one I've led. So, it is unfortunate that when my mission is complete, I'll have to leave everything I love behind, provided I'm not infinitely inanimated or killed. I'll be enabled, I'm told, to roam realms among those of my kindred, the latter something I once wanted more than anything...until I didn't.

Lozen intently watches me. Thankfully, Astral Weavers can't read minds. I retrieve an old map from the canvas of my camel saddle and lay it out for the seventeenth time over a boulder, and I know, if Lozen sees this, if miracle of miracles, nobody walks outside to bother us.

Reggie bothers us.

"Miss Barbara says you need to eat," he says.

"Ten minutes, Reggie," I say. "I want to share something with Lozen."

He thumbs his watch to set an alarm. The regimented military man embodies a part of his humanness almost as much as the hybrid part. "I'll come back to get you in ten."

I run an index finger down the map and almost immediately after Reggie, Luca shows himself in the cave entrance. "Samantha," he says. "Are you remembering?"

I look at the map and then at Luca and Lozen to kickstart my memory, but it's no use. "I'm starting to remember," I lie. "I'll be inside in ten minutes. Save a bowl for me?"

He thinks about this for a moment. "I'm saving more than a bowl for you." Luca winks and disappears again into the cave's interior. I command my knees not to wobble in front of Lozen.

"Oh, Scathatch," Lozen says. "I'll trade you ten tantalum spears and two warriors for him!"

"Spears and warriors off my fiancée," I say. "And keep your thighs locked."

Lozen offers me a phony pout as I contemplate the fact that *anyone* can be charmed by Lord Luca Harrington, this world's foremost weapons and defense contractor, even a typically restrained Astral Weaver. I remember the first time Luca and I met, how he begged me in the rain to give him one kiss...just one, after we'd walked together for miles along London's streets. It took an extraordinary amount of discipline on my part to fly away and not look back without risk to my mission—and I'll grudgingly admit, my heart.

"Why are you here?" I ask.

Lozen pulls a buckeye from the small leather pouch on her hip. "This," she says.

"I don't understand."

"You placed a buckeye seed on a small obelisk outside the Cave of Beasts, no?"

Earlier in the evening when I was alone outside, I placed a small buckeye on an unassuming rock, my small personal testament to the world that we were here. I thought the world would never find out or care.

"The Hetuk seed is the eye of the Source," Lozen says.

"Wherever a Balancer places this seed with intent, you open a temporary portal for Astral Weavers."

"My first day at Plum Hook Bay, Miss Barbara gave me a buckeye to hold in my pocket," I say. "She said it was the 'Eye of God'. She later brought up Native American burials—the ones *not* of their kindred buried on that Ohio land. She'd said they were giants, a bit like you. And she didn't seem very surprised to see you tonight."

Lozen pauses a while. "Miss Barbara is a wise woman." This is all she says. We watch a sliver of moon hover over a now star-glittered sky, just the sort of milky sparkles I love and long for, the kind of sky growing rarer on Earth. "What do you need to tell me about your intent?" Lozen finally asks, her smile fading to serious-ness. "Let's walk."

The biggest surprise of my life was Luca's public proposal at the Harrington Ball a few months ago. It made news the world over and infuriated his latest conquest, Lady Olivia Seaton. And we weren't the only ones shocked by his brazen and dangerously overt scheme. Luca cost me a great soldier in Genin. It was at the Harrington Ball that I learned Luca was more Camaeliphim than hybrid—but...Lozen and I round a corner.

I practically knock over one of the young Sherpas when I bump into him. He's balancing two waterpots on a large stick that digs uncomfortably over small shoulders. I've seen him before. He's a child, not much older than nine or ten. He reminds me of Bennie, but not in looks or mannerisms—this kid has the same depth of wisdom pooling in his almond-colored eyes—one born of having to grow up quickly if he hoped to survive—and his aura, a royal-looking purple—highly unusual in any human, particularly a child.

"My sincerest pardon," he says with a bow. "Amitabha."

I help him lower the water to the ground. "What is your name?" I ask.

"Eido."

"Eido," I repeat. "I've heard of you. You were ordered here from Nepal by your master."

"Master said it was time to put my training to use," Eido says.

"Training for what?" I ask. "Why in the hell would a grown ass monk send a child like this into harm's way?"

"Samantha," Lozen interrupts.

"This kid is a liability," I say, giving her no time to finish. "He will slow our progress." What I don't say is that he'll likely be killed. Perhaps his master hoped to be rid of him. If that's the case, my heart softens a bit, but not enough that I want this cute little bald guy to unnecessarily suffer any more than he already has in his short life.

"Samantha," Lozen says. "The child will hold his own. Our walk, shall we continue?"

"Hold on a second," I say. I squat to meet the boy eye for eye and I let out a sigh. "I'm going to send you to Nimbu's village in the morning. Nimbu refuses to venture farther with us because he says the Cave of Beasts is cursed."

"But..."

"No buts," I say. Eido stares at me, a perfect poker face, not even a wisp of disappointment or relief alighting a single hair on his youthful eyebrow. I rise. "You must be at least this tall to ride on this mission." I raise my arm to Lozen's shoulder, an impossible stretch for a kid who barely rises above her knees.

Eido finally stretches his neck up at Lozen, who smiles at him, then he looks at me, curving his lips into a mischievous smirk. "Would you let me go with you if I told you a secret?"

"What secret?" I ask. "It had better be a good one."

"Your intended lover, Lord Harrington, inserted Bezaliel mist into his blood..."

"What?!" Lozen yells, looking at me, my mouth agape, because it's true—and this clever little shit failed to mention ahead of time that it was *my* secret he'd be sharing, one I can't for the Raga of me, figure out how he knows.

"Lord Luca did it to help you because your daughter has the same mist in her blood—and needs to be thrown into the Source Vortex..."

"Asteroids," I huff, plopping myself on the ground beside him. "You can stay."

TWO

CRYPTOVARANUS

SOMETIMES I DREAM we're together, my daughter, Bennie, and me. I see the two of them standing in a courtyard in front of a grand estate holding court above the sea. Bennie is always older than I remember, dark ringlets framing the chiseled face of a fully grown hybrid—but he has the same onyx eyes. It's been nine years since I last saw Bennie. He was fifteen.

Our daughter's wind-blown russet curls drift over a cardinal cape as she waves at me. As I draw closer, I notice her eyes are hazel, like mine. Hope reaches out to me but I'm unable to cross the void, to feel the wind salt my lips with sea spray, or to hug her. I cry and call her name. Bennie shakes his head: no, not now. "It's dangerous...wake up!" His voice fades away from me like the ending of my favorite song.

I open my eyes.

The cave is dark and quiet but someone—or some*thing*—is here. I feel it. I hear no footsteps. A dim gray aura lurks above my bedside, but I can't quite make out its shape. From under the covers, Kitsune, my soul guide, pushes her warm fox fur into my hip. I hold my breath, turn up my ears, wondering who, aside from Luca or Lozen, would have courage enough to sneak into my sleeping space.

I think about what Eido said, that Luca violated sacred law by inserting himself with Bezaliel mist. "Luca can't be trusted," Lozen added in agreement. She bid retreat to her realm, *behind the veil*, before I could protest. She gave me thirty Earth days to locate Tesla's file before she must tell the Ormian Council Eido's secret.

Luca's breach of Intergalactic protocol deeply troubles me. The Ormian Council might infinitely inanimate him as punishment. While I vehemently disagree with Luca's dangerous off-grid experiment, he is Bennie's half-brother, my daughter's uncle, and my impromptu fiancée, although the lattermost is born more from duty and convenience than love.

Knife ready, I'm less of a target under this blanket.

Whoosh!

The covers are snatched away. Kitsune yelps. She makes no other sound. I can't feel her next to me anymore. I instinctively tuck and roll into blackness, counting the tumbles, *hup, two, three, four...ouch!*

I've cut my leg.

When I was brought to Plum Hook Bay years ago, I never thought I'd be desperate enough to kill again—never thought I'd have to—but now, I won't and don't hesitate. Not after being debriefed and trained by Reggie about what *really* goes on in this world—above *and* below it. I reach up and plunge the dagger...

It, whatever *it* is, hisses and flaps away. Droplets, cold and slippery, slide around my arm. I feel my way along the rock and out of the sleeping cavern. *"Kitsune!"*

I catch my breath in the main tunnel, feeling oddly spent by such a brief, practically non battle, my arm beginning to burn. I don't see my soul guide.

"Samantha, are you all right?" Luca asks. His voice rings out ahead of me, maybe ten feet of darkness away.

"It's my arm," I say, knowing I cut my leg on a rock when I tumbled, but realizing my arm hurts worse—much worse than it should. "Where's my fox? Where's Kitsune?" The wetness pools into the scars where the DOE once bolted a Dream Stealer to my wrist. I want to get past Luca, to find Reggie and Dr. Monica, but feel too weak to fight. I shiver and stop moving.

Luca waves a light stick, which suddenly, I'm thankful, chases blackness into the corners, a soft-green glow illuminating his chiseled face and lighting up azure eyes—eyes the color of a tropical ocean—but as Miss Barbara reminds me, even Lucifer, leader of demons, arrives as the Morning Star. I didn't have the heart to tell her that Christians stole and adapted a far older story about a fallen Babylonian king, into her Holy Book. The devil is a creature not even mentioned in ancient Hebrew texts but chiseled upon Sumerian stone, independent of, and not created by, *her* God.

I still don't see Kitsune.

Painted figures on rock walls stare down at us, their lifeless eyes suddenly glowing white. A case of the creeps skitters along my spine. I try to relax and remember that cave drawings are found all over the world. Yet the beasts drawn on these cave walls are upwardly topped off with as-of-yet undecipherable engravings, the likes of which none of us has ever seen—and their eyes appear to follow our direction.

Luca reaches out for me. I pull back.

"Let me see..." He stretches forward and snatches my arm. "You're bleeding."

"Luca?"

He ignores me, lost in his inspection of my arm the way his half-brother Bennie used to zone out on me at Plum Hook Bay. "Good God, Sam," Luca whispers.

"What is it?" The pain spreads in intensity up to my elbow and down to my fingertips. I stifle an urge to let out a yell and risk waking the others.

"It's..." He wraps a plastic strap around my bicep just as I stumble, half-conscious, into his arms. He gathers me up and calls for Reggie. I feel him trembling under his coat, his uneasiness foreign to me—okay, so maybe it *wasn't* Luca in my cavern—but then I remember the Scythian stories about *werewolves* and wonder if Luca's Bezaliel mist causes a sort of post amnesia once evil channels through his circuits.

Then another thought strikes my heart; if Kitsune is dead, my time here is not long either. If a soul guide dies, so too, the hybrid. I fight to keep my eyes open. Sleep. Yes, just let me sleep. I feel *soooo* relaxed now. This isn't so bad, dying. It's not as if I haven't done so before. My arm feels sticky. The wetness pools around my hands and makes me think of the honey combs I'd plunder and bite into during my summers at NASA Plum Hook Bay.

Luca shakes me—hard. "Sam!" I look up at him through half-open eyes. "Don't go to sleep! Whatever you do, **DO NOT** close your eyes!"

Reggie steps into our path, followed by his wife, and Vigo, a nearly coal-colored German shepherd that is Reggie's soul guide. "What happened?" Reggie asks.

"Cryptovaranus," Luca says. He hurries around my former foster parents, who struggle to keep up with him, and rushes me over to the ground near the main firepit. "Barbara, find me the hottest ember you can dig up in what's left of that flame." Luca pulls off his jacket and places it under my head, a makeshift pillow. He pauses a moment to look at me. If ever there was a contest for most handsome hybrid, he'd take home the trophy, I think—until his large hands repeatedly smack my cheeks. "Samantha! Wake up!" I raise my clean fist to him but the Bukhara blade, one he had specially made for me, slips easily from my palm and right into his hands.

Reggie leans over me. "What's a Cryptovaranus?" he asks.

"A modified miniature Komodo dragon with wings," Luca

says. "Hold her arms down at the elbows and keep them up over her head."

"Modified? Modified how? Did it bite her?" Reggie asks. "I never heard of a cryptovaranus."

Barbara returns, holding an orange glowing ember in her metal cooking tongs and looks nervously around the cavern. Luca holds out his bare hand to her.

"But..." Barbara hesitates.

"Drop it," he says, his voice slightly raised. She drops the hot coal into Luca's bare hand, and when he doesn't wince, but swipes the blade of my knife with it, she backs away from him in horror and makes the sign of the cross. "It didn't bite her," Luca says. "The Chinese government used to have an underground lab not far from here."

"Used to?" Reggie asks.

"Yes," Luca says. "They fled when a few of these things escaped. Horrible 1950s epigenetic experiment gone wrong. They spliced bat, Komodo dragon, and crocodile DNA. Crypto-varanus saliva is a dark blue venom that puts prey to sleep. I thought it was blood, but I was wrong." He presses the knife into my wrist. This time, I let out a scream, feeling the heat of the fire mixing with the cold liquid on my arm and taking tiny pleasure in hearing Luca, who thinks he knows everything, admit that he's wrong. Then I consider how detrimental this might be for *me* right now. "It's not working...Sam!" He slaps me again. "Stay with us! Reggie, wake up Dr. Monica. She's in tunnel seven."

Reggie doesn't move but looks down at me, worried. "I'm sure Dr. Monica *heard* her."

"Reggie!" Luca yells.

"No," Reggie calmly says. He reaches into a pocket of his Army coat and pulls out a small tin I haven't seen in years. When he twists the lid, the familiar scent of dimethyltryptamine invades my nostrils. Amazonian tribes call it "Ayahuasca yage." It's an ancient psychedelic drug that pre-dates Sumerian culture and some say it was brought to them by an otherworldly but now forgotten ice-age civilization. Years ago, Bennie added some secret ingredients to it on the NASA side of Plum Hook Bay and turned it into a salve. He once cured my broken nose with it, one he gave me, so he could remove a governmental microchip stuffed far up my left nostril. He said the chip was used to monitor my brain but hadn't yet been activated.

Luca smears a knife-swipe of the drug across my wrist. I loosen my grip on the tether to this world...

...a tunnel...it branches and divides. I pick a passageway and fly, weaving through stalagmites of gleaming aqua and white crystal until I arrive at a cross-portal, the X Point. It isn't what or where I expected it to be. I kneel beside it and settle a palm over this iridescent water-filled moon-colored round pool surrounded by a lasered stone square. Inside, I see strange gates where north is west, and east is north. I peer into endless depths of beckoning. The only way through is to jump in...I wait...I have all the "no time" in the cosmos...

"The Source is with her tonight," Luca says when my eyes flutter open. I feel fine.

"What happened?" I ask.

"You frightened a cryptovaranus," Luca says. "It fled into the caves, but it's usually never this close to the surface. They tend to remain in a small pack near Earth's mantle." He draws me close to him after wiping down my arm, and for a moment, I lose my breath, but it has nothing to do with my overwhelming attraction to him. He's crushing me.

"Earth's mantle? Wouldn't magma fry a cryptovaranus or any other living thing down there?" Reggie asks.

"Enough of the hugging," I whisper in Luca's ear. He lets up on his grip but lingers and sniffs my hair before he lets go and looks me in the eyes. I turn away. I know what happens to women who don't.

A tiny whimper in the shadows, a flash of orange pelt and

Kitsune dashes to me after being found and nudged by Vigo. She scrambles between us, paws my chest, and licks my face, her tail brushing Luca's cheek and he pushes it away. I exhale in relief, lower my heart rate, and gather her into my arms, sniffing soft, clean, ozone-scented fur. "Hey, you big chicken, I'm glad you're alive! Thank you, Vigo." I can't blame her for hiding. As a fox, she's a defenseless and easy meal for a cryptovaranus, but as a furry compass, she's better than the Sherpas at leading us through these caves.

Vigo trots around the fire, super proud of himself. I'm still not sure how Reggie, a humble hybrid, was granted such a showy German shepherd as a soul guide.

"Contrary to popular misconception, Earth's mantle is primarily comprised of hollows and rock," Luca says as he recomposes himself and stands up. He goes on, citing differences between Earth's core and crust, as well as how best to deal with unexpected creatures we might encounter, and other thorny, unpleasant underground issues he's considered. Reggie nods as Barbara presses a wet compress, one I don't need, to my forehead. I pull it away and squeeze the water over my wounded wrist—but the pain is gone. My Dream Stealer scars appear faded too—not gone—but much less noticeable.

Dr. Monica dashes into the campsite, wild-eyed with even wilder wiry brown hair, looking like a disheveled female Einstein. I stifle a laugh, knowing full well she took more than a few nips of Sullivan's Cove, her favorite whiskey. Bedouins taught her to hide it in over stretched, leathered goat stomachs. She scans the room and launches herself in my direction, moving the others out of the way. "Samantha? For bloody Cripe's sake, ya all right, mate?"

"Yes, I'm fine," I say, throwing off a light cover and sitting up. "Luca thinks I was drooled on by a cryptovaranus."

"A what?"

"Some sort of freak flying dragon bat," I say.

Monica raises an eyebrow to Luca. "Mate, didya save a sample?"

"Afraid not," Luca says. "It flew away into the caves." He makes a fluttering motion with his hands.

"Aye, ya never gets used to seein' this typo' weerd-ness," she says. "Too Bad." She squints up at the rock walls and ceiling, as if she expects a cave drawing to come alive at any moment, one she can kill with her bare hands.

Dr. Monica is a 6'2" cigar-smoking, whiskey-tipping, forensic doctor who used to serve in TAG, a tactical assault group out of Australia, until she was reassigned to Langley as part of our tribal murder task force. Working alongside her in remote regions of the globe, I witnessed firsthand how efficiently she operates. She was raised on a vast cattle ranch by a survivalist single mom, one who protected Aboriginals near the edge of the Outback. When it comes to stamina and courage, Dr. Monica possesses far more than most humans or hybrids I've ever known, except for maybe Reggie. It's what led Dr. Monica to being "read into" Septum Oculi, a branch of Komokuten that flies *above* Earthly law, and later debriefed on damn near everything "otherworldly."

"Reggie?" I ask. "Where did you get that tin of salve?"

Reggie softly dips the tip of his combat boot into the sand and draws a few lines, creating an impromptu Zen Garden. "I found it."

"Where?" I ask again, knowing full well this silver tin belongs —belonged—to Bennie. He always carried it with him at our former foster home, packed it with a weird paste, a concoction of stinky boiled lumps of congealed bark, herbs, and other unknown psychedelic matter.

"After Bennie went missing in the caves under NASA, I went to look for him," Reggie says. "I found this not far from where you brought all those kids up from that underground hellhole."

"How did you know what it could do?" I ask, trying to shake

off the visual of that secret underground lab, the one where kids were locked up in dank cages or cells.

Reggie reaches down and grabs the buckeye I left by the fire; the one Lozen plucked from the obelisk outside before she and I went for a walk. He hands it back to me and slips both hands into his trouser pockets. He pulls out an identical tin, now holding two. "I found this one," he says, holding it up. "It was the day after you arrived at Plum Hook Bay. Bennie gave the other one, this one, to Dr. Sterling, and told him to give it to me, for you, in case you got hurt." He hands me one tin and stuffs the other back in his pocket.

After all these years, Reggie still surprises me. He took down a soldier once at Plum Hook Bay when the guy got smart. One quick move, and *plop*—the man crumpled into the grass, out cold, until his cohorts carted him away. Reggie's as strong as a steel beam but the color of a comfortable walnut farm table—loaded with scratches, scars, and dents—but durable and solid, able to guard secrets, hold monsters at bay, and earn my loyalty. Yet he's also an oddity of polarity. As a warrior hybrid, use of deadly force authorized, he smokes dope and practices yoga. Sometimes he's in Rambo-mode and other times he's Buddha.

Reggie taught me, and still teaches me, how to survive in this world. He never lies to me either—but *omits* things sometimes, things I suppose he thinks I'm not yet ready to hear or learn. I wonder, *how did I wind up with this exceptionally skilled lug as my protégé?* Some Golden Bloods aren't as fortunate. Bennie scored Dr. Sterling as his teacher, and he was fortunate too. Jade Sokolov wound up with Dr. Evelyn—not fortunate. But when Reggie and I argue, which is a lot, over everything from guns and God to aliens and angels, we always call a truce, and that's about the time he tells me I was born for this mission, and I say, yes, I know—but we both walk away from each other wondering.

"Did she lose any blood?" Luca asks.

"No," Dr. Monica says. She removes her QX-2 square from

my arm. "She's slightly anemic." She hands me a patch and I place it behind my neck to replenish GBCs. Ah, what lovely golden blood I have—until I remember that it is this unique BOUO (Blood of Unknown Origin) that leaves me ripe for wounding, capture, or a potential inanimation here on Earth. BOUO possesses traces of rare element 122, *aka* "unateslium," which provides this world's military-industrial-intelligence complex an unable-to-be-cloned plasma for fueling interstellar travel—but not in the way gas is put into a car or plane—Bennie calls it "Golden Blood" for our ability to combine it with our minds and instantaneously arrive anywhere in the multiverse. The problem is, I've forgotten how to *use* it. And I lost the password.

"Samantha, are you righted?" Luca asks.

"Nothing I need to share with the group," I say, tossing him half a smile and a shrug. "Just thankful to be here—well, not exactly *here*, in these caves, but *alive*."

Luca nods and pats my legs. I stand up to stretch.

"Are you remembering?" he asks.

"Not yet," I say, putting on my best poker face and hoping my bluff will fool this handsome, ultra-perceptive hybrid, and everyone else in the caves. "But we all need some rest. Big day tomorrow..."

"She's right," Reggie says, giving me a knowing look. He takes Miss Barbara under his arm. They will part ways tomorrow, no one knows for how long, when she heads back to civilization with Nimbu.

"Barbara?" I ask. "You didn't seem very surprised to see Lozen or the Astral Weavers tonight."

Miss Barbara shrugs, looks up at Reggie, then at me, moving another reddish-gray ringlet away from her forehead. "There's a reason I never roamed those fields or walked in the woods at Plum Hook Bay," she says. "The locals disturbed Native American burials to clear land for farming...but once the government took over, and Dr. Sterling successfully split neutrinos, it opened the gates of Hell. Lozen gave Bennie some buckeyes back then and told him to keep them in an apple barrel by the house, for you...but I had a problem with that."

"What problem?" I ask.

"It happened three years before we even knew who you were," she says. "I humored Bennie, thought of him as a troubled kid with imaginary friends, until I turned around in the kitchen one evening after dinner to find Lozen standing there, looking like the devil, but not one I'd ever read about. I dropped an antique pitcher. Lozen told me she protected her kindred through the sphere. I still have no idea what she means and don't want to know. When she left, the shattered pitcher was inexplicably intact on the mantel over the fire. I'd like to pray now..."

Neither Nimbu nor Miss Barbara is trained to venture farther with us. They'd likely be forbidden by their worldly governments and the Ormian Council, having minimal secret clearances and zero "need-to-know." Nimbu raises his hands in meditation, quietly mumbling in a corner to his invisible ancestors. Barbara presses a small Bible to her lips in the opposite corner and praises Jesus for saving me tonight.

Dr. Monica, Luca, Reggie, and I exchange knowing glances. Miss Barbara and Nimbu worship deities they call by different names but fail to realize that they pray to the same God. One Source. I'm beginning to *remember*...

THREE

USTA

"They that are intoxicated by self-conceit have interposed themselves between it and the Divine...Witness how they have entangled all men, themselves included, in the mesh of their devices. They can neither discover the cause of the disease, nor have they any knowledge of the remedy."
—Baha'u'llah

WE ARE SOMEWHERE DEEP UNDERGROUND, roaming through a myriad of tunnels. Lowlight arrives in hiccups and flickers, chasing darkness that never fully extinguishes.

Straddling limbo between upper and lower Earth, I sense an uneasy, unseen, and reluctant alliance between this planet and its human inhabitants, the brink of a fallout, where ash is bound to seep and sink its way from the highest peaks topside, down to Earth's core, until everything fades to black. And we are not alone. Someone or *something* has tracked us for days. I feel *it*, whatever *it* is, hiding in the shadows. No one else in our group, except maybe Luca, seems to notice, so I remain reticent...for now...convinced it isn't another cryptovaranus, but *something* just beyond the realm of human perception and perhaps this worldly parallel, hiding behind the veil.

Special ops conduct advances ahead of us. They've yet to run into anything except rugged or damp-slick black walls, more bats than we can count, a few rats, some snakes, copious spiders, over-sized worms, and unexpected bouts of intermittent glowing green light where our footsteps tread. Our team forges ahead, some-times up, sometimes down, through arid caverns that cause the occasional cough, or deep into misty canyons where our steamy breath rises in step with our stride, our rhythmic plumes disap-pearing overhead.

Drs. Nadia Kimathi and Maxine Kanumba, an archeologist and an epidemiologist, respectively, study the strange hieroglyphs we encounter, pristinely etched on rock walls. Dr. Monica bags bits of bioluminescent glow for later study. We suspect the myste-rious plasma may be a yet unknown alga. It disintegrates in our bare hands if we hold it longer than ten seconds. As this expedi-tion's exobiologist, I'll study our collection alongside Dr. Monica later.

BOOM!

Cave walls tremble and a vibration moves through the ground beneath our feet. "This is heaps bad," Dr. Monica says as we take cover behind a boulder. "Who the hell fired a bloody weapon?"

We crouch, waiting for a signal that it's safe to move. Firing shots into the unknown is a considerable risk down here. The sound vibration could cause rock over our heads to tumble down and crush us.

Two flashes of white light finally arrive from an operator's night stick.

We move forward a hundred yards on their command and

that's when I see it... another soldier, not much older than I, face down in a puddle.

Burgundy swirls of blood frame the back of his head. From the looks of it, this soldier didn't even have time to take a breath let alone fire his weapon. I'm not a forensic physician, like Dr. Monica, but I've worked with enough corpses and crime scenes to know this.

"Turn him over," Master Sergeant Hogan orders.

Streaks of mud, blood, and water scatter back to the puddle from what's left of the soldier's face and the rest of his body. From the chest down...he's been vaporized. The intact name patch over where his heart once beat, reads, "Dolan." His M4 lies approximately four feet away, half melted into a basalt boulder.

"Packo, what happened to Dolan?" someone asks.

Packo braces his hip against a rock, gasping for breath. His gun still drawn; he stares down in horror at his fallen comrade. I can tell from his face he saw something he's never seen before. Packo, I conclude, blindly fired a shot into the depths after Dolan was partially vaporized. He's lucky he didn't suffer the same fate. Another operator steps up and wedges the weapon from Packo's hands. I scramble my eyes, looking for anything Packo might have hit, either dead or wounded around us, but come up empty.

"Packo, what happened here? IED?" Hogan asks. "Steam vent?"

Packo, a compact, yet easy-on-the-eyes soldier, looks his *team daddy* in the eye. "No, Sir." He wipes away muck, skin, and bits of brain grit from his uniform, knuckles away a small tear, and straightens himself. It's a quick recovery born of intense military training and a commitment to mission. Yet, I feel Packo's grief from where I stand. His ultra-private despair turns his aura instantaneously black. Any light left in Packo deeply stuffs under his root chakra. I fear he'll never mentally heal. No one says anything. I look again at the corpse, ghost-white pale, small, and lifeless beneath recently churned grime, everything except head, shoulders, and a partial chest just...gone.

"Packo is one lucky fucker," Hogan whispers loudly enough for only Luca and me to hear.

Dr. Monica kneels beside Dolan and scans a small ultraviolet light over what's left of him. She uses another stainless-steel instrument that reminds me of a knitting needle, to lift scraps of flesh and fabric, poking and prodding into rips and holes, through which more layers of muscle and bone can be seen. It looks, I think, as if a T-rex came out of nowhere and side-swiped Dolan before he knew what happened, making off with the lower half of his body for dinner. I know that's not what happened. In fact, I know exactly what happened, and this is, as Dr. Monica says, "heaps bad."

Dr. Monica uses tweezers to pluck blonde buzz cut hairs from Dolan's head and places them in a small zip-lock bag. If there's one thing I'll never get used to, it's the sight of dead people who didn't have time to leave Earth peacefully. This planet serves as a repository for a multitude of lifeforms...a sort of Doomsday Vault. Humans are the vessels my kindred use to store the best and rarest "star stuff." Mortals are supposed to elevate their celestial potential through the exercise of service, compassion, love, and curiosity. It raises their positive vibrations. Unfortunately, most *Homo-sapiens-sapiens* fail to clear mental, physical, or spiritual interference before death, especially if said death comes without warning.

"What happened?" Hogan asks Dr. Monica.

"It wasn't an animal," she says, looking around suspiciously. "It was a modern weapon; technology we don't have. *Do we?*"

"What kind of weapon besides a land mine would vaporize a soldier?" Hogan asks. "We have laser weaponry that might, but this isn't a case of friendly fire. Maybe it's one of our enemies, like Russia or China?"

"Maybe it's Central Asia or the Middle East," another soldier says.

"Nah," Hogan says. "They aren't that advanced yet."

"Harrington, what do *you* say? You recognize this M.O.?"

Luca and I exchange glances. I'm at unease with the inevitable. He begins to speak but stops before any words leave his lips. I stare into an abyss of blackness behind Hogan, into what has become a disturbingly ordinary and sensory-deprived view of ours for the past eight days.

"It's an Usta," I finally say, receiving a rather displeased look from Luca and a quizzical one from Reggie.

"A what?" Hogan asks, lifting the clear mask a few inches from his face and scratching his own short dark hair as he turns his head to look down the same dark cavern. "What the fuck is an Usta?" He waits for me to explain as Luca shakes his head no. I look back and forth between the two and then at the faded prong scars on my wrist.

I remember: '*We will not risk harm to this planet's heart...*' "An Usta is a terrestrial species sent here millions of years ago," I say. "They helped the Ebians seed races among the multiverse and joined Earth's Musoviis to guard its heart."

"Samantha," Luca says. "What are you doing?"

Hogan stares at me as if I need to be promptly relieved from this mission. "At this point, I'd normally ask what you've been smoking but given that I have a soldier down, and less than half of one at that, go on..." he says.

"You just violated Intergalactic Protocol," Luca says to me.

"Intergalactic what?" Hogan asks.

"Fuck the Ormian Council," I say, glaring at Luca. "Humans have been kept in the dark long enough..."

"There's good reason for that," Luca hisses.

"Whoa, whoa, whoa...hold on," Hogan interrupts. His men gather behind him to listen, their eyes still scanning our perimeter. "What the hell are you two talking about? The Ormian

Council? Intergalactic Protocol? We were read into some goofy shit back at CELESCOM, but nothing about Usta or an Ormian Council. Are you telling me this Usta thing is some sort of... alien...like an extraterrestrial?"

Dr. Monica unwraps what's left of Dolan's uniform, pays us little attention, examines the former man's wounds, and makes a face. "Give me a hand," she says. Two of the soldiers respond and she gives them tweezers. "I need ya to bag tha bits I can't reach ova' thar. Ya don' loo' like squeamish carpet beggas so here ya go." And I think, this woman probably wasn't born with an ounce of squeamish in her.

As a teenager, I used to curl into a fetal position, hands over eyes, rapid breaths, at the sight of something as simple as roadkill. But I've always been a bit of a rebel when it comes to breaking rules. If anyone lived through what I have, they'd understand. As a former ward of the court and foster kid, my "best interests" got lost years ago, along with my case number and court file. According to the US government, I don't exist. I was white-washed under *Project Bluebird,* operated by the CIA's Office of Scientific Intelligence, to determine if I could be trained in "natural acts of assassination." I passed. And so did my *squeamish.*

As Camaeliphim, I'm considered government property, but I'm not owned by the sort of political, military, or public sector bureaucracy that citizens see on the news. I belong to a *behind the scenes* regime, one that prefers the dark, and hides behind billions of "unaccounted for" tax dollars. I've grown in fortitude, able to deal with pain, guts, and gore. Reggie always reminds me that both human and hybrids can rise above their circumstances —and *do* something. Speaking of Reggie, I spy him swiping away a tear. I'm surprised he'd go soft over the death of a soldier he hardly knew, but I don't say anything. He's quieter than usual too.

When another human is killed, I can't help but think that maybe *now* is the right time to let brain-scrubbed humans in on the secret of their seeding, that things are not, in their world, as they've been led to believe. The soldiers pluck what's left of Dolan from the muck and it makes a *"splooch"* sound. I find myself wondering where they trained, what motivated them to join the military, and what criteria were used to land them here, with us, underground, in this crypto-hell, or if they even had a choice.

"Watch it, ya clumsy diggas," Dr. Monica says.

"Dr. Blake?" Hogan asks. "You were saying?"

"Usta are tasked to guard the heart of this planet, similar to the way you and your men swear an oath to protect and serve your country," I say. "They will fight to the death."

"Sounds like a great match to me," Hogan says with a stern grimace. "We'll hunt every one of 'em down and kill 'em dead."

"You can't," I say.

"The hell I can't, ma'am. They killed Dolan."

"Your plan won't work," I say.

"Killing the enemy solves a host of problems," he says, pinching his brows together and glaring at me for effect, as if laying waste to another sentient being is like playing a video game, where medals and name recognition reach top billing, only to be replaced and forgotten once another human beats Hogan's death score. "Men, get the sand out of your vaginas, let's go!"

Dr. Monica shifts her attention to Hogan. "Aye, mate, I'll havya know, a fanny is fa' more durable than your bloody wrinkle purses. I won' be havin' that sort o' backhanded he-man divisive bullshi' down here or I be challengin' ya to a kick duel."

"No time for your games," Hogan says to her, then points to me. "Or hers."

From behind us, Dr. Kimathi and her partner Dr. Kanumba release a chorus of low grumbles as they step in to help Dr. Monica keep the scene clean. I suck in a deep breath. I'll try to explain what we face without violating my clearance or putting Hogan's at risk. I'm pretty sure Hogan and his men haven't been "read into" Usta because nobody thinks they exist. "Usta hate human beings more than anything on this planet."

"Good," Hogan says. "All the more reason to wipe them out."

"It's not that simple," I add. "An Usta will kill almost any sentient being that raises a weapon to it. Packo was left to live as a warning. This might be hard for you to imagine but try to think of Earth as a living being, which it is..."

"Dr. Blake, you go right ahead and do your exobiology bull-shit, or whatever it is you do, but I hold firm to Guns, God, and country," Hogan says. "We kill on contact."

I realize Hogan is right, not because what he says is a fact, but because he *believes* in his mission down to the core of his *being*. It's the same belief Usta have—that violence is a practical solu-tion to guarding Earth's heart and their sacred space from breaches. I try another tack. "You believe in God?" I ask.

"Damn straight," he says.

"I've always struggled with how God and guns fit together," I say, thinking about the havoc humans wreak with their weapons. "Guns are a powerful tool, able to extinguish a soul faster than God forges one."

"Guns also put food on the table," Hogan says more matter-of-factly than I'd hoped. "Guns keep people free. Guns protect us from monsters. We don't have time for your emotional bleeding-heart psychobabble, Dr. Blake. I have lives to protect and a job to do." He tips his finger in a semi-salute at Dr. Monica. "Sorry if I offended you, ma'am. It wasn't my intent. We simply can't afford to be weak down here. Having women along for this ride...*complicates* things."

"Ah, bloody hell!" Dr. Monica says, looking at me and slam-ming a tool to the ground. "Ya' believe tha' pebbles on this bloke?"

"Forget the guns," I say. "You're right, Hogan, we need them. And we need you. I only ask you to consider something as we move through this underground labyrinth."

"What?"

"You believe in God, right?"

"Yes ma'am." Hogan spits at the ground by my feet. A narrow gulch between his eyes, a deep scar shaped like a pirate sword, makes him look mad all the time. Hogan's a rugged survivalist type. He has no kids and three divorces under his belt. He raises a boot to a rock and leans in to me. "Your spiritual shot at my cranial vault leaves me standing," he says. "Whatever that Usta thing did to Dolan, won't."

"The Usta know these caverns better than you ever knew the inner chamber of any of your ex-wives," I say. Hogan grimaces and uncomfortably shifts his weight. "Usta will stealthily pluck us off one-by-one and we'll be lucky to have anything left Dr. Monica can add to a body bag."

"She's right," Luca interrupts. "An Usta's weapon houses a particular type of rare plasma. It vaporizes anything the Usta sets its mind upon—it's a part of them—built into their genetic code because they see time a different way."

"Whattya' mean?" Hogan asks, now ignoring me.

"An Usta recognizes when you're going to shoot before you do...every time," Luca says.

"What are you doing?" I ask.

"Damage control," Luca says.

"Now *you're* violating Intergalactic Protocol," I whisper to him.

"They'll all be dead before any of this information *ever* reaches the surface," Luca whispers back. And the way he says this, so nonchalantly, as if life, these lives, are dispensable and mean little to him. It makes me think of *Hat Man,* a horrific dream demon with icicle hair. Dream demon wears a black cape and top hat—and sometimes shows up when I sleep, to press down on my chest and suck the life from me.

Luca elbows me out of the way and walks a few feet away with Hogan. He whispers something I can't hear. Hogan nods. Luca appears to breathe a sigh of relief. I fume, feeling dismissed and slightly frayed. Is it the air? Bezaliels? Usta? Or is it just me, being an overly sensitive and emotional *female?*

"Sergeant Hogan," I say, pushing my way between man and hybrid.

Each male shifts uncomfortably and I feel enormously odd when the memories flood back, as if a series of locks in my head open to allow forgotten moments of my foster years to pass through... *"you need to toughen up your insides, kid...you're too sensitive, emotional—and that can get you killed..."*—Lieutenant Colonel Brock Lynch.

Lynch was my weapons instructor at Plum Hook Bay—but he wasn't a colonel back then. He was a sergeant major. Today, he runs the NASA side of Plum Hook Bay, but it isn't called that anymore. It's been renamed Sky Wolf Technologies. I'm not exactly sure what they do there, but I assume it's like before...not good. Colonel Lynch never liked me. He sarcastically referred to me as, *"Princess Flincher."* I always thought it strange that such a celebrated war hero was relegated to teaching a bunch of fucked-up foster kids how to shoot. Then I realized...it was the *girls* he didn't like to train.

"I was *read* into your former work," I say to Hogan. "And you know how that goes. If we share compartmentalized information on classified projects, we both wind up in the brig...and lose our pensions."

Hogan bends his head and purses his lips. "Sounds as if you might already be in enough trouble for telling us about Usta."

"Perhaps not," I say. "Not if it means arming you and your men with intel to save our lives. At the end of the day, even if Usta despise humans, you're both on the same side."

"Against what?" he asks, looking as if he can't decide whether to believe or trust me, that I may be less credible because I wasn't born with a dick.

"Something way worse," Luca interjects, picking up Packo's weapon to examine it. "Something bloody difficult to contain or kill. These won't work, either." He props the gun next to Packo, slaps his shoulder, and gives him a wink.

"You can both cut your *correctile* dysfunction," I say, looking at Luca. "You may be accompanying females on this mission, but we are equals with different jobs, and partners on a mission. Understood?"

"So, you're sayin' you want us to make nice with these monsters?" Hogan asks.

Luca and I nod at the same time, one of the few things, lately, we finally seem to agree upon. "Don't lift your weapons at them and they won't fire at you," I say. "They only kill to protect what they've sworn oaths to die for."

"What might that be?" Packo asks.

"Earth's heart," I say. "Usta are scientist and teacher types—intergalactic researchers and engineers. It pains them to kill humans, to disrupt their time threads, even though they dislike humans. Usta despise violence. They only kill if they have no choice, for example, if humans strike first or threaten what Usta consider 'holy ground'."

"What does this, uh, Usta thing look like?" Hogan asks. He turns for a moment to check his men, observing them, I think, for signs of disbelief or weakness. He returns his gaze to Luca and me, expecting an answer.

"They're..."

I gently place my hand on Luca's forearm. "I'll tell them."

Hogan lifts a boot-clad leg and leans against a small boulder. He tells his men to keep their weapons ready if they see or hear something that isn't part of our expedition—or an Usta.

"Usta are considered a race of sovereign beings," I say. "They're telepathic but they primarily communicate through smell, which projects mental images to their kindred. Males stand between six and nine feet tall, females only a little shorter, but they're able to verbally communicate in *any* language. They usually wear dark-colored hooded robes, like Jesuit monks, so you'd likely never see them in this cave system before they saw you."

"Physical description?" Hogan asks.

"Muscular tan, brown, green, or red humanoids. They also have brown, gold, or green human-looking eyes, lipless mouths, and a flat, wide nose," I say.

"Humanoids?" Hogan asks. "Not *Homo sapiens?*"

The entire team inches closer to hear me, except for Reggie. He faces a wall, his back to us, and I'm not sure if he's listening. Some of the Sherpas whisper to the camels. I spy Eido feeding one camel a cube of sugar he's stashed in his sash. None of the Sherpas wear the bio-reg suits we do. These Tibetan and Nepalese descendants of ancient Tubo people inherited a distinct ability to auto-adapt the oxygen in their hemoglobin to extremely high or extraordinarily low altitudes. They're fully human but have learned how to control their forms, better, I think, than any other humans on this planet.

"Usta came here millions of years ago," I say. "They arrived to help create humans."

"God created humans," Hogan says.

"That's right," I say. What I don't say is the God that Hogan thinks he knows is not an accurate portrayal, but a patriarchal propagandic retelling and omission of a cobbled together half-tale that got lost in a multitude of translations and interpretations, and these days is primarily and inaccurately used as a virtue signal or war cry. "God created Usta too, and every living thing we know," I add. "And they don't exactly have skin like ours... it's...lizard-like."

"They have scales?" Hogan asks.

"Sort of..." I say.

I tread carefully here. I realize how faithfully humans cling to their particular gods or religions as the *one and only*, without wavering. Humans have been known to die for dogma. Reggie taught me years ago that I won't win such circular arguments regarding politics or religion because each is based in belief and perception passing as faith, not on facts or evidence. I decide to omit the part about how it is sentient beings that give the Source life, not the other way around. Without humans or hybrids, things like emotions, creations, ideas, or energy, good or bad, causes the entire multiverse to scatter. Form and substance, what we know as *us*, God included, is lost. The Source just is, but only if we're here to keep sharing the story...the *Truth*. And the Truth has zero to do with fire and brimstone tales, made-up sins, or which high school team will win this Friday's football game.

"You just said these creatures helped another race create humans," Hogan said.

"Usta helped place humans on Earth," I correct myself. "Usta blended human DNA into their own genetics, so they could live here as hybrid caretakers of Earth's core."

"That's the devil's work," Hogan says, and how he says this makes me think of how well Barbara did not take the same news, but firmly tightened her grip on Christianity. I don't blame Hogan, Nimbu, or Miss Barbara for having high faith or finding it impossible to believe in extraterrestrials or anything outside the perimeter of their cradle-raised religions. But they do believe in *angels,* and I know for a fact that angels *are not* of this Earth. I keep my mouth shut. Reggie once told me, *"Lots of good folks need something to believe in. It keeps them going in the right direction..."*

"It wasn't the Usta's intent to work for or with the devil," I say. "They don't even know what a 'devil' is the way we were taught. Their work was done in cooperation with ancient off-worlders known as Ebians who understood the Usta's plight as planet guardians. They helped Usta breed aggressive behavioral traits out of our races."

What I don't say is that if Hogan knew *exactly* how much our own government engages in similar epigenetic experiments, but on a far grander and mortifying scale, he'd question every aspect of his faith and likely wouldn't stand for any of it...

"What happened?" Dr. Monica asks.

"What do you mean?" I ask.

"The anti-aggression experiment," she says, standing up and wiping down some of her silver forensic tools with a cloth. "It failed. We traipse all ova' this God-forsaken planet countin' the dead and baggin' body parts. Mate, I'm tellin' ya we humans be fightin' and killin' each otha' warse than eva'...this is heaps bad." She rolls up her leather kit and hands it off to a Sherpa, who repacks it on her camel.

Finally, Reggie turns and nods at me to continue. I practically *feel* his despair from here and that bothers me. It could mean he's sensing or knows something the rest of us don't—or maybe he realizes our team is in deep shit and we will fail with this mission. As an Alphion Proximal C, Reggie's sense of perception is keener than a bloodhound on a hot trail.

"We're at war," I say.

"We're always at war" Hogan says. "You referring to the War on Terror? We got people all over the globe monitoring things. Intel says we'll be in a constant state of undeclared war for decades."

"Not that war," I say. "Another war...an unseen war."

I sit down beside Hogan and eye Dr. Monica and the rest of our group, thinking about how I can frame this in a way they'll understand.

"You know the story in the Bible about the sons of God looking down upon the daughters of men, how they came unto them and bore children with them?"

"The Nephilim," Hogan says. "It's in the Book of Genesis. Men of renown."

"Giants of renown," I say. "Allegedly bred between angels and humans."

"God told Noah to build an ark and then flooded the planet to destroy Nephilim," Hogan says.

"Some Nephilim survived," I say. "They work in government positions all over this world."

"That's not true," Packo interjects. "The flood killed every living thing on the planet except what was on that ark."

Hogan stretches out a hand toward Packo and says, "Hold on, hold on...Normally, I'd agree with you, Packo, but we saw over-sized, blue-tinted warriors at basecamp a few days ago." Hogan gestures for me to continue.

"The Bible has other texts," I say. "Omitted texts. We only have part of the story. Consider these sacred writings hidden the way our military and CIA store clandestine knowledge and tradecraft. If we don't want 'the people' to know something, do you agree we have the capability to never let it see the light of day?"

Hogan runs his finger through some dusty rubble on the ground. "Yes."

"We stamp information secret and deny it for decades, but intergalactic and sacred knowledge remains classified for eons," I explain. I study Hogan's face and conclude he was top of his class for good reason. He *listens*. He *thinks*. He leans in to hear more. I won't disrespect his faith...the spiritual side of him that helps him cope with and process the death of his comrades, his brothers and sisters in arms. I also suspect Hogan fears failing his mission more than dying, and would take a bullet if he had to, for any of the men in his detachment. Reggie would do the same for me, and I for him, so I get it.

"Some Nephilim survived," I say. "They fast-tracked human evolution through deals, first at Alinas, then Karahan Tepe, Boncuklu Tarla, and Gobekli Tepe, and later with Sumerians, Lumeria, Atlantis, Egyptians, right up through today within the deepest sects of our global governments, which by the way, actually work quite well together behind the scenes, and propagate wars with politics of profit."

"Never heard of some of those places you mention," Hogan says. "Why would sworn enemies, say China and the US, work well together?"

"They aren't really sworn enemies," I say. "If government turns our head toward war, we're too concerned with fighting one another to consider what it's really doing, say for example, when it comes to ancient artifacts, advanced technology, or free energy. And China owns more US farmland than any citizen of our country. They also monopolize our dairy and meat industry. They can't risk war on our soil."

"Why would Nephilim fast-track human evolution?" Hogan asks, shaking his head. "Wouldn't that defeat their purpose and risk revolt?"

"They need a slave race," I say. "Nephilim hope to breed a better and stronger vessel using our bodies for something that is not human."

"Now I'm lost," Hogan says.

"Nephilim thrive on a negative parent energy, something not of this world, and use it to counter compassion and keep humans infected with aggression and violence," I say. "If Nephilim keep humans divided, they're able to control and conquer them...but there's something else you need to know."

"What?" Hogan asks.

"Nephilim are not descendants of humans and angels."

"No?"

I shake my head for emphasis. "Nephilim are the children of Bezaliels, sort of...but not in a biological or birthing kind of way."

"Bezaliels?" Hogan says. He scratches his head and looks down at the small campfire beside us, one created with calm reserve by Eido, who grins up at Hogan from the cave floor, listening with what looks like glee, to my story. Kitsune sleeps beside Eido, her fur pushed up against his saffron robe until she almost disappears. I didn't even hear or see this clever little shit, or my fox, inch their way into our conversation, let alone notice Eido start a small fire. Vigo rests his large German shepherd frame near Reggie.

I take better note of our surroundings. We've landed in a large round cavern, where air, from somewhere, occasionally sweeps through—and it smells like ozone and surf—a scent I remember from my adolescent days spent at Nickel Plate Beach —and, unfortunately, on the corpses of kids Dr. Monica and I recovered with Genin among the Sentalinese a few months back. "Earth was considered *Breeding Base 1* by a highly advanced society known as Ebians," I continue. "They wanted to protect humans for the Source, or what you know as God. Unfortunately, Bezaliels followed them. Bezaliels use low vibrations as a springboard to take form. They created Nephilim for that purpose, and those poor souls became victims and slaves to Bezaliels just as humans are to Nephilim."

I decide not to mention the part about Camaeliphim, like Luca and me, being created as a counter by Ebians, to ensure all entities, including humans, behave. Camaeliphim use balance and free will, granted us through the Source, to keep peace—and sometimes that includes grand acts of compassion—or violence. We maintain universal order through Truth, not to be mistaken for never killing or lying. Sometimes we must.

Hogan shuts his eyes, tilts his head back against a rock, and breathes what I suspect is a sigh of resolve. "We've been sent on a suicide mission," he says. "We're *expendable*."

Eido reaches up and touches Hogan on the forearm. Eido shakes his head at this strong military man and smiles brightly. Hogan looks away, feeling, I sense, a bit of heartbreak because he probably doesn't experience much tenderness, and realizes he and his unit likely won't make it out of this mission alive. But he can't and won't tell his men this on the slim hope they might. And Hope is always worth the fight.

"You're definitely not expendable," I say. "You're chosen. Huge difference. You have extraordinary skill sets and will protect your assets at all costs." I look around at the men, women, and hybrids who surround us, all lost in their own conversations or tasks, the people who do, and will, depend on Hogan and his men to keep us safe.

Some of Hogan's men stand behind him, their hair too, bristle-short, and each cradles a weapon to his chest. None of them speak, but wait, not impassively. They too think. They watch. Finally, one of them laughs short and low, and there is an understanding in that laugh...a proverbial chuckle in the face of danger. Then they all get serious when Packo steps up. "Sir, what do we tell Dolan's family?"

Hogan considers this for a long while, the lines on his face trenching a little deeper when he sinks his chin into his neck in concentration. "He has a wife?"

"Yes, Sir."

"Kids?"

"Yes, Sir."

"Damn," Hogan mutters, shaking his head. "Where did he tell them he was deployed? What was his *cover*?"

"He's supposed to be in Somalia. Part of an operation to capture key allies of a warlord."

"Then Dolan dies in Somalia," Hogan says with a sigh as he looks up at the cave ceiling. "With full honors, benefits, and a recommendation for a posthumous Bronze Star. Make it happen. We'll gather in thirty to say goodbye."

"Yes, Sir."

"De Oppresso Liber," Dr. Monica says as she bursts through the somber moment, baring a wicked half-smile. She raises an eyebrow and a tanned goat's stomach stuffed with whiskey, at Hogan. Her grim sense of humor at an inappropriate time is a defense mechanism against the pain of our reality. And Hogan *gets it*. We all do.

"Just a little," he tells his men.

Dr. Monica passes each of them a small tin. "Milk or sugar?" she jokes. She pours the liquid. I wave my hand for a pass, not wanting to get too loopy or let my guard down with Luca.

"I want to ask you a personal question," Hogan says to me. I nod for him to proceed. "Are *you* human?"

"You don't want to know," Luca says with a smirk. He makes a face at me and rolls his eyes, and for an instant, I'm reminded of his brother Bennie. The thought of *him* sends a pang of "hurt and miss" through my heart, a feeling of sadness and agitation I call "sadgitated".

"Um, hmm. Yea, sorry if I—"

"Hogan," I say. "Luca is right. I've already said way more than I should."

Dr. Monica passes Hogan a small tin of whiskey.

He sets aside his weapon and takes the tin from me, downing it in one gulp. He holds it up to Dr. Monica for a refill.

"Aye, mate," she says. "You an' me? We're gonna have that crotch kickin' battle befo' ya go drinkin' up all my stash and beggin' me to nut out yo' tackle."

Hogan drops the tin with a sad laugh, shakes his head, and looks at me. "You know, I had the option to decline this mission," he says. "I could have left you high and dry."

"I suppose so," I say. "But you didn't." I press myself against a backlit cave wall and peer into the depths of another ahead of us, trying to pretend everything is normal—but as usual, nothing about this life is *normal.* An Usta softly moves back into the depths, watching us. Hogan follows my stare into the abyss, but the creature is no longer there...

"To Dolan," I say, surrendering to a small tin of whiskey and handing most of it off to Hogan.

"To Dolan," he whispers, staring into the fire.

FOUR

THE VIKING

A LITTLE GIRL lies in the back of a small rubble pile that looks out over an area of a long-deserted campsite. I stand on a boulder to reach her, move a couple of smaller but still heavy rocks out of the way, and am finally able to shimmy through the opening. I sit down beside the corpse.

Luca kneels beside me. He takes one of the girl's arm bones into his hand. He holds it a moment before releasing it, and I realize that Luca is not enthusiastic about displays of emotion or seeing dead kids. These bones remind him of his little sister. His is a small gesture of compassion that offers me hope. I notice Luca's cheek bears a graze from a wayward bat and his wavy blonde hair has lost its fresh shampoo sheen, his locks flat against his scalp. A filthy beard sprouts unkempt along his jawline. I don't look any better, my own hair a tangled mess of copper wire and my stink about as bad as his. We're all in need of a shower.

Luca looks into my eyes and in that dim moment behind the rocks, away from everyone else, I realize I cannot discern the color of his usually azure orbs...today they are not their typical tropical ocean blue...but boast of fire, almost opal-like, burning flashes of amber anger and possessed of white hues that glint and disappear when he turns away. "What's happening with all these kids?" Luca asks.

A flutter and a blue-black sheen of wings dives and bobs over our heads.

"Cryptovaranus?" I duck.

Luca reaches up with his left arm. "Vidar," he says.

Vidar perches on a rock, curiously eyeing us but mostly unconcerned. Luca takes what looks like a microchip out of his pocket and places it in a small pouch tied around the falcon's leg. He takes the bird, without any protection, and holds it up to his face. Vidar stares back at Luca, head tilting from one side to another, a robotic motion of unspoken understanding. "Go find the Usta and tell them Princess Scathatch comes with her escorts in peace. Understand?"

The raptor lets loose with a series of low, melodic, burbling screeches.

"What's going on up there?" Hogan yells. "Everything okay?"

"We're all right," I yell back. "We've got another body. Young female about ten, I'd guess. She's been here a while. Maybe a century or more. I doubt there's a next of kin to notify given the looks of her."

"What's that noise?"

"Um, it's a falcon...Luca's falcon."

Hogan mumbles to Dr. Monica, perplexed I think, about how Luca has suddenly come into possession of a falcon. Soul Guides are a long story. All hybrids have one, granted to us at birth by an otherworldly parent. Some of us used to receive dragons, fairies, or trolls, but it freaked the fuck out of humans. So...the Ormian Council decided that Soul Guides would henceforth be more of the "down-to-Earth" variety—even though nothing on this Earth is really *of this Earth*.

"Vidar," Luca says. "This is important, I need you to..." Vidar interrupts him with an impatient screech, and I laugh because

Soul Guides are supposed to be enlightened and heed, but too often come with annoying glitches like disobeying orders or chasing rabbits into holes. "I realize you know what you're doing," Luca says, falling further into his British accent as he always does when he's irritated, but looking deliciously Danish when it comes to stature, standing almost six-foot-seven and perfectly proportioned. If there was ever an Adonis on Earth, it's him—and that's a huge part of my problem...Luca lifts the bird into the air and it takes off, headed west, down a long cavern.

"Will Vidar obey?" I ask.

"He always does when it's important," Luca says.

From the darkness of a corner comes a low scratching noise. A small white shape, larger than a mouse or a rat, scurries up through solid rock. "Jesus," I say, jumping back. The creature's aura glows slightly royal purple. A pink nose without any eyes at all, sniffs the air near our feet, then runs up Luca's arm. He stiffens but doesn't flinch, trying to keep what I think is a never-before-seen species of albino rat in his periphery. It sniffs and scrutinizes the air again when I notice a small clear stone tied like a saddle around the back of its neck. I tentatively extend my hand and the animal hops onto my palm. I stroke its fur with my index finger, something it seems to enjoy, pull it to me, and tap the topside of the clear crystal.

"What do we have here?" Luca asks.

A small bubble forms on the pebble and lifts off, growing to the size of a soccer ball, suspended above the blind mole rat. Inside is a single photonic hieroglyph of Enochian communication, which contains a message. I read it and nod, Luca does the same, as we both know and understand the ancient mutating language of the universe, the one Bennie said humans have zero clearance to receive. Reggie calls us "angels of God" for this gift, again not quite accurate—we can't *always* read the messages. It just depends on the rightness of our minds at any given time.

"Es Ko," I say to the rat. The holographic bubble retreats into the crystal pebble. The blind little beast scampers down my arm, to the ground, and disappears into the shadows. "That was fast," I say. "We head *that* way." And I point down a long and narrow corridor.

"No way the camels will squeeze through there," Luca says with a squint in the same direction. He runs a hand through his matted hair.

"We'll leave the camels behind with a few of the Sherpas," I say, thinking about Eido and how this new path might be a great way to safely leave him behind, yet not shirking his mission.

Dr. Monica does her best to keep track of the day and night deep under Earth, but it's getting harder to discern time the farther we descend. It doesn't seem to stand still or move, and maybe, down here, it doesn't exist. I can't even imagine how that might work. All I do know is that it's dark almost everywhere, except for our artificial lights.

We follow a path set out by Source only knows, and now, according to my compass, walk east down a cavern system that looks more like a hollowed-out tube, the kind I once fell into through a fountain at Harrington House, outside London.

A faint glow emanates from my eye necklace, first a dot, then a small beam of light, until it resembles a tiny blue-green orb. Sometimes it divides into two globes and slowly rotates just ahead of us. It's a three-D infinity of a sideways figure 8, which tells me we're headed in the right direction—I think. The cavern is packed with hundreds of thousands of orchid roots embedded in rock walls, taking on some of Earth's negative surface vibrations and storing it here the way nuclear waste is kept in dry casks. Then we see the skeletons tangled up too.

"Don't harm the orchid roots," Reggie says. "I've seen this before."

"Where?" Hogan asks.

"Viet Nam," Reggie says with a stern look at one of the operators holding a knife. The guy slowly slips it back into his belt. "Seven miles west of Khe Sanh about halfway to the Laotian border. Shortly after midnight, an NVA force attacked our camp. Some of my unit was found in the jungle, trapped in roots exactly like this. The only soldier who lived that day was the one who *didn't* take a knife to these roots."

"Poison?" Hogan asks.

"In a manner of speaking," Reggie says.

"That deeply disturbs my sense of fairness," Dr. Kanumba says as she passes Reggie.

Reggie gently runs a palm up the length of some roots. "Ignorance and a sense of fairness can get us killed just the same as evil."

Vigo tucks his tail between his legs, whimpers, and licks Reggie's hand, his dark-pool canine eyes looking guilty, even though he's done nothing wrong. Reggie lowers his head like he's suddenly lost in thought, a pensive scowl on his face. Vigo and I are the only ones who witness a single tear land on a rock near Reggie's boot. As the others continue, I idle over to them.

"Reggie, what's bothering you?" I ask.

"Miss Barbara," he says. "I should have escorted her back to civilization myself."

"You miss her?"

"Whenever I'm away from her," he answers. "She's my best friend."

"You think she's in danger?" I ask.

"Not anymore," he says. He doesn't elaborate but I suspect he means because she returned to the US and didn't accompany us.

"You think she *was* in danger?"

"We're all in danger," he says.

"It's unlike you to cry," I say. "It surprises me because you've fought in more than a few wars and seen your share of horror."

"Not like this one," he says. "This one's the worst."

"Oh, you mean the heartache and missing her?"

"In part," he says. "The other part is even worse—what's ahead for this planet."

"How can it be the worst if we haven't yet seen battle?"

"Indications and signs arise," he says. "If the sky turns yellowish black and clouds assume terrifying forms as they hurtle back and forth carried by random winds, we directly face anti-gods—the Bezaliels. I cry for what is lost. I cry for the battle I wage inside my mind. Going soft in my old age, I suppose."

"You?" I ask. "Soft? I swear, you don't age. You look just the same as you did the day we met!"

"My physical body may slowly progress, but the mind, thankfully, matures," he says. "I consider it a curse and a blessing."

"I know this might sound weird, you being my teacher and—well—sort of like a dad to me, but if you need to talk, or if you need anything at all..."

"We should catch up with the others."

Eido walks beside me, looking up now and then with a grin, satisfied with himself, I suspect. He managed to con his way onward. He traded an older Sherpa out for himself and pleaded his case behind my back to Reggie and Master Sergeant Hogan. We enter a passage where the ceiling is littered with small holes, and I wonder what other ominous creatures might be silently watching us, ready to pounce, besides epigenetic experiments gone wrong. If it's a den of cryptovaranus, we don't stand a chance. I wish Luca had thought about this beforehand and provided drool-proof helmets.

"Your message is received," the photonic hieroglyph read when it appeared in the bubble on the mole rat. *"Zumar, suna Scathatch. Welcome her highness,"* it read. *"Ereshun awaits your*

arrival." I'm sure I've heard this name before but try as I might, it's lost somewhere in the dusty folders of my former lives.

We pass caverns full of moss and geophytes, large bulbs that are way too big to be tulips or potatoes, and that's when we see the body parts in them, an elbow, knee, or hand jutting out, each geophyte acting as a sort of bizarre amber-liquid-filled womb, orchid roots snaking into them from the holes in the ceiling like drinking straws.

"Cripe's almighty," Dr. Monica says, reaching out toward one. "This is heaps bad!" She takes a couple of pictures. "Can we cut one down for samples?"

"Hell, no," Reggie says, and the way he says this makes the hair on the back of my neck rise. "They might be just as deadly as the orchid roots."

Dr. Monica jerks her hand away from one of the bulbous containers. We pass through and hear a hum, maybe machinery, but more pleasant and low, an "Om" type sound, practically inaudible, but there. We pass a pile of discarded WWII helmets. "German," Reggie says, and this makes me shiver. We walk down what appears to be a ramp and beside it a type of door with more unfamiliar hieroglyphic symbols.

"Follow the Garden of the Dead and do not stray. Ensure no follow" the bubble message also read. I can't imagine what sort of human or hybrid would have the courage to follow us this far and even if one did, I can't help but think they'd have met a horrible and deadly end a few switchbacks ago.

We turn down a corridor and, while we've only traveled a level or so down, it's another world, desolate and forsaken, the blackness of the walls dripping with oozing sap, a narrow path little more than a vertical crevice, filled with void and gloom. We walk and I sense the uneasiness of my team, their auras dimming. We turn left, then right, and the passage shrinks us into single file.

"Are you sure this is right?" Hogan asks.

"Yes," Luca and I hiss in unison.

We've walked into a dead end.

"This is a trap," Hogan says, sounding angry. "You just lined us up in a crack without escape. We're bait."

"Quiet," Luca says. "Let Samantha focus. Sam? You've got this, right?"

"Yes," I say. I remember this passage, although I've never physically been here before. I think of my mom and how fond she was of this secretive place—although I don't know how or why I know this—she barely raised me and spent almost her entire shortened life in an asylum before Ebians took her. I'm remembering.

I hadn't noticed it until now, but a gold glow runs along a seam of rock near my feet, barely an inch in length, peering up at me with stony emerald eyes. I kick away centuries' worth of barnacles, dirt, clay, and gook, with my steel-toed boot. It's the top of a helmet, a Viking helmet. Not the kind of Viking helmet in movies with horns. Vikings never wore those. This one has a golden snake mounted in the center. What in the hell would a Viking be doing buried way down here? "*Ne tobos De-Sol untaba;* **Into the bosom of No-Time, the Viking holds the Isle.** *Strike thrice.*" This is what my mother told me the last time I ever saw her. I never knew what she meant, until now.

"Dr. Kimathi, can you hand me a mallet from your bag?" I yell. I know she's back there somewhere.

"An' how you expec' me ta do dis? I'm squeezed like a lime!" she yells back from ten bodies away. "And dis is more closeness to a man than I care to experience!"

I stifle a chuckle to subdue my rising concern. Dr. Nadia Kimathi is our expert archeologist, out of Africa. Angola to be exact. She's married to our epidemiologist, Dr. Maxine Kanumba, from Eritrea. Our team experienced a lot of back-and-forth about a couple joining us on this expedition because there's a high probability we won't make it out of here alive. But they're the best in their respective fields and we need them.

"Here," Luca says, pressing into me. I feel the hardness of him and his breath upon my neck, which causes an involuntary throbbing sensation between my thighs at the *worst* possible stink and time. I bluff and feign slight annoyance. He hands me the small Tesla coil we discovered at Port Meadow.

"What the hell am I supposed to do with this?" I ask.

"Remember Port Meadow, that's what," he whispers in my ear. "Just humor me, love."

"That makes no sense. Wha—" Then it occurs to me. At Port Meadow, this device held me down in a hole until Luca tapped three times...

... "You're a genius," I say to him with a quick smack on his lips. I don't wait to see his response. This little device, as I remember, utilizes forcefields to control matter in both biological and otherworldly systems. I turn the Tesla device upside down and lower my knees and tap the top of the Viking helmet three times. *Nothing.* Just a hard helmet. "Ereshun! It's me, Scathatch...can you hear me?" Still nothing. "*Helllooooo!*" I yell.

"This is stupid," Hogan says. "Men! Head back the way we came."

"Negative, Sir!" someone yells.

"Jesus Christ!" Hogan says loudly enough for everyone to hear. "Why?"

"The cave's closed up," comes the response. "We're sealed in from both sides!"

"Damn it," Hogan says. "Way to go, Dr. Blake, you've unwittingly sealed us in our tomb! This is what we get for listening to a female barely out of diapers!"

"Hey! Ya be stoppin' tha' sort oh' talk righ' now, ya blitherin' dickhead," Dr. Monica yells. The others grumble in agreement with Hogan.

"I can't breathe," Dr. Kanumba says. "I can't move! Oh, God, please get us out of here!"

"Shhh," I hear Reggie say. "Don't hyperventilate. Panic will make you feel worse, breathe with me....one, two, three, four. Good. Hold it for four...breathe out...one, two, three, four..."

I slide the Tesla coil back to Luca. I wish I could go home. I wish we could all go home. But I don't really have a home and haven't since I was a little girl. I think about Bennie and my daughter—then Genin and Dr. Evelyn, in the same cave system, on the other side of the world. Maybe they've already found Tesla's files and are back in the sun, ahead of us. Or maybe, they're dead.

I still don't understand how Genin betrayed Reggie and me in favor of Dr. Evelyn. It doesn't make sense. Never has...yes, it's true...Genin completely lost his gonads to Lady Olivia Ross, but I thought for sure, no matter how much he experienced Olivia's *friendly thighs*, he'd remain loyal to the cause of Septum Oculi, Komokuten, and to me.

In one molten motion, a figure walks out of the cave wall in front of me. The helmet by my feet expands, shaking dirt away, and the hand of the phantom figure catches it mid-air. "Ah, this is mine," he says. The man's white tunic and oatmeal-colored trousers might be wool and flax. His armor, typically made of iron, lamellar, I think—is fashioned from a much thinner and delicately advanced silver-like material. His boots resemble nothing I've seen on Earth, maybe the same material as his armor. His eyes glow blue like the Astral Weavers, except he isn't one, and his face is extremely pale beneath a shocking crop of firestorm red hair and overgrown similarly colored thick beard. He pats down his chest, offers me a "too toothy" smile, bows, and says, "My lady, I am indebted to you for my release and forever at your service."

"Ereshun?" I ask, leaning in to get a closer look.

"Ereshun?" he says, surprised, then laughs, palms on his thick belly. "Oh, heavens no—I'm not Ereshun—that's a place, not a person! Wait!" He leans in to sniff the air in front of me. "I smell warriors."

"They're with me," I say.

"No," he says. "That's not what I mean. Royal warriors...Ye Camaeliphim?"

"Aye," I say. "Unt de Scathatch."

The Viking immediately kneels, and I have no idea why—well, I sort of have an idea why, but the hybrid he knows as a celestial warrior goddess is a myth and may or may not be me reincarnate—and this guy? —he's not from this planet and not even remotely human.

"What in bloody hell is happening?" Dr. Monica yells.

"Shhhh!" almost everyone hisses in unison.

"I need a foking drink," she adds with a hiss-whisper. "If we get outta here, Ima' clock every one of you blokes!"

I wait for our entourage to stop grumbling. "And you are?"

"Hei, hei! Your highness, Bo is the name...at your service." He bows and tries to kiss my hand, but I don't offer it.

"Bo?" Luca asks. "That doesn't sound like a bloody good name for a Viking! You have a surname?" I elbow Luca—hard—in the ribs. *Bo* shakes his head. "Ouch," Luca yells. "That hurt."

"Good," I say. "True Vikings have no surnames. Sir Bo, it's nice to meet you. And your name can have *three* meanings: bear, warrior, or keeper. Which one say you?"

Bo paces back and forth a moment, and periodically engages me with his freaky yellow cat eyes. He leans left and right, looking at my team, perhaps appraising our abilities—or lack thereof—and stops in front of me. I wonder if Bo is a few horns short in the helmet. Maybe he took a nasty fall centuries ago and wound up here—or perhaps he's been exiled from his realm for some horrific offense. "My services are pricey, what have you to negotiate?" he asks.

"You just told the lady you were *forever* at her *service!*" Luca says low and deep, puffing out his chest, trying to lean in toward Bo but we're too tightly packed together for Luca to offer much by way of intimidation.

"Ahem." Bo clears his throat and glares at Luca. "I be of service to the Lady of Skye for releasing me. "Dritt, I couldn't give a faen what might befall the rest of you. And *you*..." Bo sniffs the air. "You're not a normal warrior..." Bo looks at me but points to Luca. "Something *off* about *that* one."

"Never mind him," I say. "Perhaps I could give you something of value if you have the ability to get us, *all* of us, out of this trap."

Bo leans in to inspect me. "Show me your teeth," he says. I do. "Hmm, you're a fine specimen of a lass and royal to boot." He polishes his fingernails on his armor, then slicks his hair with a hand, which does little good to tame his wild locks. "Your hand in marriage?"

"Oh, come on!" Luca says with a groan. "Really, Bo? Samantha is a *royal* pain in the arse. Trust me, you don't want *her* for a wife!"

I put my hand out to silence Luca but won't look at him. I'm pissed he thinks I wouldn't make a good wife—not that I would ever want to be *anyone's* wife, especially his! "With all due respect, Sir Bo," I say, flinging my engagement ring in his face. "I'm promised in official capacity to another."

"Pity for me," Bo says, picking at his teeth with a fingernail. "A king of great renown and fortune, I suspect."

"He's an arse," I say. Luca elbows me and I lunge forward, practically spilling into the Viking's grit-loaded arms, but thankfully, don't.

Bo grins like a hungry predator seeing trapped souls. Then he turns to me. "What else you got?" he asks. Bo peers into the darkness behind me. "Is that a boy? I could use a good bond servant."

I block the Viking's view of Eido, anger pooling in my temples. "The boy is not up for trade," I say, locking eyes with Bo.

"I'll take the fox or that big dog," he says. "I'm hungry."

Kitsune lets out a yelp and shrinks back behind Vigo, who growls at Bo.

"Our soul guides," I say, "are way too lean a meal and gristly."

"*Arrooooof,*" Vigo verbalizes, low and slow, so I get the message he doesn't approve being labeled scrawny pickings—or someone's dinner.

"I do know of a beautiful and strong Astral Weaver who seeks a sturdy spousal accessory." What I don't say is that Lozen's trying to find a playful souvenir for her temper-challenged sister, who does not believe in monogamy—but neither, last I heard, do interstellar Vikings—could be a match made in Raga, I think.

Bo kneels and takes a small crystal object out of what looks like a leather pouch and draws a circle with it on the rocky floor of our would-be tomb. He removes flint stones and some grassy material, piling it neatly in the center of the circle. "I'll accept the Astral Weaver and seal the deal with some mead," he says.

"I'm afraid I don't have any beer," I say. "But we do have whiskey, some of the best available."

"Avtalt," Bo says. We hold up our palms together, but don't touch, in agreement.

"What happens now?" I ask, thinking about how Lozen is going to kick my ass or kiss me once she finds out I committed her sister to a blood-hungry intergalactic Viking.

"We save the queen!" Bo lights the reedy material. The circle gives way to a deep manhole. A large crack slithers its way from the circle and between the feet of my cohorts, where a chorus of concern rises to ask what's happening...and before I can answer, we slip so far into the depths I wonder if we'll ever see the surface of Earth again.

I have no idea where we are—but it isn't our would-be tomb—and for that, I'm relieved. We're still underground, in a tunnel large and sleek enough to fit military jets—not a natural formation—too advanced. It occurs to me that although I've been read into some deep black government projects, I know little about what goes on beneath my feet. We walk slowly, and I worry we might suddenly stumble into another death trap.

Bo confidently ambles ahead, as if he hasn't spent centuries buried in rock. Whether we keep up with him is of no concern, his crystal-like torch casting massive shadows on the tunnel's walls.

"What the hell is he, mate?" Dr. Monica whispers. "He don' loo' quite human and he's damn sure not your breed of hybrid."

"I'm not sure," I say.

Each of us jogs a little. "Hmm," Bo says. I know it's around here somewhere."

"What do you seek?" Luca asks.

"Ereshun," Bo responds. "No more questions."

"Where are we?" I ask anyway.

"Lady Scathatch, you're in a world of trouble," Bo says.

"Oh, this I already know," I say. "I need to throw Raga into the Source Vortex and I've forgotten my password."

"The Crossroads of the Seven Sleepers," Bo answers.

"I don't know this place," I say. "I know the Caves of the Seven Sleepers but not the Crossroads, but even that isn't quite true because humans point to many caves as the true one."

"Recalling a password is the least of your danger." Bo holds up the torch and shows us a crude ladder made from old rope and petrified wood and begins to climb down. "But first, our deal?"

"What? You want the whiskey now?"

"A liter should do," he says.

I shake my head and roll my eyes. "Dr. Monica, please give our savior a liter of your best whiskey."

"Like bloody fokin' hell I will!" she yells.

I slightly bend my knees to stand eye to eye with her. "I promised him," I whisper. "I bartered with your whiskey to get us out of that sensory-deprived death pit."

"Aye, mate...you shoul' neva' be bargainin' wit' another person's salvation." Dr. Monica eyes the Viking up and down with a wince. "I will take one for the bloody team if ya' le' me foke him instea'."

"I already promised him the whiskey," I say.

"Ya' owe me big time, mate," she says with a glare. Dr. Monica hands over half a goat stomach full of whiskey.

Bo guzzles the entire contents like water...in six swallows. Dr. Monica and I raise our eyebrows in surprise at one another. Whiskey drizzles in a slow stream over his beard and he wipes it away with his hand. "You and me," he says, pointing at Dr. Monica. "We're gonna be real good mates, I can tell."

"Piss off!" she hisses. A scowl of involuntary loss moves across her frown line. "Ya done bellied yo'self of me best Sullivan's Cove, ya', grizzly prick."

"Follow us," I say to the others. Luca moves around me and Reggie joins him from the rear, Vigo riding his back, so I'm flanked on each side by hybrids. "Lovely," I say. I hoist Kitsune over my shoulders, her foxtail making me look overly formal and silly.

I'm a better warrior than Luca, I think, because I was trained by Reggie, one of the best Alphion Proximal C fighters sent to this planet, but sometimes each of them treats me like a fragile princess in need of saving. *Grr.* I can handle this. The rope fibers are frayed and rough against my palms as we descend. Straw and dust particles sting my eyes and make me cough. Bo blows out his torch with one heavy breath and I'm surprised it doesn't burn the ladder down. "Are we almost at Ereshun?" I ask.

"Not yet," Bo says. "We need to negotiate passage. Don't look down."

"Why?" Luca asks.

A blinding spotlight targets us from below.

And of course, I look down.

I hold tight to the ladder and stare into the abyss of an immense ravine full of light, a place that makes the Grand Canyon look like a drainage ditch. The ladder is attached to... "Is this a spaceship?" I ask. "Did I lead my team into a UFO?"

"Space capsule," Bo says.

"Is this Ereshun?" I ask.

"You've arrived at the Isle of No Time," Bo says. "Ereshun lies beyond. I travel no farther with you."

Into the bosom of No Time, the Viking holds the Isle. That's what my mother said to me a few years ago when I visited her for the last time at the asylum. "What if I secure you more whiskey?" I ask.

"Then my lady, I shall follow you to infinity!"

"How do we go from being inside a tunnel to...to...this...Isle of No Time? Are we outside?" A breeze tousles my hair. Below me are strange-looking trees, rooted into rock, hundreds of suspended glass-like shiny buildings, and far, far away, what appears to be tiny floating vehicles, a monorail conveyance unlike any I've ever seen, and miniature entities moving about—and based on their size, they're about five miles away. I lift my mask. We can breathe. The others follow suit.

"We are in *No Time*," Bo answers, and this is all he says.

"Oh, this is heaps bad!" Dr. Monica yells. She tries to go back the way we came, which makes the ladder sway. Everyone yells for her to stop. Dr. Monica is the bravest female human I know, but her courage comes with a caveat; she's terrified of heights. She remains as far away from cliffs, elevators, and planes as possible. I had a hard enough time convincing her to climb up on a camel.

"Dr. Monica! Stop. And that's an order!" Hogan screams.

Dr. Monica looks at me, her eyes as big as a twin star system, which I suspect means she's silently screaming in terror—and if she continues down—she might fall—and take the rest of us with her—but it isn't the falling that would bother her, I think. She hates that everyone is witness to her not-so-silent panic. She's frozen on the ladder with no one above her, powder white knuckles bolted to the rope, and gulping too-rapid breaths.

"What should we do?" I ask.

"I said don't look down," Bo says with a shrug. "I can cut the rope with my sword."

"Then we all fall to our death and she's left dangling?" I don't mention that Luca and I could probably get enough lift here, not to fly, but to make a survivable hard landing.

"Fair warnin'" Dr. Monica says, profusely sweating. "I'm gonna chunk mah' guts!"

"***Nooooo!!***!"

And she does...thick spew stew and Sullivan's Cove rain down like putrid fire and brimstone over our heads. None of us goes unscathed by her terror-induced vomit. She wipes her mouth with her sleeve. And now *I* feel sick. "I feel betta!'" she yells. But she still doesn't move.

"Bloody hell, woman!" Luca yells. "You have four options, Monica! You climb up, or down, or you let go!"

"You said four options!" she yells. "What's the *fourth*?"

"You can remain stuck to this ladder like a barnacle until you rot to bone!"

"Luca!" I yell. He looks up at me and smiles. He releases both hands from the rope and flings himself over Bo's head, into the canyon, offering me a parade wave until he disappears below the canopy. "Damn him," I mutter under my breath.

Reggie has already climbed *around* everyone and is now just below Dr. Monica. Finally, he reaches her, and places large hands over hers as if his body is a fleshy, furry suit of armor. Vigo whines and clings to his enormous back like a scared puppy. I'm amazed, as usual, how Reggie does this sort of thing unfazed, and so quickly.

"Move!" Reggie yells to the rest of us.

Plank-by-plank, Reggie pries Dr. Monica's hands from the rope, and eventually, we all touch foot to solid soil and catch our breath. Dr. Kanumba passes out wet wipes, so we swab away some of the chunks and stench of Dr. Monica's breakfast but not nearly enough to be presentable to anyone, especially Usta.

Away from the rest of us, Luca ambles through the foliage as if he's on tour at the Royal Botanical Gardens. It is only now I realize my heart pounds in my chest, but it has zero to do with my attraction toward him. I plan to give him a piece of my mind for dropping out on our team once I ensure everyone's okay. *Arsehole.*

Vigo lets loose with a low and intimidating growl, something capturing his attention in the brush. "What is it, boy?" Reggie asks.

Bo's eyes glow blue again. "Uh-oh," he says. And before I can ask, an unseen, angry voice shouts from some distance.

"You're trespassing, Bo. You've been barred from this place and bouldered to exile. Be gone!"

Bo mutters something under his breath I can't hear, then says, "I brought you a gift and a special guest. I hope to negotiate passage...and forgiveness." *What gift? What does he mean by special guest?* A leaden lure feeling sinks deep into my gut as I wonder if Bo is about to sell us out, maybe straight into slavery... or worse. With a rustle of super-sized purple ferns, little footsteps thump toward us. Hogan's men grip their weapons hip side and hoist them forward, ready to fire. Kitsune does a nosedive into the thicket and disappears. I strain my eyes to make out a figure and see the enormous ears first, pointed straight up like upside-down vibrant pink carrot antennae. A face, cute with a slightly pointed yet short anteater-like trunk and bioluminescent whiskers, peers out over the top of a bush. Finally, the creature breaks from the bushes to a field of gasps from our crew. It wears a soiled tunic and carries a bucket with a lid.

"I'll be damned," Dr. Kimathi whispers.

"Aye, mate...you're the exobiologist," Dr. Monica says to me. "You know what that thing is?"

I shake my head, still staring at the...animal? The body of this creature is covered in silvery fur, and it has a long black tail with a bright electro-plated tip, and walks on two bulbous hindlegs, having two short arms and long pink finger-like four-digit paws for hands. I remember Bennie's lab at Silo #57 at Plum Hook Bay, when I was sixteen, how he kept an assortment of bones, arachnids, insects, and animals, even bullet ants, and a pet cardinal named Edwin...but I've never, in all my lives, seen anything like this weird creature before me, who maybe stands five-feet tall at best, on hind legs. It lifts its snout-trunk around my aura and grunts a pig snorting sound, inspecting me.

"No, it cannot be true!" And when the words tumble out of its mouth the way any human might talk, it leaves the rest of us with our mouths wide open and speechless. "Princess Scathatch, acknu on' towdow, I thought more lifetimes would pass without us having met." It bows then pokes Bo in the shoulder with its snout. "You're another matter—I could have gone infinite millennia before seeing the likes of you again!"

I lean over. "What did you do, Bo?"

"I accidentally ate his alpha wife," he whispers. "He exiled me in stone."

"Accidentally?"

"She tried to eat my face off," Bo says.

"A cute creature as this?"

"Don't be fooled," he says. "These monstrosities are vicious."

I squint to get a better look and feeling about this fuzzy bunny-rat-anteater-kangaroo-looking critter. Its large black eyes pool with compassion. I can't detect a hint of *vicious* leaking from its pores or aura. "What is it?" I ask.

"Elemorphia," Bo answers. I sift through the catalogue of species memorized in my brain but come up empty.

"Is this smelly murderer treating you all right, Princess?" it asks.

A small patch of micro-panic ripples across Bo's cheeks and I realize that although I am Bo's ticket out of his basalt-ensconced prison, this creature may easily return him...and Bo *did* save us from our mass grave. "The Viking is a brave yet repentant host," I say. "He seeks your forgiveness." Bo puffs out his chest and smiles a too-toothy grin. "Too much," I hiss in his ear with an elbow to his ribs. Bo drops his head in feigned remorse.

"Your Highness, I'm Bilby," the creature says, frowning at Bo. He fumbles with a gold chain around his neck and stares at me. "Princess Scathatch, I'm afraid I wasn't prepared," he says. "It's been many centuries on the sunny side of Earth without nary a word on the fate of your father. We lost hope and I gave up vigil to the perpetual feast and allowed those in need among our Fluffle to eat of it."

I shift my weight and look out at the floating city far in the distance. Gleaming domes, towers, obelisks, pyramids, and I barely hear the din of what I suspect is a large city—filled with and run by...these creatures? It far surpasses, in both beauty and technology, anything I've ever seen topside. *How is this possible?*

"I take no umbrage, Bilby," I say. "It is a fine soul indeed who works in service for its Fluffle."

In the shadow of the jungle, I spot what appears to be a carved-out den, rough-hewn and mottled, with huge globs of what I think might be splattered bat scat. Bo begins to say something, but Bilby cuts him off.

"Quiet! I want no words out of you," Bilby says. "Vikings who fly ships where they aren't supposed to explore, often..." He thumps a foot on Bo's boot, making him jump and back up behind me. "...become permanently lost. You owe the Princess a huge favor."

"Bo offered to be forever indebted to my service," I say, trying to help.

"Oh, he did now? Is that all?"

"What do you mean?" I ask.

"You're a fool and a coward," Bilby says to Bo.

I'm astonished he'd say such a thing because Bo seems quite stereotypically menacing for an intergalactic Viking, almost as tall and wider than Luca. Bilby lifts the lid on his little bucket and pulls out a glowing sphere, one that doesn't look at all as if it would fit in there. It floats between us, and my eye necklace rises to the occasion, mixing its glow with the sphere.

"Do you know what this is?" Bilby asks.

"No," I say.

"Keep it safe for the Fluffle," Bilby says, without telling me what it is, and just like that it's absorbed into my eye necklace. "You didn't tell her?" he asks Bo.

"I didn't want to," Bo says.

"Probably best," Bilby says. He discards the little bucket. "Where are my manners?" He reaches his long tail up to a tree branch, wraps it around a limb, and shakes an old ship's bell. "You're quite the odiferous bunch. Let's get you cleaned up and fed, shall we? Watch the holes."

"Aren't you coming with us?" I ask Bo when he turns to leave.

"Yes, Bo," Bilby says with a sneer. "Why don't you come along?"

Bo slides back a few tentative steps, retreats through some rock, and disappears back from where he came.

FIVE

PASSAGE NEGOTIATION

I WOBBLE a bit as we reach the last step of Bilby's not-so-humble underground abode.

"Watch your heads," Bilby says as he pulls back a golden veil to a massive rustic room. Dr. Monica smashes her cranial vault into a low-hanging beam. "Damn it!" she curses. "Bloody fokin' *hare*-brained idea this is!"

We step through another short door and enter a room where a myriad of female elemorphia, wearing floral print dresses, fashioned under lacey aprons, move about. Bilby slaps his meaty paw fingers together to get their attention. "Ladies, may I present to you, Princess Scathatch, Countess of Skye." A pitcher crashes to the floor but so does every female in the room. They immediately fall silent and curtsy. My team, except for Luca, snickers. Now the room is too quiet, and nobody moves.

"What are they doing?" I whisper to Bilby.

"They won't rise until you grant them permission," he whispers back.

I don't feel the least bit comfortable with this groveling. As a former ward of the court and foster kid on Earth, I couldn't stand being expected to kiss the arses of authority figures. "At ease," I say, thinking about some members of the Ormian Council who wouldn't like this show of fawning a bit, given that a small percentage of my golden blood is humanly *diluted*. Any claims I might have to their cosmic throne—a seat I know nothing about and wouldn't care if it cracked to bits under the weight of my ass, is under *consideration*. "Please rise. Bilby is gracious and all your efforts on our behalf merit never having to kneel before Camaeliphim again."

"Is this your decree?" Bilby asks, a faint smile of approval turning up his lips.

"This is my decree," I say.

A collective sigh ripples through the fluffle and the ladies relax. The room is filled with a variety of tools, plants, potions, buckets, powders, and other garden gadgetry. A cauldron sits over a small fire inside what resembles a clay oven. Its hearth displays a variety of odd but charming mugs on hooks and it reminds me, in a nostalgic way, of Barbara's cozy but expansive kitchen back at Plum Hook Bay. Dr. Kimathi and Dr. Kanumba conduct a visual examination, mentally taking inventory of the room's contents and I join them.

"Princess?" Bilby asks.

"Oh, pardon me," I say. "I was just thinking..."

He walks across the room and I follow. "I'll bet we're quite a sight to you, my wives and me," he says, twisting a whisker with his pinkish paw.

"Wives?"

"Oh yes," he says. "My apologies. I thought it appropriate to introduce you to the wives first."

"Oh," I say. "You have mistresses too?"

"Heavens no," Bilby laughs. "That would be inappropriate. The room beyond this one houses my husbands."

"What the fu..." Hogan begins to say, but Dr. Monica slaps a palm over his mouth and shakes her head no, wagging her other finger in his face.

"What's with all the holes outside?" Reggie asks. "Booby traps for trespassers?"

"Life insurance," Bilby says.

Luca opens the door between our connected quarters and enters my room. "Something is '*off*' about this Fluffle," he says.

"Oh, something is *off* all right," I say, not exactly disappointed to see him but I won't tell him so. "Do you know how to knock? Popping into my room unannounced might get you killed." I continue brushing my hair and looking in the mirror, keeping eyes on him.

"You're *mad* at me," he says with a Cheshire grin. "You *care*."

I shake my head for effect but not so hard I come off as protesting too much. "The first hint of trouble arrives, and you fling yourself *off* harm's way to save your ass! None of our unit, except maybe Reggie, knew you could fly...but now they do! And what about leaving us to dangle? You're supposed to be a Camaeliphim warrior, not some royal pansy ass."

Luca half circles me and says nothing. It's then I realize he might be able to see through the silky gown given to me by Bilby's new "Apex" wife, Paramel. I'm still in awe of its noble tailoring and pristine sky-blue color. It glides over my skin and feels more heavenly against it than the ivory cashmere coat Dr. Evelyn once draped over my shoulders when we met.

Thankfully, my wiry hair hides most of my backside. I take a step away from the glass to avoid his gaze. "Don't," he says. "I will only touch you when *you're* ready—let me have a moment to really see you."

"Excuse me," I say, laying down the brush on a small table.

"Why in the hell would I permit your ogling when you flew off and left us hanging?"

"Samantha, you are on your way, *if* you survive, to becoming high queen," Luca says. "I know how capable you are. You had that minor hiccup handled. Besides, I loathe human puke. And this place...something is not right about this Fluffle."

I don't know how to respond to this...not the puke part, or the Fluffle, but me having today handled. I'm glad he noticed but still miffed he took a dive. "I detect nothing amiss about the Fluffle," I say.

"They're scared of something," Luca says.

"Aren't we all," I say.

"You can't have it both ways, Princess Scathatch," he adds. "You can't be both a damsel in distress *and* an independent warrior...pick one...but frankly, I don't think my coddling becomes you. And I disagree. There's something amiss about these creatures."

He's scrubbed the worst of the cave crud from his skin. His hair is again the familiar wavy flaxen sheen with platinum high-lights I envy. His azure eyes wash over me, and I observe a tenderness in them but also something raw and dangerous, a *want* he does his best to conceal...and it leaves me wanting of him in equal measure. Slowly, he reaches out and hovers his hands over my hips, looking in the mirror for permission. I slightly tilt my head and painfully discern, Luca is right...I can't have it both ways. Straddling fences always protected me when I was unsure of beastly horrors...or healthy desires.

"Secrets abound on this planet," he whispers in my ear. "So many deceptions for us to explore and expose." His hands slide around my hips. His breath and lips lightly dance along my neck. My stomach muscles contract into knots and I fight back a moan when he cups a breast. "Let go, Samantha," he whispers. "You want me as much as I do you. Let me show you pleasure."

Every fantasy I've had about Lord Luca Harrington crashes

through the gates of my reserve. I envision myself writhing under him, an ecstasy so fierce, it cannot be controlled...but that's my problem...control. I hate giving it up, appearing vulnerable and weak...going soft over a hybrid who's bedded females from here to Habibula—and even left a couple standing at the altar.

I know the rules of his engagements. Luca satisfies cravings and then leaves his ladies in waiting, never to return to them. But what of it? Genin and I shared passion yet could be apart and non-committal for months. I've had other lovers too—all human— male and female. My head leaps between hungering for Luca and the practicality of pushing him away—straddling fences.

His lips graze mine before he devours me, and I feel his desire, my desire, run like a live wire, the entire length of our bodies, securing us as one. I shudder with fear and craving, aching for him to come in unto me...to share the friendliness of my thighs...a term Camaeliphim use to describe an unbreakable bond when two betrothed hybrids engage in consummation.

My legs shake so much I barely stand. In the dim light, I fan out my arms over his chest and bury my fingers in his hair—and realize what bothers me so—I feel too much for this hybrid. The thought of Luca leaving this realm is a soul pain from which I'm not sure I'll recover. He lifts the gown over my head and pushes me down, under him, onto the bed. My Pleiades pendant pinches my stomach and zaps him with a spark of warning.

"Ow!" he yelps. "Can you take that thing off?"

"No can do," I say. "I'll compromise with a workaround." I push and twist the pendant behind my neck.

"So beautiful. I have waited millennia to feel you again," Luca whispers...and just like the first real kiss we shared at Harrington House, I melt into him and release my guard. Our eyes lock in connection and I experience the feeling of having known him lifetimes ago, snippets of déjà vu and dreams, but no solid memories. The amber light in the room casts a glow on his tropical ocean eyes, which transition to sapphire, then sable, until they're an inky flicker of otherworldly intention and venom. A wispy black arm of his aura reaches past him...for me.

"Luca?" I push back on his chest but feel only empty air.

"No!" he says. "Samantha, I..."

I reach out for him, but he hovers too near the ceiling, struggling with himself, I think. "You don't have to be sorry," I say. "We're betrothed. This isn't wrong."

Luca turns his head away in "sadgitation." He fades into the framework of the room...gone. Black tendrils of mist follow him. I sit up in confusion, wondering what I did wrong, or maybe he finds me unappealing naked. So many assumptions rush through my brain.

I can think of nothing else to do after his hasty exit except put away the hairbrush and blow out the lights. I crack the door to check the lock. I see Paramel talking with Reggie much farther down the hall. She places her paws over his hands, looks up at him and nods. How odd, I think. My doubt about Luca and his Bezaliel mist seeps into my fears, lingers, and refuses to flee.

"He can't be trusted," Reggie had said.

Somewhere in this Isle of No Time, sleep lays her cloak over my heart and offers temporary reprieve.

SIX

PARAMEL

PARAMEL RIPS OPEN THE DRAPES. I squint, sit up, and shield my eyes with a hand. Her stealthy intrusion, and what resembles natural sun, beams through a well-appointed guest room. She's brought me a breakfast of seeded jam, charred flatbread, loose tea, some sort of indescribable concoction, and a bowl of what I think might be root vegetables, and places it on the table.

"What time is it?" I ask.

"I wouldn't know," she answers. "Time is a concept used by humans to measure intervals between events because, being part human, you think and act in a linear way."

"Hence," I say, "the Isle of No Time."

Paramel tilts her head, smiles softly, and nods as I hand her my gown. She folds it neatly and places it back on the bed, even though I have no plans for another sleepover. I tie a robe around my waist. The compass I laid on the nightstand beside the bed glows and wildly vibrates, its needle spinning first clockwise, then counterclockwise, before it settles on due south.

"Your compass appears broken," she says.

"Reggie gave it to me," I say. "It's never worked, except maybe once or twice." I tap it against my palm. No change. I put it down again and tighten the sash on my robe.

"Why do you carry a useless compass?"

"It's a gift." I shrug. "It has meaning and reminds me to breathe and think before I react. Has Bilby or your parents ever given you a special gift?"

"Once," Paramel says without elaborating. An awkward silence ensues.

"May I see it?" I ask.

"I lost it," she says, looking down at the floor, not wanting, I sense, to discuss it further.

"I'm sorry," I say. "That must have been very painful for you."

"More than any sentient being could ever understand," she says, stitching her paws through the folds of her pink checkered apron. Her lips turn up into a half-hearted smile. "It disrupted my internal unity and brought disorder to this Isle. I should have paid better attention."

"I lost something too," I say, and then realize I've lost a lot of things...friends, a daughter, maybe my way...but settle on a less existential, yet still important loss. "I forgot a password."

"For what?" she asks.

"Long story," I say. "But I need the password to obtain access to a certain place."

"I see," she says. "You're a princess, right?"

"So, I'm told," I say.

"Then why don't you just change the password?"

"It doesn't work that way," I say, but wonder if it might be possible, and why I never thought of it. "And you? Couldn't you *decide* to let go of what you lost and turn your internal unity inside out?"

"Unfortunately," she says, "it doesn't work that way for me either. I am enervated, stripped of my true spirit."

"I'm sorry," I say. "Enervation for a middle-world hybrid is just as bad as inanimation for Camaeliphim. Did Bilby strip you of your Renascence?" I ask.

"Oh, no," she says. "He's been honorably hospitable. I was deceived by a jarl."

"Jarl?"

"A military leader of my territories," she says. "I was betrayed, then cursed, having to flee here for safety."

"How terrible," I say. "Where is this jarl now?"

"It was centuries ago," she says with a sigh. "He's long dead, I suspect. But never mind such matters. Bilby tells me you're the Balancer. Is this true?"

"It's what I'm told," I say. "I allegedly inherited the role from my father."

"Your status is a high honor," she says. Paramel starts to curtsy but stops short when I shake my head because I decreed the Fluffle unbound from such pretention.

"My role as a Balancer is a troublesome burden," I say.

"Aye," Paramel agrees. "It means you care about the quality of your performance not for status, but to save lives, which is noble. Power is fraught with unavoidable duty and risk of failure."

"If I fail," I say, "this world fails too."

"If you prevail," she says, "so too, many worlds."

Ripples of light float across the rumpled sheets and caress the hem of my robe near the table. "I'm surprised it looks exactly like morning sunlight coming through the windows," I say.

"An illusion we thought you might find comforting," she says, straightening the bed. "We have the ability to safely harness lava flows to capture UV light."

"Paramel, if time does not exist in the Fluffle, how can anything happen?" I ask.

"If you stop thinking," she says, her snout twitching, "the reality of timelessness is obvious."

"I'm not sure what you mean," I say.

"Time is fundamentally flawed, just as humans are," she says. "The Isle of No Time exists in an ever-changing *Now*."

"Never thought about it that way," I say. "Why do you think humans are flawed? I mean, I agree with you...they *are*...but hybrids aren't any better."

"Elemorphia are flawed too," Paramel says with a breath of resignation. "Humans are flawed because they fail to realize '*self*' is an illusion created by impulses. Worldly overlords inflate human cells with desire. Self-aggrandizement passes as 'awareness'. Elemorphia call this manipulation '*misdirected investments*. Humans fail to advance because negative energy veils their enlightenment to universal interconnectedness. It is quite difficult for humans to overcome their overlords' vibrational signals." She looks toward the window, lost to her thoughts.

"Are you happy here?" I ask.

Paramel tosses an air of sadness about her, making herself busy with nothing, and I can't help but think there is more to her story. She pours fresh tea for both of us. "If you give legs to your grievances, happiness runs."

"Clever way of hiding pain," I say.

"Or dealing with it," she quickly adds. "My parents were killed during the Ki Wars in what you'd know humanly as *centuries* ago. I miss grass and trees, stars, and feeling the sun on my face, but I do not miss war. Everything here '*just is*' and we adapt to its repetitive sameness. And you? What of your parents?"

I'm impressed by the way Paramel so smoothly volleys a question back at me. It's the perfect defense for avoiding answers. When I think about my parents, which I haven't for a while, they are enigmas. I try to remember what family, my *real* family looks like, but I carry no actual pictures. As a kid, any photographs I did have were lost during abrupt moves to new foster homes. I often wonder if caseworkers thought it best for me to forget family because my parents were too 'out there'.

"I dream about my dad sometimes, dressed in camouflage, his US Army nametag visible, but his face always enveloped in gray smoke," I say. When I think about my mom, I'm sure she's better off with Ebians. Living as a light source must be far superior to her former stint as a guest of the US government at the Tiffin Asylum for the Criminally Insane, a clandestine "zero-star" military-run mental hospital. But I don't tell Paramel this. "I met an *interdimensional* half-sister once," I say, "during a small battle against Bezaliels under a nuclear reactor at Plum Hook Bay." What I don't say is that my sister's name is Nemain. Like Lozen, she's a warrior and realm rover—but my sister escorts souls *beyond* and has never guarded Ninmah's Portals. My family is gray snippets of wilted flickers and faded shadows that glitch and disappear, like exploding stars. "Both of my parents are missing," I say, trying not to brood.

"We make do," Paramel says and pairs her statement with what I think is a soft whisker smile when she pats my shoulder with her paw. "Bilby brought me here. It isn't perfect, but I am grateful. Humans, I'm afraid, would be cruel to, and frightened of, Elemorphia. I shall offer intention that you are reunited with your birth givers, whether in this realm or another."

"Thank you."

Paramel places her floral teacup on a matching saucer and it makes a soft clink. I think about the past few days, how it feels less real...or maybe surreal. What did feel real was Luca's touch... but since there is no past on the Isle of No Time, I suppose *last night* is a previous *Now*. I replay his body pressed against mine until I'm forced to use imagination and fill in the blanks of what *didn't* happen. "I should go. I need to meet Luca and Reggie."

"I let you sleep," Paramel says. "You looked unbroken in your peace. The males of your species have gone off."

"Gone off? Where?" I ask, feeling slightly panicked,

wondering if the Isle of No Time, and Fluffles, make humans and hybrids forget whatever it was they knew before. I don't tell Paramel how angry it makes me when Luca and Reggie strategize without me. My leg fidgets under the table and I concentrate to stifle its rhythmic wobble.

"Self-care is a wonderful tonic," she says. "The males have gone off to the boundaries of the Fluffle, to drink and boast of brave deeds. I've prepared you another bath, and then if you like, I will show you around."

"Some things never change," I say.

"Indeed," Paramel says. "Change is the only sure illusion."

A rare smile involuntarily paints my lips as we share a chuckle. I lose the robe again, slide into the naturally formed lava grotto tub, which is perpetually heated from below and full of iridescent bright blue bubbles. I sink back into fantasies of Luca and how things could have, should have, gone.

Paramel leads me into the otherworldly jungle just on the opposite side of the Isle of No Time, nearer, but still some distance from Ereshun. Elemorphia guard the Isle, she says...but I suspect, given Elemorphia's industrious and gentle nature, the Fluffle is Usta bait, providing a moat, fair warning, or perhaps expendable sacrifice for Usta. I cup my palm around the Bukhara blade secured to my thigh in the event we run into something I must kill.

She swings a strange basket of something she calls '*strial hide*'. We dodge other members of the Fluffle digging holes...lots of holes. Another Elemorphia, another hole. A few of the creatures jump into their ditches under super-sized royal purple ferns and disappear. I do my best to step around each one but there isn't a lot of space between them. "What is up with all these fucking holes?" I finally ask.

Paramel outright laughs at my cursing and slips me a small test-tube vial of strange-looking liquid from her 'strial-hide' basket. "These...*holes*...as you call them, are sacred passageways," she says. "Small portals that lead just south of Ki but never meet the Sun."

"Ki? You mentioned Ki before," I say. "What is Ki?"

"My apologies," she says. "We informally refer to Earth as Ki, and scientifically as Planet D."

"Planet D?"

"Cosmic hierarchy designates Ki as *Planet D*, which stands for devastation, deficits, depletion, and distress."

"Oh," I say. "That's not good. These holes are portals?"

She nods.

"And what is this?" I hold up the strange bright violet-looking liquid.

"This," she says, holding up her own vial, "is a concentrated form of what you consider liquor. But be careful...you only require a drop to lessen your troubles."

I slide the vial into my pocket for later examination.

"You do not wish to imbibe?" she asks.

"That's not it," I say. "I don't want to fall into any holes! But thank you. I'll save it for later."

Elemorphia labor equally in silent solitude. Unlike most humans, none of these creatures yell, complain, or shirk duty with excuses. I sense no *sadgitation* over their menial and repetitive tasks. People, on the other hand, or *Kihogs,* as Paramel calls them, make noise, and squeal plenty of protest when it comes to labor. I suspect, after having lived among humans, this is mostly due to servitude passing as noble hard work for menial wages. Initially created as a slave race, humans, as part of the primate Hominin, were bred eons ago to "till soil" for Anunnaki—until Ebians intervened to elevate human consciousness and implant *awareness.* I vault another hole and pick up the subject. "Why do Elemorphia dig so many holes?"

"Insurance," Paramel says without elaborating.

"What sort of insurance?" I ask.

"Life insurance," she says. "Follow me."

We delicately dodge more sewer-lid-sized potholes in this otherworldly wilderness and find ourselves at a vaulted chamber. She wills the doors to open with a simple tap of her paw. I wipe a bit of sweat from my forehead and peer into the amber glow of a garden of orchid roots stretching their tentacles into aqueous geophytes, like the ones my team saw on our way here. Paramel gently slides one of her paws along the outside of a squishy membrane, closes her eyes, and murmurs what sounds like a chant. A hand, a human hand, presses its palm against hers from inside the bulbous womb. I jump back, trying to rein in my *shaken*.

"Don't be afraid. We are a containment Fluffle," Paramel says. "We mine lost souls and tend them for later release."

"I'm not following," I say, getting more freaked out by the moment. I recover and act as if seeing human body parts languishing in overgrown underground, amber-filled-gel-pods, and being touched by a talking rat-rabbit, is somehow *normal*. An elbow now pushes upon, but not through, another nearby pod.

"We dig holes to the underside of Kihog graves and extract corpses for later ascension."

"*Later* ascension?" I ask. "How is there a *later* if time doesn't exist?"

"This is true," Paramel says with a wink. "You pay attention. But time exists for humans, so we must cleanse their souls, scrub their memories, and extract consciousness, in this *Now*."

"I feel sick," I say. "You're grave robbers."

"We are life *re-purpose-ers*," she corrects me—without the least bit of irritation in her voice. "Human bodies are temporary containers for consciousness, which must not remain trapped. We portal our way to this world's underside of fresh graves, laser through coffin bottoms, and retrieve that which belongs to the Source."

"What if a human is cremated?" I ask.

"The essence of consciousness is easily released through cremation," she says. "It saves us a lot of work."

"What do you do with the corpses once the, uh, consciousness is released?" I ask.

"We use the containers as crop fertilizer or sell it to Usta for future soul insertion, or otherwise comfort unprepared souls, whose containers were unduly compromised, but they refuse to exit."

"Refuse to exit?"

"This happens when a human container experiences sudden expiration...the body becomes completely unusable on Ki, due to what you might refer to as *sudden death*. The soul energy is jostled, momentarily confused, and refuses to part with its broken container."

"What about bodies kept at morgues or government labs?"

"We help Ki agents pluck consciousness from those containers," Paramel says, then frowns. "Sometimes, a soul does escape our intervention."

"What happens then?"

"Humans call them ghosts," she answers. "They're cruelly forced from their vessels when government agencies steal the corpses for use as brainless cyborgs. The worst, though, is when a container abruptly awakens from what you know as sure death— it's invaded by counter-terrestrials."

"Bezaliels?" I ask.

"Sometimes," she answers. "Elemorphia moved closer to Usta to seal and guard the containers from otherworldly plunder."

"Jesus Christ," I say, thinking about Barbara and how I'm glad she isn't here to see or hear this. It would rock every foundation of Godly faith she's ever built, and I don't think I'd want to see, hear, or clean up *that* spiritual mess. "Do you house hybrids here too?"

"We aren't permitted to handle hybrid containers," Paramel says. "They pass through Usta and are escorted to the Halls of Rumnir for assessment."

"What sort of assessment?" I dodge another line of holes laid out like map dots.

"I heard it is to decide inanimation, future transition, or realm roving status," Paramel says. "But I do not know this for certain."

An involuntary shiver sparks along my spine. Inanimation for a hybrid is worse than death. No one can tell me exactly what warrants such a cruel sentence, but I suspect Luca might be a candidate, given the fact he violated Intergalactic Code with the insertion of Bezaliel mist into his Golden Blood. Then another thought strikes me. "Paramel, do *all* human souls pass through here?"

"Yes."

"Is my mother and her vessel here?" I ask.

Paramel touches one paw on my forearm and the other on a pod, closes her eyes, and chants again. Some of the pods inside the walls light up like a row of streetlights at dusk. The low "om" sound rises slightly in vibration and channels through my chest. "No," she finally says. "Anyone else?"

"My grandmother," I say. "Lorna Eda Sage."

Another long moment of silence while Paramel chants. "No," she says. "When did your grandmother withdraw from Ki?"

"Almost twenty human years ago," I say. "I was eight."

"She entered another reality."

"What does that mean?" I ask.

"Lorna Eda Sage fully engaged a new existence," Paramel says. "She disconnected her energy from this current illusion and no longer remembers Ki."

Sadness bangs on the walls of my heart. I haven't felt my

grandmother's spirit move through me for years. "Ouch," I say. "She doesn't remember me. Seems highly unfair."

"For you, maybe," Paramel says. "You should be happy for her. Lorna evolved and transcended Ki cravings and its containers."

"I'm trying to understand. Your prayers help," I say, looking at the meticulously maintained garden of corpses she calls "containers" and wondering about prayer. I don't really pray much. I meditate. I breathe. I pray when my ass is in a sling.

"I don't pray," she says. I lift an eyebrow at her. "Chants are navigational beacons. Chanting enables me to enliven and communicate with conserved energy. Craving things of Ki and its grand illusion brings suffering and unease to bound soul energy... my intent scatters mindful energy and raises vibrations for greater consciousness. It is not prayer."

"I thought mind and consciousness were the same," I say.

"The mind is connected to the body, like grounding wire for Ki," she says, "for consciousness to freely enter and exit in ongoing connection and communication."

"Antenna," I say.

Paramel tips her head up and down. "Consciousness streams through a single mind, a Source, but all Kihogs are connected, no matter where, or to whom they say their prayers. One God, if you will." We stroll through the innards of the chamber before stopping again. "Sometimes energy must be freed, but the process is frightening for souls that become too attached to their container, its mass and density. It mistakenly believes its energy is unable to exist outside corporeal form. If inner consciousness fails to elevate enough vibration to process through a container, it must be coaxed."

"Is my daughter, Hope, here?"

"Your daughter would not be kept here," she says. "She is more than human."

"I forgot," I say. "But there is one more human I'd like to find if you don't mind. Her name was Verity Lane. She died less than a year ago, Ki time."

"Hold onto me," Paramel says.

And just as I touch her, everything in my head spins and we lift off our feet. We speed toward a wall of basalt, and I squint my eyes shut when we harmlessly pass through. I adjust to bubbling magma, orange, and red bursts of blazing flames. Plasma oozes over spongy rock formations and smelt. Paramel forges *through* what she calls the lungs of Ki.

"Hang on!" she warns. "Don't let go!" Canyons, mountains, and crystal caves whiz past in streaks of color, or complete, crunchy, blackness. Rumbles, sparks, earsplitting cries, and pile-driving echoes invade my ears. We push through another wall of granite and the weight of it crushes my spirit, body, and breath into one collapsible molecule. Just when I think I can't take anymore, that I'll vaporize or irreparably split, we splash through oceans of oil, unscathed and unsoiled, and come to a screeching halt in another corridor.

I stumble into orchid roots.

Paramel patiently waits as I gently unweave myself from the gray-green tentacles that extract and contain the destructive sap of the dead. Again, she places one paw on a geophyte and the other on my arm before I fully recover, as if she didn't just transport me damn near Ki's core! My head snaps back, then forward. Amber light shimmers in the pod and I feel Verity's essence pulsing through it, an overwhelmingly sad energy retreating to the far corner of its container, refusing to relinquish its former life.

"This wasn't an easy corpse to retrieve," Paramel says. "Her body was placed in government cold storage and remanded near the summit of a clandestine military base called Mount Umunhum."

"I wonder why," I say. "How did you get her body here?"

"A high clearance Kihog," Paramel says. She places her palm

on an etched chart next to the pod. "According to her sequence grid, she arrived through a portal dug under a missile silo in the Adirondacks."

I make a mental note to do some recon on Reggie's friend Ike. "Mount Umunhum is thousands of miles away from the Adirondacks," I say. "How was she transported?"

"She wasn't," Paramel says.

"What do you mean?"

"She was teleported using cube technology through an underground artery, like the way I got you *here*. We stole her corpse from..." She sifts through a series of hieroglyphs on the wall as if reading braille. "Comm grid relays show this particular soul was harnessed from a lab run by someone named Dr. Evelyn Dennison and funneled into a holding pod at a missile silo near a United States town called Lewis in New York."

Paramel's words worm through me, looking for a place to settle, another realization I've always existed within a personal vortex of my aunt's fucked-up reality. Dr. Evelyn Dennison, *aka* the Countess of Teviot, does horrid things, but she's never held accountable. A chilly sweat trickles down my back and slithers its way into my heart. "Why a missile silo?" I ask.

"A few Kihogs possess higher enlightenment, clearances, and intelligence than others," she says. "They believe souls should never be harnessed for artificial manipulation, so they secretly help us."

Of course, why didn't I consider this before? When we were young, Verity was like a daughter to Barbara. And my "best friendness" with Verity sprouted from our mutual affinity for reading, MIA fathers, and copious unanswered questions about what brought us into this covert world of high weirdness. All this time, I figured Reggie sent Barbara to Ike's missile silo to keep her safe from Ki's corruptive influences. I've been so wrapped up in my own "need-to-know" that I never thought about Barbara, a domestic goddess, having a potentially secret clearance too. "Can I communicate with Verity's energy?"

"You can try," Paramel says. "She's folded away her consciousness and refuses our coaxing. Typical of skittish energy whose containers are prematurely destroyed. But it's atypical for her to cling so long to her container."

"I'm not surprised," I say. "Verity never did like change."

I remember how she'd toss a blanket over her head when she got scared, as if danger would overlook such an obvious hiding place. Verity used to dig her nails into my arms when we'd tiptoe through the woods at Plum Hook Bay. So many memories I have with her and about her. She saw me fly once and helped me breach Plum Hook Bay to retrieve my Pleaides pendant. I place my palm on the bulb. "Verity? Are you in there? It's me, Samantha."

A slight stirring within the watery membrane. Fingers curl along the flowery skin and disappear. Paramel stands just behind my left shoulder, and I turn to her. "Can she *hear* me?" And just as the words flow away from me, a decaying half-face practically bursts through the geophyte lining. "Christ!" I fall backward and land hard on my ass, staring up at a ghastly and ghostly open mouth trying to let out a scream, eyes wide open but not seeing, their once proud lime green goodness faded to black sockets.

"Quick!" Paramel says. "Place your hand on the bulb!"

I spring to my feet and plaster a hand over the artificial womb. The light inside slowly brightens. "Do you remember me?" I ask.

Yes. Please let me out of here.

"I'll try," I say. *I'm bloody freaking out.* "You have to help me help you," I say, steadying my breath and rapid heartbeat. "Can you do this?"

I can't breathe. Please hurry.

"I need you to try to understand something, okay?"

What?

"Remember when we were kids and you used to blend Paganism with Christianity to try to understand our fucked-up childhoods?"

No.

"Shit happens, you said, so you'd hedge your spiritual bets," I say. "Your oils and sage were a 'soul-smoothie', and your consecrated salt and crucifixes were psychic armor."

No response. God, this is worse and so much more serious than extracting a splinter, something I had to do for her all the time at Plum Hook Bay when she helped me gather firewood. I don't think she realizes she's dead!

Yes.

"Whew. Okay," I say, exhaling a sigh of relief. "You can be free from your container. Your container is the thing you know as a body and hide inside. This bulb? It's healing your energy. I know this is frightening because your visceral memory of living inside a body is still attached to your energy, the part that is really you. Take away the skin, bones, blood, your armor, and you're literally a bundle of nerves with a brain and eyes..." *Shit. Way to go, Sam. I'm sure that will help her.*

Silence.

"What I mean is, you are *not* your body...you're so much more...you're an essence."

More silence.

Do you forgive me?

"What?" I ask, surprised by her unexpected telepathic question. "You mean, regarding Hope?"

Yes.

And we arrive at *my* moment of truth: Do I forgive Verity Lane for allowing my aunt to plant my daughter into Verity's womb without my knowledge or consent? *"Do you forgive me?"* This question is probably the toughest any sentient being, alive or dead, can ask. But real forgiveness, on my part anyway, even tougher. I'm not sure I do forgive Verity...or what was once her.

But what's stuffed inside this jelly bulb is now something entirely different than it was...her, but not her. Verity is in another form, unbound and free, but too frightened to step away from what she knows. "You can leave your container," I say. "You can transition to another form, a higher form if you choose, just like you always dreamed—and float away from Plum Hook Bay and everything bad that happened to you as a human on Earth."

The bulb suddenly goes black as if someone turned out the lights.

"What happened?" I ask.

"Shit!" Paramel says. The corridor flickers. "Run!" A wisp of white mist about the size of a lamp bounces off the walls. "Did you forgive her?"

"Yes!"

The mist enters my chest, beams back out again through my eye necklace, spins in a circle and goes through my ear, comes out the other side, and whispers in my brain...*perks come with prices*...The corridor returns to normal...or as normal as a corridor of consciousness-trapped corpses can get.

SEVEN

FEWOULZ

"IS THIS ANOTHER BALANCER?" a strange voice asks.

Another Balancer? I thought there was only one after my dad went missing. *Me.*

Paramel helps me to my feet. "You did it," she says to me. Then she looks at the approaching creature. "What are *you* doing here?"

I try to unravel what just happened. *Did what? Free Verity?* She freed herself, I think. Where Verity's essence flitted away to is anybody's guess, but I hope she's transcended somewhere fantastic and far away. Damn, what a headache. I lean against a bench carved into one of the rocks near a cul-de-sac of corpses, their bulbous membranes making a half-circle around me. The compass Reggie gave me vibrates wildly in my pocket. Verity's geophyte is gone, but from the ceiling of her former holding tank, a new sprout forms, a bright lime-green bud to encase the next prematurely destroyed *container*.

The approaching Elemorphia looks straggled, his whiskers coated with fresh dirt above a red spiral twisted beard. He wears a light blue stained smoking jacket over a completely ruined orange silk tunic. His eyes are bleary and mercury silver-black, unlike Paramel's warm brownie-colored orbs—and for the first time, I feel Luca may be right—there is something *off* about this Fluffle.

"Here," Paramel says, handing him a vial of the violet stuff she calls *liquor*. With blackened paws, the Elemorphia greedily snatches her gift, cracks the cap, and sucks out the liquid in one gulp, exposing razored teeth. He slams the vial to the ground, and it shatters into grains of iridescent crystal, its pastel colors a small rainbow that vanishes when the Elemorphia steps forward. I take the vibrating compass from my pocket and glance at its face. The dial spins wildly in every direction. It makes my fingers quiver, so I stuff it back in my pocket alongside the buckeye I promised Barbara I'd always carry.

"Thank you," he says, tapping a stalk of selenite against his hindquarter, some of the violet liquid dribbling into his scraggly beard, his eyes going glassy with intoxicated ignorance. "It helps. Got any more?"

Paramel shakes her head. "I could have repurposed that vial," she says. She glares at him with what I think is disapproval, maybe even hate, the first show of negative emotion I've seen down here aside from Bilby, who seems to have perfected the art of harmlessly losing his temper. The creature shrugs at Paramel as if breaking her property is a trivial infraction. "Scathatch is here to negotiate passage to Ereshun," Paramel says.

"Scathatch? In the *flesh*? Not possible." This male Elemorphia looks me up and down, his eyes set to pity, but my senses pick up an immediate and oily schadenfreude through a Cheshire grin. "Others have tried and failed," he sneers.

"I know," Paramel says. "But they weren't really *her*."

Others?

"Aye," he says. "They're all the same to me. Even this puny Kihog."

"Excuse me," I say. "What is your name?"

"Hruumph," grunts the creature without answering. "Come on, then..." He scurries down rock-worn, garbage-strewn stairs, so unlike the tidy, organized Fluffle, and we hurry to follow, reaching a grimy rock wall at the bottom. This place is full of dead ends, I think. He holds up his paws, and the barrier slides away as if it were water. "You first," he says.

"Wait!" Paramel says to him. "Why does Samantha have to go through this? She *is* the Balancer."

"You think I'd take *YOUR* word for it?" he asks. He hacks and coughs up some phlegm and cleans off his beard with his sleeve then sways a little bit. I hold back a retch. "You know as well as I do that any disgusting beast claiming to be the Balancer must first pass a test."

"What test?" I ask.

"You inserted yourself here," she says to the nameless Elemorphia. "Usta fetter out frauds and you know it...you only have a hold in this realm because you cheat and lie."

"Paramel?" I hold out my arm for her to come along but she backs away.

"Something wrong?" I ask.

"I am not permitted past the boundary line of the Isle of No Time," she says. Tears brim around her large eyes as an overwhelming sense of dread pools in my gut.

"What the hell is going on?" I ask. "What if I decree you are permitted past the boundary?" Geez, I wish Reggie or Luca were here to mediate between these two. I could use some reinforcements about now.

Paramel turns her head from side to side. "I will wait here... and *pray* for your safe return."

Pray? I get the feeling this is, as Dr. Monica would say, "*heaps bad!*"

"Will I return?" I ask.

"I don't know," Paramel says, and the look in her eyes tells me she's so sorry about this.

"Your *decrees* hold no weight on the boundary line," the Elemorphia says with a sneery laugh, his cesspit breath floating over my nostrils. "Any princess worth her weight as a Balancer would know this..." He mutters something else about how I'll never pass this test.

"You tricked me," I say to Paramel. "I could have brought Reggie and Luca with me for negotiation with Usta."

"No," she says, looking me in the eye. "I tricked *them,* not you." She wipes away a tear. "Usta negotiation requires a Balancer to broker passage to Ereshun. He," she says, pointing an accusatory paw at the other Elemorphia, "maintains an illicit barrier between our Isle and the Usta."

"What sort of barrier?" I ask. "And why?"

The male Elemorphia's eyes gleam and he takes in a low ragged breath but doesn't say a word, waiting for her to answer, a dribble of slobber pushing over his lips, in anticipation, I think, that she will tell me.

"I can't tell you," Paramel says, hanging her head. "It goes against rules he doesn't have to follow," she says. She falls silent, closes her eyes, lifts both paws ceiling high, and resorts to a state of meditation, reciting her chants, but not moving a muscle.

"What's with her?" I whisper, wondering about this disgusting Elemorphia before me. He looks harmless enough. Gross, but harmless.

The Elemorphia gives his kindred a one-eyed-pirate once-over. "Her? She guards the Isle."

"I thought the Viking guarded the Isle."

"She *is* the Viking," he says, and looks at me as if I've gone daft and should know this.

"*She's* the Viking?"

"What? You don't think she-male Elemorphia make good Vikings?"

"No," I say. "It's not that...it's just that I thought..."

"They don't!" he yells and spits on the ground at Paramel's

feet and pushes me. "Come along. Hurry up! I don't live on *No Time.*"

I glance back at Paramel. She still stands, silhouetted in the corpse garden, arms raised, but now shuddering, tears sizzling against rocks at her feet. Quicker than I care to admit, we're alone, this overripe sewer Elemorphia and me. I adjust my eyes to the darkness but it's hard to see. *Whack!* One hard slap lands across my ass cheeks and they rumble like tuning forks. "Just as I suspected," he says with a screechy chuckle. "You ain't granted the prince friendly thigh access! What's the matter, sooty worm named *Guy* got your honeypot?"

I reach out to grab up and strangle this perverted yet psychic Elemorphia but come up empty. "You furry little fuck rat," I say, trying to see him. "I'll roast you for supper!" How he reached into the inner recesses of my mind to pluck a dimming adolescent pre-Plum Hook Bay personal trauma, I'll never know. "I killed my rapist," I say, and not a single atom of regret or remorse escapes my lips with these words.

"Big deal," he says. "You killed a pedophile. But have you ever killed a Fewoulz?"

"Never heard of them," I say.

"Ooooh," he says. "How exciting, you cut off this Guy's intro-mittent organ with your teeth! You'd make a great Fewoulz!"

Nope. He's not like the other Elemorphia...

...and then...a voice in my head...*connect to the Source, shield your mind, protect your consciousness. Paramel?* I abruptly shut down my thoughts.

The Elemorphia hisses in what I think is disgust or maybe disappointment, and scrapes his selenite stick against something that makes a rustling sound. Light sputters into form from a pleasant-smelling palo branch. He sticks his hand into the flame to adjust the glow, smiling at me with those mercury-poisoned eyes, an eerie, sadistic grin. The strange light doesn't burn him and there are no embers. We walk closely together within the small sphere of glow because it's narrow and I have no choice. I hold my breath to save my senses from his stench. This action does little to stem the utter disgust I feel from the top of my head to the tips of my toes.

"Put your blade away," he says. "Or I will inanimate you before your next blink."

"Only the Ormian Council or the DOE can inanimate a Camaeliphim," I say, pitching him a dirty, disbelieving look. "What is that?" I ask, pointing to his makeshift torch.

"A graveolens," he says. He doesn't elaborate. "You talk too much."

The farther into the abyss we travel, the more it stinks like rot and despair. "Where are we headed?" I ask.

"*Shhhh!*"

We reach a massive artificial shiny silver door. This must be the door to Ereshun, I think. The Elemorphia holds up one palm, chants something I don't understand, chants again, and I hear a rumble on the other side. The door blows open, sending us back a few steps.

"Your hand in marriage could grant you passage to Ereshun," the Elemorphia hisses.

I hold up my left middle finger to him. "Fuck off," I say. "Already engaged." I shiver and I shove disgusting nuptial bed thoughts back into the darkest bowels of my brain. Maybe I could be nicer...fake it...but, not my style.

"Oh, I could cut that finger off so easily," he says. "Problem solved."

"No, thank you," I say. "I'm pledged to another."

"This is your last chance," he says.

"Or what?" I ask.

"You're hard to kill if you're really the Balancer," he says. "But you too, have a soul. You *can* die...or...**worse**."

I push back thoughts of inanimation. "I refuse your offer of marriage."

"I'll take your eye necklace as a consolation gift," he says. Pink nostrils pinch together, then open. His hairy brown trunk sniffs around my chest. I slap it away, but it leaves a retch-worthy slime line I quickly swipe away with a sleeve.

I pitch him a disapproving look and touch my necklace, a diamond and emerald iris with a sapphire pupil, to ensure its gold chained security around my throat. This is the same necklace Dr. Evelyn stole from my mother...the same necklace meant for me that possesses some as-of-yet unknown power. It was a gift from my mother. It's the only thing I have left of her except intermittent memories.

"Suit yourself!" The elemorphia pushes me through the door with his stinky, scaling snout, and I stumble, nearly blinded by abundant light. He slams the barrier down so I can't exit, and everything goes semi-dark again. I stand in an enormous hall—alone. My eyes adjust to low, slow-moving lasers and mist. Shadowy images flit from wall to wall. It reminds me a little of the underside of the nuclear reactor at NASA Plum Hook Bay, but this place, wherever I am, is appreciably elevated in its technology.

Unseen claws scrape feather light across my chest. I back up against the door to steady my breath and heartbeat. Thousands of Eyes of Horus blink on the ceiling, watching. Stillness creeps through, joined by screaming silence. From nowhere, shards of green glass careen toward me. I duck. They fail to connect with my flesh and disappear through the barrier.

Hologram?

A looming silhouette breaks up into hasty scattered streaks and reorients itself within the door behind me. I reach for the knife strapped to my thigh but a wicked long blade already glints along my throat line. Nope. I don't think I'm in Ereshun. And this is no hologram!

"What have we here?" an ominous and unseen voice hisses...

EIGHT

BASASAEL

"The learned savant who guards the secrets of the gods will bind his favored...with an oath...and instruct her in secrets..." **- Sumerian tablet**

LUCA TOLD our team that a laboratory once existed deep under the Gilf Kabir Plateau. I now realize he is both right and wrong. Right, because it exists and I'm held hostage by some strange shadow being, and wrong, because it's a hell of a lot deeper and farther from the surface than his intel conveyed. And this place was not built by the Chinese. No way. I doubt that anyone on Earth has the knowledge to make this sort of advanced technology. It's probably more accurate that some Chinese ops stumbled upon this place not realizing what it was and never made it home again.

Blood-spattered lab coats are neatly folded one atop the other in shiny glass cabinets. Helmets without insignia hang in a perfect X along a wall. It's an octagonal room of mirrors approximately one thousand feet in diameter. If Reggie inspected this place, I'm convinced he'd give it seven gold stars for military-grade cleanliness, stained lab coats aside. Luca probably wasn't read into the entire story because he had no need to know. Frustratingly, it's how *black ops* works; everybody receives some piece of the top-secret puzzle, but nobody ever gets a complete picture. No, this lab isn't some leftover Cold War relic, but a fully functioning covert research center.

Whatever has control of this lab is not Cryptovaranus but something else, something beyond avant-garde. Malleable tables, supplies, and a host of other gadgets I fail to recognize leave me feeling slightly nauseated. I can only imagine what torture awaits. A squat shiny silver box rests in a corner. Advanced tools line up with surgical precision on stainless steel trays. This causes an involuntary volt of disquiet along my spine. The floor, covered in highly polished metallic tiles, bounces back my reflection, an invisible hand at my throat, fatal swipe ready.

Think, Sam. What did Reggie teach you?

"Why do you hesitate?" I ask.

"Killing time," the unseen being hisses, its voice deep, baritone...male.

Killing time in the Isle of No Time?

Fog rolls in and swallows up my sight, an impenetrable chunk of cloud as equally dangerous as darkness. The air lapses into chill and fear idles up beside me. *Breathe, Sam. Hup, two, three four. Hold. Breathe out...hup, two three four...* "If you're going to kill me," I say. "At least allow a final request."

Silence.

Slowly, smoky tendrils of dark arms become visible, one attached to the medium-sized sword against my throat. I'm convinced a single swipe could sever my neck as cleanly as thinly sliced deli meat. I try not to swallow too hard.

"Why?" the smoky nothing finally asks.

Some of the test tubes across from us shiver and clink.

"Last requests before death are an Earthly custom," I say.

"What do I care of Ki customs or pitiful Kihogs? Humans forget what's sacred and destroy everything that brings them life. They're oblivious to the fact that killing Source creations wounds every incarnation of God they claim to know. Kihogs mistakenly believe themselves to be the apex of cosmic advancement and evolution." The shadow shifts. "But...you're different." I feel *it* slide around me.

I wonder if this thing is a Bezaliel, only able to manifest as smog—still, quite a feat if it's true and it's taken rudimentary form. Maybe it seeks a suitable host and will use my body as a "container" once it depletes my BOUO blood and evicts my consciousness. Yet I don't feel the same negative bristle I sometimes experience around Luca—or the full-blown fury I come up against when battling Bezaliel particles. It's an odd emotion I sense in this being...it isn't sadgitation...maybe "gloomination."

A gray-blue aura pulses around the frame of its opaque onyx innards, a smoldering ghost emitting occasional bursts of sheet lightning. It's a species I've never encountered. And I think it's weakened. I can work with weakened.

"How am I different?" I ask.

"You're not entirely human," *it* says, brushing its shadow over my frame. "Nor are you Fewoulz, Elemorphia, or Usta." *It* tightens its sword against my windpipe. "And you don't tremble. Still, a pittance of a challenge. What do you want?"

"An Elemorphia threw me in here," I say. "What is this place anyway?" The Eyes of Horus over my head shift back and forth on the dome ceiling, still watching, still blinking.

"That's a lie," the cloud being says. My hands remain pinned to the wall like magnets, my Bukhara blade gone from my thigh and plastered on another wall...across the lab. I never felt a thing against my thigh. "I could slit you from pretty head to second toe, before you could blink," it hisses. "And you would bleeeeeed…"

"I didn't lie to you," I say. "That smelly little prick out there used his greasy trunk to shove me in here and said I had to negotiate passage to Ereshun! Since you're obviously not in a mood to broker crossover, I will commence my killing for you." Drawn-out deaths are the worst, I think. The anticipation of sure demise is always more brutal than the act itself. I'm positive I could climb out of my *container*, as Paramel calls them, a lot more quickly than this thing, whatever it is, plans to extend my agony. "Of course, killing myself creates a host of multiverse problems."

Another long silence.

"You have no fear?" *it* finally asks.

"Of course, I do," I say. "But Reggie taught me how to breathe. And now that I've had time to think about it, I didn't ask to be part of this stupid scavenger hunt—hell, I wasn't even supposed to be the damn Balancer—so—give me your shiny sword, and I'll spare you the energy of having to kill me if you're not going to grant my team's passage to Ereshun." I genuinely reflect on this, being killed by a vapor monster, and don't really want to die without having met my daughter in this realm.

"Reggie?" *It* asks.

"He's Alphion Proximal C," I say. "He teaches me how to enhance my skills."

"Your Balancer skills?"

"Reggie wants me to steady combat with duty. He also says I should always keep death in my thoughts. Why are you asking about Balancer skills?"

"Why would this Reggie want you to reflect on death?" *It* asks.

"He claims death weakens covetousness," I say, "and builds a stronger mind."

"This Reggie, he's your *father*?" *It* asks.

"No," I answer. "Maybe. I've sometimes thought about

Reggie being my dad. He's the closest thing to a father I've ever had. I grew up as a foster kid. My real dad went missing when I was four, in a war called Viet Nam. Yes, Reggie's like a father to me."

"And do you listen to your father?"

"Mostly...sometimes...hardly ever." I feel a little guilty and look down at the floor, not that anyone could see me in this swirling fog, not even the eyes of Horus, now blinded. Reggie and I butt heads...a lot...yet I know with every photon of my Golden Blood he'd take a bullet, laser, or even a cannonball for me, if required, despite my being damn near impossible to work with. "Reggie mentions I'm sometimes smug and take unnecessary risks."

"It is a father's duty to ensure his Source children wear the spirit of combat. Otherwise, you're nothing but a semi-Kihog in the faux skin of a warrior," *It* says. "Much like that Elemorphia outside the door."

"I fail and fall a lot," I admit. "Sometimes I'm unsure what to do."

"Honesty and humility," *It* says, "are the heart of a warrior too. The cowardly are first to boast about skills they cannot perform, and usually, the first to die."

"Of course, if I do die," I add, "it kicks off a series of unfortunate events, including, but not limited to, the Ormian Council having to find another Balancer because they're so fucked up and short-staffed since the last apocalypse, they can't synthesize or clone one. My real dad was supposed to be the Balancer, but he disappeared. I inherited the job. Hell, it could be eons before another Balancer is born, if ever. Even then, this specialized intra-terrestrial must be majority Camaeliphim and exist on *exactly* the right plane to help Earth, humans, and its realms. Shit. This sucks."

Memo to self: Shut. Up. Sam. Reggie always said there is valuable space between a reaction and a response. But then I think, so what? If this thing kills me, who's it going to tell? I think it's just as trapped as me.

"The Balancer? *You?*" *It* asks. I think it's laughing, which makes me mad. "I thought I smelled Golden Blood. And that mouth of yours. Three curse words in one breath…that must be a new record for a Camaeliphim hybrid. You're supposed to be supremely bred with noble manners and grace."

"Really?" I say, feeling a bit less scared of this creature but wondering if I possess some epigenetic deficit due to low levels of grace, an overabundance of curse words, and a penchant for bureaucratic mutiny. As for my nobility, it's about as remote and infrequent as Halley's Comet. "I'm tired of everyone finding it funny I'm the Balancer. I think symmetry of rebellion and grace serves better equipoise between wars and realms."

"You mean breaking the rules," *It* says. "And being female."

"I'd nod in agreement, but you know…there's a sharp object at my throat."

The sword floats away and disappears into the wall, *phhssst… just like that.* My Bukhara blade is strapped to my thigh, as if it never left, or was returned to me through instantaneous teleportation. "How did you lift my blade from my thigh without me feeling it?" I ask.

"I did nothing," It answers. "Sentient beings often only see with their biological eyes."

"How else are we supposed to see?"

"You don't need eyes to see what's really important," *It* says. "And you can't negotiate passage to Ereshun because I'm not the one you must kill to get there. He lies."

"Who? The creepy Elemorphia?" My hands are loosened from the door. I stumble forward but don't fall.

The creature shapeshifts and slithers around my waist, its red-beaded eyes coming into view and looking into mine before *It* focuses intently on my eye necklace. It hovers for a moment, and I swear I briefly see wings pinned against its back.

"Holy Source," *It* whispers, coming to a standstill. "You look..." It encircles but doesn't touch me, conducting, I think, a personal inspection. "...familiar." A swirling vapor wraps itself around me like a Genie let loose from his lamp. His sword disappears into the ether as misty tendrils lift but don't break my necklace.

"Maybe we met in another realm," I say, wondering if this thing can take any other form besides smoke. Maybe it's been alive for millions of years. I cough and wave some of the haze out of my face. "One of my other lives, perhaps?"

"Doubtful," *It* says. The necklace thumps back on my chest when this strange misty being floats away from me. "You've had many incarnations—but you've *chosen* this, to be human? Ah, to help humans. I dwell not long among this kind." Then it smiles but shows no teeth, only a clear canvas through to the other side of the room. "Tell me, little one of Golden Blood, why do you think **you're** the Balancer?"

"If you plan to kill me, why should I tell you?" I ask. "And by the way, I never asked to be in this position—or to be born human."

"You may be fortunate enough to live a bit longer, provided you share your Truth."

"How does that help?" I ask.

"I never said it would help," *It* says.

"I'm not sure where to begin. Is this a test?"

"Start with your birth...no!" *It* speaks. "Begin at your *conception*."

"How the hell would I know what my conception was like?" I feel sudden heat in my cheeks. "And who would want to know something so gross? Oh, wait! *You!* Geez, you're just as disgusting as the other pervert out there." I point to the door. The smoke breaks into little puffs and comes back together. "Are you laughing?" I ask.

"Begin..." the smoke says, and the way *It* says this causes the hair on my neck and arms to rise as rigid as bamboo stalks, the way Reggie's voice does when he barks orders at me.

"My aunt, Dr. Evelyn Dennison...and my mom, Avril Blake, were sisters," I say, trying to remember the story. "But they didn't know they were sisters until they met at Oxford...that's in the United Kingdom, in England, on Earth, in case you're wondering. Do you understand where England is? Never mind."

I walk to the large metal box, climb up, and take a seat. I glance around to see what I might use as a weapon, but also realize the futility. The only way to kill smoke is to smother it—but even then—its probability of seeping through cracks is statistically high. Then I notice, there aren't any cracks in the walls or doors. None. This is a room of mirrors. *Smokeface* here is only able to move through cabinets, cases, or around tables. It appears trapped. Like me. "The rest is far out there. You sure you want to hear this?" It's a stupid thing for me to ask, having met a talking Fluffle of Elemorphia, and gone through a myriad of other crazy shit up to this point, including conversing with this fully conscious vapor monster.

"Oh, but I do want to hear this," *It* says, wisps of black smoke curling around a stainless-steel table leg in front of me. "Please, go on..."

I exhale a long sigh. "According to my aunt, some other-worldly *beings* appeared inside a chapel at Exeter College...at Oxford...in the UK...aka England."

"What did they look like?" the creature asks.

"Like angels, I guess. I'm not sure," I say. "Evelyn said they wore pale blue robes and appeared as beings of light." I think for a moment about how my mom was taken up by Ebians. Bennie once shared that Ebians were the most advanced beings in the entire cosmos—and now I wonder if these creatures in the chapel that night were also Ebians, my mom's first encounter with them. "The incident terrified my mom and aunt, but the beings calmed them, and claimed my mom and aunt had been called, but only one would be chosen…"

"For?"

"Insemination." My cheeks burn red, and I banish the involuntary and disturbing vision of my mom, a human, and my dad, a Camaeliphim, having sex—although my aunt did, thankfully, share that consummation did not occur in the chapel. I leave this part out. "My aunt thought she'd be the one to carry a Golden Blood, a Camaeliphim hybrid. She was quite jealous when she discovered my father was enchanted with, and chose, my mom instead."

"Your mother," the creature asks. "What does she look like?"

"I'm not sure how to answer that," I say. "Before she was locked up in an asylum and became the property of the US government, she was beautiful—long black hair, hazel eyes, olive skin. Not like me. Afterward? Not so much."

"Locked up?"

"She was remanded to the Tiffin State Hospital," I say. "In Ohio. It's in the United States of America, on this planet. She was kept in a secret military wing on the edge of campus because she…she was…"

"From what did she suffer?" *It* asks.

"She killed people," I say.

"Perhaps she had good reason," *It* says.

"She was ill."

"*Was?*"

"She left Earth," I say.

"This human *died?*"

"No," I say. "She was taken up by Ebians. But I don't know where or why they took her."

"Your mother had gifts," the creature says, spreading out like fog in the room. "She was trapped."

"Are you telling this story, or am I?" But as the words leave my lips, I realize this creature is right. I never thought about my mom's predicament before. She was mentally fried but not by paranoid schizophrenia, a lie I was told. It was grief. My mother **was** trapped...by forces, people, and experiments beyond her control. My mom was a woman born out of her time. "She'd lost everything, *except* her mind," I whisper. "She used her mind to hone her consciousness...Humans thought my mom crazy. She saw things others didn't and spoke with phantoms. I didn't realize..." I struggle to hold back tears and bite my lip, hard. "My mom killed people—lots of people," I say. What I don't say is that an unacknowledged special access faction scooped her up and locked her away. It hoped to both protect and exploit her gifts—to siphon off her exoconscious abilities. "My mom could absorb and channel energy the way plants take in carbon dioxide," I say. "I think she overloaded her personal grid trying to help humans."

Slowly, the shadow around me transforms from black smoke to white mist and softly envelops me, a damp-morning-mist sort of hug. I wonder if this is the part where *It* kills me, even though I don't feel as if it will, which of course, would be a perfect time for impromptu execution. "Your parents," *It* says, "created an exquisite daughter. I'm convinced you have your mother's spirit. She channeled interstellar communications. Rare for a human."

"She always said I was more like my father...impulsive, hard-headed, and a bad listener." I feel an overwhelming outpouring of love from this beast and there's no escaping its odd ethereal embrace. "Why do you kill people?" I ask to change the subject.

"I kill many things," *It* says, retreating and floating across the room. "To quell misery, rebalance chaos, or protect what is sacrosanct." The creature returns to gray-smoke form and floats to another part of the lab. "But here, I am forced to conserve energy and my vibrations are kept low. I try not to lose hope."

Bzzzzzzzzzzzzzzzt!

"What makes such noise?" *It* asks.

"My compass," I say, pulling it out of my suit pocket and holding it up for him. "Damn thing never works except to spin out of control. Sometimes it vibrates for no reason. "Hey, wait a minute." My compass points due north, straight at the hazy creature. *It* slithers a foggy tentacle around my directional device and twirls, like a slow-moving waterspout, until the compass leaves my fingers and passes through its funnel. "It works! You can't have it," I say. "It was my real dad's. You can look at it, though. The Elemorphia told me other Balancers have been here before." I sweep my fingers along one of the reflective walls. I look hazy and a bit distorted as if seeing myself through too-thick lenses.

A small sphere, about the size of a baseball, rests on one of the tables. It looks like it's made from explosive hydroforming and reminds me of the suspended sphere in the caves at Plum Hook Bay, the one guarded by Astral Weavers. I casually pick it up and roll it around in my palm, smiling into its polished surface, wondering what, if anything, it does.

"Liars," *It* says, floating to and fro, here then there, my compass bobbing about in the smoky mini tornado circling the room.

"Please be careful with that," I say. "The Elemorphia are liars?"

"Fewoulz and humans are liars," *It* says. "Each is arrogant enough to believe they can pass before me as Balancers without understanding the sacredness of this conferred role." He makes an arrow with his smoke and points to the display cabinets stocked with blood-spattered lab coats. My compass dangles precariously in mid-air, tick-tocking back and forth. I hope he doesn't drop it.

"What did they do?" I ask, wondering where he stores the bones that once were upright and resided inside the bloody lab coats. Maybe this fog creature blew them into a drawer or a closet somewhere.

"A particular group of humans stole celestial codes we planted in Earth's children thousands of years ago. They created unholy, suffering chimeras," he says. "Humans never learn." A puff of smoke blows my way. "But I didn't kill them." *It* glides across the room. "Fewoulz did. Fewoulz make and break deals and then rip humans to shreds, using them as trophies and trinkets."

"That's horrible."

"Humans come willingly, mostly out of greed and with bad intent," *It* says. "Thankfully, not too many—only those of this planet with high clearances who were told another world exists far below your feet. But it's worse."

"How could it be worse?" I ask.

"Fewoulz steal the children whose codes have been compromised," *It* says.

"For food?"

"No. They seek something else."

"What?"

"I'm unsure," *It* says. "I'm unsure about most things lately. Fewoulz offer me freedom if I agree to lower my vibrations and switch allegiance."

The compass falls into my hands. It still works. *Weird.* I stuff it back in a pocket. "Will you agree to switch allegiance?" I ask.

"Never. It goes against my oath," *It* says. "But tell me...what brings *you* so close to Ki's heart? Surely, you too, risk this venture for something you deem important enough to die for."

"Yes," I say, closing my eyes for a moment, wondering how much I should disclose.

"And that might be?"

I pause and swallow. "Missing Tesla files," I say. "We need them to locate every piece of the Word, open an X Point, and throw Raga into the Source Vortex."

"I see," *It* says. "The latter is a mission of certain inanimation...or certain death, if you're fortunate."

"So I've been told," I say, staring at the smoky shadow. "But I promised *Not Who*. It appeared to me months ago as a pair of men in black suits."

"Another mission of certain inanimation," *It* says. "*Not Who.* Celestial mercenary energy of the Tall Whites. It's highly unusual for them to alter time patterns and appear to hybrids. You will not break your promise?"

"I gave my word," I say. "Although I wish I hadn't. What is a Fewoulz?"

"Fewoulz are favored pets of the Nephilim. They glide under this world's hidden side. They bottle Bezaliel energy and contain it for later unleashing inside troubled human minds. Bezaliel energy is now as prolific as wild mushrooms on this planet. Its negative properties manifest or heighten addictions, vanities, lust, greed...and a host of other internal human and hybrid maladies that will eventually destroy this valuable planet."

"What about Bezaliel mist?" I ask. "Can Fewoulz harness Bezaliel mist too?"

"No living creature has ever captured Bezaliel mist for long and lived," *It* says.

His answer sends a pang of pain through my heart and stomach. I suspected as much and fear for my daughter and Luca. While I may be trapped on the Isle of No Time, they may not have much left. None of us do. "I think humans are already screwed up enough without Fewoulz running Bezaliel interference," I say.

"Precisely, but galactic alignment goes against Fewoulz chaos," *It* says. "Order disrupts their self-absorption uptake and obstructs negative feed loops within Bezaliel networks. If they keep humans divided and fighting, it feeds them, and strengthens Bezaliel ability to take form."

"Is there a way out of here?" I ask.

"Only if I agree to switch sides," *It* says.

"Okay, so lie," I say.

"For me to utter a lie is to breach the accord I've sworn to the Source."

"What are you?" I ask.

"I am not human, the son of no man."

"Everybody is somebody's kid," I say. "Nothing sentient can exist without parents."

"You believe this?" *It* says.

"Yes, because two males or two females together cannot reproduce," I say. "It's unnatural."

"Oh, you know so much about natural order?" *It* asks. "Are you sure?"

"I'm an exobiologist," I say, feeling a bit proud. I'm a doctor... of sorts...*shit*. "Parthenogenesis," I add. I'd forgotten about this asexual reproductive avenue and now feel foolish but babble out a quick correction. "Some plants, reptiles, birds, fish, and insects can reproduce on this planet without a partner. But you aren't any of those, are you?"

"Some celestial beings not of this world can manifest without a mating ritual, but we do require your belief," *It* says. "I cannot be killed. I do not die in the way you know death. But with the right sort of holding cell, I may be contained for study."

"You're...you're..." I try not to choke on my words. I take a deep swallow and it hurts. "You're an *angel*. You're Camael. You're why my father and I exist."

The creature smiles again, its smoke turning white. "Not exactly," *it* says. "I'm the Source's, hmmm, how do I say this? Let's just say, for the sake of simplicity, I'm God's secret agent in charge. Or what some humans think of as the archangel of war. My name...is Basasael, brother of Camael, not to be confused with Bezaliels."

"*Brother?*"

"Yes." The room clears a bit, and his smoke forms a human hand. He opens a palm toward me. I touch it but feel puzzled and confused. "What's wrong?" he asks.

"I'm told you're rarely recorded among sacred texts, a fact Bezaliels count upon to remain hidden among human and hybrids...but some say you're a devil, a fallen angel, a thirteenth Watcher."

"And you?" Basasael asks. "What do you believe?"

"A friend once told me chaos cringes when Basasael is near," I say. "If this is true, you'd already be in allegiance with Bezaliels rather than contained by them for *study,* unless you're lying...but you're trapped here so I don't think you're lying. My friend Verity claimed you were endowed by God in all matters of metal and stone, a gifted artisan once in charge of herbs, oils, incense, and vestments. Bennie told me about you when we were kids. He said you went dark on Ki years ago when Nephilim put a price on your head."

"I was effectively contained," Basasael says, smoke wisps whirling. "Nephilim are your hybrid antithesis. Camaeliphim were created to counter them, another fact hidden from humans. And the Elemorphia on the other side of this door does not wear his true form."

"He's Fewoulz?" I ask.

"Yes. Your friend, this Bennie...do you mean Bennie Bathurst?"

"You know him?"

"Every **celestrial** knows the Source Bearer."

"He's missing," I say, wondering if Bennie and Hope might be trapped somewhere on this planet the way Basaseal and I are now...or worse. "Along with our daughter."

"You have a *child?* With a Source Bearer?"

I hesitate and look away, suppressing an urge to blurt out everything. "He's somewhere, trying to save her, I think. Like Fewoulz, she is not naturally made. I don't know what a Source Bearer is...I'm not even sure what I'm supposed to do as a Balancer."

"You carry the Light forward," Basasael says, swirling in the air before me.

"Hope is her name," I say.

"Fitting," he says. "You do realize that your plasma, combined with Bennie's, creates the first Horizon hybrid, what we call an Emergent. We'd hoped to wait until Ki was ready."

"Emergent?"

"Your daughter is able to freely, and without harm, instantaneously cross dividing lines between Ki and the heavens, whether in sentient or luminance form," he says, hovering near a row of neatly aligned test tubes. "She may exist in two places at once, no matter how vast the distance...like Mederonch."

"Who?"

"My apologies," Basasael says. "Kihogs recognize him under the name Enoch. His story was revised on Earth and a constellation of poetic license used to cover over the Source's true forbearance."

"I'm afraid my daughter is not like Mederonch," I say. "My Aunt Evelyn extracted Hope's celestial genetics and exchanged it for Bezaliel mist."

The smoky creature turns white, then gray, then black. The Eyes of Horus instantaneously snap shut. Plumes of ebony clouds rumble toward me and I shiver in the sudden darkness and chill. I clutch the metal sphere when lightning strikes one of the lab tables. A bolt ricochets around and through mirrored walls. I roll off the metal box anchored to the ground and duck under a rolling cart, hoping to hell this completely pissed-off angel, the brother of the head Camaeliphim, the ancestor and source of my Golden Blood, doesn't electrocute me.

"If true," Basasael says, "this is an unforgivable blasphemy punishable by..."

"Death?" I ask, looking up from under a table.

"Worse..."

"What could possibly be worse than death for a human?" I ask. "Hell?"

"Eternal life," *It* answers. "We're already in Hell."

"Ki is Hell?" I ask, confused, but realizing that yes, Earth, covered over with so much agony, arrogance, and despair, could be Hell. I can't tell Barbara this. She'd never recover. "How can eternal life be worse than death?" I ask. "Most humans believe eternal life is the greatest gift ever."

"Eternal life on *Ki*," he says. "It means no realm roving, no return to the Source. Eternal life, minus the capital 'L' is infinite biological human aging and suffering in the same container no matter how old, immobile, or injured it becomes."

"Okay, that's *waaaay* worse than death," I say, shaking my head and lowering my eyes to the shiny floor for a second. I lift my chin to the ceiling and gaze instead upon the Eyes of Horus, or what my mother used to call her Eyes of Providence, the exact same eyes Luca wears as a ring on his right hand. I place the small sphere back on the table.

"You may have that," Basasael says. "Consider it a gift."

"What is it?" I ask.

"A key."

"A key? But it's round and shiny. How can this fit into any lock?"

"It makes shadows clear," he says. "If you focus, it captures all light in a scene and enables you to see what is otherwise invisible. It is the master link between the Source and humankind. It contains the Seven Seals."

"What are the Seven Seals?" I ask.

"Let not one lamb enter a den of lions alone."

"I don't understand," I say.

"You will, little one," Basasael says. "It is the power of the seals, and the power to open them, that conveys how wrong the world is about *sin* and who, exactly, is right about judgment. This seal conveys the ability for profound cosmic, rather than worldly, religious connection."

I slip the sphere into my pocket but it's a tight fit. I retrieve the buckeye and lay it on the table. Once round and smooth, it's now the size of a prune, its rich brown hue, like cherry bark, wrinkled and shriveled. Sometimes I twist it through my fingers when I'm nervous, yet after all this time it hasn't rotted. "And you may have this buckeye seed," I say. "Consider it a gift, although it isn't nearly as cool as this sphere."

He spins the buckeye into his funnel. "The genus aesculus."

"Yes," I say. "It opens portals. Maybe you can use it to escape."

"No," Basasael says. "This seed was brought here by Astral Weavers. It is powerful medicine but would only trap the Astral Weavers in here with me. It's been a long time since I've had the honor of a gift." The seed drops to the steel table with a loud *plink*.

"It's also a potent poison if incorrectly prepared," I say. "People fall into comas or die after consuming buckeyes if they eat them raw."

"Astral Weavers taught the original humans, a previously advanced civilization on this planet, to boil and leach the poison out of them," he says. "They created a salve of hetuk meal to cure almost any inner ailment."

I finger the tin in my other pocket and think about Bennie. "Basasael?" I ask. "Is it possible to create a salve that might cure death if buckeye meal were crushed and mixed with ayahuasca bark?"

"There is no cure for a natural transition not viewed as a disease," he says. "Death is a freedom to be celebrated, something most humans fear and pretend doesn't exist...until it arrives. Birth should be mourned, for energy turned into substance heralds a lifetime of sentient suffering. However, a mixture of hetuk and ayahuasca would heal most injuries and ailments, including mortal wounds."

"Would humans know this?" I ask, feeling a bit dizzy. Thousands of strange symbols bombard my head and interrupt our conversation—packets of information, concepts of space, time, travel, and light—uploaded into synaptic networks, plumping every cell of my body until the information forces me to collapse. Basaseal traces a smoky finger in the middle of my forehead. A swirling portal, an inner vision, appears, and then recedes.

"Maybe I should return this," I say, reaching into my pocket and removing the master key containing the Seven Seals. *What was I thinking?* I steady my breath and stand up again. "What happened?"

"It is my next gift to you," Basaseal says. "You've gracefully received hidden knowledge, good intent being a necessary additive. This Reggie has trained you well. And you, I now understand, are Scathatch, also known as Sekhmet, Skadi, Skoai, Anahit, Iona, Inanna, Anu, or Samantha, depending upon Ki's timelines, a Balancer by so much more than heritage, one possessed of learning and great faith. You've fought many battles. The Seals are your birthright. Check a mirror."

A small royal purple spiral is etched into the middle of my forehead. "I'm about the most faithless hybrid I know," I say, feeling sheepish. Basaseal also called me graceful. I don't have the heart to tell him that grace is about as far removed from me as faith or the Kuiper Belt.

"I respectfully disagree," he says. "You're much braver than you realize. You are also a hub of balance in the eye of a storm, one around which all turbulence revolves. You have in you a center, a divine Source, an eye that observes and untangles chaos to recognize meaningful patterns. Your path of ascent and descent, between Ki and the Source, will help you locate Hope."

"Can Dr. Evelyn be forgiven?" I ask.

"Your aunt committed inviolable crimes against the Source and by extension, all sentient and celestial beings, including you, Bennie, me, and most importantly, your daughter."

This isn't what I want to hear. If my aunt can't be forgiven, Luca is doomed too, I think. "How do we get out of here?" I ask. "I need to find the Tesla files. If Raga captures Hope's energy before I find her, I'll have no choice but to hurl us both into the Source Vortex."

"There is no escaping this specialized holding cell," Basasael says. "Unless I agree to switch allegiance."

"But you cannot lie," I say.

"No," he says. "A lie seals me off from the Source the same as Dr. Evelyn Dennison, or as she likes to call herself, The Countess of Teviot. This is what the Ormian Council decrees."

"Geez," I say. "Eternal life on Ki seems a rather harsh punishment for an archangel in a jam...but...I can lie! I'm part human. Lying is as much a part of the human condition as truth."

"I suppose this is so," Basasael says.

"It must be so," I say. "And if I do lie, my humanness makes me legitimately imperfect and qualified for forgiveness in my effort toward personal perfection, at least according to the religious propaganda distributed all over this planet."

Silence.

I think Basasael is thinking but I can't tell for sure because he's too foggy for me to "see." "The Ormian Council has never been presented with or presided over an issue of such complexity," he finally says. "You tell a lie to save what many humans think of as an archangel, but then must ask forgiveness of the Ormian Council for helping the Source continue to flourish? What an odd conundrum for a hybrid to bear."

"Frankly, I don't care," I say. "Those snobbish sky bearers refuse to get their proverbial robes dirty, and they hand out edicts like apples while we rot in this reflective cage. Besides, their clemency is a smoke and mirror show anyway. Forgiveness must come directly from Source, right?"

"This is true," Basasael says.

"Tell that Fewoulz to open the door," I say. "We've got lives, realms, and multiverses to save."

NINE

YOU'RE NOT ALONE

MOST OF THE caverns under Ki were forged by volcanic eruptions showering the air with ash, smoke, and lava. Rainwater cooled volcanic rock, eroding it until underground tunnels, caves, valleys, gorges, mountains, and lakes were formed. It's the perfect hiding place for a myriad of crypto terrestrials who've built an entire empire under a comparatively primitive upper world of humans, in damn near secrecy.

Fewoulz, I've learned from Basasael, are transient creatures that prefer living among all manner of caustic waste and toxic materials, the landfill lords of nether regions. But occasionally, for entertainment, they'll go topside and prowl for the vulnerable. Humans call them boogeymen. This Fewoulz, masquerading as Elemorphia, appears to relish his role as bully and executioner between Ereshun and the Isle of No Time.

Paramel's empty violet "liquor" vials litter our path, as Basasael and I seek a confrontation with the unsavory beast. It's evident she's been trying to keep this vermin under the influence in a failed effort to control him. Every manner of stolen pieces and parts of others' lives lie broken and scattered on ledges, rocks, the ground, or half hidden in dark crevices, long since void of life or usefulness. Various skulls and bones, Kihog, animal, or otherwise, are thrown into disorganized, lopsided stacks. Piles of Fewoulz waste are almost as copious as Fluffle holes.

Basasael swirls behind me, absent of his true Camaeliphim form, but free...and too weak to be of much help if we must fight. The Fewoulz with no name rises from a pile of shredded rags, the light from his graveolens set low and propped between two boulders. With a flick of his paw, a handful of extracted teeth bounce past my feet, as if he's playing a monster's game of Ball and Jacks. He offers me another sneery smile. I hold the Bukhara blade in my hand, keeping eyes on him.

"How art thou, Basasael?" the Fewoulz asks. "Quite weakened, I see." Bits of unidentifiable flesh fall out of his mouth. "Have your accommodations become so crowded and intolerable you've decided to alternate your currents and change allegiance? If I'd known your weakness was an ugly, overly talkative female, I'd have thrown one into your cell decades ago!"

I step forward. "He has," I say, "since smoke can't nod."

"Your words I don't trust," the Fewoulz says without moving his trunk or paws, staring past me at the whirling mist over my shoulder, his eyes glossy, and overserved. "There is talk among the Fluffle that a certain human hybrid may be the new Balancer." He looks at me, still chewing. "I see that this stain of a hybrid has the mark of the Source on her forehead. Quite a downgrade, I'd say, from a fully-fledged Camaeliphim to a partially human *female*. Tell me, Kihog," he says, moving closer to me, "are you auditioning today for this deadly and doomed-to-fail role of Balancer?" The Fewoulz slides his tongue along the front of his grimy-gray Elemorphia teeth. "You think your puny half-human form is a fair match against a Fewoulz? I provide much more of a challenge than the humanoid sent into your motel room to kill you years ago—although you probably enjoyed his bestial thrusting." He obscenely drives his hips back and forth, and his exposed penis reminds me of a moldy and rotting stick.

I give him no anger or fear on which to feed. Although I am surprised to hear this Fewoulz refer to my attacker as *humanoid*, one I'd swear was fully human at the time. I clumsily vanquished my attacker as a teenager, in self-defense, and now I know—someone had plans to murder me before I even knew about my hybrid heritage. It's another unexpected datapoint to file away for later research. "I kill pigs with or without tails," I say with a shrug. I tighten my grip on the blade and mentally position myself for attack when the Fewoulz passes behind and between Basasael and me. I turn to follow, not wanting him out of sight.

The Fewoulz, I notice, is gaunt, and his faux Elemorphia coat matted with knots...so unlike the pristine Fluffle, whose dark gray-silver pelts are softer than chinchilla and as iridescent as opal. His lack of discipline and love of violet-colored nectar makes him conceited, empty of discretion, and ripe for unbridled rage. Arrogance and ego, I know, are two attributes that foment mistakes. Reggie taught me that hard attitude and overt displays of strength get in the way of an effective warrior, something he calls *stolen authority*, easily challenged, but not always beaten—unless the opponent, meaning me, learns to temper their demons. "I swore an oath to my Balancer birthright," I say. "And what of you? You're self-absorbed, cruel, undisciplined, and heartless."

"Thank you!" the Fewoulz says. "I'm an efficient assassin too. And oh, how I thrive on inflicting pain and controversy!"

"You do not wear your true form," I say.

"Do any of us?" he asks. "Clever disguise on my part, don't you think? It fooled *you*."

"Not really," I say.

"Oh?"

"Elemorphia will take credit in Ki's history," I say, "as the creatures who convinced a fully-fledged Camaeliphim to lower his vibrational form substantially and permanently. Not you or any Fewoulz."

A micro expression of rage flits over his face before he pulls himself upright and snarls, "Liar!"

"It's true," I say. "If your Fewoulz form remains unknown, it is the Fluffle who gain Raga's favor and elevation for vanquishing the mighty Basaseal. You'll be a laughingstock and an outcast among Fewoulz, Kihogs, Bezaliels, Nephilim, and the Fluffle."

A quick flare from the graveolens and the Fewoulz disappears among the wreckage of his lair.

My heart beats at what feels like a million RPMs per second. I turn around and Basasael is gone too. I force myself to breathe and remain calm—and steel my nerves.

A flash in my periphery.

A buzz of hushed voices overhead.

The graveolens sputters and darkness intensifies.

Shadows of low-rolling negative energy sweep over me. I experience an expanding absence of light, almost corporeal, as if darkness itself, is an entity. It swims through the sweat in my pores, slowly rolls through my mind, and laps itself around my body. Heavier than granite, its blackness wades through my lungs, surrounds my eyes, and settles so thick on my tongue I taste the acerbic flavor of nightmares settling into the deepest recesses of my brain. It presses into my chest, stealing bits of breath, the icicle top-hat man, coming to call. I loosen the grip on my blade, the way Reggie taught me, but remain corpselike still.

A low roar.

A crackling noise like the stretching and breaking of bone, muscle, and skin. Then a clunk. The putrid breath of a thousand deaths moisten the nape of my neck. I feel zaps of tingling along my spine. I yank the Seven Seals from my pocket and hold the solid shiny sphere in the palm of my free hand.

"You don't need eyes to 'see'."

The sphere gathers up all the light it can locate, offering me a three-hundred-sixty-degree internal view of my surroundings.

And what I *see* hovering over my left shoulder turns my Golden Blood to ice.

Fewoulz, I now know, are tall, winged, bat-like humanoids with razor-filed teeth, orange-yellow eyes, and ears rising over their bulbous head so pointed they could pass for daggers. Its black-and-white flesh has the sheen of frog skin. Clinging to a wall within five feet of me, its three-digit claws scrape rock until granite drifts to my feet like hourglass sand, the monster's barbed tail swishing back and forth. A weapon, maybe a throwing star, hurtles toward the Fewoulz's face. The Fewoulz tilts his head viciously fast, and the multi-blade star embeds itself into rock, tossing out gravel chips at my feet.

It must be Basasael. I strain to see his true form behind me but even with the sphere this *'archangel'* remains cloaked to me.

The Fewoulz leaps from the wall, launching a claw punch to my stomach that I narrowly escape. A cascade of firework pain blooms across my shoulders and down both arms when he slams into my back. The stench of fresh feces and old blood oozes over me when his cold, clammy skin grazes mine. I feel a fetid claw trace my cheek and the hardness of his exposed slimy penis against my leg. Beads of sweat pop up on my forehead.

A whirl of rocks and boulders comes between us, pulled into the bottom of Basasael's vortex and tossed out like rapid cannon fire toward the Fewoulz. I use the moment to roll out from under this reeking beast...

...And from out of nowhere, comes Eido...

...a flash of orange fur... Kitsune dodges past me shrieking and yipping...

...followed closely by the growls and snarling of Vigo.

"Kitsune! Eido! *NO!*" My command goes ignored. "Vigo!"

Kitsune latches onto the Fewoulz's face as Vigo clamps down on one of his grisly legs. The beast plucks Kitsune away with his claws and kicks Vigo into a rock. He swipes at Eido's robes and the child silently falls without so much as a whimper. I hear a yelp from both creatures, then nothing at all.

"No," I whisper. "No!"

Stop it, Sam.

Calm.

Do NOT let this vile beast feed on your anger or fear.

I roll the sphere in front of the Fewoulz.

Foamy spittle, *drip, drip, drips* from his raw mouth. His claws, covered in sapphire blood with golden flecks, shrink away. Eido, Vigo, and my sweet Kitsune, are lifeless heaps at this Fewoulz's feet.

My Bukhara blade is long and curved, its blacksmith from Uzbek rumored to possess otherworldly powers, an engagement gift from Luca. He said I might need it someday in case anything got too close to me that needed to "get what it deserved."

Strange creatures are carved into this blade's haft, its steel wootz serrated on one side and leanly sharp on the other. Its tip, Luca told me, weds chaos to order, but when I plunge it into the charging beast, the unexpected intensity of Light is too much...

A shadow. Wings. Something hovers over me.

"Breathe, Sam," the voice says. "You did good, kid." His eyes. So blue, with flecks of green and gray, that occasionally flicker into pools of black ink. Navy-blue veins in his neck pulse like arctic ice cracks. "I must find your mother. Please breathe."

One, two, three, four...

...rumbles and moans as the Earth cracks itself open...rock

dust settles over me but I don't roll away. Wings unfold again on a ghost-like back. Basasael cradles my head.

Camouflage.

Dog tags.

The soldier's face is fuzzy, but I can read his nametag. *Blake.*

"Dad?"

Smoke.

Fog.

Mist.

"Outwit wickedness to attain the password," Basasael says. "X your eye to realize the point of the Gods. You've been uploaded with great knowledge and potential."

Wings.

"Dad? Is it really *you?*"

The buckeye I gave Basasael sits on a rock. It cracks and sprouts until a small portal appears. The hand of an Astral Weaver reaches out...

...Silence.

I am alone.

You're not alone. You've never been 'alone'.

It's a distant, disembodied voice in my head, and comforting.

The buckeye I gave Basasael, and he himself, are gone.

* * *

"Samantha! Scathatch! Wake up!" Repetitive light taps sting my cheeks. I know this voice.

I struggle to open my eyes and rock my head from side-to-side, willing myself back to consciousness. "Eido!" I scream, the dust in my eyes clouding my vision as I struggle to sit up. I reach out to feel his body. "Where's Eido?"

"Shh," the woman says. "He isn't here."

"I must find him!"

"Lie still," the woman says.

I feel her arm and sleeve. "A *woman?*" I ask. "How can a human be so far down below Ki without risk?

Eido...he's a *child!*"

"I saw no child," thc woman says...and her voice...it's *so* familiar.

"Paramel?" I try again to open my eyes.

"You took quite a hit to the head," she says. She wipes a soft cloth over my face, and I feel a light buzz and heat.

"What happened?" I ask.

When I finally do open my eyes, I don't see the gentle female Elemorphia that I left standing back at the "container" garden, the same female who brought me breakfast and led me on a grand tour into a Fewoulz lair. I shove the stranger aside, looking at her quizzically, recognizing the voice, but not the woman. "Who *are* you?" I ask, finally sitting upright.

I pat palms across my chest, searching out the wound between my shoulders...there it is...deep claw cut to the right shoulder, slicing down my arm and almost severing a bicep. *Damn, it hurts.*

Kitsune and Vigo lick my face, their soft whines and whimpers just as much of a shock to my mind and body as this festering wound. I look around for Eido but he's still absent.

"It is I, Paramel," the woman says. She stands and twists from side to side. Her long red hair cascades in crimped perfection down her back. I search in every direction for Basaseal but fail to find him, or the freakishly friendly and brave monk-kid, Eido. Paramel kneels again beside me, gently tickling both animals away so I can freely breathe. "You freed Basaseal," she says. "He's left this realm...as he should. He'll need to heal among his kindred. You freed us both."

"I, I, I don't understand," I say, disappointment rising. I struggle to stand but the pain keeps me seated. "I saw the Fewoulz claw through Eido, Kitsune, and Vigo. The last thing I remember..."

"Shh," Paramel says. "Sit still." She unknots a leather-like strap hanging from her waist and wraps it around my arm to stanch the bleeding. The **woman**, Paramel, is adorned in a scarlet harness dress fastened by two buckles over her shoulders. Violet threads work through the tassel at the hem. Her feminine attire is overshadowed by sharp features, a strong jawline, pale skin, and intense green eyes the color and clarity of emeralds. "Don't move," she says. "That beast sliced you pretty good, but you gutted him better." She points.

The Fewoulz lies on its back in a pool of slimy gray blood, a muscled leg twisted up under its back. My Bukhara blade is lodged to the hilt through its frog-skinned chest. I edge toward him but think about Basasael. Blood trickles from the beast's half-open mouth and his arm is...missing? Ah, it's over there, pegged by a spike to a ledge a few feet away, completely skinned.

"Oh, that..." Paramel says when our eyes meet. "Roasted Fewoulz is a delicacy. This beast will feed the entire Fluffle tonight."

"Who *are* you?" I ask, reaching for my tin of salve in my pocket. I hand it off to her. "Use this."

"The Viking," she says, rubbing Bennie's salve into my wound. "I guard the Isle of No Time. You broke my curse. The least I could do was save your Fylgjur."

"My what?"

"Your Soul Guides," she says. "Although I've never met a hybrid who possessed two."

"Oh," I say. "The fox is mine...the dog is Reggie's."

"This explains much," she says. "I was confused because dogs represent a tame mind. A fox symbolizes a mind in training. Fylgjur are not changeable or interchangeable, nor can one improve or act on its own, although they mark transformations... or...portend impending doom."

"Great," I say. "What about a falcon?"

"One who has a falcon for a Soul Guide is definitely of untamed nature," Paramel says.

"How do you know so much about Soul Guides?" I ask.

"Because I am one," she answers with a shrug. She kicks the Fewoulz in its side, checking, I think, to ensure it's dead even though she's skinned most of it and cut off his arm.

"Why didn't you tell me this before?" I ask.

"I couldn't," she says. "If I told you, the Fewoulz would ensure my curse remains permanent. They do not fight fair."

"But you're a celestrial female, not an animal," I say, rising to my feet. "Soul Guides are animals, no?"

Paramel tosses her head back with a loud laugh. "Some would say the two are one and the same. I work as protector of the Fluffle and guardian of the Source vault."

"What about the boy, Eido?" I ask. "Are you sure you didn't see the little Sherpa run away?"

"I am sure."

I close my eyes and ask the dreaded question. "Is he dead?"

"Probably," she says. "If he was actually here."

"What's that supposed to mean?"

"If he *is* dead, you must make the most of this quest and your life by honoring his," she says. "It's part of the Viking code. Unfortunately, some things in life and death remain mysteries and many questions go unanswered."

I shake my head but what else is there for me to do? She's right. I have zero evidence Eido was ever here except for what I saw, which counts for everything but hard evidence. "What happened to you?" I ask. "I mean, back at the Isle of No Time, you were an Elemorphia...now you're...you're a *woman?*"

"I'm a hybrid and a Soul Guide and I was tricked," she says, spitting onto the ground. "I lost a game of cards. The deck was stacked."

I place a foot on the Fewoulz carcass and wrap two hands around the hilt of my Bukhara blade, my wound beginning to heal. One tug and it comes clean out of the creature just as Reggie taught me to do when extracting knives from wounded pigs. "How did this Fewoulz overpower you?" I ask.

Paramel spits on the ground. "I knighted my jarl controller of this province. He betrayed me."

"Your jarl?"

"My second-in-command," she says. "He sold me out to Fewoulz for a treasure that didn't exist. I knew he was a swindler. But he wasn't so lucky. He disappeared and I assume the beast made a meal of him as he did with all the others."

My wound slowly closes until it's gone. "Others?" I run a finger along fresh flesh the best I can reach. Paramel registers a look of curious surprise. "It's a healing salve," I say, "an ancient secret recipe made by a friend."

"The Fewoulz used his disguise to plunder containers and my team," she says. "And to devour the Fluffle." Paramel severs the beast's head from its body, and it makes a *sluuuurp* sound. She mounts it on a nearby iron pole sticking up from the ground. Dangling strips of ooze and muscle shimmer and wiggle like earthworms as she talks and I wonder if unnatural creatures like him wind up replanted in the *container* garden, too—but probably not since they aren't human or naturally made. "This beast threatened to raid the Fluffle nightly unless Bilby and the Elders provided occasional *Elemorphia* offerings."

Paramel pulls a vial of violet liquor from her waistband and shakes it in front of me. "I placated him with addictions instead." She spits at its head. "Betcha regret turning me into an Elemorphia now, don't you, stick face?" She stuffs the vial into its half-open mouth as if playing a college prank on a drunk roommate. Emotion flickers across her face: anger, regret, triumph, and then, a sort of resignation. I feel the same.

Basasael's sphere rolls in front of me from where, I don't know, perhaps the ether. I pick it up and hold it tightly in my palm, thinking of how fond I am of Eido and now too, this newly discovered *celestrial,* Basaseal. I have questions.

"If you're headed to Ereshun," Paramel says, eyeing the sphere. "I will take you."

"I thought as a Balancer I had to *negotiate* passage?"

"Oh, you certainly did that, and then some," Paramel says. "Are you coming? We need to get back to the Fluffle. Bilby will be surprised."

"He's your husband," I say. "You're his apex wife."

"Aye," she says. "He was a wonderful husband too..."

"*Was?*"

"When in Rome..." She trails off. "When the spell was broken, so too was the marriage. It's our agreement."

"Wait, is he human now too?"

"Bilby?" She laughs. "Oh, no. Elemorphia is Bilby's true form. He brought me into the Fluffle and gave me standing when my form was compromised, until we could figure out what to do. I was lucky the Fewoulz failed to inanimate me. He tried."

"I'm sorry about your jarl," I say. "It sounds as if he committed inviolable crimes."

"It's a damn shame too," she says, dressing out the Fewoulz with such precision it reminds me of Dr. Monica, how she grew up in the Outback similarly skinning kangaroos and cattle. "Bo, the bastard, he's the jarl who stole my fucking helmet." She foists what's left of the beast over her shoulders.

I stand for a moment in mid-squalor, then place the sphere back in my pocket. I follow Paramel wondering how I'm going to break the news about Bo, that he is alive, if not well, and claims Paramel's helmet as his own. And I wonder, too, why Bilby never told her.

TEN

SANCTUARY

WE BOB and weave through darkness, holding up every graveolens we can find among the Fewoulz wreckage. Our meandering line of humans and hybrids reminds me of a bioluminescent worm that dims and flickers, weaving its way through the ocean's depths, unable to see well but progressing forward to parts unknown, as both prey and predator.

I follow Paramel up an incline, its path worn and well-traveled, as if thousands of souls once passed through. I didn't tell her about Bo, how her jarl has her helmet, and lives. Bilby asked me not to. He was surprised and initially a bit heartbroken, I think, to see Paramel returned to true form. He was equally perplexed by the deep purple spiral on my forehead. Being the sort of Elemorphia he is, one possessed of gentle manner and integrity, he quickly recovered, happy that the curse standing between the Isle of No Time and Ereshun was properly skinned, dressed, seasoned, slow roasted, and then eaten as part of a festive Fluffle cleanse. Admittedly, the Fewoulz tasted surprisingly better than even Barbara's best Sunday roast beef...but I won't tell her that!

I still have a light headache from one too many drops of

violet-colored juice, but I wasn't celebrating. I was masking the despair I felt over losing Eido. We searched all over the Fewoulz camp for him. The one thing I'm relieved about is the Sherpas remaining behind with the camels. It buys me time to find the words to break the news to them. I should have insisted Eido stay behind, for his safety, regardless of the secrets he kept.

"Why are you headed to Ereshun?" Paramel asks.

"We were invited by a snow-white mole rat," I say with a smirk, thinking back on that moment. "I hope to find some answers there."

"You received a personal invite?"

"Yes."

"Sounds as if they might want answers from you." Paramel uncovers a metal grate and one-by-one we slip into a hole, where we meet a closed door etched in symbols.

I hadn't thought of Usta wanting answers from me. I don't have any. What I do have is a bunch of questions, a compass, a shiny sphere, a satchel full of buckeyes, a tin of salve, a Bukhara blade, an eye necklace, a blood diamond, and a Pleiades pendant, that upon inspection, looks more like a treasure trove for a fantasy role playing game, than devices for saving Ki.

Paramel taps the door using a series of raps in all four corners and then lightly presses her fingertips in the middle. The hieroglyphs glow gold, recede, and the door unseals itself with a **PSSSSHHHT** sound. Bright green steam rolls out to greet us.

Luca, Reggie, and Dr. Monica lift their weapons, alert and ready for whatever we may need to shoot or hope we don't find… or finds us. Kitsune and Vigo move in first. Vidar swoops overhead and disappears into the cavernous space. Sergeant Hogan and his men bring up the rear watching our "six." Slowly, we step through the door.

Fields of perfectly planted white glowing mushrooms unfold in front of us and it reminds me of an auditorium full of bald men. Blue and purple butterflies the size of beachballs flit about glowing green wisps of fog. In the distance, a multitude of crystal quartz obelisks, poking out of the ground like giant matchsticks, gives off an early morning light sort of energy and a low, serene hum.

Without warning, a giant reptile, a long-extinct Parasaurolophus-looking creature, thrushes past us and in one gulp, devours a small bush of unknown species.

We extinguish our graveolenses.

Intense white orbs, five of them about the size of soccer balls, move toward us in v-formation.

"What in bloody hell?" Dr. Monica whispers. "This is heaps bad!" She ducks under a mushroom cap with Sergeant Hogan, one large enough to double as a pavilion. The rest of our special ops team disperses and fans out to retreat under their own mushroom caps, weapons ready.

"Don't shoot!" Reggie yells. "Sam, we've seen these orbs before."

"You've seen *this* before?" Luca asks. "Where?"

"At my mom's asylum," I say. "And when I was a kid at Plum Hook Bay."

"They defy gravity," Luca says. "Silent and no propulsion systems."

The undersides and exterior shell of the spheres are glass-like and house neon-blue spinning plasma that sometimes glows red. Their faint fizz and crackle cause a vibrational hum in the air that lifts the hair on my forearms. "They're too small to be piloted," I say. "They're a little different than the ones we saw at Plum Hook Bay. Luca, I think they're biological in nature and possibly conscious, definitely intelligent."

"They're watching us," Luca whispers.

"Yes," I say, thinking about Bennie—how he once showed me Cutie Pie, a bio-magnetic-electric spider he created that looked and felt entirely real when he placed it in my hand at Silo #57. But his spider was something "other than" and bogus by Earthly arachnid standards. It was highly advanced and beyond my hybrid comprehension at the time.

The orbs zip around and bifurcate until the expansive cavern is full of them. They perform impossible maneuvers. "G-forces would splat a human or hybrid like bug juice if one could fit inside," Luca says. "Einstein's hair would flatten if he saw this!"

Pandemonium erupts behind us.

Our team runs in every direction. Some trip and roll over clusters of baby mushrooms and their bodies seize with a series of jerks and twitches. Just when I think I'll have to use my entire stash of salve to heal everyone, I realize the pure humans among us are laughing...hysterically. A few of the humans stop to stare at the orbs, lost in catatonic oblivion just like the patients I witnessed at Tiffin State Hospital, the day my mom went missing. Vigo and Kitsune remain close to Reggie and me. Kitsune's eyes meet mine when she looks up, letting a small whine of concern escape her snout.

"What's happening?" I ask Paramel.

"The humans?" she says with a wide smile. "They're high as fuck ...on the trip of a lifetime from the looks of them."

"The mushrooms?"

She nods, still smiling. "Why kill a potential enemy when you can disarm them with psychedelics instead? Genius."

Dr. Monica and Sergeant Hogan try to kick each other's crotch, their legs swinging high and then missing. They spin and fall together under a mushroom cap, laughing so hard tears stream down their cheeks. "I don't feel high," I say.

"You're a hybrid," Paramel says. "We swiftly metabolize the compound, only experiencing a minor sense of uplift."

"Will it kill them?" I ask.

Paramel shakes her head and I feel relieved.

"Psilocybin?"

"Of sorts," she says. "It's a bit more potent."

"Christ," I say. "How long does it last?"

Dr. Kimathi and Dr. Kanumba skip through an opening in the field holding hands and kissing until each woman collapses on the other and disappears under a mushroom a bit farther away. A couple of orbs float over them. "Reggie, please retrieve our epidemiologist and our archeologist before they remove all of their clothes and make the spheres blush," I say. He rolls his eyes at me but sets off on my thankless request without a word.

"Until we get them there." Paramel points to a large translucent building.

There's another rustle in the grasslands beyond us. The shadow of a large creature causes some of the smaller mushroom caps to bob and wobble. *Shit!* I have no idea what sort of beasts might be hiding in this field! How am I going to get a crowd of completely tripping humans to safety, especially if Fewoulz or some other deadly monster hides among them ready to pounce?

The crystal cathedral a couple of hundred yards away is immense and lit from the inside by a glimmer that casts a welcoming amber incandescence.

"I suppose the humans could stand some levity after so much time underground," I say. What I don't say is that I'm too preoccupied with their safety to pursue their sobriety. I cut, bag, and tag a few of the smaller white mushrooms for later study, my eyes darting to and fro, here and there, a half-wild attempt to be vigilant against lurking dangers and the induced laughter bubbling up inside me.

Paramel and I gather up our cackling team the best we can, and they're surprisingly easy to lead. We meander them like preschool children across a wide paved road, then wade through a pristine stream filled with multi-colored amoeba, a few neon jellyfish, and fluorescent octopuses the size of my pinky, which float freely along a soft current. The high as fuck humans in our charge stomp, splash, and disturb the marine life, causing it to dart and scatter away.

"Stop!" I scold. "You're frightening the fish!"

My words are met with child-like giggles. Hogan lifts a soggy boot out of the water. Its sole is stuck with gooey colors that remind me of a rainbow of sticky, oozing, bubble-gum. We reach a clearing hundreds of feet away from the mushroom field but when I turn to look, the orbs and the mushrooms have disappeared!

"What happened to the field?" Luca asks.

"Holographic decoy," Paramel answers. She doesn't elaborate but I have a pretty good idea what she means. Reggie once showed me a black-and-white photo from WWII illustrating a clever deception integral to the D-Day invasion. A thirty-ton Sherman tank was placed near what appeared to be a barracks. It was an inflatable tank, a decoy used in a vast and complex deception operation for the 1944 Normandy landings. Land tactical decoys like dummy armored vehicles, artillery pieces, radars or buildings, bridges, and runways are intended to deceive enemy observers, Reggie said, and have been used in standard warfare since the Trojan Horse was invented. I check my bag for the mushrooms I picked and stowed but they're gone too!

"Fascinating," Luca says. "The Usta have taken deception tactics to the caverns and canyons, applied the latest in holography, and shot it to us like a picture with added 3-D tactile technology."

"What about the hallucinogen?" I ask. "Gaseous substance released in the air?"

"Camouflage and deception has been used by the US Army for years," Hogan says. "It's a relatively simple defense tactic to augment and manipulate reality to confuse and deceive an enemy."

"It fooled you," Dr. Monica says with a laugh.

Luca glances over at Dr. Monica and Master Sgt. Hogan. "The two of you need to admit your mutual attraction and get a room."

Hogan and Dr. Monica look at each other, shudder, and then

take two steps apiece in opposite directions but don't say anything more. "2-D touch screens for training purposes and haptic holographic training displays are already possible," Luca continues. "But this ability to project true holographic 3-D objects humans can touch, taste, smell, hear, or see through the manipulation of femtosecond lasers that can be viewed from all three-hundred sixty degree angles...is mind-blowing."

"You mean the spheres?" I ask, but thinking, *Dr. Monica and Hogan?* I never noticed it before, but I think Luca is right—those two have a *thing* for one another, something they both varnish over with constant arguments, arm punches, and deep insults.

"It makes sense," Luca says. "The spheres multiply and spread out to expand the scope of our virtual reality. Source knows what sort of data those spheres gathered on all of us through scanning our vitals. Fascinating."

The cathedral is immense and covered with hieroglyphs, some I recognize and some I don't. Various coats of arms in a variety of colors flank the gigantic solid, cloudy quartz doorway. I've spent many hours among the world's greatest architectural marvels but never have I seen a sacred space this indescribably magnificent on Ki above. "Is this place a deception too?" I ask.

Paramel shakes her head. "This place is just as real as the Source. We'll have to secure our weapons in the vestibule."

"No, ma'am," Hogan says.

"It's like a *church,*" I say. "We can't carry our guns, blades, or lasers into an Usta holy place. To them, this space is sacrosanct."

Hogan spits some tobacco at his feet. "Ain't my church," he says. "God knows what we'll meet inside and I'm not gettin' caught with our crosses down!"

"They worship *God,*" I say.

"They don't worship *our* God," Hogan says. Most of his unit nod in agreement.

"Oh?" I ask. "What god do they worship?"

"I don't know," he says. "But it damn sure ain't my God with all that Satanic gobbledy-gook carved in the damn door. Look. That ain't Farsi or Hebrew or any other language I recognize."

"It's Enochian," I say.

"It's what?" he asks.

"The mutating language of angels," I say. I point to some of the figurines on the frame. Color and light wash over each one as I run an index finger along the symbols and read aloud. "*And from the days of Idris until now, the kingdom of Ki suffereth violence, and the violent taketh Ki by force. Follow peace and holiness, without which, no sentient being shall ever see the Source. Strive to enter the strait gate with Love. Many will seek to enter but only few shall be able. Do not despise your kindred, animals, children, or this planet. For in the heavens, their angels face the Source.*"

"I'm not sure how you deciphered that mess, but we'll wait here," Hogan says.

"What's the matter?" Luca says with a slap to the sergeant's back. "Can't take it on *faith* and trust God to enter a church without your weapon?"

"I'll take refuge in the Lord Jesus Christ over trust in any man...or in your case, hybrid or beast," Hogan says. "My men and I will wait here and guard the perimeter. Don't lose radio contact, and for insurance, leave your weapons with us."

Luca pushes against the crystal door but his hand slides through as if it were made of air, and I wonder if it's another hologram. "We may not have much of a signal in there," he says, yanking his hand back.

"We wait with Hogan," Dr. Kanumba says, pointing to herself and Dr. Kimathi, fear evident on their faces. The only thing behind them is complete darkness but I'm not going to argue. They're human—and Usta despise humans—something each of these people may intuitively sense and fear. No humans, as far as I know, have ever made it this far or this close to Ereshun and lived.

"Aye, mate," Dr. Monica whispers to me. "I go where you go, death be damned."

"Vidar," Luca says. "Go on ahead and relay any danger." The falcon flees his arm and its wings vanish through the door.

"Vigo," Reggie says. "You're next. Get in there. Take Kitsune with you."

The rest of us, Reggie, Luca, Dr. Monica, Paramel, and I, step through. The vestibule is pleasantly lit. An incandescent glow, like millions of candles, washes over us when we step into the nave, the main worship area. Luca turns to me and softly smiles; the vivid blueness of his eyes takes on flecks of gold from thousands of small white orbs floating around us.

Paramel touches my shoulder. "Welcome inside the border of Ereshun. I have business to attend. Sjáumst."

"But..."

Paramel taps her forehead and points to mine. "You'll be fine. Fare thee well." She gently bows and slips away through an oversized pillar.

The rest of us stand in our thoughts admiring the architecture. *How could we not,* I think. This place is exquisite and ancient. An immense feeling of peace and benevolence, so unlike anything I've ever felt above ground, sails over me. It is quiet, serene, and sane, and in a myriad of ways, soul-stopping. A low hum, like the "OM" we've heard off and on for weeks, rumbles through my chest—but there is no instrument attached to such a glorious and improbable sound. Somewhere in the distance, chanting, like monks maybe, but ethereal and comprised of a yin-yang equilibrium is some of the sweetest music to ever bless my ears. Baieidō incense, its scent of herbs and agarwood, captivates my nose.

Rows of iridescent windows host panoramic views of the universe and perhaps beyond, boasting nebulas, planets, comets, asteroids, stars, various ether and other unrecognized but glorious horizons beside twin and triple star systems. There are no stone or bronze images of Buddha, Jesus, Yahweh, Allah, or any other images of gods or goddesses gracing an altar because there isn't one. No pews, crosses, swastikas, or pentagrams either. There's zero indication that this space is designed for any single religion, belief, or Creator, yet it is, I feel, within every fiber of my current iteration, elevated in sacredness, precisely due to its absence of dogma. It is holy space filled instead with unseen, but undeniably felt interconnectedness and genuine love—sans judgment. It makes me want to weep with joy and curl up forever within the sanctuary of its bliss.

I wander through the grand hall as if in a trance. I can't even guess how many beings might belong to this "congregation" if I can even call it such. A few hundred thousand? Maybe more? It's mind-blowing to consider such an advanced civilization has existed for what appears to be thousands, perhaps millions of years, right underneath a large and mostly unsuspecting human population. Hogan and Barbara should see this, I think. I wonder what their opinion of this place might be and if they'd too experience the same level of transcendent awe and emotion.

A large crystal slab is adorned with polished gemstones of every shape, size, clarity, and color, their facets glinting and flickering under the golden glow of transparent floating spheres. Another slab is stacked with small strips of metal from iron to ore, steel to platinum. A third holds piles of every seed imaginable from pumpkin to pepper, poppies to primrose, each one distinctly unique from the others but all planted on the same Earth, needing water, air, sun, and food to produce their own fruits or flowers—interconnected with the exact same God—so they may one day bloom.

The storage slabs appear endless, each holding a treasure of words, herbs, symbols, equations, or materials, organic and otherwise, yet possessing spirit in its own special way. One clear slab even contains lightning zipping around inside, its opening at the top a perpetual flame—and another holds light blue clear water, like an oversized ice block. And then we stumble into the "container room," like a wax museum, but the life is gone from these endless rows of forms, both human and not. Embryos and fetuses in various phases of development are housed in clear vats, alongside every mammal species known and unknown.

"This gives me the creeps," Dr. Monica says.

Luca wanders into a dark part of the cathedral and out of view.

Some of the spheres pulsate, expand, and then materialize into shadowy hooded figures lined up in formation, each holding a plasma-loaded fluorescent tube. One phantom tilts his head at me. A faint glow emanates from my eye necklace, first a dot, then a beam, until it forms a small blue-green orb that floats directly between the creature and me, then divides into two globes, its rotating three-D infinity symbol glowing to life. The creature bows and lays down its weapon. Other Usta follow.

"Zumar de Scathatch," *It* says. "Unk zen."

"Zami, Unk zen," I say.

"What in bloody hell did you both say?" Dr. Monica whispers in my ear.

"It called me 'your highness' and said it's lived hundreds of years, but never did it believe it would live long enough to see my return. It welcomes me to Ereshun, and I accepted the greeting." I look around for Luca but still don't see him. Thankfully, today at least, I'm able to understand Enochian. Reggie steps up beside me. Kitsune and Vigo hover near my feet, bowing before Usta, without a whimper, growl, or whine, docile and submitting, I think, to show respect—or hide fear.

"*You?*" Dr. Monica asks, taking a deep swallow. "Her *highness?* This bloody monk said o' that wi' sa few werds?"

"It's Enochian," I explain. "Packaged concepts. It's a language that predates Sumerians and even Kaharan Tepe. But Usta prefer telepathic communication. She also asked if I needed her to kill you. Get behind me, please."

"Wha…"

"You're the only one of us in here who is fully human," I say. "Usta are deeply distrustful of humans."

"Can't say I blame the poor blokes," she says, and does as she's told. "That thing is female?"

"Kedu kan pai?" I ask the Usta.

The seven-foot-tall creature peels back its bulky hood to reveal a hairless oversized head the texture and color of crocodile skin, its ears lobe-less slits and gill-trimmed cheeks. "Ak-shune dob-lay, Skresh."

"Whoa," Dr. Monica almost falls over but quickly recovers and looks around for a safe space. "What the bloody foke is that thing? I've…ah… seen a lotta freaky creatures huntin' in tha Outback and travelin' with you, mate, bu' I neva' seen a gator beast dressed like a monk!"

"Dr. Monica," I say. "Meet Skresh, a crypto terrestrial whose kindred once guarded the Musoviis, the initial Earthers who helped Ebians seed races among galaxies."

"I'll buy the bio-engineering crap," she says, righting herself and smoothing out her suit. "But this Panspermia E.T. seedin' shat? That's goddamn Looney Tunes!"

"You sound like Hogan," I whisper to Dr. Monica, and she makes a face.

Skresh extends three long claw-like digits toward Dr. Monica and speaks, perpetually poised as most Usta are. "You are born of a blood that has protected our descendants for untold years."

"Huh?"

"I think she means your mother," I say. "Didn't she protect Aboriginals near the Outback?"

"Aye. My grandmother and hers before that, too." She nods, then sways, as if she's suddenly dizzy. "Stop doin' that!"

"What am I doing?" I ask.

"Not you," Dr. Monica says. "The Shelia creature! She's pitchin' telepathy crap into ma' brain!" She takes a step toward Skresh, but the Usta holds up a claw, and I can tell, Dr. Monica is confused. She also hesitates to physically engage in what she no doubt realizes is a losing battle. I'm struck by Monica's reaction, how human and akin it is to Genin's. He acted similarly when we met a different Usta in the caves under Harrington House.

"Dr. Monica means you no harm," I say. "Raga turns the eyes, hearts, and ears of humans inside out. Speaking of Raga, do you know where I might find her?"

The cathedral fills with hisses and the pleasant *Om* sound abruptly ceases.

"Who the hell is Raga?" Dr. Monica asks. I forget that although she's been granted a cosmic clearance into most of our unacknowledged special access projects and clandestine operations, she wasn't read into Raga. More hisses echo through the large chamber.

"Our minds close on the bitterness of such knowledge," Skresh says, eyeing Dr. Monica with interest. "Beware of chimeras...to even mention or think about such energy invites curse." She makes a ritualistic gesture with her claws and bows her head.

Dr. Monica visibly shivers.

"This subatomic particle Queen whose name we can't utter already cursed the upper world," I say. "Humans, like this one, Dr. Monica is what we call her, are mostly decent creatures... unaware of the dangers they face. You recognized that her mother helped your descendants, and as we say above, the apple doesn't fall far from the tree."

Dr. Monica looks back-and-forth between the Usta and me.

"We care little for the plight of cruel and violent humans,"

Skresh says, looking at Dr. Monica. "They deserve the consequences of their largely ignorant actions and decisions."

"Most of them don't," I say. "A few humans decided for the majority to hoard celestial gifts. Most humans know nothing of this war."

"War?" Dr. Monica asks. "What war?" She plants a fist on each of her hips and looks at me then Skresh. "What the hell sort o' beast are ya?" She waves her hand up and down. "This can't be bloody true," she says. "Are we in anotha' virtual reality, mate?"

"Skresh is just as real as you or me," I say. "And so is this war. But if you tell anyone *up there*..." I point to the ceiling for effect. "They'll demote and discredit you, take away your clearances, and say you're crazy. You'll wind up in a mental unit at Walter Reed, overdosed on psychotropic meds, and wondering if this was all a bad dream."

"Well, that's just foking cruel mate...I'm supposed to carry this cosmic overload to me grave?"

"It's unfair," I say. "But I suspect we can trust you with this sort of knowledge. After all, you've come this far."

Skresh lifts her arms in the air. "We will not tolerate subterranean war and risk harm to this planet's heart. But the one called Saratu encourages us to welcome you, even this human...fully."

"Who's Saratu?" Dr. Monica asks. "Another Usta?"

Reggie steps up. "May I?" he asks me.

"Of course," I say. "Dr. Monica's already been read in this far. We might as well take her all the way."

"It will be the first for any human to know so much," he says, holding out his elbow for Dr. Monica. She pinches her eyebrows together and politely declines his chivalry as they stroll a few steps away.

"I'm beginning to think this planet's penchant for non-disclosure may be a huge mistake," I say to Skresh. "Maybe we should share our secrets with a few more humans in the hope they'll improve Earthly stewardship."

"Careful," Reggie says over his shoulder. "Our celestrial ancestors felt the same about Atlanteans, and before them, Lemurians, and before them, Actomarians, and look how well that didn't turn out." He and Monica walk and talk through the cathedral until I can't see or hear them anymore.

"You wear the Eye of Sakhet," Skresh says. "You're the one before whom evil trembles."

"I think you're mistaken," I say. The necklace settles into place against my chest, its light finally dimmed. "Evil trembles before Basasael. I'm the Balancer."

Skresh gives me a funny look. "Child," she says. "I'm rarely mistaken. Did Basasael confer your birthright as a Balancer?"

"Yes," I say. "My father was supposed to be the Balancer, but he disappeared during the Viet Nam War."

"Oh?" she asks. "What was your father's Ki name?"

"Brice," I say. "Brice Blake."

Skresh abruptly stops walking and turns to me, imposing, but non-threatening. "How many Ki names do *you* have?"

"It depends," I say. "I go by a few according to Ki's linear timelines. In this life, I am Dr. Samantha Ryan Blake or according to very few, the Countess of Skye. To those of my kindred, I am Sakhet, Iona, or Scathatch."

"Hmmm," she says. "It seems **you** have not been *read into* your entire Truth."

"What do you mean?"

"As they say above ground, 'the apple doesn't fall far from the tree'."

Her words feel heavy, like dumping a load of fresh gravel into my brain. Shock trembles along my spine as Skresh watches my reaction. Reggie taught me to temper my emotions but sometimes they are not so easily quelled, even with breathing. We, Camaeliphim, go by many names...

Smoke.
"I need to find your mother..."
Wings.
Dog tags.
Camouflage.
Brice...Basaseal...Brice...Basaseal
"Dad?"

Before we enter Ereshun, we must pass through *Sanctuary*. It isn't a city but more of a base camp for every wayward creature unknown to humans—a literal 'no-man's' land—and from the looks of it, a quasi-market. All manner of beasts, terrestrials, and interplanetary travelers commune in ad hoc manner among their ilk, trading, bartering, talking, eating, drinking, praying, or gaming. If it weren't for the fact, they *aren't* human, they might be considered the personification of cosplay.

The Agarthans look like they just arrived from ancient Greece, wearing long white robes and tunics, some standing more than eight feet tall but rather human-looking, except for their thin strips of white hair. The typical Greys are just what any Earthling might expect to pop in for an abduction. Albino-like Andromedans are androgynous, hairless beings surrounded by a visible blueish-white aura. The Bezanoits hide insectoid bodies under gray spacesuits and steampunk-like goggles. Polished mantis-type beings flit in and out of existence with triangular heads and extremely bony exoskeletons. Still hundreds of others, I'd guess, the menacing ones without names, possess scales, scutes, tails, or bony plates. These latter creatures, I can tell, are built to fight, with clawed fingers, flaming yellow or orange eyes, and a slightly pungent but not unpleasant odor, like reptiles. They nod, wave, or spit when they see us passing through, including the creatures covered in hair who remind me of Bigfoot and probably also pop up for semi-fresh air in our forests and farmlands every so often, to scare the humans—or deliver a dead drop message to a topside military outpost.

"Mate," Dr. Monica whispers in my ear, "what are these beasts and how di' they get here?"

"They're from other dimensions and planetary systems," I say. "They come here below Earth because they can't risk being seen by civilians or getting captured by Nephilim, or our militaries, who'd lock them up for study and then deny they even exist."

I wonder how we hybrids and a lone purebred human might appear to these otherworldly creatures and when I begin to ask questions, many of them bow, avert their eyes, or move away. Then I wonder what humans would think if all these creatures suddenly decided to take a topside tour. It occurs to me how right our governments might be in keeping E.T.'s hushed up and classified to prevent mass pandemonium. The beasts, creatures, humanoids, and various terrestrials found in Sanctuary are the stuff of both vivid dreams and lucid nightmares.

Dr. Monica steps back to avoid an Irigan and accidentally bumps into a giant Sulzu, an intraterrestrial well over ten feet tall, bald, and with wide black eyes and alabaster tombstone-shaped teeth. "Excuse me," she says with a gulp. The giant silently picks her up by the scruff of her collar, moves her to the other side of me, gently puts her down, and moves along. "This is heaps bad," she whispers. "I used to think I wa' tough for a Sheila, mate, but, aye, I'm beginnin' to hav' ma' doubts."

"You're still tough," I say. "The Sulzu that just picked you up is from Earth. They were here before humans. Stick close—none of these beings are used to seeing or smelling pure kihogs down here."

We pass a few silver and gold-colored pods, where some of the beings barter in outdated or human technology. There are beepers, computers, old books, battered art deco lamps, wires, bulbs, or scratched CDs being sold as if they're antiques. I pick up a signed copy of Rudyard Kipling's poems. I guess even celestrials can appreciate Kipling's genius and soul, which gives me hope for humans. I thumb through Kipling's poem, "If," one of my favorites, and reread, *A White Man's Burden* about governmental takeover and control of the masses through force.

Some of Kipling's verses bother me. But I suppose that was his point—for the reader to feel disturbed—to rise to vigilance and circumspection—to think—and maybe to realize that art, sentient beings, or disparate worlds are not always meant to feel fuzzy and comfortable—and that we're all more entangled and similar than any of us might care to notice or admit.

Another pod, shaped like a flying saucer, and as big as a circus tent, appears to be acting as a sort of "government center" where small chips the size of rice are implanted in claws, fingers, paws, or talons. We steer around it and continue toward the edge of the camp.

"You need a magical spear or some secret knowledge?" a kneeling creature asks. He's covered in a long scarlet robe with a hood. "I got pulse point swords, vortexes, ether axes, electromagnetic bows, and plasma shields."

Luca stops, turns, backs up, and closely inspects the creature. He curls an index finger at me to quietly join him. "I got laser lances too," the creature says without looking up.

"We aren't permitted to bring weapons into Ereshun," I say. "Why does everyone else get to carry or sell weapons so close to the city?" What I don't say is I kept my Bukhara blade strapped against my thigh having snuck it through. This creature's robe reminds me of something a wizard might wear. Its gold-threaded border shimmers against fresh blood-colored velvet. An array of impressive-looking armaments lay scattered about.

"Because we are a human and three hybrids," Luca says. "We're considered more dangerous than any of these celestrials due to our inbred genetic propensity toward violence." He yanks the hood away from the beast's head, who flops backward and tries to crawl away without looking back, but Luca pushes a boot hard against this creature's ass, and the hybrid falls face-first into the dust, a familiar firestorm of fuzzy red hair splayed out like the sun.

The creature lifts his head and mumbles, "You need a sphere of symbols?" He sits up, rubs his eyes, blinks a few times too fast, and looks at us. "I've got screwballs, spoil-sports, oddballs, and sad sacks too, if you be in the market."

"Jingoes, mate," Dr. Monica says and points at the creature "The squib lives!"

"Bo?" I'm gob smacked.

Beneath the robe, Bo still wears his white tunic and oatmeal-colored trousers under advanced silver armor. His eyes glow blue like the Astral Weavers (except he isn't one), and his face is extremely pale beneath a thick orange beard. He pats down his chest, offers me a too-toothy smile, bows his head, and says, "Your highness, I am forever at your service." He tries to shake my hand, but Luca swats it away. "I scored some high-quality wet blankets and a few souped-up egos. Give ya a real good price on 'em," Bo says with a sheepish grin.

"Actually," I say. "I'm in need of a special helmet."

"Hang on," Bo says, jumping to his feet. "I have, let's see... here!" He picks up a dented brass helmet covered in patina, one that looks as if it came from a costume shop, as the helm is small enough to fit a child. "This one was worn by Napoléon during the battle of Heraclea...it has special powers."

Reggie, Dr. Monica, and I burst into laughter. Luca just looks pissed off.

"Something wrong?" Bo asks. "What's so funny?"

"The Battle of Heraclea took place in 280 BC between the Romans and the Greeks," Reggie says with a smirk. "That helmet looks as if you fetched it out of a toybox from 1970."

"So?" Bo says. "Napoléon was there at Heraclea."

"No," Luca says with a frown. "He wasn't. Napoléon fought in the battle of Austerlitz. You're off by about two thousand years, give or take." He waggles his palm back and forth.

"He...he...Napoléon," Bo says. "He reincarnated."

"He was human," Reggie says. "And I know for a fact Napoléon did not return to Earth, because my brother Makonen escorted his energy to Gliese B, twenty-four light-years away."

"We can always have Paramel check the container grid back at the Fluffle garden to see if Bo is correct," I say. "He can come with us. From the looks of him, he's not thriving so well for a mighty Viking. Oh, and this helmet will never do. I'm in need of a golden helmet, one embossed with a serpent sporting stony emerald eyes, the one you retrieved out of the dirt when we released you from your granite prison."

Bo trembles a little and loosens the cord of the robe around his neck. "I got other helmets. I got body parts too. Need a replacement beak?"

"No."

"Some fingers or claws?"

"I want the golden helmet," I say. "What in the hell are you doing with body parts?"

"I find them here and there..." Bo says. "You know, after battles and other stuff."

"What sort of *other* stuff?" I ask. "Never mind. I don't want to know. I'd like to see the golden helmet."

"It's not for sale," he says. "It's **mine**!"

Bo stands up, dusts himself off, and starts to walk away but Luca reaches out and snags him by the shoulder. "That's no way to treat a Princess," he says to Bo. "I'm sure we heard you say back in the caves, and here just a minute ago, that you were forever in Scathatch's service."

Reggie and Dr. Monica nod. "You want me to clock this bloke?" she asks, taking a step forward. Bo backs up and I hold out a hand to stop her.

"Scathatch can't have the helmet," Bo says. He stomps his boot to the ground like a frustrated toddler. "I stole it fair and square!"

The four of us cross our arms and glare at him. "Bo, I'm going to give you to the count of three to produce Paramel's helmet... one...two..."

...A rickety carriage from the Steampunk Era passes between Bo and my entourage...and by the time the dust settles, and we get around it, he and his battle gear, including the helmet we never actually saw, are gone.

ERESHUN

PEACE WITHIN USTA civilization means everything and Ereshun, beyond the suburb of Sanctuary is tranquil, its beauty beyond compares. Crystal spirals rise hundreds of feet in the air and most of the city hides within a forest of pure white stalagmites and stalactites. We are not permitted to touch the tapering columns of lava, pitch, or sand, because oils from human and hybrid skin weaken such ethereal structures.

Usta are also intensely tribal creatures, private, and difficult to tell apart, a bit of a hive mentality where they work for the greater good of their commune and all existence, including humanity—even though they loathe humans, who they claim, "sorely lack compassion and are overstocked with self-service."

Usta are forced to remain hidden beneath miles of granite shields that protect them from the Nephilim, which might use human militaries and mercenaries for infiltration, and because Usta's true form frightens humans. They have large heads covered in scales and their faces are sort of reptilian with diamond-shaped eyes and amber-red faceted pupils. A protruding brow ridge of varying degrees lends them a menacing appearance.

Dresh and Nesh, our male Usta guides, are not much different-looking than the females, except for a thorny sexual organ on their thumbs used to attract and arouse mates. Their hands, if I can call them such, are like bumpy clubs with claws. The thing I find so funny is that Usta males also adorn their cheek gills with bright pink pigment from the remains of billion-year-old molecular fossils of chlorophyll. They tell us it's part of a sacred ritual. It comes from organisms that inhabited a long-vanished underground ocean and it gives the males an effeminate quality.

The two Usta exchange mind concepts without breaking eye contact. It's a completely silent conversation that looks downright weird and involves zero gestures. Dr. Monica shivers and moves closer to me. "I'm roomin' with you, mate," she says. "These beings give me the heebie-jeebies."

"They're peaceful unless they detect harmful intent," I say. "Try to relax...breathe in, to the count of four, hold for four, and breathe out. Let the music wash over you."

"Stop wi' tha bloody fokin' breathin' exercises, mate," Dr. Monica says. She pulls a vial of Paramel's purple liquid from her pocket, snaps the lid and taps a drop on her tongue. "That's better!"

A soft nonstop series of harmonious chants drifts into the chambers and surrounds us, a sound bath of such ethereal beauty it brings tears to my eyes. Ferny-looking vines snake around and over ancient granite walls, guarded by soccer-ball-sized white spheres that bob and float around us. When Dresh and Nesh conclude their business, Nesh approaches me, relaxed. "Thank you for respecting our quietude," he says telepathically. "Usta do not like the feeling of *loud*."

"I can see why," Luca whispers telepathically into my brain. I internally flinch, not expecting his voice in my head. "These entire grounds would likely collapse from the sneeze of a cricket."

I briefly smile up at him as we're led to the inner sanctum and turn down the volume of my mind. We've been so busy, he and I haven't had time, or opportunity, to connect. I want to ask him what happened that night back at the Fluffle after he kissed me and then so abruptly withdrew. His finger lightly traces the nape of my neck and I involuntarily shudder. It appears his psychic abilities are quite acute in Ereshun. I speed up to keep up with Dr. Monica and Nesh, who's giving us a mental tour of the place.

"Ereshun is approximately three million years older than any topside civilization on Ki," he says. "Although a small group of us did arrive more than five million years ago, around the time we split humans from primate seeds. Usta were trying to calibrate human DNA to minimize aggression. Unfortunately, we experienced a few unexpected setbacks and visitors. Our work continues...*wiring* energy wirelessly through sentient containers is quite complex."

"What are the floating spheres?" Dr. Monica asks.

"They are us," Nesh replies. "In our highest meditative form. It is a state of light we strive to achieve. And it's less frightening for humans when we must, on rare occasions, roam among them. Humans can accomplish this transition too, although we've only seen a handful possessed of enough discipline to reconfigure their inner bio-hardware and appropriately connect to outer consciousness."

Spheres bump or join as one or break off into hundreds of tiny spheres the size of nightlights. None seem in a hurry to do anything except exist in this *Now*. The fresh scent of ozone, oxygen, and surf fills my nostrils again. A small streak of silent lightning, what Kihogs above call "heat lightning," travels along the underside of majestic-looking royal purple and sapphire clouds.

Nesh leads us into a hall, onto an open floor. I'm not sure who he's taking us to see because hierarchy among Usta, from what I've been led to understand, constantly rotates. I wonder, too, if I'll be able to appropriately convey my appreciation for recognizing a human in service to us and not killing her. Allowing Dr. Monica this far into their sanctum is something they consider a great risk and probably a sacrilege. When the spheres and the Usta part to create a path for us, a small being, clad in a saffron robe, sits atop a clear crystal craft. I'm engulfed in shock.

"Eido?" I ask.

He opens his almond-colored eyes. He looks pleased to see us but not at all surprised.

"Holy Source!" I say. "Eido, what are you doing here? I mean, how is this possible? I thought you were dead!"

Relief washes over me but I'm pissed off too because Eido just...*poof*...disappeared. I've been agonizing for days, reciting my grief speech to the Sherpas, and thinking about how I'd have to travel in person to confront his Master and break the horrible news. But here he sits alive and no worse for wear, after throwing himself at a Fewoulz. I must admit, his dangerous action gave me time to plunge my blade into the beast, likely saving me from perpetual imprisonment.

Eido smiles the bright grin of a child filled with free-spirited joy. He rises and floats to me, inches off the ground, staring into my eyes. "It's lovely to see you too," he says. And the way he says this, without pain or suffering, and far beyond his age, makes me wonder how hard he hit his head back at the Fewoulz's lair. Eido tilts his head back and laughs. "I suffer no concussions," he tells me telepathically.

I silently glare at him and mentally speak. *"I'm happy you're alive but wish you'd let me know you're okay. I was worried sick!"*

"It was too great a risk," Eido says out loud. He doesn't elaborate.

A few of the Usta, elders I think, because of their lighter almost translucent scales, float in a circle, deeply engrossed in telepathic conversation. Luca and Reggie stand near them. I strain to connect to their thoughts. They civilly debate our arrival, whether it's a safe or intelligent decision, especially since humans and hybrids carry war in their hearts wherever they seem to tread, disrupting elevated vibrations and canceling enlightened progress. One Usta lowers and shakes his head while another balances three spheres on a single claw. A third lumbers in what I think is contemplation.

"What's happening?" I ask.

Eido smiles again, studying the creatures without looking at me. "They are concerned that *you*, dear Princess, are in over your head as a Balancer—and I tend to agree."

This troubles me. If Usta feel the promise I made to *Not Who* is beyond me, they're probably right. "I'm not sure how to respond to that," I say.

"Balancers *should* be over their heads to effectively carry light forward," Eido says, breaking into a wide smile. His words cause a stir among the Usta, who all turn to look at or float around him. "This is a job *beyond* the human mind."

"Oh," I say. What I don't say is that I agree with him, that maybe a hybrid like me must be *out* of her mind to take this job.

"We have a Balancer," Eido says to the others. "We are no longer auditioning for a role that is Scathatch's birthright, conferred to her by Basaseal himself. Look." He points to me as the light on my necklace turns up.

"The spiral on your forehead glows and spins," Luca whispers in my ear.

I don't feel a thing.

When I turn to look again at Eido, he is gone. Just...vanished! I yank my head around to see if he hid behind a slab or pillar, looking for a piece of his robe or for his head to peek around a corner. Nothing.

"Why do you come *here?*" an Usta finally asks, using his voice.

"I was invited," I say.

A collective internal gasp causes the hair on my forearms to rise.

"By whom?" another asks. "We did not extend such an invitation."

"By me," someone says, her voice authoritarian enough that we all turn toward the sound. "We should not question our guests but make them comfortable." The creature is shrouded by her robe and floats to me. She reveals herself, raises a bony ridge on her brow, and lightly cocks her head to one side.

"Eresh?" I ask. "Is it really *you?*" I haven't seen her since the night I fell into a fountain with Genin in the UK. We landed in a tunnel under Harrington House chasing after an entirely different creature, one I haven't yet spotted in the bowels of Ki, but I know it's down here somewhere.

"It is well known in Sanctuary that you freed the Viking and the Fluffle from a Fewoulz," Eresh says, tossing her cape over a sphere, one that glides off with it. "And broke a centuries-old curse."

"This is true," I say.

"And how is your human...the one I met...what was his name?" she asks. "Your lover, Genin?"

Blush, about as hot pink as the male Usta wear, floods my cheeks, and I refuse to look at Luca. "Genin betrayed me," I say.

"I see," she says. "But an act is only a betrayal if it violates existing trust."

"I trusted him," I say.

"Presumptive contracts and psychological conflicts are a hindrance for hybrids who cavort with humans," she says. "Kihogs are not to be trusted."

"Tell me," I say with an eye roll. "How is Eido, a human child, permitted among you unharmed? Do you trust *him?*"

"Eido is compassion made corporeal," she answers. "He is a wisdom king in temporary human form who precedes the Balancer. He is neither omniscient, omnipotent, nor an object of refuge, worship, or harm. Eido makes himself Light, a symbol of the divine in sentient beings, sent here at the request of Saratu."

"***Saratu***?" Reggie and I ask in unison.

"She is Eido's master teacher," Eresh says.

"What the bloody hell did she just say?" Dr. Monica asks.

Eresh hisses at her, and Monica jumps behind me, her fingernails digging into my shoulder. I feel her trembling, but despite this, I consider her courageous. It's not every day humans meet far-advanced non-human, highly intelligent creatures that defy comprehension and are capable of evaporating life with a single crystal-stick-loaded mind-swipe.

I haven't thought about Saratu since the last time I saw her in Nepal at Tetana's funeral. We shared the same foster home at Plum Hook Bay. She originally lived in the Sahara Desert. Saratu locates underground water using her feet, but that's not all she does. When I was a foster kid, Reggie and I watched her get taken up by a sphere a lot bigger than the ones here at Ereshun. Reggie and I didn't understand it then, but we do now. Saratu is a celestial douser, a Ceitan from a galaxy millions of light-years away. She guards and communicates with crypto terrestrials the world over from her perch in Nepal, orb-plucked by the Usta to monitor Ki tensions.

"Scathatch," Eresh says. "You're about to embark on a journey unlike any other."

"Um," I say, looking around. "I think I've gone about as far down the rabbit hole as I can go."

"Not yet," she says with a lipless grin. "You will need help for your biggest challenge, throwing Raga into the Source vortex."

Luca and I look at one another in surprise but purposely exchange no words. I am relieved Bennie hid our daughter so well that even Usta, at least for the moment, are unaware of

Hope's Bezaliel mist or the fact Raga may already be sharing space with her container.

The room erupts in hisses, the spheres amplify their magnitude and surround us.

So much for mental privacy. *Shit!* I have a hard enough time keeping my mouth shut, let alone my mind too! "Um, okay, so you now know about that," I say. "That my daughter has Bezaliel mist."

"Your daughter?" Reggie asks. "What in the hell are you talking about?"

"Fallopian egg heist, 1984," I say. "Compliments of Dr. Evelyn Dennison."

"She forced you to sleep with a Bezaliel?" he asks. "That's not even possible."

Luca looks almost amused.

"No," I say. "It's complicated."

"What's a Bezaliel?" Dr. Monica asks. "I don' remember ya eva' mentionin' being prego, Sheila. Is Genin a Bezaliel? Where's the carpet begga' you mothered?"

"No!" I say. "I've never been pregnant."

"Who's the father?" Reggie asks.

"Bennie," I say. "The child was conceived in a test tube and then placed under heavy guard at Plum Hook Bay without our knowledge or consent."

"I knew that woman was foul," Reggie says. He folds his enormous hands into fists at his sides.

"Our little reunion with Verity and Evelyn at my mom's asylum prompted the embryo to come out of storage."

"What are you saying?" Reggie asks.

"When Verity and I were foster kids at Plum Hook Bay, Dr. Evelyn made Verity an offer," I say, "in exchange for American citizenship, a job with the CIA, and a college scholarship... Verity would someday carry Bennie's and my child...Verity named her Hope."

"This is criminal," Reggie says. "Evelyn violated every oath she swore to Septum Oculi. She was hired to save you from that hell hole, not throw you Plum Hook Bay kids to the wolves...but wait a minute...you said your daughter has Bezaliel mist. Bennie is not a Bezaliel."

"Right," I say. "Dr. Evelyn injected our daughter's DNA with Bezaliel mist, without Verity's knowledge or consent, in the hope of adopting, raising, and feeding off Hope's power. I suspect, but can't prove, she also used that fucked-up mind of hers to blow an artery in Verity's brain."

"Jesus, Sam, why didn't you tell me sooner?" Reggie asks, pinching his brows together and running a hand over his whitening beard. "Evelyn has committed inviolable crimes."

"The timing was never right," I say. "And yes, she has."

"Sam," Reggie says. "There's something I need to..."

"Where did Dr. Evelyn take this child?" Dr. Monica interrupts. "How old is she?"

"She's about eight months old, Ki time," I say. "Evelyn doesn't have my daughter. At least not anymore."

Luca looks no longer amused but deadly serious. "We believe Bennie now has Hope."

"Bennie? He's *alive*?" Reggie asks. "How do you know this?"

"I confided in Luca," I say. "Back at Harrington House."

"You confided in *him*?" Reggie asks, a hurt look on his face. "Wait...are you two...? You entangled yourself with this beast, didn't you?"

"No," I say. "And if Luca and I were to mutually agree to such a decision, it isn't your, or anyone else's business."

"Oh, Christ!" Reggie says, throwing his hands up. "That would fuck up everything!"

"Enough!" Eresh yells, giving Reggie a stern look. And for the first time since I've known Reggie, he stands down. "You require otherworldly warriors," Eresh says. "Hope is an Emergent, the first. Our wish is to save her rightful container for this life and enhance her mind."

"Enhance her mind, how?" I ask, feeling suspicious.

"By preparing her to understand and visit the root of reality," Eresh says, "one that conserves and conveys information through a zero-point field of subtly fluctuating energies from which all things arise."

Luca lets out a low whistle. "Fascinating," he says.

"Why?" I ask. "Why would she need to understand such a thing?"

"You don't know?" Eresh asks.

Her words echo through the halls of my head but I can't come up with an answer. I grudgingly shake my head no.

"Think," Eresh says. "Your mother and Verity are human *Receptors,* able to process cosmic knowledge, your friend Bennie is Source Bearer, and you're a Balancer. Your daughter holds the history and future of all that has happened in the cosmos and can relate it to all that is yet to happen, provided she is appropriately reared to do so. She is the bio-electro-magnetic record keeper of the Source—or in simpler terms, the eternal self-realized mind of God made manifest, but only if you contain Raga and her corruptive energy within the Source Vortex."

"No pressure," I say, feeling heart heavy.

In all my years as a half-human on Earth, being coerced and controlled by humans, cryptos, or celestrials, slides to the forefront of my mind. As a kid, I lived in deep denial about my otherworldly visitors, skills, and involuntary travels. I'm convinced Eresh is correct about my daughter's ethereal potential and identity; it leaves me unnerved about the methods, intentions, and lack of compassion government operatives might use to manipulate Hope and hold her "above top secret." My daughter needs her parents. Bennie and I can help her align her humanness with her celestial abilities. If not, Hope's gifts will leave her terrified and confused—perhaps enough to act out, without control, fearful of what she doesn't understand—and surrounded by strangers.

"What if Raga seizes Hope's form?" I ask.

"If this happens," Eresh says, "you know what you must do."

"Then we have no Emergent because I've killed my own daughter," I say.

"And this world will collapse," Eresh says.

"Cripe's, I'm confused, mate," Dr. Monica says. "What's an Emergent? Wha' happens if you don' succeed?"

"Game. Over," Luca says. "For Earth. For us. For everybody and every multiverse from here to Michotu."

I feel an oppressive wave of gloom pass through the room as if we collectively concentrate and transmit our thoughts into one telepathic voice to Eresh, but I can only make out fuzzy static and garbles rather than details.

"Well, that is heaps bad," Dr. Monica whispers.

"They deserve amnesty," Eresh says.

"Who?" I ask.

"The humans with high clearances who've broken their promises," she says. "The ones in your above governments who've kept our secrets. We need their help."

"You expect me to *forgive* the humans who've broken their agreements with celestrials?" I ask. "They may have kept our secrets, but they also violate every single treaty we ever make with them! Those humans to whom you want to grant amnesty are the reason I lost my mother and father. Scores of other decent humans on this planet have also been discredited, badly hurt, or lost their lives sharing celestrial truths. We deserve justice."

"Your 'above governments' claim the vast majority of the human population is not ready for our otherworldly knowledge," Eresh says. "We remain hidden to protect the human population. But yes, I agree, the *'silent secreter'* humans do lie to keep their families and fortunes safe. It is easier to treat celestrials as a threat to national security than it is to admit knowledge of us. Yet disclosure also risks global riots or innocents being held liable for past deeds. We must work together for Ki and the realms to survive."

"Any celestrial warriors who fight alongside me risk inanimation," I say.

"It is a risk many are willing to take," Eresh says.

"I heard," a voice says, breaking through the silence, "the Usta put a call out for celestrial warriors, damn near unheard of from them."

"Paramel?"

She's dressed in futuristic battle gear, her long red hair braided down one side over a breast shield, wearing the same advanced silvery boots Bo does. She approaches me and bows. She looks at Eresh. "Pardon me, madam, for appearing without head covering, but the helmet you bestowed on me has been stolen."

"Who will guard the Isle of No Time against Fewoulz if you accompany us?" Reggie asks. "It's our understanding the Viking holds the Isle."

"The one you call Hogan, and his men," Eresh says. "We intercepted them on the cathedral steps and escorted them back to the Isle of No Time unharmed. Bilby met them at the Fewoulz lair. They are in advanced training against all manner of human or intraterrestrial foe."

"Why would they agree to this?" I say. "What did you tell them?"

"We felled them with sleep and appeared to them as angels in the mushroom field," she says. "They've been touched by what they know as the hand and spirit of God, to act as warriors for Jesus Christ."

"Bloody ridiculous," Dr. Monica says.

"I agree," Eresh says with a rapid flash of her blueish tongue. "It's about as absurd as the Bible story about a gang of rapists suddenly descending on Lot's home in the middle of the night to defile archangels. But Lot hands over his virgin daughters instead? Do you think God would condone such violence against a child, or bless the human who makes such a ludicrous offer?" Dr. Monica shakes her head no.

"It makes little sense to Usta, either" Eresh continues, "but the capacity to believe some nonsense, while discrediting universal Light, unfortunately, is the line of demarcation between humans and advanced beings."

A commotion ensues behind us and when I turn to look, two connected spheres toss out Bo at my feet.

"Bo?" Paramel asks. "Is that *you?*"

Bo lifts his head, stands up, and reminds me of a cowardly lion, his knees clamped together as if he must pee, wringing his ridiculously out-of-place robe in his bulbous hands. He looks around to make sense of his ethereal surroundings and jumps behind me to hide when he spots Paramel.

"I heard," Eresh says to him, coming around to my other side, "you're in possession of a golden helmet belonging to this female warrior, one I gave her."

"It's mine," he says. "I found it fair and square."

"If I may interrupt," I say, stepping away from Bo. "He told three hybrids and a human back at Sanctuary that he *stole* Paramel's helmet fair and square." My team nods and Luca offers me a solid wink, one Eresh doesn't miss. Paramel steps forward to kick Bo but Eresh hisses her back.

"I see you wear the blood diamond," Eresh says to me. "An eternally flawless red shield that enables you to exercise flexibility within your form."

I glance at the ring on my left hand and look again at Luca. "I wasn't aware of your description, but yes," I say. I silently wonder what flexible forms this ring might enable and how to activate them, and why Luca really put it on my finger. I wish I could recall and upload all my memories, but try as I might, the celestrial lives I've led are sometimes about as solid as a faded black-and-white television with a faulty antenna.

"And this hybrid here," Eresh says. "Hello, Lord Harrington, it's semi-wonderful to see you again...he is your betrothed?"

"Yes," I say.

"Lord Harrington, do you *love* this female Camaeliphim?" she asks.

This space couldn't suddenly get any smaller or quieter and I'm positive, after Eresh's unexpected question, that everyone can hear the rapid beating of my heart about as clearly as a helicopter rotor.

I won't look at Luca.

I won't.

I refuse.

I look at him.

Luca wears a smile about as bright as a sphere, looking back at me. "With all of my heart," he says.

I melt inside and look away, feeling foolishly giddy, trying to hold onto my poker face, but it gives way to a royal flush.

Eresh taps her crystal stick to the floor with a loud *thwack!* "And how much of that, your heart, is actually left?" she asks, glaring at him.

And this question is how I know *she* knows...that coursing through Luca's hybrid veins runs the same Bezaliel mist as Hope, a secret Eresh holds back from the rest of her tribe, for what purpose I can't say—except that if the other Usta were to know—Luca would likely be in more danger than Dr. Monica.

Luca appears a bit unnerved and looks up at the ceiling. Hers is an unexpected question, a brilliant question born of the fact I suspect that she somehow senses or smells Luca's Bezaliel mist where her kindred can't—or maybe she was read into something we weren't. Eresh turns away from him.

My heart plummets just as fast as it soared with her question.

He LOVES me. But... although Luca is part human, he's infused with Bezaliel mist, even more reason for me to exercise extreme caution. *He can't be trusted.* Then it occurs to me; maybe humans and hybrids can't trust themselves. Perhaps humans and hybrids congregate in churches, stadiums, or packs...for reassurance they're not entirely dubious and beyond repair—and maybe too, why Usta do, despite their claims of enlightened advancement. *Presumptive contracts and psychological conflicts are a hindrance,* Eresh had said. I only need to remember what happened with Genin to know this.

"Eresh, you have not asked Samantha if *she* loves *me*," Luca says.

Eresh spins the stick and abruptly turns to face him again. "I do not need to," she says. "Her intentions are perfectly clear. Lord Harrington—you shall fight Bo for Paramel's helmet within the Cage of Savagery."

"Cave of Savagery?" Luca asks. "Seems a bit inconsistent with this whole Zen realm gig you've got going on here—I mean, outside of the vapor sticks you wield with impunity."

"The *CoS* is contained and doesn't leak into our realm," Eresh says, raising a severe brow ridge at him.

Reggie and I exchange glances and I feel utterly confused. *"What is the Cage of Savagery?"* I mentally ask.

Dr. Monica interrupts me with her own thoughts. *"Ah shat, this is heaps bad, I promise ya Lord, if ya let me live through dis I'll neva' be settin' foot or openin' me mouth where it don' belong, eva' agin! I'm gonna piss ma britches..."*

"Dr. Monica! Quiet your thoughts!" I direct to her and her alone. *"I can't mentally 'hear' Reggie!"*

Dr. Monica puffs out her cheeks with a large sigh and abruptly silences her mind chatter.

"The Cage of Savagery is a barrier that keeps violence contained and prevents it from leaking into Ereshun. I suspect we're already in it," Reggie says. *"I don't think Usta would risk*

humans or hybrids free-roaming through their realm no matter how friendly they appear."

"Bo is extremely dangerous," Paramel whispers to me. "He may appear cowardly but it's an act. And he doesn't fight fair..."

...And just like that, Bo and Luca are sequestered within an electrical boundary, a *Cage of Savagery,* subject to certain inanimation or death should either of them get thrust against the thick ropes of green glowing plasma. They're forced to circle one another like angry, trapped animals. Weapons appear and disappear around them like magic. Bo seizes what looks like a small tornado while Luca opts for a...a pair of rubber tires?

Oh, come on!

Luca's choice of weapon is absurd and makes no sense. I'm beginning to doubt his standing as this world's formidable and foremost defense contractor.

Bo conducts a series of jumps and hand movements, cartwheeling in and out of his swirling maelstrom until Luca lands a swift kick to Bo's wrinkly twins and the jarl pitches over like a broken tent pole. Near Bo's hand suddenly appears a Morgenstern, a ball with spikes attached to a club. Bo grabs it and winds up his tornado, sending the weapon out the top, incoming to Luca's face.

I can't look!

I look.

The Morgenstern is set to smash Luca's temple, but he flings a tire up with his arm to render the weapon completely stuck. He lets loose of the other tire and whips it into the green energy field, instantly breaking the connection between our world and the Usta. The weapons disappear and Eresh swiftly taps her crystal cane a few times to reconnect the cage.

My heart and head silently root for Luca, hoping—praying, for his safety, yet wondering about our union, if it's really something built to last, like the Source—but hell, even that's in question now and can't survive without sentience. Watching Luca fight, I'm awed by his level of skill, as if Reggie himself, one of the best warriors in the galaxy, spent years teaching Luca everything he knows. It's a surprisingly even match between Lord Harrington and Bo the jarl, like watching an anaconda fight a crocodile, quick bursts followed by concentrated strikes.

My Bukhara blade is suddenly in Luca's hand, and I gasp. This is the second time a Camaeliphim has successfully and secretly heisted the weapon from my thigh. The Usta try but cannot force it to disappear. Luca swings his legs to knock Bo off-balance. Bo lands with a loud thud on his stomach and his mini tornado vanishes through the ceiling. Thankfully, none of the icicle-shaped stalactites fall on our heads. Luca straddles Bo's back, lifts Bo's head to the crowd, and holds the blade so close to Bo's throat that a single drop of blood bubbles up but doesn't drip.

"Enough." Eresh taps her stick three times.

The forcefield vanishes and Luca smashes Bo's head to the ground. The impact breaks the jarl's nose and sends blood gushing. Luca's display of violence both discomforts and thrills me at the same time, reaching deep into that ancient and primitive part of my human brain, one of lust and competition, feelings I fight to subdue. I let out a cheer.

Reggie pitches me a scolding look. "Part of your job is to restrain nasty species," he says. "Not act like one."

But I'm not so secretly happy for Luca even if I do wipe the vicarious victory smile off my face.

"Enough," Eresh says. "Who brings this weapon into a sacred house?"

"I do." I step up. "I also question how sacred this house when you possess a Cage of Savagery."

Paramel walks over to Bo and kicks him in the side. "Produce the helmet," she says. He wobbles to his feet and swings his own knife at Paramel, who handily dispatches it from him, and now it is *she* who holds the weapon. "Did you bring this blade into a sacred space?" she asks with a sneer. "Give me my fucking helmet."

Eresh stops me from intervening when I take a step forward. "Wait," she says. "Intergalactic Vikings must sort this out themselves."

"Can they inanimate one another?" I ask.

"No..." she says. "Only the Ormian Council may inanimate hybrids or celestrials. The Vikings may be above human, but they can still die by one another's hand, like humans or hybrids."

Paramel grits her teeth, kicks Bo in the jewels a second time, and she pulls an arm up behind his back. "In case you did not hear me the first time...produce...my...helmet."

The helmet instantly appears on her head, and she stands to straighten it. She rolls Bo over and raises the knife in her hand, ready to plunge it through his throat. Gone is the gentle Elemorphia who rendered such fair and gentile hospitality back at the Fluffle. The Viking who holds the Isle fights violently and with skillful competence, a stellar addition to our team, I think.

"Wait!" I yell. "Paramel, don't kill him!"

"Why?" Paramel asks.

"I promised him to Lozen's sister."

"The Astral Weaver?" Paramel asks. "But she's..."

"I know," I say, cocking my head at her and speaking slowly. "She's... in need of...a spousal accessory."

Paramel slowly tilts her lips up and releases Bo. His face hits the ground a third time. "You unlucky bastard," she says to him. She points at me. "Summon Lozen."

"I can't create a portal," I say. "I gave my last buckeye to Basasael."

"Nesh," Eresh says, "conscript a buckeye from the repository..."

We walk back the way we came, through the cathedral, the virtual mushroom fields, and into Sanctuary, which is now practically empty, its markets packed up and put away, and its participants making all manner of interstellar merry within various brothels or bars. Any evidence of enlightenment is erased but the ethereal quality of the place still wafts through the cavernous city. A few creatures, their arms filled with wares, or vials of violet liquor, teeter through and over cobbled paths, waving or staring at us with bleary-eyed smiles. Two female creatures lead another male on a leash into a large tent near the government center. Others vanish into caves or the folds of rock formations.

"Eresh," I say, "do under dwellers ever make it to the surface of Ki?"

"Yes," she says. "We sneak up sometimes to watch the stars."

"Do humans ever see you?"

"Sometimes," she says. "It's usually by accident or because humans inadvertently build or develop too near our gateways. When this happens, we're forced to relocate or camouflage the ingress...or worse, unfortunately."

"You kill them?"

"Never topside," she says. "It's Kihog natural territory."

"What do you mean by *worse?*"

"We strip them of their memories," she answers.

"That's not fair or fun," I say. "I know how that feels."

"Relax," she says. "We only extract the moments they actually see us and then we plant doubt into them about what they think they saw or offer *alternative* memories."

"Alternative memories?"

"We replace unexpected Usta sightings with memories of owls, bats, bigfoot or sometimes aliens or ariel phenomena," she says.

"Do non-clearance humans ever make it far enough into Earth to see all of this?" I ask.

"Never," she says. "We've installed *preventative* measures

against Kihog breaches. Of course, if they spot us underground nearer the surface, we take measures."

"I've seen your measures," I say, thinking of Dolan, how half of him evaporated into nothingness when we started this journey. An involuntary shiver lifts the hair on my neck.

"That was mercy," she says, as if reading my mind. Then to Paramel, "You will monitor your helmet more closely going forward?"

"Definitely," Paramel says, touching the emerald eye of the golden serpent attached to her head.

"The helmet, when activated, enables us to monitor and mold our meditation, to keep all of you animated and protected, if we so choose," Eresh says.

Luca abruptly stops and his azure eyes flicker over us with concern. "If you so *choose*? I thought only the Ormian Council made such decisions."

Eresh ignores him and walks across the bridge that leads back to the Fluffle. The ferns are wet with dew and amber light glimmers from hundreds of holes in the ground. "We may not be able to save *all* of you," she finally says without looking at him. "I want to visit old friends now. It's been decades since I've last crossed over into the Fluffle."

I stare out over vines, plants, flowers, trees, and violet roots. If it weren't for the fact we're miles underground, keeping company with intelligent non-human biological entities, the atypical scenery would not appear too far off from *normal*. It's quiet way down here, almost sane in its simplicity and natural order—and its brutality. For a moment, I wish I could stay and forget about being the Balancer, maybe live with the Fluffle, take daily grotto baths in a forever *Now* and sleep away this life. It won't happen, I know. Hybrids, like humans, are built to feel the sun and wind on our faces, smell pine trees, watch the rain, marvel over stars, and hear the lull of ocean surf. I'm no longer a fully-fledged celestial able to roam realms. This place, this planet, all of it, is the only home I know. It needs a retooling for sure, but I'd like to think Ki is not a lost cause on the distant wispy arm of the Milky Way.

"I'm tired," Dr. Monica says.

The rest of us don't say anything. Luca mulls Eresh's words, I think, his face drawn and pensive. Paramel scouts for Bilby, and Reggie looks concerned. I can only imagine what's going through Dr. Monica's mind right now, our telepathic abilities greatly diminished outside Ereshun. I place my arm around her, and she surprisingly leans into me, and takes a deep swallow. "I don't know wha' *normal* is anymore," she whispers. "I'll neva' be the same or sane after this. I'm no' the same now..."

"You can return to the surface," I say. "I know this isn't what you originally signed up for."

Paramel takes Bo's knife from her belt and uses it to cut some violet roots snaking along the ground. She hands one to Dr. Monica then approaches her home hole, takes a deep breath, motions to me, and climbs down.

Dr. Monica pulls away and scratches the side of her head. "Samantha," she says, "I'm learnin' tha' humans live compartmentalized lives—the life an' personality we show the world *up there*," she points, "and an internal life we hide in both our heads and down under, mate. I may not understand what it means to be hybrid like you, or all of this, but Ima' part o' this team, and by extension, one of ya'." She holds up the violet root and watches its sap *drip, drip, drip* to the ground, allowing a potent nightcap to go undrunk. "I'll finish ma' duty because I made a promise, but mo' importantly, I consida' you a friend, mate. I'd take a bullet for ya'. Don' wan' to...but I would." She lays the root on a rock and climbs down another hole.

Luca touches my arm before I crawl into Paramel's den. "Hang on," he says. He goes first and ushers me down, catching me in his arms. It smells like herbs, soil, soap, and soft fire in Paramel's space. Luca stares into my eyes, my heart beating fast. "Kiss me," he says. "I need to feel...human."

"No."

He pulls me closer. I don't resist but I don't press against him either. "I'm not sure we're meant for each other," I finally say. Thoughts of Bennie trickle into my mind, how much I've missed him since our time at Plum Hook Bay. Sadness pours over my heart. Luca and Bennie are brothers, the same levels of intelligence and cockiness, yet so different. Where Luca is outspoken and arrogant, Bennie is reserved and gentle. Luca kills. Bennie revitalizes. Then there's my daughter. I've not said much, but she's *always* with me, occupying most of my mind, most of the time, even within a perpetual *Now* on the Isle of No Time.

Luca releases me, spins me around, and places both of his hands over my shoulders. "This life we lead is not for the weak," he whispers in my ear. "There's no walking away, heading back to the surface, and pretending we can go on the way we used to before we knew we were hybrids. Up there, on the surface? Very few humans know we exist. We *pass* as human. And those who do know about us? We frighten them."

He's right. And we've reached a cerebral junction, that place where desire, duty, and destiny come together. Which path we choose means no looking back. I linger for a moment under his firm rub.

"You've got this," he whispers. "I'll be here...as lead or behind the scenes...as you wish." I turn to face him again. He smiles and it doesn't *feel* phony or insincere, yet I still sense that confounded Bezaliel mist coursing through him, getting in our way. I once felt I could trust Genin too, but he proved me wrong. "You'll find your answers," Luca says. "I won't get in the way of your search." And with that, we reach the doors to our respective rooms, and he retreats without pressure.

I lean an ear against the wall of my room to hear the echo of his footsteps, the quiet removal of clothes, a quick rush of water, and a light squeak of his bed.

"Damn," I think.

Alone with the silence and my darkest thoughts, I finally and freely weep, but it does little to relieve my stress.

"Heroes have no time to cry," Paramel says. I quickly wipe away my tears. She hands me a vial of purple liquid. "But cry we sometimes do…"

TWELVE

ENTANGLEMENT

THE FLUFFLE FEELS vacant and dim when I climb out of my guest hole. I meander through ferns and tiptoe over dens to avoid disturbing anyone. This is about as close to "fresh" air as I can get, and I need to clear my head. I sit down on a small bridge of vines and roots and dangle my legs over a shallow trickle of water that runs into a narrow cavern, where Paramel once showed me a waterfall. Lava lamps are set to dim and some of the crystals embedded in the obsidian above me glisten like stars.

Asteroids, I think. It's been a strange *Now* in the Isle of No Time.

Bo tried to flee from the Astral Weavers when I used the buckeye to open their portal. He headed straight through rock and jumped over so many holes in a single leap I was impressed. He snaked through shadows and ran to the place we'd first met, until he was out of options. I think his idea was to restart Paramel's interdimensional craft and dodge into a black hole until she forgave him, or until Lozen's sister decided he wasn't an appropriate spousal accessory after all. Bo never expected to get caught and failed to even consider *Plan B,* something I now find myself seriously pondering.

We discovered battle gear, valuables, and food Bo had stolen and stashed throughout the Isle for Fewoulz. His intent was to help Fewoulz terrorize the Elemorphia and separate them from Usta to disrupt balance in favor of Bezaliels, not an inviolable crime. It was cheating Paramel out of her destiny and encouraging a "no time" curse on the Fluffle and Usta, through Paramel, which sealed his fate—the inviolable crime for which he stood judgment.

"You're the most cowardly jarl in the cosmos," Paramel said when we surrounded him. "You betrayed this Fluffle, the Isle of No Time, Ki, and me. I trusted you."

Instead of taking Paramel's words like a Viking, Bo dashed again, down the path, through the caves, and then re-climbed the unstable ladder that got us here. I still see him, soaked in sweat. He huffed and puffed. His loud clatters and clanks echoed over ridges, valleys of rock, and through folds of sediment, clumsily giving away his super dusty position to any creature within a hundred-mile radius. He missed his footing on the ladder and tumbled to the end of his rope. When he reached bottom, we were there, waiting. Bo fumbled for his blade and called Paramel a "cursed bitch."

I'll never forget the look on his face when he remembered she'd reclaimed her weapon at the Cage of Savagery along with her helmet. Paramel cut off a piece of his ear as a souvenir, and as a reminder to Bo, she said, "'Tis' better to listen than it is to be 'overly' heard." Bo was out of time, friends, influence, and power. He'd burned too many bridges, as humans might say.

A magnificent light engulfed us when Lozen's sister stepped through the portal in her finest wedding attire. It was difficult to see anything when she swooped in on Bo with her beak, beast, and talons. He let out a terrified shriek I'll always remember. And by the time Lozen's sister concluded her ceremony, pronouncing him a stellar spousal accessory, it was as if Bo never existed, every drop, bone, and inch of him plucked so clean he didn't even leave a stain.

Luca is in my head. I walk a middle line in my mind, leaning against common sense, still straddling fences, and it leaves me frustrated. He retreated from me tonight without pressure, his words unexpected. *"You'll find your answers."*

Lord Harrington confounds me. I hate to admit he's opened a door to my heart. I find it difficult to ask for help, or depend on others, but what I find most difficult to do is love, or should I say, *allow* myself to love. Oh, but this hybrid, how he challenges and chafes me. On one hand, if it weren't for him funding this venture, I'd still be ambling around topside, in a covert lab, running into walls and dead ends on the global tribal murders. On the other hand, I love him despite myself. I don't want to love him. Love complicates things and experience reminds me that the *fantasy* of bedding a human, and I would assume this goes for hybrids too, is usually better than the *reality*.

Asteroids! I kick away a small rock, watching it roll over the edge and make a soft splash, its ripples licking my toes.

Luca and I tumbled together into this abyss—and I want him —but can I, or this team, afford my desire? It's foolish to go to him now, after he faded from me, and then I rebuffed him tonight—or *Now*. The regret creeping into me feels worse than the wanting lump tightening my insides...

...Luca raises an eyebrow when he opens his door. "You've found answers so quickly?" he asks.

"Perhaps a temporary one," I say.

Luca sits on the edge of the bed, half-shrouded in darkness on one side, and on the other side, closest to me, he's gently illuminated by the harnessed substance that makes the Fluffle glow.

I wonder how much further over my head I can get. Up until this point, my life has prepared me for battle, distrust, and a myriad of other unpleasant or life-threatening tasks and realities. But Reggie's training failed to prepare me for the entanglement of intertwining my body with another hybrid. A look crosses Luca's face, showing zero discomfort when he smiles. I wish I had his confidence. His eyes rage from blue to black and back again. *Is he capable of love? How much of his heart is left?*

An interconnecting cosmic field stretches out between and around us to meet in a place where balance and chaos lightly mingle. He stands, approaches me, and the feelings I've kept frozen and safely out of reach melt into savage longing. Tiny green sparks of static electricity dance along my arms, visibly giving away my desire.

Luca is three steps away.

A swooshy feeling unlike any I've ever felt surges across my hips. It causes everything female within me to involuntarily throb in anticipation of his touch.

But he doesn't move or speak.

He watches.

I memorize his features, his breathtaking hybrid-ness and a silent hopeful madness that gives itself away in his eyes. I struggle to tamp down my heart's eagerness. Danger roils around him, black wavelengths of darkness that advance and retreat in concert with my sparks, a place where order and chaos reside in a void and can't help but collide.

Luca removes his shirt, then the rest of his clothes.

I'm...speechless. Every statue of Greek Gods does zero justice to the Camaeliphim who stands before me, a flawless fusion of human and celestrial. For a moment I fear I may not be able to handle him without splitting in two! The muscles along his chest involuntarily flex when he sees the look on my face. He tosses his head back and laughs, then takes a slow step into my orbit.

"Take off your clothes," he says. "...slowly...I want to see you..."

...Everything spins when his hand reaches for my throat. He lifts me off the ground and dangles me over the bed. Geometric shapes and lightning explosions shiver through me. This is how half-mortals conduct foreplay I instinctively know, erotic and natural for our kind.

Luca releases me and I fall to the bed, not letting my eyes off him. He cocks his head to one side, lifts off his feet, hovers over me, and then slowly presses his chest into mine. "What treasures will I find within you?" he whispers, his breath teasing my ear. "I dare you to tell me what brings you pleasure." He inhales against my hair, and I feel his breath upon my nape.

I brace myself against his heaviness, in awe of his solidness, my heart beating wildly. Icy -blue veins throb against his neck, and it reminds me of the pulsing river that rushes through Plum Hook Bay. I solidly strap long fingers around it, imagining I'm a cobra, depriving the evil inside him of its host.

Don't.

Let.

Go.

He gazes into me with eyes so aqua, I see everything worth saving. I feel his compassion and maybe what's left of his soul, but a darkness resides in him too, one I hope to forever extinguish. I squeeze harder, feeling his heartbeat along arteries under my finger pads. He closes his eyes in rapture. Luca undoes my grip and wraps his hands around my wrists, lifts off me, and raises my arms overhead, sucking in a couple of deep breaths. The imprint of my fingertips upon his neck leaves a fading tattoo.

Levitating over me, he stares into my eyes and slowly drags an index finger from my forehead to my navel. *He's not to be trusted,* I tell myself. The executive decision that led me here seeps through my desire. My want is so great I can barely contain it, but there's a motive behind my ardent madness.

I've been taught that when two Camaeliphim share the *friendliness of their thighs,* they are forever entangled, my energy in him and his in me. This calculated action may enable me to internally harness Luca's contradictions, to share control of his Bezaliel mist...but it's a two-way reception...he may also control a part of me...the good and the bad.

Light, I'm learning, doesn't always trump darkness or drive it away on command. And some hybrids, like me, are fine-tune bred to be warriors. We're blessed to be unhinged and free from innocuous half-truths, unfelt prayers, or a "safe" life led behind monasteries or homey hearths. I'm able to mingle with darkness and come away mostly, if not completely, unscathed—to *pass* through this world with less attachment to safety than most.

As a Balancer, I traverse the line between demons and deities, tuning each like cosmic strings, according to the direct will of the Source, to which I must attend, atone, and attune. My treacherous gamble is to better understand Luca and the enemy I'm up against. The stakes for the Source, multiple realms, Earth, my daughter, Bennie, and my heart, couldn't be higher.

"Do you like this?" Luca whispers. He kisses me long and deep, our tongues intertwining before release.

I nod into his azure eyes now pooling with unbridled intensity.

"And what about this?"

And so, it goes...methodical and sensuous...he explores every part of my body until passion overrides any sense of control. We seize one another, gripping, grasping, twisting, and spinning until we lift off the bed. My light struggles against his blackness. The room expands and contracts. My hips are taut against his...and the thickness of him, when I open my legs, and he pushes up into me, sends a flood of heat through my abdomen.

"Oh, Samantha," he whispers when I take on his energy. "No!" He tries to push me away when darkness falls over us, but I refuse to let go and wrap my legs around his waist.

We slam against a wall. Vases on the shelves shatter. Shards of multi-colored glass and sparks from blown-out lights float around us. We are in the *Now,* on the Isle of No Time, and this... our surroundings, glide in slow motion, our impending entanglement imposing push-pull gravitational effect for control. Luca tangles my hair in his hands, pulls me closer to him and I yield... until I don't. I push off his chest to the other side of the room right before we reach irreversible ecstasy. He traps me in a corner with a devilish smile.

"How much do you want me?" I ask.

"You naughty Camaeliphim, I will make you beg for pleasure," Luca says. A quick flick of his wrist and he's curled his hand around my ankle, pulling my legs up over his shoulders mid-air, the rest of my body free-floating where gravity bottoms out. I'm unable to yank away and find myself fully exposed to his lips...

...Raw...uncontrollable...oh... "Oh, my god," I breathe.

Luca ceases pleasuring me. "Beg," he says.

"No."

"Samantha, I have the power to make you feel better than you've ever felt in any of your lives." His lips graze the most intimate part of me, his cheeks against my thighs. He resumes, slowly, teasingly...and I'm completely lost in a cascade of pleasure. Random symbols, shapes, colors, and stars race through my head. He stops again.

"Please...don't stop..." I beg.

He continues, harder this time. Everything fades into the mist...such...indescribable...oh...I pulsate and writhe under him... losing control...*mayday!*

He stops.

No!

"Say it," he says. "We must together, agree."

"Entangle yourself with me," I whisper. "Please." It takes every ounce of sense I have left to disengage from him and try to lower my legs, but he holds firm. "Repeat it to me," I pant. "We must together, agree."

"Entangle yourself with me," Luca repeats.

Our need is feverish and rises when I arch into him. We spiral upward, our bodies together, until the ceiling catches his back. I close my eyes in delicious rapture, every ounce of pleasure pulsating through me in repeated waves of ecstasy until I collapse against him, shaking, tears running down my cheeks. He embraces me until I calm. I recover and guide him into me once more.

"Luca," I whisper, "I have the power to make you feel better than you've ever felt in any of your lives."

Our bodies and minds shudder in concert, our wounds and tragedies laid aside and momentarily forgotten. He's lost in rapture and Light, taut, and sleek, the two of us in perfect V formation until *his* moment of no control. He cries out with raw male pleasure, unable to hold back, shuddering as we fall from ceiling to bed, and it collapses under our weight. Shockwaves ripple through the room. I look at him dreamily and this tall hybrid with tropical ocean orbs stares back from a perfectly etched face. He hugs me tightly. "We are entangled," he says.

"Yes."

"As always, you make me wait," he laughs. "And as always, we tend to lay waste to our accommodations."

I wish I could remember our previous lives together but do not. The DOE once embedded a Dream Stealer in my wrist and stole vital memories. My mother, a *receptor*, tried to restore them, and sometimes they arrive in my brain like zappy glitches. Between the pale-pink-gray morning of a new *Now* and my sleep-heavy eyes, Luca kisses my cheek. "And as always, I have loved you..."

———

What I know as morning in the Fluffle trickles through a skylight and tap dances against my eyes. I roll over, stretch my arms above my head, and stretch a hand to other side of the bed. Luca is gone. I spring into a sitting position, pull the sheets up to my neck, and glance around. The bed is a pile of kindling. Broken vases and bulbs lie shattered and scattered about the room—along with any whimsical notions I once held about the hybrid to which I'm engaged.

This mission is one I never wanted or requested. I was thrown into the role. It's another black mark on the Ormian Council—and on me too, for allowing my hand and heart to be so easily forced and played. My anger grows from the realization that the Ormian Council has crafted all my lives while I perpetually hang in multiple quiescence. This endless feed loop of re-existence is an exercise in futility. The Council continues to follow fruitless patterns in the hope of a different outcome, which is about the same as living in a forever *Now* on an Isle of No Time. I'm resetting the clock, installing a change of plans, and forging a new direction.

The powers who dictate our fates want me to conquer Beza-liels, vanquish them one-by-one while Raga makes yet another escape. Luca, I now realize, is only one part of my problem. I'm remembering. And *Now* is the last time I play this game. But first, I need to repair the damage I've done.

My feet tap the Fluffle floor, there's a throbbing ache between my legs, and what makes Luca male, his neon blue life force, flows out from me.

THIRTEEN

THE ORMIAN COUNCIL

HUNDREDS OF TINY WHITE SPHERES, like fireflies, float over a great cobalt river that runs behind the waterfall, its splash and roar muffled by rock and moss below. We stand on a docking station, in a cup-like depression that's been laser-etched into a basalt platform. On every side, pillars of clear crystal tower over us, smooth and faultless, as if buffed by angels. A fearsome torrent of deep underground turquoise sea descends from the brow of raven-winged cliffs, at least a half-mile free-fall. It strikes a mass of limestone boulders then churns into enraged froth. The pristine water finally spills over mossy stone, and its foam radiates pink, green, blue, and violet hues over spatter-polished surfaces.

Some of the Usta in their simple earthen robes are here to see us off. Gleaming green-blue frogs and luminous dragonflies plop, buzz, and croak as brown leeches larger than footballs anchor themselves to granite walls. I wish Dr. Kanumba and Dr. Kimathi were here to help me tag and catalogue this previously unknown to us flora and fauna.

"Well, would you look at that," Reggie says.

"Wow," Luca whispers. He lets out a low whistle as we gaze

upward and I can tell by the look on his face he's impressed, which is often a hard feat where he's concerned.

Poised above our heads is a large transparent bubble that shimmers hues of white, pale powder blue and gold. As it gently draws near, I notice a thin, seamless gilded band encircling the craft's equator.

"Your chariot awaits," Eresh says.

"This?" Dr. Monica asks. "Mate, how are we suppos' to ride in this contraption? I don' see any gears! Thars' no controls or equipment at all! And wha' if we hav to take a piss? No privacy or toilets? How do we shower?"

"The Amunettica has everything you need," Eresh says. "Come, inspect the craft for yourself."

We step through the gel-like material, but it doesn't stick to us, and it isn't wet, but soft and squishy, like the cathedral doors we crossed to get into Ereshun. We amble into a clear lift void of cables.

"How do we ascend?" I ask.

"Use your mind," Eresh says. "Work together."

"Oh, this ought to be fun," Reggie says with an eyeroll. "Like herding cats."

The five of us lock eyes in agreement. The craft shimmies and tugs upward, plummets, and then jerks to a stop. "Strooth!" Dr. Monica shouts, white-knuckling my forearm. "This is heaps bad! We need to work in tandem, ya clumsy blokes!"

Eresh intervenes as our "flight instructor." She maintains control of the craft while the rest of us turn off our egos, coordinate our brain power, and *will* the Amunettica to rise. "As all terrestrial bodies have rotational energy, so too, your minds," Eresh instructs. "Objects on Earth, including this craft, can be utilized in the simplest manner to furnish motive travel anywhere in multi-dimensional worlds, as long as you come to agreement on a fixed point." She invites us to stop at a level on the craft that houses six smaller bubble craft and other equipment.

"This is genius," Luca says, stepping off to look around. "I've worked on and flown a lot of craft, but never have I seen one such as this."

"One of our best designs," Eresh says. "It's a bit obsolete by our standards but should suit your human and hybrid needs just fine."

"Aye, if this is obsolete, mate, I can't even imagine what your most updated craft can do," Dr. Monica says.

"This space is a storage unit," Reggie says. "How many levels?"

"However many you need," Eresh says, tapping her temple.

The next level shows us gardens, a lab, free-floating columns of what Eresh tells us is fresh drinking water, a meeting space, and shelf after shelf of stacked flat crystal chips no larger and less thick than military challenge coins or maybe Catholic communion wafers. The room also has see-through walls where I notice the waterfall emits sparks of bright yellow photons now and then. "What is this?" I ask, pointing to the screens and picking up one of the crystal chips, holding it between my thumb and index finger.

"Your library," Eresh says. "That particular seed you hold contains all of Earth's geological history, replete with samples and 3-D models."

"How is this possible?" I ask, inspecting a what looks like a silicon chip smaller than a grain of rice.

"Place the crystal against your forehead, between your eyes," Eresh instructs me.

And just like that, I'm presented a "mind trailer" to the contents of the crystal. *Wow.* I could potentially retain and recite cosmic information at will, I think, using these. "They're not labeled," I say. "How do you know what's what?"

"Focus on them as you take your journey and you will know," Eresh says. "You don't need eyes to 'see'."

"So, I've been told." I put the chip down on a sticky slide and we continue.

The next level shows us living quarters, each to his or her own private suite.

"Where's the shower?" Reggie asks.

"Step through here," Eresh says.

"You mean this empty doorframe in the middle of the room?"

"It's called a Pristeril," she says with a nod. "Go ahead, try it."

Reggie steps through the glowy frame but nothing happens. There's no water, soap, or noise...but when he steps out the other side, it's as if he, his suit, his boots, and his hair, were spit-shined, double-waxed, and run through ten washing cycles. He smells fresh, like peppermint and linen, his hair and beard trimmed to perfect precision. He could pose on the cover of *GQ* Magazine!

"I've got to try this," Dr. Monica says, her mouth agape. "Ya loo' spiffy, mate!" She steps through and comes out the other side just as clean as Reggie, her dark hair a modern razor cut that looks better than ever, her face artistically enhanced, a living filter! "Wha' a time saver! How do I look?"

"How is this possible?" I ask.

Eresh taps her temple and then her heart and gives me a lipless reptilian smile.

A mirror suddenly appears in front of Dr. Monica. "I look gorgeous!" she yells.

Of course, Paramel, Luca, and I try this amazing Pristeril too. My hair turns from frizzy copper wire to perfect coils of shiny red ringlets that bounce and spring when I walk. Luca gulps as I come out the other side and I burst into laughter when Reggie gives him a protective fatherly scowl.

We ascend to the top level, an exposed center space, where a round raised platform, almost like a couch, enables us to sit, facing outward. And to my blood-curdling surprise, as Dr. Monica so astutely observed below, there are no controls at all!

"How are we supposed to drive this thing?" Reggie asks.

"With our minds," Luca says, tapping his temple with his index finger. "Remember?"

The Ether V Luca built topside, one he once used to fly me from Harrington House to Oxford two hundred miles away, in under two minutes, didn't run on propulsion either. Luca used his DNA and distortion, a melding of bio-electromagnetic energy mixed with anti-gravity and his brain. And we crashed it!

"Our energies must synchronize and connect with the craft," Luca says. "We use resonance, which creates a vacuum in one hemisphere of the craft. It's a bit like an artificial gravity field. The propulsion is self-contained and basically creates its own slope, enabling us to move faster than the speed of light without fuel, propellers, engines, or the like."

"How?" Reggie asks.

"You need to get off of Earth more, chap," Luca says. "We create a positive ion cloud ahead of the bubble, which forms a gravity well that attracts matter."

"I saw something once," Reggie says. "Some scientist, Brown, I think his name was. He performed a demonstration before Air Force brass decades ago, showing how discs could fly using high voltage."

"What happened?" Luca asks.

"It worked," Reggie says. "Damn things violated every law of physics we knew. A colonel immediately ordered the two-stars in charge to shut down the demonstration. The science behind it was abruptly classified."

"Of course, it was," Luca says. "This is a bit different...this craft uses the electro-magnetic gravitational field but also *transmutes* elements so efficiently, it conveys several million units of horsepower through a channel less than the thickness of a human fingernail."

"Yea," Reggie says. "You lost me at transmutation...speak English...but not *your* English. Use words I understand."

"This craft can go anywhere. It renders distance and time obsolete," Luca says.

Dr. Monica scrunches her brows with doubt. "Mate, it's one thing to make a lift rise using our minds and anotha' thing ta shower withou' wata', but to fly a focking craft inside the planet havin' to agree in mind with tha likes o' you blokes? We rarely agree on anythin'."

"We'll have to agree," Luca says. "Or we crash."

"Wouldn't flying faster than the speed of light squish us like bugs?" Reggie asks.

"Gravity can actually adopt two polarities at once," Luca says. "Something most humans are left in the dark about. Subquantum kinetics shows that gravity can attract and repel at the same time. As occupants, we should feel no stress regardless of how sharp we turn or accelerate. Sentients respond equally to wave distortions of the gravitational field."

"There are two avenues for propulsion," Eresh says. "The Ocron Configuration and the Alta Configuration, the latter meant for interstellar or parallel realm travel. The craft works most efficiently if you tip its gold equatorial band vertical."

"Huh?" Dr. Monica says, tilting her head, searching in vain, I think, for controls that don't exist, and then scrutinizing the "gold band."

"We roll down the slope of a perfect right triangle," Luca says, trying to explain it to Dr. Monica, the same way he once did to me when we first met. I'm only partially able to grasp the concept even now, and I'm half-hybrid. I can only imagine how mind-boggling this must be for a pure human like Dr. Monica. Sure, the concept of faster-than-light travel has been around a while, but to witness something even faster, in action, where speed becomes as fast as thought, must be mind-bending for her or any other Ki-bound mortal.

"Aye, mate," Dr. Monica says with a shrug of doubt. "Whateva' you say."

"The thought power which operates this craft is the same as above," Eresh says to Dr. Monica, pointing to the ceiling. "It is based on *faith*, like that found in your sacred texts to move mountains or part seas. It is free for use by any sentient being if they choose to believe it's possible."

"Uh-huh," Dr. Monica says. "Faith. Got it."

Eresh's words remind me of Makonen, the Alphion Proximal C who once rescued me from a military hospital in Washington, D.C. It's because of Makonen that I'm even here. He used his mind to release the Dream Stealer bolted into my wrist. He said his ability to both harness and focus power was a skill every sentient being possesses, but only if they precisely tune inner frequencies toward the Source. Of course, Bezaliels cause a lot of static and interference, but Makonen claimed that sentients could rise above that too, if we brought their mind and bodies into full agreement. It's too bad he pulled a grenade on himself to save my life. "*Some of my elders are able to part oceans, even planets,*" he'd said. He also mentioned that very few humans have the discipline to learn the secret knowledge of the Akashic Record, a compendium of universal history, energy, and intent, stored in the Akashic Field. When I asked him where this Akashic Field was located, he said it was a bit like Shambala or the Kingdom of Lo, difficult to find because it's everywhere and nowhere at the same time, and mostly veiled by what he termed *common humans.*

"You drive." I point to Luca. "And train the rest of us. We can give up control if we agree, right Eresh?"

"This is true," she says. "But I also thought it a good idea to bring you a co-pilot."

"*You?*" I ask. "Oh, please say it's you."

All of us descend and exit the craft.

"Oh...not me," she says and points over her shoulder. "*Him.*"

I lean around Eresh to look behind her. A man bounces down wide stone stairs and ambles closer. Reggie and I look at one another in wide-eyed astonishment. "Is that…?" But Reggie fails to finish his words as the man strides toward us, tall and confident, his face looking less taut with worry, the lines receded, but his eyes just as bright and steel-blue as I remember.

"I thought you said no humans got this far into Ereshun?" I say, wondering if Eresh withheld the truth, which would go against Usta philosophy because they claim they don't lie. Yet I'm learning that Usta, like humans and hybrids, equally bend nature and honesty if it suits their agendas.

"You asked if any *humans* made it down this far," Eresh says. "You did not ask about hybrids who were invited or granted asylum."

"Hybrid? Dr. Sterling Dennison is a hybrid?" I ask. "Reggie, were you aware of this?"

"I was," he says. "But neither of us could blow our covers at NASA. He's able to pass as human, like you, me, and Luca. Dr. Sterling is Alphion Proximal too, like me. What I don't know is how the hell he got all the way down *here*."

It didn't register with me as a kid, but Dr. Sterling being Alphion Proximal now makes sense. He used to be Bennie's handler at Plum Hook Bay, the way Reggie was mine, and probably why Dr. Evelyn was so excited to marry Dr. Sterling, which I now know had zero to do with love and everything to do with controlling and learning from us hybrids. Every Camaeliphim sent to Earth receives a teacher, a Ki guide. It's typically a hybrid from some other planet or realm, but not always.

"I asked Eresh to grant Dr. Dennison asylum," Luca says matter-of-factly. "She only agreed if outside contact was forbidden, for his and the Usta's safety."

Dr. Sterling Dennison is probably the smartest nuclear engineer on the planet next to Luca and Bennie. When I was a foster kid at Plum Hook Bay, scientists successfully split neutrinos. It was Dr. Sterling who registered something very strange about these energy-less subatomic particles; neutrinos change form when they oscillate. They can also alter dimensions. When this happens, strange things, in the form of unknown matter, objects, and entities, ones that bend every law of science and nature humans know, jump in and out of Earthly existence.

A short pang of sadness zips around my heart. I remember how Reggie told me that Dr. Sterling sacrificed his entire life for the sake of a greater cosmic good. Yet he doesn't show a trace of arrogance, resentment, or exaggerated humility. He and Reggie did everything within their power to ensure Bennie and I, and the rest of the Plum Hook Bay foster kids, spent limited time at the mercy of Dr. Evelyn and her *experiments*. Dr. Sterling kept us out of yellow body bags too. Some other kids and creatures she worked on weren't so lucky.

To say I'm not comfortable with bureaucracies due in part to Dr. Evelyn is an understatement akin to describing comets as flashlights. A shiver skips along my spine just thinking about her. She used to force-feed me psych meds and shove me into rabbit holes for extended stays. In Dr. Sterling, I still see, just as I did as a child, all that is good and the opposite of Evelyn.

Dr. Sterling stretches his lips into a wide smile, more comfortable and at ease than I've ever seen him. His black hair mostly covers a few wisps of wiry gray that strain from his temples; and it reminds me of a steel wool pad I used to use to scrub pans with at Plum Hook Bay. His sapphire eyes float over me with the same compassionate concern he always showed and radiate familiar "happy to see you again" intelligence.

"Samantha," he says, and I hold out my hand...but he sweeps me up into his arms with a tight hug. "Oh, kid, how I've missed you! Let me look at you...wow!" He sets me back on my feet. "You're all grown up!" Sterling and Luca slap one another on the back and shake hands. "Great to see you again, my friend," Dr. Sterling says. "I wasn't sure if it would happen. I see you relocated Samantha."

Relocated?

"Great to see you too," Luca says, dismissing the comment. "We have much to discuss. Like the fact that Samantha is now Dr. Blake, exobiologist, with a degree in Foresight from the University of Oxford."

"Wonderful!" Sterling says. "Happy she's learning about her human and Camaeliphim ancestry and getting reacquainted with her British heritage."

Reacquainted?

"Reggie?" Dr. Sterling asks, moving toward him. "Is that you, dear chap? Well, I'm gob smacked! Never thought I'd see you this close to hell, knowing how much you hate caves, especially after what happened last time."

Last time?

This is news to me, and I'm surprised to hear Reggie doesn't like caves.

"What *last time?*" I finally ask.

"Plum Hook Bay," Dr. Sterling says. "Reggie refused to come up out of those caves until he found *you*. He ignored nuclear sirens, bats, rats, the surging heat, and every other unsavory danger known, or unknown, to man or hybrid. It was the first time we encountered strange beasts on site. One would have killed me if Reggie hadn't mortally wounded the creature first."

"I had no idea," I say.

Reggie doesn't look at me. He won't admit it, but inside that gritty crust he shows to this world is a teddy bear who will charge like a grizzly, all claws on deck, against those who threaten anyone he cares about. Reggie never uttered a word about the effort he made to save me on the NASA side of Plum Hook Bay or about encountering lab-mutated chimeras. But that's Reggie. He goes beyond duty without the expectation of medals, attention, or accolades—and he keeps his mouth shut. He says it's part of the Septum Oculi code. He's a better hybrid, I think, than I'll ever be, but I won't tell him that.

Paramel coyly peers over my shoulder, listening to our conversation. She looks intently at Dr. Sterling.

"And who is this lovely lady hiding behind you, Dr. Blake?" Dr. Sterling asks, standing on tiptoes to get a look at her.

I slide to one side and introduce them. "Paramel, meet Dr. Sterling...he's a nuclear engineer, a fellow Camaeliphim. He was once my guardian and science teacher. Dr. Sterling, meet Paramel, the Viking who holds the Isle of No Time."

I feel tiny electrical charges pass between them. "Paramel." And the way Dr. Sterling whispers her name practically sings on his lips. They shake hands and stare into one another's eyes a little too long. "You're *human?*" he asks.

"Hybrid," she answers. "More celestrial soul guide than hybrid and a lot less human than all of you, well, except, perhaps, for Lord Harrington. Samantha killed a Fewoulz and broke my curse."

Dr. Sterling swivels around, looks at me quizzically, and says, "You're the Balancer..."

"Yes."

He turns his attention, all of it, back to Paramel, struck by something in her and she appears equally fascinated. Luca raises an eyebrow at me when we exchange side glances, a shit-eating grin on his face. "It's probably been years since Dr. Sterling's been laid," he whispers in my ear. I elbow him in the gut. Reggie shakes his head and Dr. Monica laughs.

I've seen worse matches, I suppose. Sterling and Dr. Evelyn, my aunt, being a perfect example of a couple who *never* should have married. Hmmm...a Viking who guards the Isle of No Time, and a nuclear engineer hybrid who successfully harnesses split neutrinos. Theirs would be an unusual entanglement indeed, but when Source energy so blatantly passes between two souls, it is wise for others to step aside and allow the natural order of things to progress...except I've never known celestrial Vikings to practice monogamy. Alphion Proximal Cs, like Dr. Sterling, are faithful to a fault.

"Dr. Sterling, what are you doing way down here?" Reggie finally asks, a pinch of confusion between his bushy eyebrows. He waves an index finger between Luca and Dr. Sterling.

"How do you two know each other?"

"Dr. Sterling is Luca's silent business partner at Harrington Technologies," I say. "Sterling wooed and seduced Dr. Evelyn to learn everything he could about Plum Hook Bay and to get closer to Bennie. We need to keep him MIA. He's the only nuclear engineer on the planet who reasonably understands Bennie's work about as well as Luca. And Dr. Evelyn put a price on his head."

"Treacherous woman," Dr. Sterling says. "Inviolable crimes."

I notice that my mention of Bennie causes tears to pool in Sterling's eyes, a sadness impossible to hide. Bennie was like a son to him.

"Why did Evelyn put a price on Dr. Sterling's head?" Reggie asks.

"She hopes to sell Earth's security to the highest bidder," Luca says.

"This is heaps bad," Dr. Monica says. "She's the Sheila who tried to steal your joey, right?"

"Baby?" Dr. Sterling asks. "You have a baby?"

I nod.

He sits on a nearby rock to steady himself and stares at the ground and then looks at me again, all serious. "Dr. Blake, a child unduly complicates your cosmic obligations."

"I know," I say.

"Is Genin the father?"

"No," I say. "Genin is a traitor and he's underground in another part of this world with Dr. Evelyn and her team."

"Why?"

"We're in a race to find Nikola Tesla's lost files," I explain.

"They were brought to the Cave of Seven Sleepers by Verity's husband."

"Where's Verity? Is she with you?" Dr. Sterling asks.

I shake my head and now it's my turn to look at the ground. "She's dead to this life," I say. "Tetana, Fensig, and Pa Ling are dead too." And just saying their names causes a lump in my throat to grow so large it's hard for a moment to swallow, talk, or think.

"Evelyn killed Verity and the other Plum Hook Bay kids? Why?" he asks. "What about Jade Sokolov?"

"Indirectly, Evelyn killed them," I say. "I suspect it's because we all know too much about her experiments and classified programs, but there's a far more sinister reason she doesn't share with her colleagues at the DOE. Verity was a surrogate mother to my child, a baby conceived in a lab at Plum Hook Bay without our knowledge or consent and kept under heavy guard. I'm not sure if Jade Sokolov is alive or dead...but Priyanka and Rakito are safe in Burundi the last time I checked. Saratu is in Nepal."

"Saratu is Ceitan," Dr. Sterling says. "She can't be killed and possesses the capability to leave Earth at any time. As for the others, I think I'm going to be sick..." We give him a long moment of silence, to let all our news sink in. He stares off into the waterfall and then asks, "Anything else I should know?"

"Bennie is my baby's father."

Another long silence...

... "Sam, I am so sorry...Luca...you must...Jesus, this wasn't the plan. This was *never* the plan," Sterling says as he wipes away a single tear. "What has Evelyn done to and with this child?"

And now I'm wondering, *what plan?* "Evelyn doesn't have Hope," I say. "That's my daughter's name."

"Fitting," Dr. Sterling says with a frown. "We'll need Hope... in more ways than one. Who has her?"

"We have some good news," Luca interrupts, and for once, I'm thankful he does.

"I could use some good news," Dr. Sterling says. "Go ahead."

"Bennie is alive," Luca says.

"Alive?" Dr. Sterling stands up and an involuntary look of complete shock widens his eyes. He clutches both of Luca's shoulders. "How? He never came out of the caves at Plum Hook Bay!" He stomps away a few feet, turns, and then walks back to us.

"We think he hid underground at Plum Hook Bay, maybe with the help of Astral Weavers," I say. "Bennie knew Dr. Evelyn created an embryo using our biological material. He waited for the right opportunity. He resurfaced after Hope's birth with the intention of…"

"Killing her," Sterling says.

"No!" I say. But now that he's blurted it out, fear twists its way up from my stomach to my throat. "Hope was relocated to the Antarctic," I say. "Luca found her through his contacts."

"Let me guess," Dr. Sterling says. "611 Norad."

"That's right," I say. "How did you know?"

"Clandestine ops is a small world," he says. "And neutrino detectors are my specialty. I once worked there."

"She's not at Norad 611 anymore," I say. "Bennie manipulated bureaucracy for a BOUO transfer to Norad 611. He later escaped and took Hope with him. We don't know where they are…somewhere, I assume, far away from Dr. Evelyn. The Source can't directly intervene without destroying everything. But the worst news is, Dr. Evelyn likely transferred Bezaliel mist into Hope's DNA."

"A tri-bred," Sterling whispers, running a hand through his bristly hair. He and Luca exchange glances and it causes warning bells to go off in my brain. "What is Evelyn hoping to accomplish?"

"The same thing she's always wanted," Luca says. "If she controls a Bezaliel-loaded Emergent, she controls this world, and by default, other worlds, and every creature from here to Habermas."

"Playing God doesn't end well for humans or hybrids," Dr. Sterling says...and the way he says this causes an involuntary shiver to roll down my spine.

"Maybe not," I say. "But Evelyn's gotten closer to realm domination through her underhanded practices than any other human since Adolf Hitler."

"Do you know the password to assemble the Code of Everything and open the Source Vortex?" Dr. Sterling asks.

"I can't remember it," I say. "The Ebians buried it so far into my DNA that even the DOE couldn't extract it...they tried."

"Then it's my turn for some good news," Dr. Sterling says.

"We could use some," I say, looking around at our solemn crew.

"I am in possession of Tesla's lost file," he says. "Perhaps it will help you remember."

FOURTEEN

MERAMIANS

Journal Entry #33

MY DEAREST SENTIENT,

I've been reading Nikola Tesla's previously lost files and wish I could have met him. This underappreciated celestrial hero writes that a cosmic cure for humanity exists within the X Point, otherwise known as the Source Vortex, a small space beyond the portal where energy particles condense to such a degree there's zero probability for escape—but plenty of opportunity to warp space, bend light, and twist magnetic fields, solidifying something Bennie and the Usta knew all along—traveling faster than the speed of light is not only possible, it creates "bubbles" of realities capable of "popping" in and out of Ki's existence—and the potential to change and charge our destinies...

"Turn this way," Dr. Sterling says to Luca and gestures for him to head into a calm pond of bright aqua below us.

"How do you know where to go?" Reggie asks. "Every gorge, valley, tunnel, and cliff look exactly the same—like a fractal inside a labyrinth."

I lay aside my journal and the Tesla file, having loaded most of it into a crystal chip that fits perfectly inside a portion of the Pleaides pendant under my shirt. We gurgle down into a trench *beneath* the Mariana, the surprising blue brightness of it igniting my eyes enough for me to don tinted goggles with the rest of my crew. Synchronized silver, green, and white flashes zip and turn. Paramel watches from her seat, in awe, as does Dr. Monica, neither of them moving or making a sound. Reggie takes a seat near them, fighting his underwater seasickness again.

"We must be out of our minds," Dr. Monica finally says.

"Probably a good thing," Luca says, steadying the craft, his eyes locked straight ahead.

"Bank a bit to the left," Dr. Sterling says. "Good."

Through the water comes a rumble that rocks our precarious but sturdy craft. The brightness turns instantaneously black. Luca maintains the stabilizers to steady our drift.

"Crickey," Dr. Monica says. She visibly shivers. And I don't blame her! Above our heads passes a crocodile, but not quite a crocodile. It's a prehistoric monster of such ginormous proportions, a blue whale would pale in comparison! "Mate, that thin' mus' be over ninety fee' long! Will it eat us?"

We're relieved and thankful when it glides out of view, oblivious as we float beneath. Frigid turquoise water reappears. Our vulnerability and insignificance in this deep-sea world leave me feeling like an amoeba sample stuck between the glass plates of a microscope slide.

"We're deep under the center of Antarctica," Dr. Sterling says. "Near Hercules Dome." Silver and white flashes whizz past our craft, small Tic-Tac-looking biologicals without fins. They don't resemble any fish, crabs, or shrimp I've ever seen. Peering into the vastness, I stumble backward when an eerie human-looking face suddenly pops into view on the other side, meeting me eye-for-eye.

"Jesus, Sam, ya' all right?" Dr. Monica asks as she thrusts out a hand and helps me up.

Another flash of a face and a look of terror rolls across Paramel, one she quickly secures, and the three of us jump back and recover. We gather up the courage to move closer to the creatures on the other side of the clear crystal for a better look. Eresh told us this craft is impermeable. I hope she's right. Curious faces periodically press into our bubble, their webbed hands pushing off again and low echoes of sonic-like chatter vibrate through my chest.

"Now I know what fish in an aquarium feel li', mate," Dr. Monica says. "Thar's no such thing as merfolk, right?"

"Sure Monica," Luca laughs. "Just as there's no Fewoulz, Elemorphia, anti-gravity craft, extraterrestrials, or ...Australian Akurra."

"Australian Akurra is an Aboriginal myth painted on cave walls," Dr. Monica says.

"It's a huge water snake," Paramel counters. "It has sharp fangs and a mane of razors. Only experienced Shamans may approach it for knowledge, but even they don't walk away unscathed." She lifts the sleeve on her suit and shows us a deep scar of dots resembling a flame. She yanks the sleeve back over her scar. "Pray you never meet one."

"Why did you need to meet one?" Reggie asks.

Paramel pulls a violet vial of "liquor" from her pocket and waves it back and forth before she stuffs it away again. "I needed a recipe." And the way she does this makes me wonder what trial Bennie had to pass to obtain the recipe for his ayahuasca salve.

Strange humanoids tap the crystal on our craft and point at

us, indicative of an intelligent self-awareness that gives me the creeps. Sometimes they resemble fish more than people, having small noses and mouths but no ears, only expanding and contracting slits, like gills. Their eyes are large and wideset, almost drawn out near the temples, with a bony ridge that runs through the center of their bald heads. Their skin is pale and appears seal or dolphin rubbery, their torsos extra-long and thin, compared to humans or hybrids. And rather than having the tail of a fish, they use two leg-looking appendages with completely webbed feet to steer through water, yet maneuver over our craft like cetaceans, with curving, fluid, crab-like movements. Their arms appear shorter than ours, and their shoulders condensed toward an almost nonexistent neck. But it is their song, an ethereal series of whistles and rhythmic clips and warbles, which most astounds and unnerves me.

The lights in our cabin blink on and off as buoyant chirps reverberate through our craft.

"They're excited," Dr. Sterling says. "The way this craft is made, they can't crack it."

"I'm not taking any chances," Luca says. "Let's get us where we need to be before those soundwaves damage our echolocation systems."

"What are they?" I ask.

"Meramians," Dr. Sterling says. "Surviving ancestors of Atlantean miscreations, part homo-sapiens-sapiens and part dolphin, with a pinch of megalodon."

"A *pinch* of megalodon?" I say. "But they're not much bigger than us."

"The *pinch* is their hunting ability," he explains. "Highly instinctual predators. If it weren't for a mimicking scent surrounding this craft, we'd be dinner."

"Oh." I pull my hand away from the glass.

"I still find it hard to believe there is a congregation of Usta way down here," Reggie says.

"Only a few, not a congregation," Dr. Sterling says.

"Why here?" Reggie asks.

"Guard duty," Dr. Sterling says.

We reach a massive solid black wall that extends as far as my eyes can see, up or down, a waterfall of sand in front of it.

"Now what?" Luca says.

Dr. Sterling directs a series of photonic beams into the rock. The falling sand disappears. Hieroglyphics swell from nothing, a series of symbols so old I have no idea what they mean when I struggle, without success, to decipher them. Dr. Sterling then places a small crystal pebble against the glass, and it communicates with the beam and characters.

We slide the craft through an opening and enter a tube-like tunnel, the water behind us gone, and with it, thankfully, the Meramians. We reach a clearing where four Usta await our arrival. We climb out of the craft and walk to a much smaller chapel than the grand cathedral just beyond Sanctuary.

"Who are we meeting?" I ask.

Dr. Sterling pats some dots on a wall. "Someone you haven't seen in a while," he says.

"Who?"

"Your uncle."

"My uncle? *Here?* My mom never had any brothers," I say. "Well, at least none I knew about."

"Your father's side of the family," he says.

I involuntarily shiver. "Please tell me he isn't Meramian."

Dr. Sterling chuckles and shakes his head.

"I've never met my celestrial uncle," I say.

"You have," he says. He doesn't elaborate and I search my brain trying to locate a lost memory of meeting an uncle from another world...an uncle who wouldn't have an ounce of human in him. A shiver ripples through my solar plexus and settles uneasily in my gut. I don't even know what a fully-fledged celestrial relative might look like—Smoke? Mist? Frankenstein's monster?

We pass through an open area that feels cosmopolitan yet nostalgic at the same time, a bygone era that meets and mingles with the future. *Asteroids!* Ancient shipwrecks and war era submarines are leaned against one another or stacked as far as I can see, along with more derelict space vehicles than I've ever seen in all my lives. There are gadgets, gizmos and all manner and make of mandalas, fractals, beams, rocketry, and lots of suspended seaweed.

I don't know anything about my uncle, especially if he resides down here in the bowels of Earth...or Ki...or Planet D...as every celestrial from here to Haapavesi prefers to call this remote terrarium. I smooth my hair. I wish I'd walked through the Pristeril before we disembarked.

An Usta plays an instrument I don't recognize but the music is soothing and surreal, unlike the Meramian, a tattered captain's hat perched over its head, and it looks comical atop such a fearsome face. We stop in front of him...or her...or it...I can't tell, but there's no bright pink powder on its face, and I'm afraid of being offensive if I ask!

"It's Netesh, right?" Dr. Sterling asks with a wide grin. The serene music trails off into the din of the caves and the Usta warily nods. "I've seen you play at Cathedral. We're here to see the Camaeliphim and his court."

"On whose orders?" Netesh asks.

Dr. Sterling stuffs his hand deep into the chest pocket of his suit and pulls out a crystal pebble, hands it to Netesh, and draws out another. "Do you know what this is?"

"No," Netesh says, narrowing his eyes. "I smell humans." He looks among us and sets his inky orbs on Dr. Monica. She steps behind me, hands at her sides, trying, I think, to make herself small and invisible.

"This," Dr. Sterling says, "contains every song ever written in all of mankind's history…"

Netesh snatches the crystal from Dr. Sterling and examines it between his claws.

"So? What use is that to me?" Netesh says. "I am already familiar with Kihog music…and most of it is dreadful. And I still smell humans." It licks the air with a slender-forked blue tongue slurp.

"I'm here on orders from Eresh," Dr. Sterling says. "She's in Ereshun."

"Oh," Netesh says. "Things must be bad topside if she's traveled so far underground to Ereshun." The creature places the crystal against his forehead.

"This crystal," Dr. Sterling says, producing another, "contains the music of angels, but there's more." Netesh perks up to listen.

Dr. Sterling's charm is the stuff of legend for covert operators everywhere. And now I understand how he so successfully seduced Dr. Evelyn to keep her close, not the other way around. He reaches back into his bio-suit of tricks and hands the Usta a compact of bright pink powder. "Please let the Camaeliphim know I've arrived with his niece."

The Usta raises the ridge on his brow with surprise. "Princess Scathatch?" He abruptly stands, walks around me, and bows toward a trembling Dr. Monica. "Your highness." He rubs the bright pink powder into his cheeks.

"Get a lo' of the queen," Dr. Monica chortles, regaining her courage. "He thinks I'm a princess! Hey there, mate, a little o' tha' stuff goes a long way."

Netesh shares the powder with two other Usta. The remaining Usta, the ones who don't wear bright pink powder, suddenly appear rather, um, turned on…hmmm…so I guess this is how Usta mating rituals work. The males *need* this pink powder to attract females.

"Not her," Luca says, then points at me. "*This* is Princess Scathatch."

The creature bows again. "Please stand," I say. "I decreed to the Fluffle they no longer have to bow before Camaeliphim, and I decree it before Usta, too."

The Usta hands Dr. Sterling an old ship's map that Sterling unfolds and scans. He nods and rolls it up again.

"The human must remain here," Netesh says, looking at Dr. Monica.

"Like hell I will," Dr. Monica protests. "*Sam?*" I feel the fear in her voice, its vibrations coursing through me.

"You don't understand," Netesh says as he flings a dismissive claw at her. "For a pure human to directly view a fully-fledged Camaeliphim...it's certain death."

"The Camaeliphim won't kill her if she's with me," I say.

"No," Netesh says. "He won't. She will kill herself."

"I don't understand," I say.

"Gazing into sacred knowledge overloads Kihog brains. She is unprepared to view a Camaeliphim in true form."

"How do I prepare?" Dr. Monica asks.

"It takes years of practice, ritual, and initiation," Netesh says. "Sometimes drugs help too."

"Sounds like Dr. Evelyn's bag of tricks," Reggie says, and I give him a knowing nod.

"Any way to advance my training right here so I might tag along?" Dr. Monica asks.

"A human cannot override what is sacred using pseudo-science," Netesh says, rolling his eye slits. "That's the trouble with you Kihogs, you're always trying to find a quick-fix work-around. You can't simply pop a pill or take a potion or recite some words to meet a fully-fledged Camaeliphim. Why do you think he dwells so far below humans? To keep them safe from him, that's why!"

Luca brushes past all of us and starts down a long corridor.

"We'll pick you up when we get back," he says. "Try not to get vaporized."

"Luca," I say, pinching my brows. I slowly trail him, then stop. "Not funny."

"This is heaps bad," Dr. Monica says. "I'll stay here and take care o' your soul critters." She paces between two Usta and peers over the edge of a platform, runs a hand through her dark hair, and it springs up again in one spot.

Dr. Monica is unlike any pure human I've ever known. She shrugs and walks toward the craft. Her resigned expression reminds me of Priyanka, a Plum Hook Bay foster kid I once knew, who now lives on a Burundi coffee farm with her husband, Rakito. I was always in awe of the way Priyanka stared out into and appropriately assessed the world with courage, even if she was cold, hungry, or facing abuse. Dr. Monica seems to take hardship and danger in stride much the same way as Priyanka, except Dr. Monica was raised in the Australian Outback by a single mum who protected Aboriginals. Monica knows how to wield weapons better than words and doesn't challenge the Usta.

"I'll remain here with her," Paramel says, looking back and forth between Dr. Monica and the impending darkness of yet another series of caves. I can't say I blame Paramel either, for wanting to remain behind. Luca slips into blackness, and I no longer see him. Reggie looks at and then taps his watch and jerks his head toward the blackness for us to get going. Dr. Sterling lightly taps the map in his hands, patiently waiting.

"Dr. Monica can hold her own," I say. "But stay with her if you like." A micro expression of relief washes over Dr. Monica's eyes and she involuntarily sighs. "Netesh, ensure Dr. Monica and Paramel remain fully intact and un-vaporized, do I make myself clear? If you fail, I will instruct Eresh that you and the others are quarantined here on duty in perpetuity, that none of you ever receive another atom of pink powder. Understood?"

"Yes, your highness."

"Wait in the craft," I say to Dr. Monica. "We'll return for you, I promise."

"Here," Paramel says. She hands Dr. Monica four vials of violet liquid and gives her a tight hug. "If things get sketchy, we'll drink 'em...mate."

CAMAEL

DR. STERLING lightly punches his fist a few times against an oversized granite door embedded in a mountainside—*under* the Mariana Trench. Nothing happens. I can't imagine we'd come this far to meet my Camaeliphim uncle, and then he doesn't even bother to answer the door. Maybe he's too old or decrepit...maybe he has servants who didn't hear the knock...or maybe he's inanimated, the Bezaliels or humans with high clearances having gotten to him first. And just when I'm about to suggest we turn back, *phssst*...the strange door unseals from jagged rock and opens a few inches. Red glowing eyes peer out at us over a reptilian-like snout.

"Who are you?" The creature asks, giving us a one-eyed, side-glance once-over. Normally, I'd be stunned by a talking dragon but after everything we've encountered since embarking on this journey into Ki's depths, little surprises me anymore.

Through the tiny opening, I spot a pulsating orb—but it's a lot different than the Usta spheres. Its shimmering display is an unpredictable blue-white glow that fades and dances into vividness, like an uncontained lava lamp about the size of a small car.

An overwhelming feeling of peace surrounds me, which is weird because this place is the creepiest-looking royal court I've never seen. Not that I've been to many, but it's nothing at all like the Usta Cathedral overstuffed with sparkly treasures, sanctimonious scientists, and high-brow philosophy.

"Princess Scathatch to see Camael," Dr. Sterling says. "And part of her team."

"*Camael?* Wait! *What?*" I ask, jerking my head toward Dr. Sterling. "Camael is my *uncle?*" And just like that, my heart speeds into hyper tick-tock mode, and sweat creeps along my hairline.

"You remember him?"

"Not exactly," I say. "Bennie told me Camael was an angel of war...but not just any angel. Ancient texts claim he's God's 'secret angel in charge'. Bennie told me he went dark years ago when the Nephilim and humans joined forces to put a price on his head." I shiver and take a deep, painful swallow. If Camael is my uncle... *"My name...is Basaseal, brother of Camael, definitely not to be confused with Bezaliels."*

The door turns into a swirling pool of water, and we step through into Camael's court just as dry as if we'd crossed a threshold to someone's home...but in doing so, we're relieved of a small bit of gravity, able to semi-float. My toes drag the ground toward the stretching plasma, so I tip myself horizontal, and flap my arms a little like chicken wings to prevent falling forward.

"Brilliant defense system," Dr. Sterling says. "Intruders are rendered practically weightless the moment they come through the door, unable to hurl weapons."

"The swirly on your forehead glows like a flare," Luca says. "It's spinning too."

I touch it but don't feel any heat or pain.

As we move toward the inner sanctum of this space, gravity continues to diminish. A few repurposed pillows from some of the derelict ships outside, float by, hand-embroidered, no less, and

I'm certain created by humans who have long since passed on to other transitions. I reach out and lock arms with the nearest person, who happens to be Luca, and he looks positively mesmerized by the plasma glow in front of us. I finally turn myself upright.

Zap!

A beam of light shoots out of the plasma and lands a target right between my eyes! It punches my head backward until I regain my bearings. *Whew!* I'm not inanimated or dead...I don't feel any different at all, but I've never seen an energy form like this. A sudden burst of intense love expands through me. Then, dizziness and a wave of nausea ebb and flow along my insides. I feel egg-shaped fear expanding through my plexus. Steadying my breath, the way Reggie taught me, helps me fight an urge to turn and run, not that I could while half-floating. I check my bio-skin to make sure all organic systems still run green...

...I'm okay but must turn my eyes from this wild sphere now and then. I notice that Dr. Sterling, Luca, and Reggie do the same. A clammy tingling causes the hair on my neck and arms to stand at attention and I stuff an urge to puke. My brain is uploaded with rapid scenes and symbols, people in pale blue robes, trees taller than skyscrapers, pearlescent stars, three pale moons, and oddly colored planets, going in and out of focus like a hazy television channel.

"Breathe, Sam," Reggie says. He takes my free arm as Luca holds firmly to the other.

"I think I'm going to be sick," I say.

"Look away as needed," Reggie says.

The reptilian being who liquefied the front door has the tail of a sauropod, although not nearly as large. I've seen it before. I sift through my head trying to remember the dinosaurs I once charted for Dr. Evelyn when I was a kid. It plods down the aisle away from us and hides behind the orb, successfully out of view. I remember. This is the same beast I saw at Harrington House the night I flew out the window and followed it to a garden fountain. It jumped in and disappeared!

Netesh sits on a tattered floating pillow and begins to play one of the songs from the crystal chip Dr. Sterling gave him—a soothing, ethereal melody. The reptilian beast peeks around the plasma again and snorts with what I think might be approval and looks at me, then behind me, to see what's coming, so I turn to look too. At the far end of the aisle, I spot two small yellow lights, ambling out of darkness...attached to...

"*Randolph?*" I ask.

The wolf approaches, regal and large, his ample silvery paws padding the ground, unaffected by the decreased gravity. The wolf's head almost reaches my chest and I semi-float boulder-still. He sniffs my hand, lifts his snout, and lets loose with a soulful howl that sends a chill of sadness through my soul. He trains his eyes on me and barely moves another muscle in his well-bred silver fur body, except to lick my wrist. Then he turns in a circle and lies down for a nap at my feet. It's Randolph, all right—and for the lives of me I can't figure out how he got here—unless...Is Bennie here too? "I don't understand," I say. "Why on Earth would Bennie's soul guide be *here*?"

The plasma grows brighter as hushed whispers pass over our heads. Photonic symbols float off the plasma entity and disappear, but I can't understand a thing, and this frustrates me. "I think it's communicating," I say. "But I can't translate...wait! I think it says Randolph is *his* soul guide for Ki. This plasma is a *he*? I feel so sick... what is happening?"

"It is our humanness," Luca says. "It makes a Camaeliphim in its natural form difficult for us to view. Humans may describe such beings as angels...or extraterrestrials."

"Same thing," Dr. Sterling says.

When I look again, flowy strands of white light, like tentacles, sprout from the plasma and grow into limbs. A set of two hazy arms and two legs stands before us. A low rumble vibrates under my feet. It morphs into a face with pale powder-blue navy-colored veins in its neck, like crackling frost that meanders upward and spreads across its cheeks. Pure white eyes turn deep night-black for a moment before they adjust to the color of steel spikes, boring into me, through me, testing, I think, for mental leaks. A phantom hand strokes amber-gray tufts of feather-like hair that pokes through its chin, coming to corporeal form inside the uniform of...a *police officer?* A shiny silver badge, polished shoes, gun belt...but no name tag. My heart sinks to my toes with shock.

"Cameron?" I ask. "Cameron the Cop?"

"Only when I have to go looking for promising souls like you," he says with a laugh. "My cover, up there," he points, "my *legend,* is Cameron. Down here and everywhere else? I am known in my true form as Camael."

"Define *promising,*" I say. *Keep your balance, Sam.* Whoa. I'm so dizzy.

Cameron the Cop arrested me for shoplifting when I was a sixteen-year-old runaway. He bought me McDonald's, dropped me off at the Cuyahoga County Juvenile Jail, and brought in Dr. Evelyn to make me an offer. Little did either of us realize back then, the extent of Evelyn's covert training as a double agent, or the fact she was my aunt. The *offer* was to go with her for "special training" or stay behind and rot in juvenile jail. Of course, I chose the latter. I had no knowledge at the time that Cameron was sent to locate me after the Ormian Council voted I should pick up my father's destiny.

It was Cameron the Cop, aka Camael my uncle, who saved me from that hell hole on the NASA side of Plum Hook Bay—but only after I rescued a multitude of kids and killed a reptilian-human chimera. It was a test. I passed. That beast was a Nephilim hybrid hell-bent on stealing kids for experiments so ghastly humans didn't want it to be true. Painful memories. Nobody believed me, said I made it up, that Cameron had never been to NASA Plum Hook Bay—but I know better. I stuff my grief over losing Bennie and Luca's sister Brigdhe in those Ohio caves. It feels forever ago. I was a runaway—but not the kind humans know. And I'm not the same hybrid I was before. I'm a survivor. *No.* I'm a *thriver.* I'm remembering.

"Hello, Scathatch," Camael says, giving me a warm grin. He leans forward to get a better look.

"Why are you *here?*" I ask.

"I accepted an offer," he says.

"What *kind* of offer?" I ask. I sway and feel my grip loosening from Reggie and Luca. *Stay upright, Sam. Breathe!*

"We're going for a ride," Camael says to me mentally. "I see you have the mark of your father and he's conferred your right as a Balancer."

"**Samantha!**" Luca yells.

It's the last thing on my usual side of the realm that I hear.

A council gathers. People in pale blue robes swoop down from a dusky sky painted with pearlescent stars and strangely colored planets. Three pale moons of different phases keep watch over this odd meeting of translucent beings.

It's neither warm nor cold, frightening nor comforting. Trees stand taller than skyscrapers, the veins from their flesh-colored leaves pulsating with hundreds of bubble-sized orbs that break away to hover over me.

One being glides up and gently wipes an open palm, softly as a cat's whisker across my forehead. "Nemain?" I ask.

"My sister lives and is well," she says, turning to face this strange court of beings. She looks back and smiles down at me. Wait one second. I've been here before...

...Whispers, like low whistles that get caught in seashells, echo around me. This otherworldly court beyond the veil of this underground trench deep within Ki continues its conversation...in Enochian! Strange symbols, etched into plasma, breathe and fold away like a pulsating puzzle—it's alive—and it's Camael! Am I

dead? My body feels lighter. When I look down at the ground, my feet aren't there!

"Plug in her conduit," someone says.

A razor-thin laser light plugs itself into the base of my spine. It sputters and sparks the way blowtorches taken to metal might do. "Relax, Scathatch," Camael says. "Nothing matters in matter."

The vastness that I always thought of as *me* is not. As a sentient being, I am inconsequential, a microscopic part of a far greater whole, but necessary for the transmission of information from the Source and back again. What I think of as *me* collapses into a heap of material insignificance, like a pile of hastily unzipped clothing unto the ground, a nothing compared to grander cosmic singularity. I look for Luca, Reggie, and Dr. Sterling but don't see them.

"Nemain," a male voice says. The voice is attached, I think, to a celestrial in charge. His avocado-sized green eyes register reserved alarm, but I can't tell if he's sentient or a hologram for my benefit so I might make sense of the form.

"Yes?"

"Shall we redeem her and make known?"

My sister, Nemain, makes a scan of my spirit, curves her lips into a light smile, and it is then I see her third eye, a multi-faceted crystal staring at me from the middle of her forehead. I know her. She was with me that day at Plum Hook Bay, under the nuclear reactor, on the other side of the Earthly veil, fighting off Bezaliels to weaken the Nephilim beast Brigdhe threw into the abyss.

"You will alight," she says to me, mind-to-mind, in a language that sounds like dolphin chatter, yet I understand her ancient Enochian completely. Her sapphire eyes flicker and remind me of moon-glittered ripples on the ocean, and we connect, first eye to first eye. "I shall fight for you again when the Bezaliels breach your skin line."

"I understand," I mentally say in Enochian.

Nemain addresses the court. "I've laid our plenty upon her and made known, the realm has ripped, and the Infinite Field calls for the return of this Balancer to fix Ninmah's Portal—but there is a problem."

"What problem?" a voice asks.

"A female Emergent has been created between this sister and the Source Bearer," Nemain says. "Unfortunately, Bezaliel mist may course through this celestrial child's bio entity."

Gasps all around.

Shit!

"And this comes to you how?" someone asks.

"The Red Bird," Nemain answers, flitting about, without any feet, the bottom half of her nothing but light. "Bennie's soul guide."

I knew it! I always thought Edwin the Cardinal was a better fit for Bennie as a Soul Guide than Camael's wolf. Camael must have sent Randolph to watch over us when we were kids because he couldn't remain topside himself. A rumble vibrates in my chest as I stand before my father's kindred, *my* celestrial kindred, the Ormian Council, and its Court.

"The Emergent's parents *do* understand what must be done," someone says.

"Aye," I say, and float forward. "I made a promise to *Not Who* that I'd throw Raga into the Source Vortex. If she has taken form through my daughter, I shall keep my word."

"*Not Who?*" a female spirit asks. "It showed itself to you?"

"Yes," I say. "It slid two plates of time near a space boundary, so I could jump through, to somewhere else."

"Why did *Not Who* help you?" Camael asks.

"It gave me an escape because my BOUO was being drained by the DOE at a clandestine military hospital topside on Ki."

"That's the third time we couldn't find you. If I may intervene," Camael says with a bow before the Council "We may have an alternative."

"And this would be?" someone asks.

"Scathatch has agreed to marry Lord Luca Harrington," he says, circling me. Flashes of my night with Luca pass through my mind and I don't even blush because...well...I can't in this lighter form. The passion that transpired between Luca and me is just a normal consequence and vibrational exchange of our being hybrids—albeit with rare and elevated levels of pleasure the likes I've never known until we entangled.

"Theirs could have been a mighty match for untold eons of Ki time," the man with the green eyes says. "Lord Harrington and Scathatch might have accomplished much for the benefit of multiple realms. What do you have in mind?"

Could have? Might have?

"Lozen has shared some rather disturbing news," Camael says. "It seems Lord Harrington, with the aid of an Alphion Proximal C hybrid known as Dr. Sterling Dennison, allowed Bezaliel mist to be inserted into his form too."

Shit.

A look of distress skitters across Nemain's face.

"Preposterous!" someone yells.

"Treason!"

Lozen promised me thirty days! *Damn her.* And then I realize...her idea of thirty days and my idea of thirty days are probably two entirely different frames of reference because she's on Ninmah Portal time...but still, where is Camael going with this?

"If this is so," the being in charge says, "Lord Harrington and Dr. Sterling have committed a universal violation!"

Crap.

"Lord Harrington could take Princess Scathatch's place and sweep himself and the child into the Source Vortex," Camael says. "Dr. Sterling could be inanimated."

"No!" I yell. I turn to Camael. "How could *you*?"

"You're the Balancer," Camael says. "And the Ormian Council has decided universes may remain synchronized without humans. Consider it a sentence of mercy, to let you live out this life on Ki."

"Oh, really," I say. I turn to address the Council. "If the Ormian Council has voted for human genocide, it perfectly sets up Bezaliels for complete victory," I say. "And what sort of life would I have on Ki if you wiped out humans? My sentience would be short-lived...then what? I join you on the Ormian Council? Removing humans from Earth's equation means inanimation for all of us."

"How?" someone asks.

"Widespread uncontrolled chaos with no sense or patterns," I say. "It would kill humans, as intended, but it also annihilates plants, viruses, bacteria, oxygen, water, fungi, and animals too. Balance. Gone. The Source would then suffer extensive multiverse collapse when Bezaliels raid and destroy Ki's repository seeking additional energy. Nobody wins. Game. Over. This tiny marble of a planet lost inside a black hole holds *everything* in order, even if it appears to all of you as randomness."

A thousand lights pummel my spirit until insight is lost, shrouded again beneath layers of blood, bone, and skin, and I'm stuffed back into the half-human form I recognize as *me*...but... I'm still here, on the other side of the veil!

A look of shock crosses over some of the beings on the Ormian Council and others in the court just *poof!* Disappear! "Chicken shits," I whisper.

"Let me look at you," the being with green eyes says. "Come, come..."

I float up and meet him.

"I am Annunan, Earl of Ormia. It was unfortunate what happened to your father," he says. "Your families have suffered much in their lifetimes because of duty and..." He trails off. "I've always been fond of your father...and your uncle too. It's my understanding you freed your father from a Xaradin cage and killed a Fewoulz in the process."

"Yes."

"Where is Basaseal?" Annunan asks.

"He said he had to find my mother," I say.

"Not a wise thing to do," he says. "You have a rather troubling and low-bred human pedigree. Your mother is a receptor and her sister...what is her name?"

"Dr. Evelyn Dennison."

A low buzz of troubled mumbles permeates what's left of the Council.

"Ah, yes," Annunan says. "Evelyn the body snatcher. Evelyn the celestrial thief. Evelyn the Countess of Teviot and treachery. She has abused her human Source gifts and shared sacred knowledge with other less than desirable humans."

"Sounds about right," I say, folding my arms and straightening my back, feeling suddenly less ragged and drained, my nausea and terror replaced by something strong and familiar. "You're my father's friend," I say. "I'm not sure how I know this, but I do."

"That is correct," Annunan says with a smile. "You must be remembering. And pardon the others, but this is the first time we've banished a hybrid back to Ki for insolence and it didn't work. You're still here! How extraordinary. I've known your father for what you'd understand as hundreds of Earth years. We trained together. I knew your grandparents too, esteemed Camaeliphim...but stubborn and evasive...like your dad...and you, too, I see."

The Council and what's left of the Court plunge into silence.

"If Luca is thrown into the Source Vortex with Hope, I will consider it an act of violence against my Camaeliphim family and Ki, whether I have a *troubled* pedigree or not. I am still half celestrial and a princess." I stare up at Annunan, feeling defiant.

He tugs a bit on the top half of his robe, agitated I think, but hiding it well within ancient and powerful eyes as we float in deadlock. "You may or may not be a princess," he reminds me.

"We aren't sure if your title is even valid due to your humanness."

"The Ormian Council gave me this iteration," I say. "I didn't ask for it. And then you veiled my celestrial memories. You want me to help you, yet none of you would dare dirty your own robes with an Earthly intercession to save yourselves, or humans, and then you have the gall to count yourselves as superior." I spit on the ground. "None of you, it seems, make great Ki tenders either and remind me instead of self-serving, pompous overlords."

More rumbles of discontent.

Rows of blacked-out windows are lined up like soldiers behind Annunan. I see nothing but darkness through them except for an occasional firefly-sized glow that occasionally flits by and disappears. Annunan lightly sinks to the ground, patting Kitsune on the head with a tentative tap. I wasn't even aware Kitsune had or was able to enter this realm, but her sudden appearance shouldn't surprise me. Soul Guides are adept at finding their way, especially her. She wanders over to Nemain, who playfully teases her with a wand of light, and I float down to join them.

"Camael," Annunan says. "Is there a reason you intervened in Scathatch's current iteration and brought her here?" He plays with a small bolt of lightning in his palm, running it through his fingers as if it's a tiny snake. I try to imagine Annunan and my father training together hundreds of years ago, my dad a brave warrior "*angel*" and Annunan an intelligence strategist, a bit like the balance Bennie and I used to strike at Plum Hook Bay. And like my Uncle Camael, Annunan isn't a celestrial I'd want to double-cross. But I will challenge him, to learn, and perhaps discover a win-win between Kihogs and Camaeliphim.

"The Source Vortex," Camael says with a small bow.

"Humans and Nephilim are close to finding the Word," I say. "If they get their hands on the Code of Everything...the COE... the Ormian Council won't have to consider genocide. Humans, unfortunately, behave like unremitting children. They'll squabble and divide one another right into certain death and planetary destruction as they fight for planetary dominance. You won't have to help them along. This is what my team and I are trying to prevent."

"I understand," Annunan says. "Your father too has a lot of ideas about how to contain Bezaliels and Kihogs, including allowing Camaeliphim to share intimacies with humans and appearing to them in damn near true form. The Ormian Council doesn't trust humans to do the right thing. It seems that you too agree."

"And what might the *right* thing be?" I ask. "You need humans. Without their belief or their forms, Camaeliphim and the Source lose vibration and frequencies, and along with it, our existence. We are...*interdependent,* all connected. Like it or not, we are them, and they are us."

"A dangerous liaison indeed," Annunan says. "As Drs. Dennison, your father, Lord Harrington, and even the Nephilim have so carelessly proved. I've always considered cavorting with humans beneath Camaeliphim or other advanced celestrials. No offense."

"None taken," I say. "Annunan, do you believe in the power of a human mind?"

"In its hollowest and simplest, most primitive form," he answers.

"If a human mind is the binding agent of all matter, it must be sentience that provides life to the Source—not the other way around. Without human observers housed in corporeal forms, consciousness scatters, like photons...and we fail."

Annunan tips his head to one side and nods as if I've said something profound or maybe that he's forgotten. Power and influence will do that to celestrials—make them forget that they too are not invincible and all-knowing. He rests his small ball of light on my shoulder, slides a manifested finger across my cheek, and lifts a few strands of my hair. "I strongly suspect you provide Lord Harrington quite the challenge. Do you love him?" He drops the curls on my shoulders, and it causes me to shiver but I refuse to budge. He retrieves his strange toy.

"Lord Harrington's decision to allow Dr. Sterling to insert Bezaliel mist into his hybrid DNA was certainly stupid," I say. Annunan nods with a smile. "But he did it to help, not harm, Camaeliphim or Kihogs. He did it to learn from the energy. And I love him—more deeply than any being I've ever known."

"Oh?" Annunan says. "You are sure your love runs so deep for only a single wayward Camaeliphim? What has Lord Harrington learned from his stupidity?"

"Control," I say, narrowing my eyes at Annunan.

"Every bit your father," he says. "He, too, lacks discipline and allows his heart to rule over his head. We are aware that a few humans have successfully back-engineered some celestrial technologies."

"Yes," I say. "Some Kihogs secretly move large boulders using sound frequencies and some levitate their bodies. Others harness the astral power of crystals, tapping free energy derived from Earth, fed to it from space. And others build machines that defy physics. They tell 'the people' our craft arrive from outer space. Other human factions claim our kind are dangerous and a threat to international security. Still, other human *Secreters* deny that both we and our technologies exist."

"It was agreed by the Ormian Council to never share such knowledge with humans again," Annunan says. "Especially after what happened at Lumeria, Gobekli Tepe, Kaharan, Meteora, Lo, Shambala, and Atlantis. According to our calculations, humans are not spiritually evolving and the technology they create will one day overtake them."

"I disagree," I say, and I'm surprised by my sudden defense of humans. "The Bezaliels will overtake them *through* the technology. And while it's true most Kihogs fail to register even a blip of enlightenment on the intergalactic spectrometer, I've met many humans with higher-than-normal levels of compassion, awareness, or elevated consciousness."

"You know about the intergalactic spectrometer?"

"Yes," I say. "Luca told me."

"Figures he would. What do you want?" Annunan asks.

"Nikola Tesla and my grandfather, Ian Windsor...one human and one extraterrestrial...built an advanced lock and key device that would have enabled them to leave Earth with the Code of Everything and hide it in a new location. It opens the X Point that leads to the Source Vortex. They launched off Ki but were forced to leave the COE behind."

"Tesla was a celestrial genius," Annunan says. "And he was dangerous. He was taken up by Ebians."

"My mother," I say, "was also taken up by Ebians...and she was pure *human*." I don't ask if Annunan considers *her* dangerous too.

Shock skitters across Annunan's face, but he says nothing because I suspect he fully realizes that Ebians are far ahead of even Camaeliphim with their advancements. His look also tells me he may not have known the Ebians removed my mother from Ki.

"I know that Tesla and my grandfather received *otherworldly* help to control matter in both biological and artificial systems. This little piece of jewelry..." I pull the Pleaides pendant from my bio suit and show it to him. "...is one part of a whole that generates a beam using nanoparticles that assemble themselves into conduits to create X Points or powerful forcefields. It also helps us travel twenty-thousand times faster than the speed of light. This pendant opens the heart of that lock and key device."

"Where did you get this?" Annunan asks.

"I need a couple of things from you first," I say.

"What?"

"Lord Harrington and Dr. Sterling Dennison are the only

two hybrids within a million multiverses that know how to put Tesla's device together. First, I need them alive and kept animated. Second, I need a sphere held under guard by the Astral Weavers at Plum Hook Bay. If I have that, I can put the coil, this key device, and the sphere together..."

"To locate the Source Vortex and throw Raga into it..." Annunan says.

"Yes, but we can also get COE off this planet."

"You cannot take COE off planet," Annunan says.

"Why?" I ask.

"If you separate the Code of Everything from Ki, it will mutate, much like the Enochian language and your golden blood," he says.

"Oh, my God..." I say. "The Ormian Council prevented Tesla and my grandfather from taking the COE off planet! It was *YOU*!"

"We relocated those two beings," Annunan says. "We gave them a new existence. We did everyone a favor. If the COE mutates, Source only knows what may happen. We couldn't take that chance."

"But Raga needs to be thrown into the Source Vortex," I say.

"Not exactly," Annunan says. "Raga needs to be thrown into the Source Vortex to avert multiverse chaos and prevent Bezaliels from taking corporeal form, hence your father's job as a Balancer. I see he's passed on his birthright to you, a first for a *human* hybrid. Of course, some Bezaliel energy will remain here on Ki...It keeps humans appropriately divided and distracted."

"Don't you prefer peace?"

"Of course," Annunan says. "But as previously discussed, the majority of Kihogs remain woefully unenlightened and primitive, and therefore the COE will remain scattered, on Ki, until Kihogs elevate their consciousness, understood?"

"Yes. But I need a third thing."

"And what might that be?" Annunan asks, releasing a puff of light out the top of his head like a discarded heavy sigh.

"I forgot my password," I say. "The Ormian Council clouded too much of my memory. I need the password to obtain the sphere from the Astral Weavers, and I only get one chance."

"And if you fail?" Annunan asks.

"I won't."

"But if you do..."

"I'll be inanimated or die."

"If you succeed, you become *my* wife," he says. "And I ensure your princess-hood among the Ormian Council."

Nemain abruptly stops playing with Kitsune. She looks from Camael to Annunan to me, just as surprised as I am by this sudden and unexpected *offer*. She slips into the darkness of a tunnel and is gone.

"I care not for empty titles," I say. "And even less so about serving as your trophy spouse."

"Annunan," Camael interjects. "What are you doing? Scathatch can't make such a promise after sharing her friendliness with Lord Harrington. Theirs is a bond only broken by..."

"Inanimation or death," Annunan interrupts. "His."

"No," I say.

"This is blasphemous," Camael says. "You're Basasael's best friend! Their bond can only be broken by..."

"Basaseal will approve the match," Annunan interrupts. "Lord Harrington is contaminated with Bezaliel mist, and the entanglement is null. I will enforce *Sakar* upon Scathatch for strategic purposes between Kihogs and Camaeliphim. And Scathatch, if she's more Camaeliphim than human, will honor such an intelligent offer."

"What's Sakar?" I ask.

"*Sakar* is a mostly forgotten and rarely enforced misogynistic Ormian tradition," Camael says. "This ancient law is no longer in force. It's been unenforced for at least thirty-six thousand Nibiru orbits!"

"But it hasn't been repealed," Annunan says. "I call it into play, as humans might say. You know as well as I do, the Council and the Court would welcome this match for Scathatch's sake."

The thought of losing Luca to death...or an unwanted marriage to Annunan, breaks my heart. But our cosmic obligations are higher on the scales of Balance. "I need not my father's approval for anything," I say. "And I have zero duty to you or the Ormian Council. You care so little for humans, and I am part human. No number of chants or prayers or unnaturally forced nuptials behind your veil can ever change this. The entire Ormian Council should be ashamed."

"And you already have a wife," Camael says to him, a look of disapproval and disgust roaming his face.

"Yes, her name is Alondra...beautiful soul," Annunan says. "But under the law of Sakar, I am a celestrial noble and may look upon any Earthly sentient I find fair and collect them as I so choose. It is a secret agreement made with Kihog leaders in possession of cosmic clearances. I've never partaken of a human hybrid. We could grow to love one another very much, or at least have some fun."

"Does Alondra get her choice among humans too?" I ask, arms folded across my chest, holding in my disgust.

"She does not," Annunan says.

"Why?" I ask.

"It would be dishonorable," he says.

"And if you lie with another, it's not dishonorable?" I ask.

"Males are able to enjoy a variety of fruits strictly as a source of recreation and increased vigor," he says. "Females not so much —females engage in pleasure as a service to males or because they think they're *in love*."

"I feel sorry for Alondra," I say. "And for the humans forced under the law of Sakar into abduction and rape."

"It's seduction," Annunan says. "It's the best experience of any Kihog's pitiful life to be seduced by what they know as *angels*."

"This arrangement reeks of rotten fish," I say. What I don't say is that I understand why Annunan does this. If I succeed, he gets a large share of what is sure to be my fleeting glory and prestige—increased power and name recognition among the Ormian Council. At least until history is re-written as if it were *he* who threw Raga into the Source Vortex, securing his legacy for ages. If I fail, he can mark the female human hybrid as exhibit number one of his sorry excuse for multiverse collapse.

"You do this for your personal glory," Camael says to Annunan, anger rising in his voice, along with a low rumble of thunder. "You cannot enforce Sakar on Scathatch!"

"I can and I will," Annunan says. "If Scathatch agrees."

"And she must agree," Camael says.

"Never thought I'd receive more matrimonial proposals underground than surface side," I say with a heavy sigh. "Or that Camaeliphim would harbor similar desires to humans." Annunan bristles when I compare him to humans. "Understand this, Annunan, I **do not** agree to our match and need not my father's approval to decline. You will give me the Source Vortex location and reinstall my password memory...and your word that zero harm comes to Luca or Sterling whether I fail or succeed."

"Or what?" he says. "Are you threatening me?"

"Agreeing to marry you would be a threat," I say, narrowing my eyes at him.

"Because Lord Harrington is a possessive and jealous hybrid?" Annunan asks.

"No," I say, meeting him eye to eye when I step closer. "Because *I* am." And with those words, I focus on his translucent form until a bolt of energy congregates in my head, enters my necklace, blows through my mind's eye, and short-circuits his form, causing him to sputter and spark until I relent.

"Sam," Camael says. "What are you doing?"

"Restoring balance," I say. I release my focus and Annunan rights himself, floating mid-air, acting as if he's felt no pain—but I know otherwise.

"Done," Annunan says, visibly shaken. He looks at Camael. "See? Was that so hard? Scathatch may have her father's fortitude after all." He reaches into one of the dark windows behind him and seizes a small buzzing sphere the size of a hard candy. "Swallow this," he says, handing it to me. "It will lead you to the Source Vortex and help you remember the password."

"Thank you," I say.

"I'm going with her," Camael says.

Annunan shrugs. "Suit yourself."

"You've already risked enough by coming topside to help me," I say. "The Nephilim put a price on your head. It's why you went dark in the first place."

"I went dark to bide my time until you were ready to act as a Balancer," he says. "You've proven that today. There's a time to come out of hiding and that time is now. And my apologies for offering up Luca to the Source Vortex—I was thinking of you and your father. And your mother. I love her too, you know." And the way Camael says this makes me wonder if he's *in love* with my mom.

"Off with you both," Annunan says. "You've got work to do." He shoos us through the wall of a tunnel that pops and hisses as we pass through.

When we come out the other side, I find myself lying on the ground where I fell, staring into Luca's eyes. And no matter how much I try to look away, I can't—Annunan's self-serving proposal masquerading as honor, still rings in my ears. But even worse, the Ormian Council wants Luca dead or inanimated. I don't trust Annunan to keep his word.

And Camael is nowhere to be found...

SIXTEEN

THE SEVEN SEALS OF ME

"The only reason for time is so that everything doesn't happen at once."
--Albert Einstein

BY THE TIME we return to the Isle of No Time, the cloudless "sky" set to *evening* mode, transitions from pink and yellow hues to golden orange. From my perspective, it pales in comparison to the real sunset found topside and makes me longingly miss almost everything above my head, including fresh air.

Fluffle sunsets are not unique like snowflakes. A Fluffle sky is predictable with its pre-recorded tones always set to *Now*. Of course, I realize Elemorphia adjust the light now and then for our team, to be hospitable. But what is *home*? As a hybrid who loves to gaze upon post sunset stars, I wonder about home...and family...and Hope. Sometimes I wish I could fly away, to somewhere else, to home...but I'm not sure where *home* might be for me. Has Ki ever been my home? I flee its traps as much as possible but here I am, still bound to this terrarium, dependent upon it for survival and my sentience.

I settle next to Paramel "outside," near the Fluffle community center, a place of camaraderie and fellowship. Tiny Elemorphia play and weave their way among us, their chitters and giggles bubbling up from that space in them where innocence and wonder still dwell, "un-evicted" by life's hardship or holes.

The Fluffle, according to Bilby, has changed little over the past thirty-thousand years. It was gouged out and terraformed by his ancestors to escape creatures *Homo sapiens sapiens* don't know exist—and to flee from Ki's numerous wars. Time just sort of went away in the Fluffle, because for Elemorphia, there is nothing down here to measure...only holes to dig and human corpses to snatch. I find this confusing. If there is nothing to measure, then nothing should happen... "Time is an illusion and not fundamental to *our* existence," Bilby told me. The concept of a perpetual *Now* where things *do* happen is difficult for this hybrid to grasp.

I look away from the "sunset" to study the beryl polished central floor of the Fluffle, its various sheens of yellow, blue, and green, it's said, reflect evil onto itself. The Elemorphia believe beryl keeps their demons at bay. I suppose it works because Fewoulz have never actually entered the Isle of No Time or Ereshun. Fewoulz loiter between the two realms to prey on non-solicitous souls.

I consider my Uncle Camael. I can't for the lives of me figure out where he disappeared.

He told me that fully fledged Camaeliphim remember a time when Kihogs lived elevated lives, beyond oppression. Humans were happy in communicative consciousness with trees, rivers or oceans, trading and laughing in peace, with simple homes, style, and food. It was a time when there was *enough*—a sort of Garden of Eden or Shambala or ancient Kingdom of Lo, now out of reach and veiled from humans, and impossible to physically reach. There was a time on Earth—way before what modern humans recognize as *the Beginning*. It was a time void of pain, suffering, or war.

Basasael once echoed his brother's sentiment about Ki's current situation. "Ki is just noise. And war. And disease. And hunger. And poverty. And pollution. And politicians. And lots of shade that has nothing to do with trees. And more war."

Today, Ki is a mostly cold and heartless place of high-rises and higher egos, all determined to crowd out, influence, or lord over one another. It is a place of dank offices, dirty streets, unkempt minds, and secret clearances. Living here means a serious lack of privacy paired with an overabundance of greed, self-absorption, and fear. And Ki absorbs it all...the human resentment and bitterness...the trash...the pollution. Earth takes whatever human nature drives through her soiled flesh...ah, but those sunsets!

The last wave of deep purple fades to dusky sapphire. Bilby covers some of the holes with the other Elemorphia to prevent souls from passing through and getting lost if they leave their bodies before the Fluffle can extract them. He checks some of the fires, says hello to a few of his husbands and wives. He picks up a spoon to taste some root vegetables in a pot.

Paramel taps the tip of her sword in and out of our own small fire.

"How's he holding up since you've transformed back into a Viking?" I ask.

"He's got plenty of spouses to heal his broken heart," she says with a smile and a wink. She looks down the end of her sword and points it toward him. "See?" Bilby climbs into a hole with two other Elemorphia, male and female. "He's quite prolific." Her eyes wander over to Dr. Sterling, engrossed in conversation with Reggie, Luca, and Hogan, his eyes flashing as he regales the males with tales of all things crypto-terrestrial. "Did you tell Lord Harrington about Annunan's offer?"

"No."

"Males," she says. "I loathe their androcentrism."

"Aye, mate," Dr. Monica says. "I couldn' agree more! Cheers." She places a drop of violet liquid on her tongue. "The poor blokes never got over the fact they can't birth carpet beggars, and without *Mother* Nature it's all for naugh'."

"I thought you quit drinking?" I ask. "And the males would disagree with you. They'd probably claim patriarchy is the result of logic and brawn being able to dominate emotion."

"I thou' I did too, mate," she answers with a slur. "But afta' bearin' witness to all this high weirdness, I decided ma life's too shor' not to tip 'em back. And ya forgot male egos, mate. Fragile creatures."

A chuckle ripples through the three of us and it feels good to laugh.

"What are you going to do?" Paramel asks.

"Honor my agreement with *Not Who* and throw Raga into the Source Vortex," I say. I can't look at either woman. "I do not view males as superior to females."

"Got that righ'," Dr. Monica says. "But they do."

"I view us as equals of different strengths," I say. "Ki needs comparable measure of males and females in order to thrive. It's Bezaliels that get in the way. They dilute clear thinking. Every human or hybrid, no matter their sex or gender, possesses a probability for cruelty...or kindness."

"Spoken like a true Balancer," Paramel says. "I agree with you, but I also tend to like it when males underestimate me."

"I need a favor," I say. I reach into a strial hide bag and pull out Basasael's sphere, the one he gave me when we were trapped in the Xaradin cage. Its shiny metal feels cold to the touch. "Do you know what this might be?" I softly toss it between my palms like a baseball.

"May I?" Paramel takes the object from my hands, rotates it back and forth in her palm as if it's a crystal ball, which it sort of looks like, but isn't, until her eyes almost pop out of her head. "I saw you put this in your bag at the Fewoulz lair...Holy fucking asteroids!"

"*What?!*" Dr. Monica and I ask in unison. We sit a little straighter and lean into Paramel.

"This is the master link between the Source and Ki!" Paramel whisper-yells as she kneels and scrutinizes the sphere more closely. Her eyes flicker between me and Dr. Monica, who looks over my shoulder with great interest.

"Master link?" I ask. "What does that mean?"

"Centuries ago, Vikings used Iolite spheres as navigational tools through winding astral paths...but *this?* This sphere is different from any other on Ki...it possesses a much higher vibrational power. Where did you find this?"

"Basaseal gave it to me," I say.

"Oh, Samantha..." She cups her free hand over her mouth, lowers it, and whispers, "He's your father! Legend says it is passed from one Balancer to another, a birthright."

"You know Basaseal?" I ask.

"Who is Basaseal?" Dr. Monica asks.

"He is renowned among celestrial Vikings as a great Drengr, a fearless warrior," Paramel says. "The sphere only passes through kindred. During the Ki Conflict, before the fires, floods, and plagues, and *waaaaay* before Lumeria or Atlantis, it is said an angel, a warrior of God, carried this sphere to an oracle, a high priestess named Avgi living in Theopetra's Cave outside Thessaly in Greece. He ordered her to take it to the monks of Meteora. This sphere, it's known as 'God's Rock.'" Paramel trembles, looking at her reflection in the sphere.

"Meteora?" I ask. "Annunan mentioned Meteora to me...said it was destroyed."

"'It's a place 'suspended in air' with monasteries perched atop vertical peaks," Paramel says. "Monks used to climb these soaring stones to settle in the caves and hollows, to serve as intermediaries between Kihogs and celestrials and to hide from war. Elemorphia went *underground* while the monks *elevated* their ground."

Dr. Monica makes the sign of the cross. I roll my eyes at her because she's not even remotely Catholic. She's an atheist. But her action makes me think about Eido and if she's having a change of heart about God. Eresh said Eido is a wisdom king in temporary human form who precedes the Balancer. "*He is neither omniscient, omnipotent, nor an object of refuge, worship, or harm. Eido has made himself Light, a symbol of the divine in sentient beings, sent here at the request of Saratu.*" It would only make sense if Eido came from Meteora, along with some of the other Sherpas.

I lean over and pull a map from my satchel, roll it out, and trace a finger along the route from Nepal to Meteora. The distance between the two is about 3600 miles, give or take, but that isn't what strikes me. Every country between Nepal and Meteora is a damn near straight line through Central Asia, the Near and Middle East, and the border of Western Europe. Our team is deep underground exactly between the two, somewhere under Iran, close to the ancient city of Verkana, which means "wolf" in ancient Avestan, an old Persian language.

"Theopetra's Cave is said to be the oldest human construction on Ki, dating back 250,000 years," Paramel says. "But it's actually much older...and not built by humans." She hands the sphere back to me. "This sphere has the power to plunge Ki into complete darkness but enables a Balancer to see what is otherwise invisible. Legend also claims Basaseal hid the sphere from Nephilim and Bezaliels. It's considered a master link between the Source and Ki. This *Me'* contains the Seven Seals and restores profound cosmic connection."

"It's pronounced 'may'?" I roll up the map and put it away, taking up the sphere for another look.

"Yes, but spelled M-e'. They're known as decrees of the divine housed in physical objects," Paramel says. "You've got the master *Me's* in that sphere."

"This is heaps bad," Dr. Monica whispers. "Ya can' jus' go carryin' around a rock o' God in your strial hide, mate!"

"I don't disagree with you, Monica, but I don't exactly have a lot of safe storage options near the center of Ki."

"What are the Seven Seals?" I ask. "I've read about the Seven Seals in the Christian Bible in the Book of Revelation, but Basaseal wasn't very clear about that."

"Mate, it **must** be the Seven Seals in the Bible," Dr. Monica says.

"Human males rewrote the Bible to convert the masses to monotheistic patriarchy," Paramel says with an eyeroll. She sighs and looks up at the phony sky, now glittered with faux stars and planets, trying, I think, to remember. "The way I understand it," Paramel says with a furrowed brow, "is that some Christian scribes took great liberties with the apocalyptic Seven Seals vision by John of Patmos in the Book of Revelation. My parents taught me that the ancient Seven Seals hail from Sumer, and they aren't seals at all, but forty-nine divine decrees, divided into seven groups, all having to do with Apocalypses."

"Apocalypses as in plural?" I ask.

"Yes," Paramel says. "Unfortunately, Kihogs added, subtracted, or completely twisted divine decrees with subjective interpretations, phony *Me's*, and mistranslations. In other words, humans and their Nephilim handlers muddied the plot. Truth got lost and we don't understand Me's for what they really are. Kihogs and Nephilim also launched a discredit campaign against Basaseal, claiming he was a fallen angel...well, he was in a way, but he was never a Bezaliel, Nephilim or devil the way humans might think of them."

"Basaseal must have retrieved this sphere from Avgi," I say.

"Avgi was tasked to guard the Seven Seals and bless them if a Balancer turns them over for safekeeping," Paramel says with a sage nod. "She was a monk of the highest order. Meteora serves as a gateway to a place humans sometimes call Shambala but I know it as the Lost Kingdom of Lo—and still others call it Alinas. Your eye necklace is glowing and so is your forehead."

I lift the necklace off my chest and feel the warmth of its light on my neck and face. "What did Bilby send into my necklace the day we arrived?" I ask.

Paramel stands and brushes some of the lava dust from her thighs and steps down a ledge toward the fire pit. "Let's hope you don't have to use it," she says.

"Well, how am I supposed to know if I'll need to use it?" I ask. "I don't even know what *it* is!"

"You'll know," she says, walking toward Dr. Sterling and not looking back. "And you'll know what to do with it too." And with her words, she hops the ledge to Dr. Sterling, where he creates a spot for her next to him, and they nudge one another in a way future lovers do when the energy between them is just right.

"Samantha?" Dr. Monica asks, stretching her legs and looking out across the Fluffle. "Has there ever been a female Balancer?"

"I don't think so," I say. "Never a half-human one either."

"Maybe your kindred sent a bloody Sheila this time to get it righ'."

I shake my head and grin, staring into the fire.

She pulls her hat down to cover her face. "Night, mate."

<hr>

We take a different route toward the surface. The camels, what's left of them that haven't gone missing or been eaten, plod along carrying minimal supplies, guided by the Sherpas, who walk, again, mostly in silence. Like Saratu, the Sherpas exude an air of calm I find soothing. They appear to me as breathing examples of grace under fire, true servants of the Source, who live by the guidance that comes through their visions and meditations. They crave not *things* and strive for nothing—or nothingness as one of them told me. Observing them, I realize I still have much to learn about sentient transcendence.

Occasional posters along this trail near the opening of Ki offer kids for sale, *in all manner of age, size, and demographic,* available for experiments, slavery, sexual servitude, or to work as child warriors. Some of the metal or leather posters are shredded, dented, decades old crime relics, dating as far back as the 1940s and as recently as 1989. I rip one lagging poster from its last hook and stare at it in disbelief. This path, now abandoned by traffickers and their commodities of kids, is a discarded place...and when we confront a pile of small bones, the collective heartbeat of our team stops. I continue to look on them, bearing de facto witness to what must have been the horrendous final moments of these children. I make note of the grisly details, kids stripped of their futures, lives, and dignity—these exceptional universal miracles of the Source cut short.

"Aye, mate," Dr. Monica says. With a flick of her wrists, she expands an evidence bag. "I neva' get used to seein' this typo' cruelty."

"In my country," Dr. Kimathi says, moving in to help, and taking the bag from Dr. Monica, "this sort of cruelty is, unfortunately, quite common. Food shortages and poverty lead people to do unspeakable things."

"This level of human barbarity doesn't surprise me anymore," Reggie says.

"What? You don't feel dis' suffering?" Dr. Kanumba asks, one hand on her hip and the other arm outstretched to emphasize and draw our attention to macabre details.

"Oh, I feel it," Reggie says. He shakes his head. "It makes me angry as hell, but it doesn't surprise me." A tear trickles down his cheek. He's been *off* for weeks, quiet and withdrawn. I figured it was the caves and he's probably missing Barbara more than he'd ever admit.

The echo of our work bounces off walls of the ravine and through the caverns. I can only imagine how horrendous the terrified screams and sobbing were when these kids lost their lives. We bag a few of the bones and cover the rest, each of us taking a moment of silence. I think about the parents of these babies. Did they spend their lives wondering what happened to their children? Did they die with tremendous loss and heartache forever embedded in their own bones? Or did they maybe sell their own children out of a sense of despair and desperation? I feel a push of air blow past me and hear a hushed whisper echoing from a nearby tunnel. Vigo's ears point to attention, his eyes latched into the darkness of another cavern. Kitsune leans in close to me. Our crew falls into abrupt silence. Hogan and his team ready their weapons. "Luca," I whisper. "How many tunnels around here like this one?"

"Around seven, according to my calculations," he says. "Four of them are no longer accessible due to rockslides or hardened lava."

Movement in the shadows near the edge of a trench seizes every fiber of my senses. A large rat scurries past to hide among some rubble and a few bats follow. Where there's rats and bats, there's a surface nearby—we're almost topside.

"Hello, Samantha," a man says, stepping into the light, his arms raised in surrender. "Please, don't shoot." He staggers but quickly rights himself. He's alone...and almost unrecognizable.

"Genin?" I ask. "Is that *you?*"

"It would be me..." he says, leaning against a wall, appearing weak.

"Aye, neva' though' I'd see this dobber's face again," Dr. Monica says with a scowl. "Ya must 'ave some crocodile clangers to be showin' up 'ere, ya' traitorous bloke...I oughta skin ya alive for what you did to Sam!"

Luca doesn't say anything, but he doesn't have to—the look on his face says it all. He takes three steps toward Genin.

Dr. Kimathi and Dr. Kanumba hide behind Hogan's team, backing up until they're safely out of sight.

"Luca, wait," I say. I step forward and block him from seizing Genin.

Genin looks as if he's done battle and couldn't handle another one even against an earthworm. Enlarged heavily bruised biceps, slightly damp with sweat, bulge beneath torn sleeves on his camouflage. His heavy black beard makes him look as if he's been stuck down here fighting a war for at least a decade. I hold in a bank of tears to keep them from bubbling over the edges of my eyes for all the anger I feel.

"Where's Dr. Evelyn?" I ask, searching behind him, expecting her to emerge from the shadows too, along with Lady Olivia Ross, the spoiled London "it" girl who financed their mission. Maybe Olivia and Dr. Evelyn are dead, which would serve them right traipsing into crypto-terrestrial territory with polluted intentions. All of this comes rushing back to me; the games, the angst, the jealousy, the horrors, our Ayahuasca trip into the caves below Plum Hook Bay as teenagers. It's far away, our past, yet our adolescence rushes forward in my mind like an avalanche. I trusted Genin. I loved him. He deceived me. He led Dr. Evelyn's team deep into Ki for the Tesla files on the other side of the world. *But how did he end up here?* The stakes are too high to let him slide away unscathed.

"Dr. Evelyn is headed to a Buddhist temple outside Nepal," he says. "She left me for dead."

"Not surprising," I say. "Why?"

"Why did she leave me for dead?" he asks.

"No. Why would she head to a temple near Nepal?"

"Nepal is a center for spirituality," Paramel says. "It has the most unique geophysical effects on the planet. And most celestrials pass through Nepal in physical or ethereal form from other worlds or parallel realms."

Shambala. The Lost Kingdom of Lo. Alinas. "Why would Dr. Evelyn head to Nepal?" I ask.

"It's a transit point," Paramel says. "Of collective agreement, entanglement, wisdom, and passage…"

And with Paramel's words, I remember:

We enter the monastery through gigantic iron gates. Monks in orange robes mill about an oversized veranda. We're led to a stone courtyard near the top of the building. Nuns in bright pink robes ready a feast. Each lay red, orange, and yellow print block cloths on the ground. A bounty of rice, goat meat, cheese, dumplings, and peppers settle over delicately handwoven or blocked fabrics. Below us rests a large square pool. Lotus flowers bounce and float around it like fish bobbers, tightly closed, save one that bursts open wide and white, opening symmetrical petals skyward…

"Saratu locates water in the desert through her feet," I say. "She sends and receives messages to crypto terrestrials all over this planet. Genin." I take in a deep breath to brace myself against what I hope he doesn't say. "What does Dr. Evelyn plan to do?"

"She plans to close the Source Vortex after she retrieves your daughter."

"Jesus Christ," Reggie says.

Genin collapses. And everything rushes at me at once in slow motion. Bennie escaped Norad 611 with Hope. What better place to hide an Emergent than in a mountaintop monastery under the care of a fully-fledged Ceitan, one able to adopt physical appearances that mirror cultures across this universe? And what better place to hide a Source Vortex?

Saratu had called her ability, "multiplicity of universality" to be able to expand from spark to any form and back again. Ceitans deliver curriculums of light to planets to help raise intelligent forms out of duality. Unfortunately, Kihogs, according to Luca, haven't budged a bit on the spectrometer of enlightenment. And Saratu is understaffed and overworked, her Earthly cause to raise human vibration a thankless and never-ending job. Ceitans are known to take on the harshest of challenges, even in remote places like a wispy arm of the Milky Way Galaxy.

"We've got to get to Nepal," I say. "Saratu's in danger. Luca, I need your help to beat Evelyn to her destination."

"I can call the Ether V, but it only has room for two," he says.

"And it's unstable," I say.

"We didn't exactly crash at Oxford," Luca says, a pinch of irritation seeping into his voice and traipsing across his brow. "Problems occur any time the Ether V flies over Earth's gravity field."

"We don't have time for problems or crashes," I say. "We need another way."

Reggie and Hogan each hoist one of Genin's arms over their shoulders, and their height difference makes Genin look like a lopsided scarecrow, his chin rolling along his chest.

"Leave him," I say. "He betrayed us."

"He didn't betray us," Reggie says. "I asked him to switch sides."

I practically drop my blade. "What?! You *asked* him to?"

"Recon," Reggie says. "I knew Evelyn was up to something big when she showed up at Harrington House. I just didn't know *how* big."

"And what about Lady Olivia Ross?" I ask. "What sort of trust was Genin exercising when he decided to nut out his wedding tackle on *her*?"

"Um, mate," Dr. Monica says, latching onto a camel harness. "Not exactly how we use tha' phrase..." I toss her a dirty look. "Ah, neva' mind..."

"All part of the plan," Reggie says. "He's quite the raven and it was *your* idea."

"My idea?!" I say. "I didn't plan for him to fuck Lady Olivia! What do you mean he was quite the *raven*? You had him *honey-trap* that spoiled bitch?"

"You requested Genin as your plus one for the Harrington Ball when you were at Langley and Abar ordered you to go!" Reggie says. "You *knew* he'd stack up well against—" He looks at Luca then drops his head.

"Reggie!" I yell.

"Samantha, hello?" Luca says, lightly waving his arms. "Fiancé over here!"

"Not now, Luca," I say. "Reggie, why in the hell would you withhold this information and make me think Genin was a traitor?"

"You had no need to know," he says. "And Vor wouldn't allow the clearance. I needed you to be genuinely upset. I thought it best under the circumstances."

"Me, of all hybrids, had **no need to know**?" I ask, feeling rage bubble up inside. "*Asteroids!* I hate this compartmentalized bureaucratic bullshit." I can't decide if I want to hit Reggie or shoot him, but I switch gears to avoid doing both. I suck in a deep breath and settle on a low, measured tone instead of stomping off. "Luca, I don't care which one of your inventions you pull from your arsenal or your arse, but we need to get as many fighters to Saratu as quickly as possible."

"I know a quick way to Nepal," Paramel interrupts. "But you're not going to like it..."

We're outside, in the night air, running down a path toward Saratu's monastery outside Nepal, a herd of hybrids, humans, camels, and about twelve Elemorphia carrying an unconscious Genin. I'm still trying to right my atoms after being shoved down a Fluffle hole, scrambled into nanoparticles, and teleported directly here. The technology isn't perfect. We're about a mile away, a steep climb. Paramel told us that teleportation, at least at this time, is something humans and hybrids can only do a few times in their sentient lives without going mad or getting killed.

But oh, the stars! Real stars! Cool evening air bathes my face and I suck in oxygen and ozone, happy to be topside but dreading what's about to happen. A few chickens strut and peck and flap their wings to a chorus of squawks when they bumble out of our way on a dirt road. People will get hurt tonight, I think, and that always bothers me.

I thank the Source we're too high up for the provincial towns-folk below to see this ramshackle spectacle of humans, hybrids, and otherworldlies about to converge on their sacred place—the monastery perched high above.

Our privacy is short-lived. My heart hammers its way through my chest when a wide-eyed farmer and his wife round a bend and startle us with their straw-stuffed wooden cart pulled by an ox. Their eyes widen in shock, but they swiftly put their heads down, pretending not to see us and scurry the animal downhill, trying to shrink from view. I fear they'll tell the entire village. Then I realize how silly they'll sound. I imagine people would have quite a laugh at their expense if they mentioned they passed an overly tall intergalactic female Viking, camels, a camo-clad special ops team, and a bunch of hybrids in spacesuits, accompanied by a dog, a falcon, and a fox—and a small contingent of utterly bizarre-looking Elemorphia.

"Let's move off the road and disperse, shall we?" I say. "We'll reconvene at the base of the monastery, near the west wall.

We reach the gates to the grand feat of human ingenuity built into the side of a mountain. A late summer storm blows up from the valley and lashes trees lining the road. A funnel cloud in the distance stretches a fat dark finger from the sky and grazes dancing rice fields below. But the specter of sudden violent weather isn't the most chilling element I see. It's the little girl far up in the tower looking down on us with a smile, her long wavy hair and pale skin hauntingly out of place among a site known for head-shaved Buddhist initiates.

I strain my neck to get a closer look at the little girl. She's too old to be my daughter Hope. I let out a sigh of relief until I wonder why in Source's name a little girl might be in Saratu's tower.

"Saratu is throwing a party tonight," Reggie says. "Look."

"What?" I turn away from the tower for less than a second, but when I look back again the little girl is gone.

A gate guard examines invitations and checks them off against a list in his hands. Tuxedo-clad men and evening-gowned ladies point and laugh at us, then clap. *Shit!* So much for remaining incognito. Another guard waves us through. "You must be the entertainment," Camael says with a wink, the only stray he gives away from his cover as private and convincingly human-looking security. "Go around this way and take the back stairs..."

RAGA

"I'M FEELING A LITTLE PRESSURE," I whisper to Dr. Monica.

The vast corridor of Saratu's private chamber is supported by immense blood-red round columns. A cold front tiptoes through and a light breeze tousles wisps of our hair. The chill causes a natural shiver to slide down my spine. Through glassless windows, distant snow-capped mountains crowd into one another and stretch their pointed white peaks through misty clouds, as if vying for the sky's attention. Birds chirp from *inside* while the monastery's bones, its timbers and floors, rattle and creak. Stone chiseled steps feel cool and comfortable under my bare feet. Ceremonial silk paintings of deities ripple overhead. We ascend the tower around another winding path of carved stairs. Thin tapestries gently sway, pushed by the air of our passing. A variety of orchids hang suspended by their roots all over the building. And somewhere in the distance, I hear the pounding beat of techno music, seriously out of place against this ancient rustic décor.

"You've got this, mate," Dr. Monica whispers as we climb.

My tension rises with each step until we arrive at a large crackled green double door decorated with heavy brass knobs. I haven't been here since Tetana's funeral, months ago. Tetana was Saratu's Ki wife, an American fighter pilot killed in an F-16 during an advance directive under Operation Vigilant Warrior. The report stated, 'mechanical failure of unknown origin'. Her last word, according to aircraft carrier control, was a calmly uttered *"fuck."* Tetana's funeral was the only time I saw Saratu the Ceitan cry. All three of us share the distinction of graduating from Dr. Evelyn Dennison's Plum Hook Bay academy for fucked-up foster kids.

Two monks, one on each side, pull thickly braided ropes.

Slowly, it creaks open...

...but Saratu the Dorje is not here.

The wooden altar and the ivory pillows are the same. Candles litter the floor, leading up five steps, accompanied by the soft glow of hundreds of oblong paper lanterns. But there are no saffron seated monks chanting on each side of this incandescent path like last time. Crystal bowls stuffed with tightly fisted lotus buds, go unattended. Dr. Evelyn always said if Saratu was left to wander the world, she'd either be crucified within minutes or make so many friends she'd start a new religion. Instead, she won favor with the Dalai Lama and was crowned as a Dorje, a White Tara, a goddess of wisdom and compassion made manifest. A single monk approaches us from out of the shadows, "This way," he says.

"Jampa?" I ask, remembering him from my last visit.

He presses an index finger to his lips and motions for us to follow.

"Not you," he says to our team. "You." He points to me. "And...him." He points to Luca. "The rest of you please wait here for instructions. Tinley will be along shortly."

"Tinley?" I say, feeling incredulous. "Tinley died last time I was here. He inhaled one of my mom's cigarettes. I saw him myself, a blue and rigid corpse in the courtyard after a failed mission to assassinate the Dorje."

"Lots of Tinley's here," Jampa says with a smile, the kind of serene and calming smile only monks seem to master. "Ex-Chinese mafia members make good monks...and warriors."

"Oh."

Luca and I follow Jampa into Saratu's personal quarters behind the altar. "If we make it out of here alive," Jampa says, "I'll make you the best mushroom tea you've ever had in any of your lives."

"Comforting," Luca says.

Thick purple cushions sit plump under a sheer ivory canopy. Beyond this, Luca momentarily marvels at the opulent room housing enough amenities to incur the wrath and jealousy of gods. It certainly rivals Harrington House...in a different, less dripping traditional Ralph Lauren foxhunt sort of way. Gold chalices, ancient artifacts, and bronze figures settle with the dust on smartly placed shelves. A highly detailed tapestry of Shambala hangs over her colorful hand-carved teak desk, a visual feast.

Saratu rounds a corner, adorned in green and golden robes, wearing a small tiara of black pearls and copper armbands attached to exposed biceps. She's bedecked in a light layer of white scarves. "Samantha," she says, arms outstretched, and embraces me in a tight hug I don't refuse. "I have missed you many days and nights." Kitsune jumps up and down and pounces around her. Saratu slips a treat from her garments and gives it to my fox, who snatches it and hides under a table.

"I have missed you too," I say. "Unfortunately, our reunion isn't a pleasant one."

"I've been planning," she says. A visible white aura surrounds her, typical of Ceitans. It turns from pale cloudy blue to defined low-glow gold. "Camael filled me in on what has transpired. We are as prepared as we can be. Dr. Evelyn is the guest of honor for tonight's party."

"If that's the case, we're going to need all the help we can get," Luca says. "Odds are not in our favor."

"Pardon me, Saratu," I say. "This is my fiancé Lord Luca Harrington. Luca, this is Saratu the Dorje."

"Ah, the notorious Lord Harrington," she says through squinted eyes. "I can smell your Bezaliel mist from here. You fight it mightily and hide it well."

"And the renowned Ceitan made manifest on Earth," he says, crossing the room and lightly kissing her hand. "An exquisite inaugural entry to corporeal form as a Dorje."

"Careful," Saratu teases him. "If I were straight, I might push Sam out of the saddle, but then again, rumor has it you're contaminated."

"Highly," he says.

"The question is, can you be trusted?" she asks.

"I don't know," Luca answers. "Can anyone ever be fully trusted? Can we even trust the reflection we see staring back at us in the mirror?"

I take the glass of consecrated water she pours and we clink hammered goblets.

"I need your help," I say.

I walk over to the window and look down at the unassuming lotus pool, square in shape, and typically a space reserved for reflection. Like the fountain back at Harrington House, the lotus pool has a normal shallow bottom—until it doesn't—and rather than it leading underground to Usta—this thing goes asteroids knows where, into a swirling bottomless vortex—the Source Vortex, where space and time goes off-scale, and may lead to doorways of alternate realities or tunnels to other universes—or perhaps, anything that falls into its event horizon shrinks away to non-existence. The white lotuses floating about are knotted tight, not even one petal peeping toward a descending night sky. The pool has evaporated a few inches.

"You have my help," Saratu says without hesitation. "I also heard you recovered your memories."

"Most of them," I say. "What do you know about Dr. Evelyn and her team?"

"I know she failed to locate the Tesla files," Saratu says. "She's enraged. Her entire team, except for Genin, I heard, was vaporized by Usta...but Eresh said Evelyn had a band of Fewoulz kill her team to maintain their silence." A shiver snakes up my spine. Genin's still unconscious and being cared for by some of the Sherpas near the nunnery. They don't know if he'll live but I did swipe some of Bennie's salve on his wounds.

Saratu continues. "My monks tell me Dr. Evelyn succeeded in retrieving the sphere from the Astral Weavers at Plum Hook Bay—and she has made many Kihog and Nephilim friends, some here with us tonight."

"Only a Balancer with a password can earn the sphere," I say, feeling overcome by dread. The Astral Weavers would never hand it over to a human, especially a human like her."

"They would if it was a decoy," Saratu says, her eyes clear and wide. "Lozen said Dr. Evelyn thought she was very clever with her extraction."

"Who planted a decoy?" I ask. "*You?*"

"Not I." Saratu points behind us into her office. "He did."

Camael steps out of the shadows, and how he got here so quickly from ground zero, only fully fledged Camaeliphim know.

"Remember when you and Genin went into the caves at Plum Hook Bay?" he asks.

"We were sixteen," I say. "Bennie concocted a brew of Ayahuasca and we..."

"You stole a gold pendant cube buried in the roots of a buckeye tree." He picks up a small bronze statue of Buddha and runs a finger through some of its detailing without looking at me.

I touch the Pleiades pendant under my suit. Still there, still intact—and scan through memories of Plum Hook Bay. I remember that night, that trip to the caves *under* the NASA side of the farm:

A gust of wind sweeps over our heads...a thunderous boom... cave dust. Without warning, one of the mummies opens its eyes, and there is no pupil, no iris—just eerie royal blue lights emanating from ancient sockets. The glowing sphere they guard goes cold-steel dark. Something pushes me—hard. I fall...and mentally toss Genin into the circle...Black wings flap overhead... breathe, Sam! One...two...three...four... A man...an Army uniform... the hazy out-of-focus face of a soldier. I can't read his name tag. As fast as Genin and I fell into this cave, we're sucked out of it, through a kaleidoscope of lights, tunnels, and diagrams, spinning... I sit up disoriented, hands black, blistered, swollen, and covered in Bennie's salve.

"That was *you*?" I ask.

"It was your father," Camael says. "As a Balancer, he was the only celestial on the planet who could touch that sphere without getting killed. When Lozen told me what you and Bennie were up to, I pulled Basaseal out of hiding and into service to switch out the spheres. Unfortunately, for your father, it was a prime opportunity for Fewoulz to capture and imprison him."

"Why would you risk pulling Basasael out of hiding?"

"You barely understood you were a hybrid," Camael says. "You weren't ready for the power of the sphere or to act as a Balancer. And besides, you're my niece—you're family—and while we may not always be visible to you, we try to be there for you when needed."

"I thought my dad gave the sphere to Avgi at Meteora," I say, feeling odd. Outside of Reggie, Vigo, Luca, Dr. Monica, and Kitsune, I never felt like part of a family, especially an ethereal family I barely know. "For safekeeping."

"Impressive you'd know the story," Camael says. "I can only surmise Paramel listened to the oral histories of her ancestors and shared them with you."

"She was helpful," I say.

"Basasael retrieved the sphere from Meteora a century before your rebirth. He gave it to the Astral Weavers who remain under the Earthly protection of *Firelanders* on the other side of this world. We didn't realize it then, but keeping that sphere right under the nose of Fewoulz was the safest place for it to be...and then you came along..."

"Firelanders?" Saratu asks.

"Descendants of Druids," I answer. "They moved from the UK to America and settled in northeastern Ohio near my hometown after the American Revolution. They're typically a nonconfrontational and pastoral sort of people. I came along and ruined everything, didn't I?"

"Au contraire," Camael says. "You were right on cue, just as you are tonight and just as you were when I first found you in an American drugstore stealing lipstick."

"I don't do that anymore," I say. "Steal, I mean."

"Hybrids learn not to do a lot of things as they grow in body and mind," he says. A look of understanding and compassion crosses his brow. "And now I need the two of you cleaned up and ready for a horror show at ground zero. Sources tell me Dr. Evelyn will be here within the hour."

I'm nervous about our strategy, but Reggie says a slight case of edginess is a good thing because cocky overconfident leaders typically experience certain defeat.

Luca and I clean up and dress for the party, an art exhibition put together to draw out my aunt. The art is brought in by curators the globe over, Luca said. This event, usually held annually and elsewhere, is attended by humans with obscenely obnoxious wealth and connections. I wish this were just a party but... Dr. Evelyn. People could get killed. People *will* get killed.

Lots of them. So many things could go wrong, probably will go wrong.

Saratu picked out my pale blue dress with detachable full-length skirt. It's quite the bustier showstopper lined with Luca's latest invention of bullet-, fire-, and poison-proof fabric—a silicon-elasto-polymer—mixed with a bit of her Ceitan powder—space dust that she says offers a degree of protection against negative energy. This dress will do me little good if I get hit or shot in the face or cleavage...or get flung into a Source Vortex. It's a ridiculous get-up to marshal troops. I'm surprised Saratu picked such a bold and seductive statement.

Breathe, Sam.

I slide my arm through Luca's. "Damn, you look hot," he says. "I could take you right here and now."

"Not bad for serving as your arm candy," I say. "You ready?"

"For their reaction, or seeing Dr. Evelyn?"

"Both," I say.

Without hesitation, we walk straight into the party. People gasp, point, whisper, or stare. We knew they would. The last this world had heard, Luca and I got engaged at the Harrington Ball in the UK and disappeared after his ex, Lady Olivia Ross, went missing.

Funny, I don't recognize anyone here. I thought at least a few people from the Harrington event would show, maybe Sir Harry Fairchild or the Duke, the upper echelon being a small world. I spot a trickle of D-rated celebrities, a couple of over-hyped musical artists, a "compromised" comedian, a few washed-up sports figures, one suspect filmmaker, and some moguls from one industry or another. A few religious types, not monks, stand surrounded by a bunch of glittery clingers-on, who wear too much makeup and too little clothes.

"Champagne?"

We snag two glasses from a passing silver tray.

Techno music blares too loudly and drowns out conversational voices of the affluent and artistic. Their bright robes, capes, sparkly jewels, fur, and bejeweled walking sticks are a cornucopia of excess. We pass through the din into a quieter part of the party. "Do you know who I am?" someone asks another someone. I feign charmed delight and join them, one hand plastered to my strial hide bag, which I thought would be seriously out-of-place, but oddly isn't, given the absurd spectacle of flamboyantly dressed guests.

Luca and I hold our own among a throng of deeply curious onlookers, who press in on us. I'm thankful paparazzi is barred from this event. The partygoers, I notice, exert their pretension on one another, each giving in to their vices in a similar yet personal way. I observe them, study their auras, their snobbish delusions of elevated exclusivity, and common frailties, hidden under glittery baubles, shimmering silks, faux laughter, and fluffy feathers. They'd be instant casualties on the front lines of a galactic war, I think.

"Do you see her?" I ask.

"No, this is a bit like playing spot the criminal at a prison," Luca says. "Yet a whole lot more repulsive. I'm not sure why Saratu thinks it's a good idea for us to attract this much attention. We've entered a den of lions."

"I only see celebrities and rich people," I say.

"Demons walk among us," Luca says. And the way he says this, as he scours the room, causes goosebumps along my arms and thighs. "I'm concerned about your glowing spiral."

"Compared to what?" I ask. "That guy over there holding a cobra?"

"You're a walking target," he says.

We're approached by a girthy man who reminds me of an overfed rottweiler, except his curly hair is too gunmetal gray for that—maybe an overstuffed poodle. He extracts a cigar from his mouth, its stubby tip soaked in saliva. "Lord Harrington, old chap! Where the hell have you been hiding? The whole world still talks about your absence! We all thought you were dead! Good god, man, you don't look a single day older! We haven't seen or heard from you in years!"

Years?

"Nice to see you, Skiggens," Luca says. But he doesn't smile. In fact, nothing about Luca's demeanor conveys that it's nice to see anyone tonight, especially this guy. I feel Luca's muscles tense beneath his tuxedo. I wish he'd lighten up—but then again— there's nothing to be light about. The darkness swirling around him is positively chilling. This is not an opportune time for his Bezaliel mist to kick in.

"Ah, this must be the mysterious lassie everyone's talkin' about," Skiggens says, eyeing me up and down as if I'm a rare steak newly punched with a sales sticker. "We thought you were dead too!" His shirt cuffs are trimmed in orange and white fox fur. He elbows Luca's free side in the ribs. "Ya old devil! Tender bonnie flesh. I knew you liked redheads but didn't think you were into..." He looks around the room and puckers his oily bugle lips. "...*this* sort of thing."

Skiggens reaches out to run two thick fingers along my upper arm, but Luca grabs them before they contact my skin and bends them backward until I hear a crack. "You refer to my fiancée as tender bonnie flesh again, Skiggens," Luca seethes, "and I'll have your ballocks mounted on a plaque and hung over the entryway of Harrington House. Understand? This lady is *the* Countess of Skye. You will treat her as such."

Skiggens clears his throat but doesn't utter a sound, not even a grunt or moan of pain escapes his mouth. He refuses to look at or recognize me. He fades through a few shades of white until a low-grade tomato color tints his puffy cheeks. It's the only giveaway he's hurt and trying to recover. He replants the cigar stub with his healthy hand, glares at me, and walks off without another word, hiding cracked fingers inside a trouser pocket.

I wave away remnants of swirly stinking cigar smoke. "Luca, you were a bit harsh on that old man."

"We're surrounded by society's worst," he says. "And he must be going senile because I ran into him at Sir Harry Fairchild's gentlemen's club in London before I left the UK a few months ago. It hasn't been years since I've seen him. I don't like this crowd."

"Pity," I say. "You fit right in." I lift my skirt to take two steps forward, but Luca touches my elbow.

"You know as well as I do that when it comes to clandestine work," he says, "we're sometimes forced to walk among the intuitively noxious—although usually not so openly and unprotected."

I yank my elbow from his grasp. "True," I say, looking up at him with defiance. "To reap intel, but it shouldn't be at the expense of broken bones without just cause. Take your hand off me."

"I disagree," Luca says, tugging me closer. "You think I was too hard on him?" he whispers. "He's an arms dealer."

"So what?" I say. "So are you."

"True," Luca says, his eyes darting around the swarm. "I arm people with the right to defend themselves against governments or gangs' hell-bent on mass bodily harm. But I have not nor will I ever...how do I say this to you...spend quality time with old men who defile and then dismember children." He presses in on me. "I told you when we met, I prefer fully grown hybrids, but only one in particular, and that is you."

I almost spit out my champagne and set it down on a passing tray. "Skiggens?"

"Not just Skiggens," Luca whispers in my ear. "Look around. It's true these people are here for *art*. Go ahead, take a closer look at the *art*."

I lean into a piece positioned on an easel next to us. It reminds me of something Salvador Dali and Picasso might create together after a night of heavy drugs and an orgy, full of flesh tones and red paint, garish and gauche with a single eyeball mounted in a cube staring blankly into the crowd.

"Look very closely, Sam. Tell me what you *see?*"

The piece is entitled, *Suffer the children, and forbid them not, to come unto me...*my shoulders tense and a deep pang of sorrow punches my gut as another shiver sprints through me. "This isn't a painting," I gasp. "Luca, I'm going to be sick." Rage and vengeance race through me, leaking out of my pores with heightened unbridled anger and sweat.

The *canvas* is human skin and the dark eye, once belonging to a child, preserved in an acrylic cube. Glancing around the room, I spot another *piece,* a little girl, maybe two or three years old completely dipped in wax, her pale dead arms mottled with needle marks, bruises, and grotesque lesions, and with gouged-out cheeks. It is unquestionably at the top of the list of the most horrible things I've ever seen—even worse than the underside of the nuclear reactor at Plum Hook Bay—and that was more than bad. I struggle to control my gag reflex and push the involuntary bile back down my throat with a hard swallow.

A strong desire to drain the blood from every being in this room percolates in my head. I'm precariously balanced between states of stand down and slay. I can't believe I'm witness to this atrocity, confronted by unspeakable final moments and remnants of intense suffering. It's raw, direct, and intolerable to every fiber and faculty of my being—but not to these humans or Nephilim—they appear enthralled and sickeningly giddy. I turn my face into Luca's shoulder, tears of compassion and fury breaching my eyes.

"Do. Not. React," Luca whispers. "Hold onto me if you must but please put on your best 'we're here to buy' poker face."

"But...*buy?*"

"If you want justice, we must completely maintain our composure." He twists my upper arm, as if dialing down my mortified reaction. "We must act as if we enjoy this sort of thing. Play your best poker, Samantha."

"Nobody would believe this," I whisper. What I don't say is that I want nothing but swift suffering for the barbarians in this room. I latch my arm through Luca's again, boiling over with rage.

"These people count on nobody ever believing it," Luca says. "It's how they continue to successfully operate under the radar."

"Why would Saratu engage this? She abhors violence and loves children. She's not..."

"No," Luca says. "It was arranged by Sir Bob. Saratu is an absent host. At Sir Bob's request, Saratu lent her space. When you want to capture a secretive global enterprise of predators, the best way to do so is corral them and infiltrate their base camp."

"Your comptroller at Harrington House arranged this?"

"Yes."

"I, I, I don't understand..." I say, my heart plummeting to my feet. "Sir Bob served in a military task force with Reggie...he doesn't seem like the type of man..."

"He isn't," Luca says. "This is a highly secretive event. The show goes on with or without us, every...single...year...and has for decades. Sir Bob thought if he secured the venue, it would flush Dr. Evelyn out of her hole."

"*Decades?!*"

"This party is only one small revolting display of depravity. Dr. Evelyn is its self-interested curator of corpses," Luca says, shifting his eyes over the throng. "She is also, as we've learned, in the business of human and hybrid trafficking, gliding under a ruse of upper echelon respectability. These *pieces* are high-value trophies for society's most noxious and deadly."

Yellow body bags. This is what I remember about Dr. Evelyn at Plum Hook Bay. She had them delivered to her on the other side of the farm by the van-full. She's been a corpse collector for years—and now it appears, a murderer too.

"Why would you finance *this?*"

"I would *never* finance *this*," he says, his eyes glaring with disgust. "I was missing, remember? Sir Bob figures, and I agree, that by getting these bastards together in one space, if all goes well, we can kill...oh, about three hundred human and hybrid traffickers and scores more pedophiles tonight...give or take."

"And you don't think Dr. Evelyn will see right through Sir Bob's convenient and highly coincidental charade?" I ask. "She *knows* he works for you."

"She also knows I have Bezaliel mist coursing through me, and I suspect she can't resist our direct challenge," he says. "Evelyn is here to sell kids, and pieces of them, to the highest bidder...and she will use the crowd's energy, combining it with Bezaliel mist to close the Source Vortex. In her mind, if she kills a few hybrids and humans using her revolting collection as bait for an undeserved celestrial promotion, it sweetens her plans."

"She's sick," I whisper.

"Evelyn is beyond sick," Luca says. "And there isn't a court of law or any enforcement agency on this planet that can or will tap her out with justice."

"How can she get away with this for so long and not get caught?"

"Evelyn is the gatekeeper to walk-in closets full of skeletons, many in notoriously high places of power, influence and connections," Luca says. "Her contacts kill to keep these deaths covered up and graves unmarked," Luca says.

And then it occurs to me. "If Dr. Evelyn extinguishes the esteem and energy of kids, it diminishes the power of the Source Vortex," I say. "It enables Bezaliels already here to freely roam until she figures out a way for them to take form, whether it's parasitic or something else, a new species entirely. The lotus pool is evaporating."

A look of terror crosses Luca's face and he backs away from me. "As much as it troubles me," he says. "I must leave your side for a bit."

"Why?" I ask. "Did I say something wrong?"

He shakes his head and turns away, scouring a buffet table.

"Luca, we're on the same team," I say, feeling negative energy emanate off his skin like sparks. It gives me a horrible feeling. "Tell me what's wrong."

"We're always on the same team, Princess," he says, closing his eyes, then opening them again to look at me. "I struggle to contain my fury."

"Me too," I say. "It's difficult not to reach out and kill someone here."

"That's not it," he says.

"It's your Bezaliel mist," I say. "Is it drawing you into *liking* this sort of thing?" I ask, mentally readying myself for an unexpected battle against him, if necessary. "Is that what's happening? You're starting to feel and think like *them?*"

"Not in the way you may think," he says.

"Talk to me, Luca. Tell me what you're feeling, what you anticipate. Maybe it will help."

"It's...how can I describe it...unadulterated blood lust," he says. "If I start killing, I won't stop. I see the way these men and women ogle you, fantasize, and imagine putting their hands, tongues, and pieces of them on you and into you...and it infuriates me to my core."

"Breathe, Luca. Your reaction isn't inappropriate given the crimes they've committed. You're above this. You just told me to play poker. Come now."

"What's inappropriate," he says, breathing harder, his words echoing in a way that reminds me of a primal and barren desert wind, "is that I want to make you suffer for their desires...to push up against you even if you fight back, to dominate you, control you, force you under me, and demand your unwavering love, even if it hurts you, so they understand you're *mine.*"

"Okay," I say, my eyes locking with his. "That's inappropriate."

"Paramel warned me days ago that my Bezaliel mist would be a danger to you," he says. "I didn't want to believe her. And it's why Paramel was given express permission from the Ormian Council to leave the Isle of No Time and fight topside, to protect you—from me—as needed. The Ormian Council says I must accept my fate of infinite inanimation for inviolable crimes."

"So, you stood before them too."

"Yes."

"Luca," I say. "We've had to *accept* a lot of things...the death or disappearance of our parents and loved ones, illness, murder, struggle, abuse...and our duties. Acceptance can go fuck itself. I'm not giving up on you."

His wide blue eyes turn a lustrous anthracite and fix upon me as cold and polished as obsidian, but he doesn't say another word, and I'm not sure if it's because he can't or he won't.

"Leave me unattended," I say, not wanting him to leave my side, not here, not now, not ever.

"I am a hybrid of few regrets but inserting Bezaliel mist into my DNA and losing you all over again is my biggest and most painful." He hangs his head a moment before he recovers.

"I need to tell you something," I say, taking his hand. "I love you." I blurt it out...just as fast as if I'd snapped my fingers. "Love is a partnership. To be healthy, it must be interdependent."

"Samantha," he says, the rage in his eyes melting away. "I love you beyond time and measure...but the primitive mist coursing through me, and the human blood helping it along, render me a beast even worse than the ones surrounding us now."

"Before you go, you must know something else," I say. "I promised my hand in marriage to Annunan if I succeed with this mission."

"Annunan? He's married."

"I know," I say. "I mentioned this. He cited Sakar and said my father and uncle would approve the match, given that your blood is, um, compromised."

Luca's eyes glaze over. "Sakar is never enforced among Camaeliphim anymore."

"It's never been officially repealed either," I say.

Luca's blue irises disappear into inky black rings of rage, as if a sudden, severe storm passes through, one that promises untold damage. He crushes his glass into dust, without a drop of blood or other injury to his hand and looks away. "You're able to hold your own," he says. He pecks my cheek, and his lips feel ice cold. "Oh, look over there. The Countess of Teviot has just arrived."

And with that, Luca is gone.

EIGHTEEN

DR. EVELYN DENNISON, COUNTESS OF TEVIOT

DR. EVELYN STROLLS in and my heart dims. Traumatic memories leave a wake of turbulence in my gut. *Yellow body bags.* When she was a psychiatrist at Plum Hook Bay, I was sixteen and stole into the NASA side of the farm, the one place none of us foster kids were allowed to go—unless remanded there to a secret lab *under* the nuclear reactor and against our will. I remember *hiding on a cliff ledge. Three windowless black vans pulled up. Through the entry lab door comes Dr. Evelyn, dressed in blue scrubs, unzipping yellow body bags to check the lifeless limbs of corpses...*

...The huge hall of the monastery is held up by massive pillars that rise to the roof and disappear into murky blackness. The human part of me wishes I could climb all the way to the top of them, into deep space, and never return—but the hybrid in me refuses to thwart my calling and an opportunity, even if fleeting, for justice.

Across from me, a gentle splash of red liquid, a gruesome bucket-sized handmade fountain. Attendees dip their fingers and dab their cheeks, leaving blushed stains of what I don't want to imagine, and hope isn't real, but know to be true—the blood of innocents.

I accidentally back into a sculpture of two small, intertwined hands, their tiny wrists fitted with bronzed rope. It wobbles and I'm forced to catch it before it falls. Lamps sputter, flicker, and flare. I struggle to contain my fury along with the lights, which recover.

Maintain your composure, Sam.

I gently center the grotesque arrangement back on its precarious pedestal. Luca, I hope, will lose his composure after I lied to him about agreeing to marry Annunan. I'm betting that a pissed-off hybrid carrying Bezaliel mist might prove the fiercest of warriors. I just hope he isn't tempted to switch allegiance. I study the little hands before me and wonder about the life once attached to them. I've listened to survivor stories, and I have my own. The healing process and the guilt and shame are painful but their deaths even worse. My own trafficking experiences are often and unexpectedly relived through tears and flashbacks and bouts of post-traumatic stress. When I was a child, Dr. Evelyn made me an *offer*. I didn't get a choice to decline. My hands, head, and power were much smaller than hers at the time. Not anymore.

I exhume memories, alongside remembrances of friends, some of them unceremoniously buried and forgotten. These victims deserve more than thoughts, prayers, or willful blindness...they deserve due process and justice. Today, the *Now,* is just as good as any other to open the floodgates of retribution.

The monks are nowhere to be seen. It's then I notice that almost everything belonging to this monastery has been removed from the exhibition hall, as if Saratu purposely created a boundary, like a Cage of Savagery, for evil to loiter and remain contained. No one is allowed to roam up any of the stairways that lead to her quarters or the lotus pool.

Dr. Evelyn is taller and much younger-looking than I remember, dressed completely in white, a dress cinched hornet-tight at her waist. She's mimicking an angel of light, which we both know is a farce. Her complexion radiates vitality, the opposite of everything else slowly degenerating or artificially preserved in this room. In fact, Evelyn's positively beaming, and this unnerves me. Everything about this "party" is wrong, but her eerie yet beautiful countenance is even more so. She nods proudly at the turnout, her charm on high volume. She strides through the hall. Onlookers and bystanders step aside in awe. She goes around a pillar, through an exhibit marked *Veils of no Mercy,* and runs her hand over the knuckles of a half-rotted board littered with rusted nails and...small human thumbs.

Dr. Evelyn inspects her *work* with what I think is admiration, sniffs a decomposing piece of flesh carried along on a silver tray, and lightly fingers a small stack of razors. Someone in a burgundy cape clears space off a seriously out-of-place Victorian chair, its wood carved trim layered over with too much gold leaf. Evelyn sits down with every thread of luxurious overkill she can muster. People pay homage, bidding her devotion, to their death, effusively kissing her ass and hand with promises, but hoping, I suspect, to considerably underdeliver. Next to her, a live monkey is strapped in a box, virtually immobile up to its exposed head poking through a small hole. It spins and screeches in terror. It grows quiet after a few attendees bash it in the head with a mallet, cracking its skull like a walnut to extract and consume the spongy brain inside.

"What a scrumptious delicacy," some woman coos as she oyster-slurps white matter.

Until now, I thought eating monkey brain was an urban legend—but most things too horrible or supernatural to imagine, I suspect, are deliberately relegated to the annals of myth. Normal humans are still offput by such barbarity, which gives me hope for Kihogs, that the majority still possess compassion and shun this sort of thing. Evelyn dips a finger into the hole of the now dead simian's skull and brings it to her lips for a taste, as if testing vanilla cookie dough.

Eventually, Dr. Evelyn stands and grabs a passing bottle of wine and two crystal glasses. She steps through a free-standing double door of tiny blood-smeared handprints and heads toward me. She taps her heel-clad foot down two steps and flashes a huge insincere smile. "Hello, Scathatch. I think it's time we have a heart-to-hybrid chat. Holy water?" She lifts the bottle and light refracts a detached eye rolling around the bottom. She carefully pours a couple of inches of liquid, as if she's a monk performing a ritual, and hands me a glass.

"*Do. Not. React.*" I internally repeat Luca's mantra like a feed loop through my brain, but really want to fling a glass at her and lunge. I don't. I breathe and shake my head to decline.

"Oh, pity," she says wistfully. "This vintage is called, *An Eye for an Eye,* bought and bottled in Auschwitz post World War II. I thought you'd treasure the opportunity given your penchant for revenge and your covetousness of nice things." She sets the bottle on a simple rustic wooden bench and points her blueish fingers at my eye necklace for effect. "Ah, well, I'll toast for both of us...to bygone days!"

A voice inside me screams at Dr. Evelyn's nonchalant depravity. This can't be happening. I tell myself this is a night-mare—that I'll wake up in a hospital bed any moment, sixteen again, at Plum Hook Bay, the recipient of one of her drug-infused "down-the-rabbit-hole" concoctions. But another voice, that cold, sodden, wet blanket of reason, born from Reggie's relentless and regimented military, martial arts, and meditation training, has taught me to trust my instincts. And my instincts scream that something is terribly, awfully, wrong here—something well beyond what I'm able to *see.*

This world, I have learned, is full of secrets and evil, actions and things, that defy common or scientific knowledge and discredit Truth. Gifts of discernment, supernatural skills, visions, and trans dimensional and otherworldly beings exist, no matter how ridiculous they might initially appear or sound to the populace, or how much humans bury their heads in denial or time —"*angels*" DO walk among us, capable of turning a cheek or delivering wrath according to our oaths and allegiances. But so too, roam the opposite of angels. And this is my calling—to fetter out what unbalances Ki and cast it back to where it belongs, far away from this outpost of a repository known by humans as Earth. I remember.

A small brass bowl of water ripples on the floor next me, clear and collected—the *real* holy water, because without it, Life is impossible. Water is an astonishing natural element, able to extinguish fire, quench earth, or energize ether. Water is equal parts order and chaos—a Balancer's ally. To my right is an open door set between two additional pillars, craggy and worn yet still doing their job despite ages of weathering and expectation, a bit like Reggie. "So," I say, "you want to have a heart-to-hybrid chat, but you have no heart. This can only mean one thing. You, Raga, have taken corporeal form within my aunt."

"I claim nothing, Scathatch." Her voice is low and warm, and chilling beyond my bones, like a night spent swimming naked in the Arctic.

I sense a source of pride in her telling me this. "Then why bother with chit-chat?" I ask, not taking my eyes off her, wondering how Raga got into Evelyn and why.

"Bennie is such a smart boy," she hisses. "But a Source Bearer compromises chaos."

"As does a Balancer," I say. "But I'm told I'm not easy to kill."

"True," Evelyn says with a smirk, looking at nothing or thinking of something, I can't really tell. "But with the right sort of holding cell, you can be *detained* like your father, or better yet, *inanimated*. Your blood of unknown origin, your *BOUO* is worth more on this planet than all its resources combined. A millionth of a drop of your blood infinitely powers interstellar travel," she says. "And reverses biological aging."

"So, you harvest hybrids like me to sell to the highest bidders—to reverse Evelyn's naturally aging container."

"I harvest humans too. I repurpose their containers into high art or as alternative food sources," she says with a slick wink. "I'm resourceful." She casts her manicured hand out to showcase her macabre display.

"Why the kids? The human kids, I mean. Why kill them?"

"You already know."

"Their terror feeds your negative vibration," I say. "You harvest them because the Ormian Council coded their DNA with star seeds and you're looking for something...a certain power I suspect."

"Bingo!"

"My father was given the opportunity to switch sides," I say. "To work in concert with you and Bezaliels."

"And you freed him," she says, taking a sip from her glass. "And killed a Fewoulz in the process. You really fancy yourself like him, as one of *them*—a Camaeliphim—an angel?"

"I'm aware of my humanness," I say. "I know that while I'm hard to kill, I have a soul. I can die. And we both know, Camaeliphim aren't *exactly* angels."

"Your death would be a waste," she says, "of precious resources."

"What are your plans?" I ask.

"This realm will be the first I have conquered in sentient form," she says, admiring her arms, checking her manicure, and then staring through the crystal glass. "And you'll be able to do little about it."

"You're probably right," I say. "The Source can't directly intervene without giving you exactly what you want, energy through uncontrolled chaos. And pure humans, although they may claim otherwise, even against their better judgment and survival, encourage pain, loss, and suffering, which feed you and your kind."

"You have had your share of loss and pain," she says, giving me a gratuitous smile and a hiss, wanting me to share more, I think—for me to spoon-feed her my suffering.

We walk toward the corridor.

"Yes," I admit.

"I'm not sorry about it," she says, then stops. "I can read your aunt's soul. She's not sorry either. She wants you to know she was abandoned and abused by humans to manage her own losses."

"I know," I say. "But her pain is not a free pass to impose it upon others. Did she expect you'd take full form in her body?"

"She welcomed me," Raga says. "She reached out to me for years through her dedicated practices. It's what led us here, like a beacon. We now have a temporary arrangement. She gives me space to rent inside her body and I teach her things, until I find a substitute vessel. She retains her youth and beauty, and her mind, indefinitely, along with a grander title, the ability to visit other worlds, and more money than your precious Lord Harrington."

"Why not just kill Evelyn and keep the body for yourself?" I stare directly into her luminous steel gray and violet eyes for the first time and confront irises that have borne witness to countless universes, galaxies, and planets.

Raga has seen multiverses expand and contract, implode or collapse, rise to host intelligent life or remain extinct, and her orbs remind me of my father's, but hers, unlike his, are chillingly void of soul and don't belong on this planet or in this realm—or in any of the multiverses beyond it. I fight back bile and nausea chugging its way up my solar plexus. Bezaliels, it's been said, can make Camaeliphim feel ill—but it's also said my kindred has the same effect on them. But if Evelyn the Raga is getting sick, it doesn't show.

"Evelyn will roam within me on Ki until we locate the perfect container, young, innocent and oh, so malleable. And I will give her this newly refurbished form—and then another—and another—as long as she'd like. I have another body in mind." She raises her eyes to the ceiling. "I'm bored. What do you want?" Raga asks.

"I want you to leave this planet and my daughter alone," I say.

Raga, co-hosted through the body of my aunt, lets loose with a party of shrill laughs that sounds like fingernails raking a chalkboard, only louder—and not human. "I can confidently claim without risk that you are in no position to bargain. The Ormian Council doesn't want to acknowledge you. Even the parents who conceived you scrambled off to parts unknown. You have no authority as a lowly half-human hybrid."

"I understand," I say, trying to act untroubled. "But you might be interested in this."

I reach into my cleavage and pull out the gold Pleaides pendant, displaying it to her. I didn't know it when I stole it from the roots of a buckeye tree that this collapsible cube of other-worldly circuitry, separated into three main fragments of light with unknown inscriptions, has a clock-like cube of settings and a series of symbols. It serves as a key to create portals, to open the Source Vortex...but it needs a sphere, the right Me', to work.

Dr. Evelyn, or should I say Raga, involuntarily screeches and reaches for my pendant. ***BZZZZZT!*** She's catapulted against a pillar. Mountain dust sprinkles down over her head, but I remain, thankfully, unscathed. She brushes the grime crumbles from her scalp. I pull the pendant close to my chest and drop it back under my dress.

"Tsk, tsk," I say, waving a finger at her. "It's not that simple."

"It isn't?" she asks, her milky eyes fixing on me and her lips curving up as she straightens her dress. "With the click of a finger I could have you dismembered and scatter your pieces all over Ki. And then I could take your pendant and use it with this..."

She reaches into the designer purse loosely hanging against

her hip and tosses a malleable metal sphere back and forth between her hands like it's a baseball and she's readying to throw the first pitch. "As you see," she says when it grows to the size of a small melon. "I have been known to acquire unique pieces." She holds up the sphere. "You could be wealthier than Lord Harrington if you were willing to sell your pendant."

"But you know I'm not," I say. "However, being part human, and stuck on this backwater terrarium, I'd consider temporarily joining your cause, provided you return a favor."

Evelyn the Raga drops her sphere back into her bag and purses her lips. She folds her arms across her chest. "All humans have a price," she says. "Even if it isn't money. And you, little girl, are not your father. Defeating me is a job for a Balancer, a fully-fledged Camaeliphim. The Ormian Council sent a half-human scruff mutt to do a celestrial's job. You. Will. Fail."

I hold my poker face, something that's never been easy for me, but is necessary, since everything, and I do mean *everything*, depends on it. It's possible I may be able to pull off this elaborate ruse, even if the probability is infinitesimally smaller than a neutrino. "You're willing to barter," I say.

"Not willing," she corrects me, "mildly entertained. What do you want?"

"Safe passage out of here with my daughter and her life," I say.

"Favors work two ways," she says. "Have you seen your daughter? An utterly ugly child by my standards. She looks too much like you. But I like...her energy."

I blink.

"Ah," she says. "So, you don't know Bennie brought her to Saratu for safekeeping. And by the way, she's not a very smart four-year-old."

"She isn't even a year old yet by Ki time," I say, trying to maintain calm.

"Ah," she says again, and I find it annoying. "You spend a few days underground, no time at all," she clicks her fingers, "years pass. Four of them."

The Isle of No Time. A perpetual *Now*—but only for those who are actually there.

Shit!

I consider the little girl peering over Saratu's balcony. So, now I know, thirty days on the Isle of No Time constitutes approximately four years topside on Ki. It stings my heart to think I've missed so much. I was looking for a baby, an infant. But— why didn't Evelyn use that time to snatch Hope instead? "What do *you* want?" I ask. "Aside from stealing a form to call your own."

"You get Saratu out of my way and serve me Luca on a platter. He'd make a powerful Ki ally...until he serves his purpose." She glances toward some of the grotesque abuse she calls art. "After that, scraps of him would be as valuable as slivers of Orion rock and sell for millions. His BOUO would fetch even more among this world's leaders. Let me slowly drain this planet, and him, Samantha. Humans will do it anyway, with or without our help, so you might as well stand down and let me close the Source Vortex. We share the spoils and clone your little one. I'll take the alternate star seed and make off to another realm. You get to keep your daughter and rebuild this putrid planet. I'll hold your eye necklace in trust to seal our deal."

"I'll give you my Bukhara blade," I say. I unsheathe the blade from my thigh and hand it to her. "Luca is Camaeliphim. The oath in his genes wouldn't allow him to switch allegiance. I want this back."

"As you can readily see," she says, twisting her tight waist as if she's a runway model when she stands. "Energy is not bound by DNA but may be changed. Look at me! I'm a goddess made manifest and irresistible to any human on this planet!" She laughs but it sounds like echoes of hisses and deep voices. My arm hair stands at attention, but I offer no other indications of fear. "Luca is morphing into something you'll never be able to balance or conquer," she says. "Volatile human blood helps him along. I bet if I collared him, he could take me to the zephyr of pleasure. You think he likes collars?"

"And if I change my mind and back out of our deal?"

Evelyn lowers her head and runs a finger under her chin, then glowers beneath an oily smile. "Reggie dies," she says nonchalantly and with a shrug. "Just like I killed his precious Barbara. And just as I'll kill your daughter."

NINETEEN

REGGIE

I SPRINT through the monastery as if chased by Hell hounds. I wind my way back to the top toward the unassuming lotus pool under Saratu's balcony. Exhausted, clammy, and alone, I detach the long skirt from my body suit. Drops of chilly perspiration creep down my neck. Evelyn the Raga drained a heavy portion of my energy. I slap an iron patch to the back of my neck, anemia being another inconvenient hybrid curse on this planet. Three minutes have passed since I learned she killed Barbara.

The wilderness of Nepal retreats for miles in all directions when I glimpse out a window. And although it's not humid, I'm drenched in sweat, pushing my way upward toward the rest of my team, too weak to fly. Nepal smells of incense and sage, mango, and marigolds. It is dark and my route upward is illuminated not by candles, but by wisps and patches of green plasma that appear and disappear in glimpses along the walls, followed by hushed whispers. "I know you're on the other side of the veil, Nemain," I say. "Thank you."

I pause against some masonry to regain strength and wipe

away a few tears. Nemain sends me a pulse of green light. If it were blue light, it would be Lozen. "How in the hell am I going to break the news to Reggie that his wife, his best friend in the entire cosmos, was murdered by Evelyn the Raga?" Another pulse of light.

Then, I fly...

... I've almost reached the top of the monastery, just a little farther...

...Reggie taught me how to find the freshest berries under a bush, recognize wild mushrooms, and cut off chicken heads. *"There's a natural hierarchy in life...some chickens are sacrificed so others may live,"* he once told me. *"Some chickens peck other chickens so hard they kill them, and then stand on the dead ones to take more than their share..."* He also taught me how to castrate pigs. His life lessons escaped me at the time, but as he said, *"The skills aren't learned for those you plan to kill, but for those who get hurt along the way you might be able to save."*

I swipe away another tear.

If there was ever a woman on this planet who loved me like a mother, it was Reggie's wife. Barbara was a human female completely devoted to her God and Jesus Christ. I always struggled to buy into her cradle-raised religion built on a foundation of patriarchal bullshit. But Barbara believed fully that humans can be saved—that repentance and forgiveness lead to human transcendence...she believed I, too, could be delivered from evil and redeemed. She served as a beacon of light through compassion rather than a bullhorn for hypocrisy. But even more importantly, I loved her—still love her—and she taught me that there is nothing on this planet more important than the exercise of Love, no matter what our beliefs.

I remove the metal sphere from my strial hide and wonder if my hands are anything like my father's, when I examine them. Humans and hybrids die—sometimes too soon. Death offers no rhyme or reason for this transition, usually taking souls unawares. I sift through life's years of tutoring and squeeze it into one lesson, one hand, one password...

The sphere is heavy, possessed of Seven Seals, centuries of intergalactic code—to everything—held within super elastic memory. Portals always want to open, I think. I just need to let go and let it happen, the way Barbara stood back and gently encouraged me to fly.

Reggie leans against a wall and stares at the steps leading up to Saratu's quarters. He checks his M-4, Vigo at his side. There's a slight shimmer and shift in this world when Evelyn the Raga unexpectedly steps around the corner behind him on the stairs. I freeze, the hairs on my arms rising to attention like soldiers. Vigo whimpers but holds firm between the two of them and refuses to budge.

"Hello, Reggie," Evelyn says. Her voice is low and gravelly, and it echoes through the halls until it abruptly dies away.

Reggie blinks at her in a micro moment of disbelief, then recovers, but doesn't say anything. She surprised him. He doesn't like surprises. Reggie laughs out loud, slapping his knee. Vigo looks at me, then at Reggie, then at me again.

"I'm just as confused as you are, Vigo," I say.

"Is something funny?" Evelyn asks, slowly wagging my Bukhara blade back and forth in the air at him, as if it's a magic wand filling the pit in my stomach with all sorts of tangles and knots. Vigo growls at her, low and menacing.

"You are!" Reggie says. "Look at you! Wavin' Sam's knife around like you already own the world. Your victory is a bit premature. And you look like a pageant reject! Runner up! Ha, ha! A bridesmaid but never a bride! Even your marriage to Dr. Sterling was a complete sham—his!"

"Don't I already own the world?" she asks, mocking him. "Pageant reject? You'd fuck me in less than a heartbeat if I let you. Will you squeal like a pig the way your wife did when I killed her?" She wiggles her tongue at him and then runs it along her teeth. The beat of my heart rises into my throat.

Reggie's eyes grow dark, but he doesn't flinch. "I have it on a much higher authority than you that Barbara received a nonstop first-class pass to the heavens of her choice. And unlike you, she transitioned from this planet with honor." And the way he says this, with sincerity and quiet confidence, rather than malice, causes the hair on my neck and arms to stand at attention. So, he knows...

"Phssst," Evelyn the Raga says. "You sound positively human. So beneath you, Reggie. Honor. It's such a conforming but shallow standard of conduct for Kihogs, one with little meaning before an Earthly apocalypse."

"Barbara lived up to and fulfilled the terms of her agreement," Reggie says, keeping his eyes fixed on her.

"Reggie," I interrupt. "How long have you been carrying this around? Wait a minute. You knew Barbara was gone when we were among the orchid roots in the caves, didn't you?"

"The soul connection between Barbara and me was strong," he says. "I knew the moment Evelyn killed her."

"How?" I ask.

"I taught Barbara to remote view too, same as I taught you," he says. "Barbara came to me in spirit. Then our bond was extinguished. I asked Paramel to retrieve and then help me release Barbara from her container."

"What agreement did Barbara honor?" I ask.

"To give up her life, if necessary, to protect you," he says. "The same agreement I made with your parents and uncle."

Reggie stands poised at the bottom of the stairs, holding his gun. He's forty-nine in Earth years and practically raised me in every martial art known to human or hybrid. He's protected and trained me, tolerated my nonsense. He's alert but not tense watching Evelyn the Raga, almost relaxed. The air feels thick enough to taste and the stone beneath our feet is warped with centuries of weather and walking meditation. I remain as still as Reggie.

Inky pools of anger shine through Evelyn's eyes. Without hesitation, she lunges and tries to plunge my blade into Reggie's neck. It's a miss and he's on the other side of me. Packo comes out of nowhere and seizes her from behind. She turns on him and with one quick motion there's a crack. Packo drops to the floor, his carotid arteries torn and his dead eyes lingering on us. With full force and accuracy, Evelyn launches the blade in our direction. I duck and hear the crack of bone against knife blade. Blood spurts from Reggie's plexus when Evelyn yanks the weapon away.

Time
Stands.
Still............
....
....
....
....

My heart pounds its way through my chest, keeping time with the pounding in my head. "**_Nooooooo!!!!_**"

Vigo lunges at Evelyn but seizes and falls over like a stuffed animal. His eyes roll back in his head, and then Reggie's Soul Guide goes rigid on his back, four legs straight up in the air.

The clack of guns and a heavy thud of encroaching boots sound miles away. Suddenly, there's gunfire and splintering wood —shattering glass. The room skids to slow motion. My team shifts itself in my direction and fences me in, weapons drawn.

Reggie hunches deep into his jacket. He staggers but doesn't fall, looking down at Vigo lying motionless at his feet. Tears well up through his eyes when he looks at me. Color flees his face. He smiles widely. "Sam," he says. "Stop this bitch." His knees buckle and his eyes flutter. Like a strong walnut table, full of dents and scratches, his legs finally give way from under him. A crumple of the sturdy hybrid I love and think of as a father lies lifeless on the floor.

Evelyn the Raga hisses with deep laughter. "See?" she says, looking at me, her eyes glowing. "Now, you're free! I did you a huge favor killing these useless slugs." She grabs one of Reggie's ankles to drag him up the stairs.

"What the fuck is *that* thing?" Dr. Monica asks.

"Beyond human," Hogan whispers. "Sweet Jesus. Shoot on command."

"Do. Not. Shoot," I say as the moment slides back into focus. "Evelyn the Raga feeds off our anger and fear." But even as I say this, I feel my BOUO practically boiling in my veins.

Reggie's head thump, thump, thumps up each step. I leap after Evelyn, pulling the tin of Ayahuasca from my suit. Instinct dictates fate when I smash open the tin and plunge it into Reggie's wound. Evelyn reaches for the Pleaides pendant stuffed under my suit, but its charge causes her to retreat up the stairs, closer to the Source Vortex. I roll down each step with a thud and when I run up the stairs again, Reggie's body is gone.

I career midair with Paramel, crashing into her shield. She yanks me into a dark hallway, both of us bouncing along a bulwark of walls. She shoves me into a prayer niche and presses her finger to my lips. "Remain quiet," she says. "Like a monk."

I fall into my friend, and we sink to the ground together. I sob so hard and silently, it feels as if Earth may shatter at any moment.

"Get it outta' your system, mate," Dr. Monica says, leaning down, one hand on my shoulder, the other wrapped around a handgun. "The best way to honor a fallen brother or sister is to save our arses, live our lives with honor, and tell their stories."

I wipe away the snot and tears, hoping the tin of salve I

shoved into Reggie's wound didn't enter his body too late. What I don't understand is why he didn't fight back. There's no way he didn't see Evelyn's attack coming. Hogan and his comrades watch me, not knowing what to say, awaiting orders—and dealing with the loss of one of their own. Packo's sudden death is definitely a hard loss to our team. But evil offers no time to grieve, especially when a multitude of other lives is at stake—and Packo understood, agreed to, and accepted the sacrifice. Looking at our seasoned unit, feeling their anguish and desire for justice, I stand up and turn off Reggie's death like a faucet. It's not because I don't feel immense grief, but because, as he would say, there is no crying in battle.

"How many fighters does Evelyn have?" I ask, righting myself.

"About four hundred, give or take," Hogan says.

"How many do we have?" I ask.

"About fifty," he answers, "if we include the monks. Saratu says some of them are highly trained in martial arts."

"Might do some good against unarmed humans," I say, "but against Bezaliel particles, they're somewhat useless. Weapons?"

"Our semi-autos, a couple of hand grenades, your swords, a few handguns, and Luca's ray sticks," he says.

"How much time we got?"

"Not much," Dr. Monica says. "That lunatic is headed to the lotus pool."

"Where are Lord Harrington and Dr. Dennison?"

"Waiting for you one floor above the pool," Paramel says. "Evelyn can't close the Source Vortex without your pendant."

"True," I say. "But I can open it without her. The problem is that she's going to throw about four hundred obstacles and two valuable pawns in our way. We need reinforcements." I pull a buckeye from my strial hide, set it on a nearby ledge, and set my intention.

"You callin' those creepy blue creatures and that *lieutenant* from Ninmah's whatever, to join us?" Hogan asks.

"You mean Ninmah's Portal and the Astral Weavers? Yes."

"Good," he says. "We can use those ruthless reinforcements."

And just like that, his men gather in a circle, hand over hand, to pray. I get it now, Gods and guns.

TWENTY

THE BATTLE

WAVES OF FIGHTING crash over the monastery walls about the time that storm reaches us. It sends a nervous system of lightning across an omen darkened sky. I observe the pandemonium of battle as I hover twenty feet or so above ground zero. There's fire, plumes of smoke, and the hollowed-out skeletons of burned-out buildings. The voices of my unit ring out clear and distinct. Others, villagers, and children, scream in terror as soldiers slice and shoot through the enemy.

Luca scrambles out from under a pile of humans and hybrids. The Nephilim have him surrounded. *Damn it!* I'm forced to swoop into the fray as Tinley tosses me a tachi sword. I slash, duck, and fight, making my way to Luca until he and I stand back-to-back. With one slice, I take out a Nephilim in my periphery who raises his arm to fire a weapon into Luca. The hybrid falls, eyes full of surprise that he's cut in two, and what little is left of his life empties away.

"Thanks," Luca says.

"No problem."

Luca slashes another person hell-bent on taking off my head.

"Thanks," I say.

"No problem."

"Where's Camael?" I ask.

"Holding Evelyn the Raga at bay," he says. "She's a lot stronger than we expected."

"Well, well, well...look what we have here." Skiggens grins at the two of us, his suit, and his demeanor undisturbed by the blood, gore, and cacophony rising around us. He eyes me up and down, licking puffy spit-shined lips. "Kill Harrington and let the lassie live," he says to his oversized bodyguard. The bodyguard flashes us a mouth full of gold-capped teeth and expands his chest in a display of menace. He unhitches what looks like a laser gun from his snakeskin clad waistband. "But...kill Harrington slowly," Skiggens adds, settling his hand over the other man's weapon. "I want the last thing this Lord sees is me enjoying his *bonnie lass'* tender flesh."

"Cheerio," Luca says to me, launching himself at Skiggens. "I have a pest to exterminate."

With one swipe of my sword, and before Skiggens or Luca can even react, the bodyguard lies dead, his throat severed nearly in two. "Never underestimate female Camaeliphim," I say. "We may appear weak, but our handlers train us well." I launch a hard kick to Skiggens' crotch and drive the tip of my tachi sword into his thigh. "Kill him slowly," I say to Luca. "I want the last thing he sees is you enjoying his final moments in the flesh."

Skiggens crawls on his belly, leaving a trail of blood in his wake. He rolls over, the lines of his face etched with black dirt and tear smears. He looks up at Luca for mercy and pleads for his life. Before I can stop him, (I don't really try), Luca slowly reaches a bare hand into Skiggens' chest and tediously extracts the man's still beating heart just enough that it's still attached to Skiggens.

"I don't see any remorse or redemption in here, do you?" Luca asks.

I lean over for a look. I'm surprised the heart is about as black as soot. I actually *feel* evil with every sputter and beat. "No," I say. I look closer as if scrying through an obelisk mirror. "This man's heart is blind to the suffering he's caused, even though he has full comprehension of his life's history."

"What say you?" Luca asks.

"Call his 'this life' back to the Source," I say. "We'll want to advise Bilby and Nemain that any future containers carrying this bad energy should endure the same tortures he's bestowed until his vibration reaches absolution."

Luca shoves the beating heart into Skiggens' mouth. "Chew on this," Luca says with a growl. He then pitches Skiggens' body over a wall, where it lands on rocks below with a violent crash. "We have to retreat," Luca says. "We're outnumbered and outgunned. The Nephilim have called in a lot of human favors and firepower. And you're not marrying Annunan."

"To retreat is certain death for these humans and for us. Why aren't I marrying Annunan?"

"I will die before I let that happen," Luca says. "Sakar be damned."

"Um," I say, thinking about my lie, "I think that's the plan... you're wanted, dead or inanimated, by all factions in this fight."

"*That* marriage is not going to happen." Luca strikes down three more Nephilim with a flick of his ray stick.

The Nephilim, our counter hybrids, look a lot like Camaeliphim who pass for human, but aren't. The giveaways I notice are glimpses of scaly clawed feet they try to hide in specially made combat boots. Their eyes flash reddish yellow, so unlike the opal pearlescent blue, green, or hazel hues bred into Camaeliphim orbs. And they don't have BOUO. They don't exactly have Bezaliel mist either. The Nephilim receive micro-bulb implants of synthesized particles that mimic and attract Bezaliels.

"Most of Hogan's men are down!" Luca yells over the din.

"Hogan too?" I ask. Luca shakes his head but I'm not sure if he's telling me no or if something is wrong. I lose sight of Luca again when a panicked crowd pushes through and separates us.

Damn it!

Strike one.

Strike two.

Strike three.

The gong sounds and this is my signal that Evelyn the Raga nears the lotus pool. I need to get there. She may not be able to close the vortex without me, but I'm concerned she may possess the power to permanently disrupt or negate its power.

I crouch and slay my way through the crowd. Without warning, a Nephilim wraps large hands around either side of my ribcage. Pain rips its way up my chest when he squeezes and tosses me at least twenty feet against slick terrain. He bashes his way through a small crowd of fighters and tightens his grip around me again, lifting me high in the air. I struggle to kick him, without success, going weak as he saps the breath out of me. Brief scenes of my lives flicker like stars in my mind's eye. A sword pokes through the front of his plexus, sending a waterfall of blood and pus to the ground. The Nephilim and I fall with a sharp thud.

"You need to get to the lotus pool," Paramel says as she slips the rest of her blade out of his body and pockets his implant in her strial hide.

I nod at her and scramble back toward the monastery. "Thank you!"

Monks hop out from hidden spaces to drag injured soldiers and humans away. Hundreds of bullets punch through a fleeing black helicopter, one that lurches into a violent spin. It skims a thick canopy of trees and strikes a tower, then bursts into flames, raining debris and shrapnel. A piece of metal slices into my shoulder, separating me from my sword. I leap, jump, and glide around corpses and the gravely wounded. We're losing ground and this fight.

And just when I think Luca was right about a retreat, my eye necklace lights up. It lifts off my chest and wildly vibrates. A rumble beneath our feet shakes the foundation of the monastery down to every last block. The fighting abruptly ceases as everyone struggles to make sense of what's happening. I use the time to pull Ayahuasca salve from a pocket and spread some around my wound. It's a pity I don't have much left and Bennie never taught me how to make more.

The sky turns orange, then purple, and the land is suddenly pockmarked with hundreds of holes. Scores of wild beasts rush out from makeshift buildings or push through rock and dirt, or grab the legs of partygoers, and yank them underground. Some traffickers take cover in the jungle. Hundreds of dark kangaroo-bouncing monsters collide with wispy tentacles of Bezaliel mist as blue-skinned Astral Weavers thunder down to us from the sky, and Usta rise out of the ground.

My eye necklace releases a beam of light toward Lozen. I snatch a hand over it just as an oversized black beast bounces past me, fangs bared. It latches onto some Bezaliel mist directly over-head seconds before the dark cloud nearly engulfs me. The creature inhales the black fog into its mouth, then thumps the chest of an approaching Nephilim with its clawed feet, stopping its heart. The beast leaps over me. I strain my eyes to see what it is when it turns. It stands at least two feet taller than I, its enormous ears severely curved like a serrated scythe. A face, ugly, with a slightly pointed yet short anteater-like trunk and bioluminescent whiskers, wears a soiled tunic, holds a corpse in its paw and carries a small...*bucket?*

"Bilby?" I ask.

Bilby lifts the lid on his little bucket and pulls out a glowing sphere, one that doesn't look at all as if it would fit in there. It floats between us, and my eye necklace rises to the occasion again, mixing its glow with his sphere.

"Do you know what this is?" he asks.

"No," I say.

"Probably a good thing," he says. "You kept it safe for the Fluffle." And just like that, what he put into my necklace when we met is sucked out again, reabsorbed into the sphere and returned to his quite ordinary-looking antique bucket.

"What did I keep safe?"

"What did you keep safe? Oh, your highness! You marinated the **Morph** in Elemorphia," he says, blood and mist dripping from his whiskers. "We're forever in your service, Queen Scathatch."

Bezaliel mist hovers over our heads again but Bilby sucks in a breath until the mist disappears down his throat, along with the slime. He runs a pointed tongue along an imposing row of fangs. "This is a real treat for us! It's been centuries since my kind has morphed and we've inhaled Bezaliel mist. It's a Fluffle's most prized delicacy, like your topside truffles!"

"Doesn't inhaling Bezaliel mist negatively affect Elemorphia?" I ask, feeling confused...and wondering about him addressing me as *Queen*, not *Princess*.

"It enhances *us* and neutralizes *them*," he says. "Raga loses power with each one we consume!"

"Why didn't you tell me sooner?" I ask, feeling hopeful.

"You weren't read into it and had no need to know," he says, inhaling more of the mist as it sweeps through and over the grounds. "But when I met you, I knew...oh, how I knew!"

"Knew what?" I ask.

"Why," he says, hopping away and getting positively high on Bezaliel mist. "That you are your father's daughter! And only the daughter of high-ranking Camaeliphim can control the spheres!"

"What?" I ask.

"It's true," he says. "Your mother asked for the decree as a wedding gift from her betrothed ones."

"Betrothed ones?"

"Camael and Basasael," he says.

"She's married to Basaseal!" I say.

"Yes, him too," Bilby says.

"What do you mean *him too?*"

"Receptors and Balancers take more than one spouse, and it's typically divine siblings," he says.

"What? That's ludicrous!"

"Is it? Says who?"

"Everybody!" I yell. "It isn't natural. Well...maybe multiple spouses are normal for Elemorphia but not for humans or hybrids."

"No?"

"No!"

"Perhaps not for purebred humans," Bilby says. "Although human males did twist the context of their religions to allow the men of their species to take more than one wife."

"That's not natural either," I say. "Are you telling me my mother has two husbands?"

"Sort of..." he says.

"Mate!" Dr. Monica yells from a nearby bush. "I coul' use some healin'". She points to her leg.

Shit. She's taken a bullet. When I turn to look back at Bilby, he's gone. Luca was right...there *was* something *off* about the Fluffle, an oh, how I thank Source for this!

Pushing past the dead, I make my way to Dr. Monica.

When I check my surroundings to ensure I'm not stalked, I watch two partygoers capture and drive a nun to her knees. She sees me and distracts them from my cover until her eyes briefly bore into mine for help, which I'm unable to give. Suddenly, she smiles up at her torturers. Amid this terror, she's *chosen* joy in her final moments. Her eyes turn glassy and vague with a single blast to the back of her head, and she falls face-forward into the ground, her "this life" extinguished.

"Nemain," I whisper. "For Source's sake, take care of that one. She deserves Valhalla." I fire off two rounds from Dr. Monica's gun and take down the nun's executioners. "You can leave the other two souls for the Fluffle to dispose of as they see fit."

Behind me, a few monks hurry initiates, some as young as three or four, toward the jungle. When they're cut off by a couple of black- suited characters holding AR-15s, Paramel swoops in from behind and slashes their knees away, then drives her sword through their necks. The monks cover the children's eyes. She orders the monks and nuns to surround the frightened children, about twenty of them, and provides their personal escort to safety beyond the trees. Damn, she's one of the best arch warriors I've ever met.

"Bullet missed your artery," I say to Monica, tearing her trouser legs at the thigh. "But it tore the shit out of your muscle. Hold still, and don't scream. This is going to hurt." I plunge my fingers through flesh, blood, and bone to extract the bullet with two fingers. "Got it!" But when I look down at her, Dr. Monica is unconscious. I check her pulse. She's alive! I rub some salve into her shredded flesh, nearly all I have, and tourniquet her wound just like Reggie once taught me to do with wounded pigs. She'll be safe here, I think. I snatch another weapon from a dead guy beside her and sneak around the perimeter.

A bullet whizzes past my head.

Genin!

He's taken cover, playing sniper behind a fortress wall. But the Nephilim that had been creeping up behind me lies dead. Genin points at the beast and gives me a thumbs-up. He continues to take out any being who isn't part of our team, true to his word, to me, and his mission. He hand-signals me and I kill three more enemies sneaking up from behind. I sorely misjudged Genin due to my pride. I make a mental note to work on my ego. Reggie always said that too much makes one ripe for compromise —or killing.

One by one, former partygoers choke, burn, or scream, their blood loosed from corporeal containers and running over. But we too, suffer casualties. A couple of Hogan's men are down, and I can't tell if they're wounded or dead...

...And in come the Bezaliels on the other side of the veil, swooping wisps of tentacles desperately reaching to strike violence into anything sentient. The Elemorphia inhale all they can, but probably not enough to put out the inferno.

TWENTY-ONE

SOURCE VORTEX

EVELYN THE RAGA drags Reggie's body along the courtyard, the sounds of jerks and clunks echoing throughout the now nearly empty monastery, *down, down, down* three stone stairs.

It seems such a short time ago—yet so far away—our time together at Plum Hook Bay. Muttering and complaining, Evelyn the Raga slumps Reggie over a half-wall, or the last remnants of what it used to be before chaos erupted. She walks on. His container is limp and devoid of life. Bilby was right—Raga's weakened in human form—but how much I can't discern. She might be as powerful as a large wave—or a record-breaking tsunami—and—it appears—may have taken the life out of Reggie again if Bennie's salve even worked, something I didn't think through. She heads toward the lotus pool.

The Nhat Hanh Monastery, where the lotus pool is guarded by Saratu and the monks, was built on the orders of Buddha in 503 B.C. The villagers claim the mountain upon which it sits is sacred and possessed of Source magic. It took hundreds of years to complete but when finished, was the size of a small city, imposing yet serene, and open to anyone for the study of philosophy, yoga, transcendent meditation, art, music, theology, science, history, or martial arts. In an oddly comforting way, I find Reggie's death here fitting. He was killed in the line of duty, fighting for the greatest of causes—Life—within the walls of everything he most held dear.

I reach into a pocket and tuck a buckeye into Reggie's stiffening hand when I reach his body. "You, brave hybrid, why'd you have to go and get yourself killed? I may need to phone a lawyer," I whisper. Only this time, he doesn't offer me a smart-ass comeback to our long-standing old joke and his dead silence stings my heart. "I'm going to miss you."

The moon peeks out from behind a small cloud, high in the now chilly night, diamond dust constellations glinting opposite her in a sapphire sky. I can just make out the details of the countryside and the village below: Smoke rises from hearths inside warm homes, the glow of life and light, humans either oblivious, ignoring, or hiding from the war above their heads. A broad river laces through the green jungle and winds its way toward ethereal mountains. Three rivers run into a larger one and it makes me think of Barbara's Father, Son, and Holy Ghost, all connected to a single Source, but this landscape looks more like a nervous system of roots spreading off into Earth's myriad of directions.

A red crested cardinal flutters onto the stones, examines Reggie's corpse with a twitch and bob of its head, gives off a short chirp, and then flaps away into the night. I place a finger into Reggie's stab wound, wishing I could heal it with a simple touch. I remove the tin of salve. Clouds move in to cover over a multitude of sins and bloodshed below, my only light the sputter of a few paper lanterns handmade by humans who still have heart.

Evelyn the Raga stands between two large pillars, by the lotus pool. She lays her hands upon tree branches, bushes, and flowers. Each wilt and die with a light graze of her fingertips. She slowly meanders around the courtyard the way a vampire, overly confident and sure of draining its prey, might do. Her footsteps follow the barefoot patterns of monks that have worn over centuries of cobblestones, her energy leaving a jagged edge that fails to dovetail within a gently scooped surface. When she reaches the pool, she sits on its benched edge to touch the water.

"Wait," Camael says.

"Why?" Evelyn the Raga asks, a menacing smile curving her lips upward in a forced sort of way. And once again, the depth of her evil stuns me. "You won't last long surface-side in such a weakened human form or in your true form."

Camael gently nods at her in agreement. "If you inanimate me, other Camaeliphim will never let you rest."

"Humanness hardly becomes you, Camael" Evelyn says. She looks at her nails as if she's bored, then glances at the lotus pool, which appears to tremble and slosh.

"Nor you," Camael says. "I will send you back from whence you came."

Evelyn the Raga's shoulders rumble like distant thunder when she laughs and tightens her face. "You can't. You're not a Balancer." A flicker of anger gallops across her brow ridge and passes through her eyes. Before a warning rises to my lips, a band of shadows drops down upon Camael's head. The cobblestones beneath his feet crackle and then explode.

Bezaliel mist covers him completely, pile driving Camael into the ground until he lifts two mighty arms and bursts through the pall. He rolls and spins into his true from, a glint of opal plasma and scales, moonlight burnished unto white plumage. I retreat a few steps, forced to cover my eyes until they adjust to the power of my uncle's raw awe, the likes of which I've never encountered in a fully-fledged otherworldly being. A blue tongue flickers in and out of his mouth, his slitted nostrils flaring below sapphire diamond-shaped pupils ensconced in glowing royal blue quadrilateral orbs.

Camael's fist locks over Evelyn the Raga's half-frozen hand. Everything darkens except a shaft of moonlight. He slows his breathing and everything in me tingles and merges into a seedbed of fear and frustration, knowing that multiverses hang suspended on this imbalance.

Evelyn hisses incoherently and flings herself forward toward him. Camael leaps backward and vaults a wall seconds before Evelyn's laser fire, one she conjures from the tip of my Bukhara blade, just misses him. Camael ripples through rock and rises above Raga before plunging toward her. He teeters slightly off balance and reaches solid ground just as Evelyn the Raga's second fire from my blade tags its mark. It severs his eye into milky white blindness and half tears off his scalp. Camael sinks to his knees, his noble body warped and bowed like driftwood, a portion of his majestic pinions singed to gray ash.

"Belor lehana," Camael says when I rush forward. "Tanari." He swirls into a mist of smoke and disappears!

Evelyn whips the blade in my direction and almost sweeps my feet out from under me when she commands it to fire another ray. I jump over the beam and spring out of range. Slowly, she reapproaches, a sardonic smile pasted above her chin. I dodge her first two attacks and tuck and roll on her third. Troublingly unbalanced, I glance up.

Evelyn the Raga towers over me, shifts her grip, and brings the blade down on my head. I twist but catch enough of the blow on my right temple to daze me. Geometric symbols and stars explode behind my eyes. She tosses the blade aside and hovers too near, secures a hand around my neck, and lifts me off the ground. I tilt my head to clear my mind. I then look down into her molten eyes, into her madness and rage, unable to see anything redeeming of what was once my mother's sister. Evelyn is almost completely consumed by Raga, but she's in there, I know. I sink my fingers into her arms, which feel almost fluid. Raga recoils, the bit of humanness left in my aunt fearful of a hybrid's touch, and the *not human* part trying to repel our polarity.

"You'll need this," I say, releasing a hand to pull the Pleaides pendant out from its hiding place between my breasts. "You can't permanently close the Source Vortex without it...or me."

She rotates me through the air for a closer inspection. "Reggie's death was too easy," Evelyn says, cocking her head to one side. "It appears even easier to kill a half-human twit sent here to do a real Balancer's job."

Orchid roots slither over stacked stone walls and creep along the ground toward the pool. Evelyn the Raga reaches out and summons them to retreat before she kills them too. And I remember—Evelyn forced me to choose therapy with her—once —at Plum Hook Bay. My anger that day levitated a lamp and sent it smashing through a window. She was visibly shaken back then. I didn't understand the power of a gift I was unaware I possessed —until now—and it's lain dormant within me for years.

I will have to fight Evelyn the Raga and know only one way to do so. I close my eyes and slow my breathing—the way Reggie taught me. I monitor the severity of my wounds and slow my Golden Blood. If the US government can drain and control my BOUO, and use it for interstellar travel, it must mean that I can use it for the same purpose—and much more naturally. I visualize and reassemble the chaos of my mind brought on by Raga and her subatomic Bezaliel particles. Each particle latches onto another until they appear as an opaque mist the way a school of fish or flock of birds might do. Patterns. Dr. Sterling taught me that universal truths and patterns rarely break rank in a grand cosmos, and that even chaos, which initially appears completely random, isn't necessarily so. I carefully and mentally carve away at their control, willing each of Raga's fingers around my neck to loosen. I render some of the Bezaliel mist static. I don't know how long I can control the stillness before rebalancing order to this planet.

Evelyn withdraws. I hover in the air over her, having successfully blunted her negative vibrations. She looks tired, weakened in human form. Perhaps if I provoke her enough, her humanness will cave to the limits of Ki's physics, even if that limitation is about as feeble as nuclear fallout.

Evelyn pulls my father's decoy sphere from her purse, running a black-tipped finger along its metal cheek, smiling with delight.

My breath steams in the chilly air but my body sweats with clammy anticipation, and somewhere inside me, warning bells shriek. Evelyn reaches a finger toward the lotus pool.

"No," I say—but it's too late.

She lightly touches the water...

It begins to freeze over but then...a shadow crosses over the pool......and the water zaps her the same way my necklace did.

The pool doesn't wither, crack, or turn to glass. The shadow hovers over us and I'm unable to make out a form. White lotuses hold firmly together, refusing to open, wilt, or die. Evelyn the Raga tries again, but this time, the pool defiantly bubbles and breaks up the slush she tries to lay. Evelyn's face flushes bright red and she appears confused. She's unable to exert the same will over the lotus pool she did to almost everything else in her path.

"Hello, Countess," Luca says as he lowers himself to the ground. "What a blood-curdling and unpleasant surprise. Something wrong?" The palm of his hand is held out toward the lotus pool gleaming like a hot ember—a standoff.

Dr. Sterling watches from a balcony above, his arms leaning against the rail. He looks spellbound and doesn't move a muscle.

"Clever to use your own Bezaliel energy against me," Evelyn says. "Camaeliphim play in the prohibited obsidian arts now?"

"We're schooled to deal with a myriad of minor nuisances," Luca says, stepping between Evelyn the Raga and me.

"Then deal with your inner demons," she says, raising a palm to him.

Luca falls like a dropped stone. He's suddenly paralyzed and suffocating under the weight of Bezaliel mist, his own and what she sends into him. It rises out through his ears and mouth and encircles him like a small tornado. "Do not give in to her, Sam. I will find you wherever you're sent, no matter how long it takes."

Evelyn laughs in such a way it causes the hairs on the back of my neck to rise. "Not if you're inanimated."

It takes my entire reserve to stay in place and not rush to comfort Luca, although from the looks of it, there is little I could offer by way of relief. "Aunt Evelyn," I say, trying to retain my calm and save Luca. "If I close the Source Vortex, you're stuck here, in human form, sharing corporeal space with a host you cannot trust. Raga will destroy Ki but in doing so, it also limits any opportunity for her or your multiverse dominion. You wouldn't risk such an impotent and mortal existence, would you?"

"Give me the Pleaides pendant," Evelyn the Raga says. "Now. Or I *will* kill your daughter."

"Is she really my child?" I ask, slowly rounding the pool and approaching her—but not too close. "I mean, it's true she shares some of my DNA. But we've never met or bonded. Hope's birth is off paper and grid thanks to your misguided amplitude. This world and those beyond it aren't ready for an Emergent like her, especially one contaminated with Bezaliel mist. You count on my maternal instincts to *save* Hope—but that's exactly what you want. Go ahead, kill her."

"You don't mean this," Evelyn hisses. "It's not in your nature to destroy your own blood."

"Saving my daughter gravely injures a multitude of worlds," I say. "You don't want to close the Source Vortex. You're hoping I'll open it for you so you may take her with you, absorb her, and wield her as the ultimate cosmic weapon."

"You're too clever too late," Evelyn says. "It was your own government who invited me here. Of course, it was an accident and they have absolutely no idea what I am. It was their experiments on invisible negative energy that presented entry to this planet."

"I'm aware," I say. "The neutrino experiments were designed to keep humans divided and under control—humans—I'll give you—did open the gates of Raga when they split neutrinos and allowed you in."

"It's a perfect plan," she says, "because humans, with or without clearances, remain distracted by obsolete technology that our respective kindreds give them. Kihogs truly are lower life forms, Samantha, nothing more than easily led and trainable primates who *think* they're capable of intelligence and self-awareness. Most of them can't grasp what's really going on in their own little world let alone 'out there'." She looks up at the stars. "They're too primitive. Bezaliel mist has its effect on hybrids too. Let's look at you, for example. You'll open the Source Vortex for me because you're dumb enough to keep a worthless interstellar promise you made with *Not Who*."

"My aunt was always the sort of dissatisfied human who bathes in the blood, misery, and the tears of others," I say. "She was never content to come in second or go with less. Evelyn lured you into *her*. Granted, this took decades of practice, murder, mutations, deadly experiments, and deception, but she did it by studying Bennie and me first, then Hope's embryo, implantation, and birth—until Bennie was able to rescue Hope. Bennie is a Source Bearer. His having Hope throws a kink into your cosmic travel plans."

What I don't say is that I suspect Evelyn reverse-engineered Bennie's, my, and Hope's DNA, not wanting to become Camaeliphim, but a fully formed Bezaliel, the first ever in corporeal form. What Evelyn failed to consider is that Raga devours both positive and negative energy—throwing every system off-balance—until it's impossible to discern Dr. Evelyn, the Countess of Teviot, from Raga the Bezaliel. And now I see—the willing host has almost cleanly consumed the desperate predator. It's a match made in Hell, on Earth.

"I asked earlier why you both bothered to share bodily space," I say, "but you never answered me. The answer is you got impatient. And you made a mistake. You can't completely possess my daughter *because* she's an Emergent. While any mutual information between her entangled particles *can* be exploited for energy, any Earthly *transmission* of such energy at faster-than-light speeds is impossible through a human host. You and Evelyn are both stuck in your own paradox."

"You're *dead* wrong," Evelyn the Raga says.

"As a sentient observer," I continue, "you are forced to relinquish assumptions and knowledge beyond our conscious horizon —to *dumb down*—to experience what it is to be what you refer to as a primitive primate. The problem you now have, and it's a serious one, is that you've become a human-level observer running on a massive quantum computer, and therefore, cannot, despite your intelligence, harness Ki's physical world within your mental constraints, to realize multiverse chaos."

"You. Will. Fail," she says, holding the sphere out at me.

"You think so?" I ask. I lift the flap on my strial hide and hold up the Me'. It's the first time since we started this deadly game that her face cracks with concern. "You're holding a decoy, bitch. This Me' is the genuine Ophanim, the ones who never sleep, the beings who guard the gate of the Source and complete knowledge. Theirs is one realm you will *never* enter."

"***Now!***" Dr. Sterling yells.

He tosses the Tesla coil from the floor above. I slap the *Me'* over its top, latch my Pleiades pendant into the bottom, and turn the key. I fly head-on at Evelyn, yank her from the ledge, and take her with me into the lotus pool. I leave nothing behind. And the last thing I see is a little girl with russet ringlets peeking over Saratu's balcony...

We splash down like stones, sinking fast. The pool feels paralyzing and chilly. It suffocates me and sizzles my lungs. I seize Evelyn hard by the neck. I hear the rush of water and then a maddening hum of white noise when we enter the vacuum. She wriggles and hisses in my arms, tries to spit, then scratch. I refuse to release my grip, and I increase pressure on her as we pass *through* the portal into empty, whirling space. My eyes sting, my skin is scraped, and my heartbeat echoes in my ears when I expel the foulness of Raga's chaos from my lungs.

The tears in Evelyn's human eyes slowly turn to ice, her expression one of shock, like a desperate demon slowly deprived of its host as it meets a sudden and unexpected fate. My eye necklace glows brightly as I secure the sphere between us. The lid of the Source Vortex reveals itself—and surprisingly, it isn't dark—but light and intelligent, locked on us, and loaded with controlled, caressing fury. I close my eyes and stop fighting the vortex and my fear, ignoring the searing pain tearing through my mind and body.

Evelyn's phantom beauty fissures under the howling maelstrom of blinding intensity, that space where crossroads meet behind the mirrors of reality to form an X Point. And for a moment, I wonder if I'm doing the same, my reflection, my force, and my hybrid-ness fading away. Evelyn the Raga clings to me as we careen toward the opening whirl. And hatred, as adulterated and cold as I've ever witnessed, void of everything that makes Ki a sacred repository of Life, struggles to hold onto me.

Evelyn's bony fingers try to force their way into me, a last-ditch effort to escape this potent space. But hers is a futile endeavor. Silvery spheres race to surround us, latching on like stubborn thistles. Some yank Evelyn the Raga away from me. Evelyn's hands gesture frantically, a plunging figure shrinking away into the abyss. She releases one last shriek through the void and tumbles helplessly into the blinding gulf of the Source Vortex. She's forcibly separated from her sentience when it swallows her up, blotches of blackness that burst and disappear into non-existence, her information and energy completely lost.

I'm violently snatched in the opposite direction, into a sea of churning color.

And then...there is nothing.

Nothing.

Nothing.

Nothing.

TWENTY-TWO

AILITH & BENNIE

THE SOUL of the sea is calm, its mood serene and placid. Staring over a cliff, I think about those fortunate souls in her rippling embrace, their sun-kissed skin exposed to glistening life. Centuries of passengers and crews are baptized with brine and foam, the blessings of whales, and their wave shined, smiling faces thrust up at blue horizons, a chorus of sentient souls, their nets cast toward new lives.

"What's the password?"

A little girl, about five years old, blocks my entry through a small gate to a majestic castle. Russet ringlets meet the hem of her cardinal-colored cape, dancing in concert with an incoming breeze and the high-pitched songs of seagulls. So, this is *Hope*. I want to hug her. I'm compelled to hug her. She stands defiant, hands locked on hips, the wind tossing thick rusty spirals about her cheeks as she searches my eyes for an answer, the *right* answer. I have the answer! I knew there'd be a test!

"What's your name?" I ask.

"I have no name if you have no password."

"I was at least twelve before I could launch such smart-ass comebacks," I say. I offer her a thumbs-up and the little girl, *my* little girl, cocks her head and crinkles her nose in confusion, as if she's never seen such a silly gesture and has no idea of its meaning. Near the cliff's edge, a commanding limestone fortress stands strong, its sleek exterior partially covered by leafy green ivy that grows around meticulously maintained window frames. The estate holds watch over a vast sapphire ocean, its bluff secure as new sand tumbles in brought along by frothy waves. Late afternoon shadow meanders through tamed thickets of thistle that stitch verdant ground with royal purple and are expertly trimmed like acres of Bonsai trees.

"Where are your parents?" I ask, looking around, knowing exactly how I got here. It's a beautifully safe and secure place to raise a child, this parallel realm just on the other side of Ki.

Hope produces an oversized silver sword from beneath her cardinal cape and positions it between us—quite a remarkable feat for one so young—but an easy feat for an Emergent. Again, she demands a password. "I take no prisoners," she says. Her weapon pitches a glint of light into my eyes. This time, I see it coming. The little girl's bottom lip juts out to blow a wayward ringlet from her eyes, a curl that repeatedly returns, against her frustration, to its original position...just like her father.

"*Grrr.* Dad says I can't cut my hair, or I'll lose my strength... like Samson in the Bible."

"Your mom lets you play with a sword?"

"This isn't playtime," she says with a frown. "And besides, this is my mom's sword. I'm saving it for her until she returns." Her golden-green orbs flicker with raw determination as she carefully measures me, her trespasser, eyeing me up and down with pursed lips, a perfect clutch on her sword handle. Bennie trained her well, I see. Hope is as comfortable wielding a blade as most other kids might be holding a teddy bear.

"The password," I say, "isn't a password at all."

The little girl slowly lowers her sword and stands a bit straighter, intently watching me.

"It's a safety dance," I say. I move my arms and legs the way Bennie taught me when we were kids stuck inside Silo #57.

"You're not doing it right!" she yells.

"I know." I smile. "Your dad told me when we were kids at Plum Hook Bay that he'd show me how to do it right someday. But the answer you seek is Love."

"***Mum?***"

I tip my head a few times, knowing she won't miss the point, and crouch with my arms wide open. Hope drops the sword and plunges herself into me.

As a child, I never believed in angels. And as an adult, I've never believed in angels...or their angles and agendas. But my daughter? I believe in her. It's hard not to believe in her when she says, "mum" and I feel her pressed against me, her hair tangled in mine and our hearts intertwined on some sacred maternal scale. Worry, love, and helplessness unbind within my instinctual affection. A tumult of anguish and joy expand through my heart, leak out of my pores, and cause a tangible release of tears to tumble and splash against Hope's cape. When the dam of tears runs dry, I release her and rise to my senses.

"And you are Hope?" I ask, my hands on her shoulders, knowing it to be true and wanting to memorize this moment, all of her, those wiry russet curls, hazel eyes, pale skin, and dark pink lips; the way she blows ringlets out of her face like Bennie used to do, her curiosity, her questions, and her bubbling personality, so unlike me or Bennie. I wonder where she inherited this, until I remember Luca and his charm. Of course! She's just like her uncle. *"The apple doesn't fall far from the tree," They* once said. I heard them...those church people. And for once, they're probably right.

"My dad said you'd call me Hope, but here... I am known as Ailith."

"Your name means *rising warrior*," I say.

"Like you!" Ailith yells.

"Where, exactly, is *here*?" I ask.

"You don't know?"

"I know I've been here before," I say. "A very long time ago, I think."

"You were!" she says. "Come on, I'll show you!"

Hope/Ailith grabs my hand and yanks me toward the castle.

The gleam of pride in her eyes is evident. What I don't say is how much I have failed and fallen as a warrior, or how painful its burden of loss. Camaeliphim have heavy crosses to bear. It's hard to imagine this child, my child, will serve as a Balancer one day, an Emergent no less, able to change form and freely roam realms at will, sort of like a Ceitan, but even better.

Bennie crosses the lawn and strides toward an outbuilding, a stable, and threads a bridle through the mouth of a brawny gray steed. An unexpected and surprising surge of love overwhelms me. I fight to keep my balance.

Seagulls glide overhead, their white feathers a whir of flaps and floats along the pristine shoreline. Bennie the Source Bearer radiates peace, an attribute I find difficult to reconcile or manifest as a Balancer, tipping between order and chaos and back again until...well...until *then*, I suppose...whenever *then* might be. And my, how he's grown. Standing nearly six and one-half feet, he firmly grasps a saddle and launches it over the steed's back, securing leather straps, looking just as handsome as his brother, but with long dark curls hovering around his face. Another swoosh of desire moves along my hips. And then he looks up...

"Daddy!" Ailith yells. "Mummy is here just like you said she'd be!"

"Bennie," I softly say as we meet. It's all I can say. My hands shake. My heart beats. His dark eyes study me and I try not to stare at his broadly tanned chest under a partially unbuttoned shirt, a chest that slopes down to a V like an upside-down triangle.

He stops what he's doing and stares at me.

"Are you gonna kiss?" Ailith asks. "Because that would be *reeeaaaally* gross!" She rolls her eyes.

"Ailith's got your mouth," Bennie softly says. And I can't help but laugh. "You've fared rather well despite having passed through a vortex. Do you understand where you are?"

"Behind the veil on Isle of Skye," I say. "A land of caves, caverns, crevices, and cliffs."

"The perfect place to keep an Emergent safe," he says. "It's your old battleground, the place where you once put my brother and his men through an ultimate test of battle."

"I guess I didn't win," I say.

"Scathatch," Bennie says. "You and he were the only two left standing."

"Daddy," Ailith says. "What's an Emergent?"

"You haven't told her?" I ask, using a finger to toss a curl out of her face.

"Mum," Ailith says. "Will you *pleeeeaaase* braid my hair?"

I nod.

"Not yet," Bennie says. "I thought we could tell her together...when she's *older*."

Ailith falls asleep in my lap, and I carry her to bed, tucking her in and thinking about how angelic she looks, that despite Bennie's and my uninformed consent, she's perfect, and maybe the sort of creation some intelligent force outside of Evelyn *knew* should exist. I pick up her sword to return it to the mantel and notice it's *my* sword...from another place...another life...another time...long ago, and almost, but not quite, forgotten. I challenged her uncle with this sword and lost...my heart. A couple of thrusts midair for old times' sake and then I lay it up for her. Ailith will need this fine blade someday...but I hope not as early as I had to take it up.

She stirs. "Mummy?"

"Yes, Ailith?"

She reaches up to touch my eye necklace. "May I have this please?"

"Someday...yes..."

Ailith smiles, buries her curly head in a fluffy pillow, and floats off to slumber.

Bennie leans in the doorway.

"Is she...normal?" I ask.

"That's a loaded question," he says. "Are you *normal?*"

"You know what I mean," I say, stroking her hair and moving another curl from her face. I lightly tuck it into a braid, hoping not to wake her. "Does she have Bezaliel mist coursing through her blood, or were you able to extract it?"

"Ailith is *all clear,*" he says.

And then Bennie draws down the ambient light and I breathe...just like Reggie taught me.

* * *

After dinner, Bennie and I retreat to his study, sharing a glass of what he calls Bamuri, a clear ambrosia-like liquid that slides down my throat like a perfect melody. Earth and time feel so far away. We sit next to one another on the couch. I avoid eye contact, feeling aroused and guilty at the same time. I don't know if Luca survived on the other side of Ki. I hope he has, but I can't feel him or our connection on this side of the veil.

"This...this isn't there," Bennie says. "This is an entirely different world and different rules apply." He looks at me intently as if he's read my mind, and he inches closer. I sulk a little, mostly out of embarrassment, and avert my eyes.

"Do you want me?" he asks. His question is soft, neither a challenge nor a come-on.

Confused by my unexpected attraction toward Bennie, I withdraw a little more.

"If I said I wanted you too, would that help?"

I stand up, lean against a wall next to the doorway, and cross my arms. "We aren't entirely human."

"We're more Camaeliphim than we are human," Bennie says. "If you want to share yourself with me, just tell me so."

I fall silent and stare back at him.

"It costs you nothing to say you desire me," Bennie says. He strips off his shirt, exposing a damn near perfect chest. He stands up and walks toward me.

I feel him staring at me the same way he used to back at Plum Hook Bay when we were kids, as if trying to sift through my soul to see what's "*in there.*" I tighten my arms around my waist, practically hugging myself as the sensual strain between us intensifies. I've waited so long to see him and always, on some level, loved him, but never did I interpret or expect this—to *want* him. *Asteroids! Why am I doing this?*

"I shared the friendliness of my thighs with Luca," I blurt out. "I am forever entangled with your brother. We're engaged to be married!" I fling my ring in front of his face as if it's a weapon, as if it will stop him...stop me...stop us.

Bennie shifts sideways and leans against the wall too, looking at me thoughtfully, giving me space and the freedom to run away, his gaze set to compassion. "And in this realm, which isn't Ki, will you share the friendliness of your thighs with me?" He's so close I feel his body heat. His energy is stronger than I ever remember it on Ki—but we were kids. And kids grow up and change—and some, like him, even move to other realms. Damn, he even smells sexy, like vetiver and bergamot mixed with fresh air.

"I belong here," he says, as if reading my mind. "This Skye has always been my home."

"Huh?"

"As a child, I was accidently drawn into an X Point that led straight to your Ki," he says. "It was opened by two gentleman scientists who built a very special device...the same one that brought you here. We were surprised to discover how quickly Kihogs had advanced your world."

"Who's we?" I ask.

"Alterians and Ebians," he says.

"These two gentleman scientists, did their names happen to be Ian Windsor and Nikola Tesla?" I ask.

"I see my brother told you the story."

I nod. "Are they still alive?"

"Oh, yes," Bennie says. "They have a realm-roving lab that locates additional potential repositories like Earth."

Disappointment settles in my stomach. I thought maybe I could meet my grandfather and this Nikola Tesla—but like most of my relatives—we don't tend to stick around in one place for too long. I bet my family tree can be traced all the way back to the first Ormian Olympics.

"What happened?" I ask.

"As a child, I was tossed out of the X Point at Port Meadow in Oxford," Bennie says. "Tesla and Windsor were sucked into it from there trying to escape with a piece of the COE. They needed to get it off planet. I was immediately located via military radar, remanded to Vor custody, and carted off to a clandestine facility for study, where humans figured out that our kindred, Camaeliphim, is far advanced compared to them. A deal was cut that I could return to my home realm after sharing what I knew of Alterian and Ebian technology, but..."

"The deal was broken," I say. "You became a prisoner instead. Is this why you always looked so puny and weak at Plum Hook Bay, because Earth was never your home world?"

"Probably that and Dr. Evelyn spiked our fruit cocktail with psychotropic medications," he says. "But I never forgot you. I knew then, when they brought you to Plum Hook Bay, who you were and that you were destined to be the next Balancer."

"How did you know?"

"You look just like your father," he says.

"You mean, like wispy smoke?" I say with a huff. "Because that's all I've ever seen of my dad—well, that and some blackened wings and red eyes—before he flew off to find my mother and left me alone to fight off a skeevy Fewoulz."

"You're part human," Bennie says. "It would make you very sick to see Basasael in full form on Ki."

"So I've been told," I say. "The Ormian Council needs to remedy this sort of malady, especially for part human hybrids related to celestrials."

"They're working on it," he says. "You can be here *or* there, so that's progress. Ailith can exist in two places simultaneously, and that's a first too."

"How is that possible?" I ask.

"How do two hybrids create a gifted child capable of existing in two places at once with full awareness?" he asks. "Part of it is tapping into universal knowledge and part of it is a combination of coincidence and genetics."

"Ailith was a fluke?" I ask. "I thought Dr. Evelyn created her on purpose."

"Evelyn did," Bennie says. "And her probability for success was high...but not guaranteed. And no one expected we'd create an Emergent. Even the Ebians are awed. If hybrids with human stock create such advanced celestrials, it's only a matter of centuries before Kihogs shed their need for physicality and sentience too."

"And then we'd be like Ebians or Ceitans," I say. "Able to roam realms at will. And they don't want that."

"Not yet. Humans are not ready." He lifts his hand and

lightly touches a finger to my temple and then draws it to my chin with a slow tease. "Now, about this thigh friendliness. You never answered my question. Do you want me?"

"I don't want to hurt Luca," I say.

"Do you love my brother?"

"With all my heart."

"Do you love me?"

For a moment, I lose myself to the lull of the waves outside and the wind off the water, which lightly blows through extended windows. "With all my soul," I finally say.

"Is it true that on Ki, some human and hybrid men take more than one bride?" Bennie asks.

"Yes," I say. "Women don't like it much, or they convince themselves they might like it because they have no choice."

"Do women ever take more than one husband on Ki?"

"In some cultures," I say. "The Bororo in South America, Tibetan peoples within the Nepal parts of India and China, the Massai of Kenya, Irigwe of Northern Nigeria, where women traditionally acquire numerous co-husbands, the Marquesas' Islands of the South Pacific, the Inuit, the Bari of Venezuela. If I recall correctly, about fifty-three Ki cultures practice polyandry."

"Why do you think they do this?"

"Land scarcity, a shortage of females in a particular area, or to keep resources in the family," I say, trying to remember some of my research on the subject.

"What about as a means to initiate, reinforce, or guarantee peace between realms?" Bennie asks.

"What do you mean?"

"Let me show you." Bennie places his hand against my cheek then wraps it around the back of my neck. He leans in, and kisses me, silent, long, and slow, until I find myself under him, over him, and completely ungrounded—because we float to the ceiling locked together. Passion unfolds not in a torrent, but with gentle, teasing extraction until I surrender and collapse on him in tears.

Any anger, trepidation, or fear I felt is warmed away, peace returned.

"Earth and Skye," he whispers.

"What?"

"You're a Balancer, the Horizon between Earth and Skye."

My thoughts drift in the hazy afterglow...Luca, bound to Earth, has eyes the color of sky, while Bennie, bound to this parallel realm, has orbs of basalt. It seems backward or inside-out...in physical contrast anyway. And I, with hazel eyes, float between each hybrid, keeping breath and natural boundary between domains, belonging to neither, but unto myself and Source.

I think about a small painting my mother once gave me, a hazel eye of blues, golds, and amber, with a black iris. A single swipe of red showed a cardinal staring into the void. "Bennie?" I ask. "Can I stay here, with you and Ailith?"

He offers me a light smile. "Luca would desperately miss you, and you, him," he says, pulling me to him, and I know this to be true.

"But I've desperately missed you too," I say.

"There is a feral-ness in Luca you require," Bennie says. "And a rationality in me you can't live without."

"And this is, okay?" I ask. "Isn't sleeping with two celestrial hybrids, especially brothers, some sort of unforgivable sin?"

"We aren't sleeping, and you sound incredibly...human," Bennie says. He plants a soft kiss on my head. "We aren't children anymore, Scathatch. Sin implies ownership and control, and you, my lovely, belong to no man, hybrid, or celestrial... only the Source. Humans make rules on Earth because it's a far-flung outpost with finite resources...and because humans, tragically, get greedy, and carve out their pettiness and jealousies, which, unfortunately, often include other humans—or hybrids—and a thing known as *marriage*. You may visit Skye, but you can't remain—just as it is for you on Ki. You're part of both. Maybe it will help if you think of me as your grounding wire and Luca as your alternating current. As a Balancer of positive and negative energies, you'll always need us both to thrive."

"The curse of the Balancer," I say, sadness creeping in as we rest by the fire. He strokes my hair and I run my hand along his chest, which is smooth as velvet.

"It's known as the '*Blessing* of the Balancer'," Bennie whispers just as I drift off to sleep...

A glowing sphere, an oversized egg about the size of a dresser, emerges from the air just above our heads. It expands and bifurcates. I nudge Bennie to rouse him, but he doesn't awaken, as if suppressed by some force that keeps him at rest. Flowy strands of white light sprout from each floating egg then grow into limbs, a set of four legs now standing in Bennie's study.

Two men in black suits hover before me, eerie chalk-colored skin, eyes so cold clear blue, I once didn't know if they were peril or protection. **Not Who**, as this particular *being* is known, is unlike anything most humans have ever seen. *It* takes the form of Air Force or Naval Intelligence officers who've been "sheep-dipped"—who used to be military but got discharged and immediately brought back as private contractors. They bend or break Earth's laws against those who witness things not meant for human eyes. Yet this weird-looking entity pretending to be two men-in-black are not them. *Not Who* is a celestial mercenary of the Ebians. It's not even close to being human or hybrid—and I know—it's here for me, to collect on the promise I made.

Not Who's double trouble form stands shoulder-to-shoulder, staring at me, each in possession of a red balloon tied around its wrists, the same sort of welcome balloon Barbara once gave me, and Bennie stole my first day at Plum Hook Bay. Dread settles with a thud in my stomach as I rub my forehead. *Not Who* says nothing. "I suppose you're here to make good on our deal," I say.

"We promised you freedom from your humanness if you threw Raga into the Source Vortex," *Not Who* says. "Freedom to travel among your kindred as a fully-fledged spirit being. Freedom to move about planets, galaxies, universes, dimensions, and perhaps, at times, to return here, to Ninmah's Portal, closer to the Source."

"This is Ninmah's Portal?" I ask. *Not Who* tips its chins up and down. "I still don't know what your offer means. The only thing I really know and remember is *being* hybrid, on Ki."

The black suits look at one another quizzically, then at me. They shake their heads in unison but remain silent, looking down, literally burning a hole in our blanket. There's smoke...

"Has anyone mentioned you're annoyingly creepy?" I say. "Stop doing that! Why are you here?"

"I have orders to break my promise," *Not Who* says. "I regret to inform you...you may not roam realms among those of your kindred at this time...if you so wish."

"What?! Whose orders?"

Not Who extinguishes the small flame with a dual stomp, and I throw off my part of the singed blanket. Bennie still sleeps, which I find bizarre, as if he's been drugged or purposely put under. I put two bare feet to the floor and slowly walk around his large mahogany desk, the one piled high with maps, artifacts, crystals, books, dried purple thistle and one silver case, which I'm sure contains the bio-electro-magnetic arachnid he made at Plum Hook Bay and named Cutie Pie.

"Your mother's orders," *Not Who* says.

"My mother? How is that possible? She was taken up by Ebians."

"Basasael made her a celestrial queen, gave her a realm as a belated wedding gift, and granted her a star system too, one she used to make a wish," *Not Who* says.

So, Basaseal found my mother.

I think about this for a minute...how Basasael helped me, then fled this realm to find his celestrial companion, my mother, leaving me on Ki to fend for myself. Then it occurs to me, crisp and clear, as if I'm hearing it sung by angels; and as Kahlil Gibran once wrote, children should be raised to fly away, like arrows—to hit their marks and flee the safety of the quiver, to find their loves, discover their destinies, and let go of the hand that keeps them. At first, I was bothered by my parents' abrupt flight from my current iteration on Ki and felt abandoned. Now, I understand. Just as I've been forced to keep my distance from Hope, so too, my parents from me, for the sake of our Earthly protection. And while I've always longed for a *normal* family, the absence of my parents made me stronger, self-reliant, and balanced, able to color outside of lines and open to risk.

"What was my mother's wish?" I ask.

"Your freedom to choose," *Not Who* says. "Free will..."

"We both know that when it comes to *free will*, cosmic terms and conditions apply," I say, looking at a compass on Bennie's desk, one just like mine.

"The Ebians would like to make you an offer," *Not Who* says.

"I knew there was more to this story," I say. "What sort of offer?" I sway and reach for the corner of the desk.

Stay upright, Sam. Breathe.

"Samantha!" Bennie yells.

It's the last thing I hear.

TWENTY-THREE

RETURNING

"SAMANTHA! Samantha, wake up! Please wake up. Come on, love...I know you're in there."

"Ailith," I whisper.

A tug on my dress and I'm foisted over the edge, out of the lotus pool. I'm too weak and wet to fight. I feel pruned from so much time in the water...lips press against mine...I choke, spit, and cough...coming back to life...to Ki life—to being human and hybrid again where I last fell, taking in gulps of air to quench instinctive human panic, sentience returned. As I lie splayed out like a fish that's flopped from its bowl, my eyes flutter open. Initially, I make out the hazy blueness of a tropical ocean—until I focus and realize Luca's eyes appear very much concerned.

"Oh, thank God," he says, pulling my upper body against his chest. "I thought we'd lost you forever."

I melt into him, exhausted, and sleep the sleep of a thousand slumbers.

When the sun peeks over a mountain, there is little left to indicate a monastery was ever built here. The main hall, the vault of violence I stood in with Dr. Evelyn three nights before, is obliterated. The grotesque displays passing as art...gone...taken by the Fluffle for decontamination. Saratu told me the souls will be embraced by what humans know as *angels,* taken up and healed, offered realms of their choosing. I draw the fur blanket tighter over my shoulders. I fix my mind on receding darkness. I've slept an entire night and day.

Nothing remains except the remains of humans and hybrids strewn across the landscape, their bodies bloating in cold pools of thickening blood, picked at by the beaks of rare Indian spotted eagles. The nuns and monks tend to what's left of the living, on the fringes near the edge of the jungle, the wounded, and the frightened.

Sentient beings die of this life in a myriad of ways, I think... some are murdered, poisoned, or starve, others freeze to death on mountains, some suffer sudden, unexpected accidents and illness, or they go off to, or get caught in, the crosshairs of war, and never come *home.* I scan my eyes over the battlefield. Even Genin didn't survive this raging battle. I never got to thank him.

One part of my heart grows exponentially in appreciation for Life and humans, while the other, less optimistic side, ticks away at how long humans, as a species, can cling to their feeble existence. Time, something humans require in order to flourish, is fleeing this planet. When the last of humanity is gone, and Earth's rhythm dries up, vibration, frequency, and energy will fade away —and all, including my kindred, and our multiple realms, will cease "to be."

It pains me too, when I think of Barbara and Reggie, how each died apart from the other when they wanted nothing more than to *be* together. Death, I've learned, doesn't accommodate humans or hybrids but works on its own timeline, every moment a potential and perpetual *Now* like the Isle of No Time.

From my vantage point on Saratu's balcony, I see Dr. Monica, hobbling along on her now bandaged leg and helped to a crumbling bench by Hogan. Reggie's body is gone from the ledge near the lotus pool, likely carried away by the monks for later internment and military rites, or perhaps cremation, something he always wanted. I'll have to contact Agent Abar at Langley to get Reggie's dress uniform shipped here, along with his decorations, medals, badges, ribbons, and insignia. Reggie and Barbara never had any children of their own and lived mostly *off paper* so I'm not sure if they wrote a last will and testament. Reggie would want Vigo's remains placed on the funeral pyre alongside him too.

Paramel briefly exits the jungle, squints up at me, and offers a sword lift semi-salute. I return the gesture before she shakes her head over the carnage, turns away, and recedes into the brush to care for the children she saved the day before. They've suffered trauma. She tells me she can modify her violet liquid to erase their most painful memories, things children should never have to see or bear.

My head swells with the low rumble of after-battle sounds, the clink of debris and discarded weapons, the grieving blare of monk horns, soulful and sad, as they lament misfortune over the mountains and through ambling valleys. The sharp smell of spilled blood and smoke invades my nostrils. I struggle to listen to some of the muted conversations going on around me, but I'm disinterested in the slices I hear. And then...I notice...the white lotuses in the pool have relinquished their tight grip, each unfolded like outstretched dove wings, straining toward a dusky sky.

Kitsune tries to comfort me with a soft lick against my knuckles. She whimpers until I give her a light scratch on the head. Then she trots forward a few steps and gently paws the ground. She's lost her pounce, I think. She lifts her snout in the air, tail down, ears laid back against her head and whines. She picks up a single twig with her mouth and drops it at my feet. Kitsune then gathers another and piles it over the first one until she's made a small monument to what I'd guess would be Vigo's memory. She's lost friends too. Animals, Bennie told me, grieve just as people do. How I will miss that handsome hybrid until our cosmic horizons meet again. Should be a couple of hundred Ki years, if I correctly calculated.

Tears freely and silently flow from my eyes, soaking the ground at my feet. I heave a sob to pull it inside and tuck it away. I half succeed, thinking mostly, about Ailith. I imagine her angelic face as she sleeps, oblivious to my world and life on Ki. I know this is a memory I've been permitted by *Not Who* to keep. Yet this forced parallel realm separation from my daughter causes an indescribable angst and sadness to take up permanent residence in my plexus.

"Samantha?"

And here is Luca, for the rest of this life I have, without Bennie or Ailith, Reggie or Barbara, Vigo, Genin, Verity, Pa Ling, Fensig, or Tetana.

I will remain with Luca tonight and we will spend the morning at Reggie and Vigo's memorial service. Then we'll get what's left of our things together and make our way to…I'm not sure where…I'm thinking Burundi. Luca tells me I've secured my position among the galaxy, holding court on Ki, but having domain over suburban realms from here to Hermia, and perhaps even as far away as Parabolian. Ours will now be a neutral life. Not great but not bad either. Tepid. Lukewarm. Temporarily secure. A hybrid's life, I'm learning, is rarely a fairytale, and this human incarnation is one I hope to never repeat.

A rising chill accompanies the setting sun. It's like a splash of water against my face. The taste of cold air on my tongue blunts the smell of corpses.

Luca leans against what's left of a wall in the shadows. "I've always preferred silence to words," he says. "But would you like to talk? I'm learning that friends talk. Or we can walk in silence if you prefer."

I go to him, and he drapes a large arm over my shoulders to secure the blanket. We amble away from the rotting butchery, into a portion of Saratu's mostly undamaged quarters, me feeling guilty about many things.

"Is there ever more to our lives than pain and loss?" I ask.

"Pain and loss pretty much sums it up for hybrids and humans," Luca says. "It's what we do, manage pain and loss—along with chaos—and minor moments of joy."

We walk and talk along lesser-traveled corridors of the monastery, sometimes between rooms, or through closets and storage spaces. We float together down long halls and over altars. I share with him how Dr. Awoudi found me years ago on the streets of Cleveland, and how Dr. Evelyn made me an offer to accompany her to Plum Hook Bay, and how Reggie and Barbara were there through it all...I tell him about how I met Bennie and Verity and the other foster kids at Plum Hook Bay, and all the things that have happened to me, between or since, on Ki.

We find ourselves in a rustic kitchen where Luca fires up a clay oven and proceeds to make proper steaming mugs of mushroom tea. He sits and listens—and then I sit and listen—to how he lost his mom, found his memory, made it to Ki and made a fortune, and then looked for Bennie and me. We suck down our last drops of boiled herbs and fungi when Luca looks at me and says, "The purple spiral on your forehead is gone." I try to remove the blood-red diamond from my finger to return it to him, but it won't budge. "Not even Annunan can break fate," Luca says. He takes my hand in his. "Saratu can marry us before we appear at the Ormian Council...if you desire to remain entangled with me ...and Bennie."

I jerk my head back, surprised he knows about his brother and isn't upset.

"I'm Chaos," he says. "Bennie is Order, and you, dear Samantha, are Balance between celestrial half-brothers," he says. "I don't like sharing you, but I do understand how this works. Here is not there and vice versa."

"Fate doesn't exactly work this way," I say.

"Perhaps not, but your sister Nemain did get word to Basasael regarding Annunan's nuptial order. It's my understanding your parents weren't very happy with him and refused to confer their blessing when he tried to enforce Sakar."

"Bilby referred to me as Queen on the battlefield," I say.

"You balanced forces and threw Raga into the Source Vortex. Your coronation is assured."

"I suppose this means if I marry you—you become king," I say.

"Queen consort," Luca says. "You're still the boss...as much as it pains me."

"Oh?"

"Your mother insisted."

"I see."

"Marriage doesn't have to be our goal," Luca says.

"I've never considered marriage a goal," I say. "I think of it more as a state of mind in which two beings should simultaneously arrive."

"You'll make a wise queen."

"And what of your Bezaliel mist?" I ask.

"We have secured temporary peace on Ki," Luca says. "When the scales tip again, you'll need my feral-ness."

"And how do you expect the scales to tip?"

"The Elemorphia were unable to inhale every Bezaliel," he says. "Some of their mist escaped. Bezaliels will hibernate, regroup, and create a new Raga. Could be centuries from now—could be tomorrow."

"If we tell any humans about this outside of Dr. Monica and Hogan, they'll think we're insane," I say.

"All the best hybrids are," he jokes, a slight smirk gathering in the corners of his mouth. "But seriously, Septum Oculi and our respective Ki governments are already aware of most of what's transpired here and are...*en route.*"

"Why?"

"To mount the biggest coverup since Roswell and Rendlesham," he says. "Humans aren't ready for the truth."

"It frightens me that you're probably right," I say. "How long do we have to disappear?"

"Abar bought us a couple of days," he says. "After the bodies are bagged and tagged, the Army Corps of Engineers will help Saratu and the monks rebuild. Our country's governmental spin teams will label this otherworldly battle a local civil war and blame the Chinese. I figure the short attention span of humans will render this entire business into the realm of conspiracy theory or myth, classified on Ki for centuries—or until humans are ready for disclosure."

"Will disclosure ever happen?" I ask, hesitant to know the answer but wanting to hear it.

"It will happen when humans become okay with not knowing where they might eat or sleep every night and that they won't have a job to go to on Monday mornings. It will happen when they forget what *weekends* are and remember how to look up instead of slouching with their heads buried in technology. It will happen when chaos overrides monetary and religious systems. The Ormian Council's simulations reveal that any celestial disclosure at this time will cause widespread panic among those who never learned that Ki already provides everything they need, rather than everything Kihogs think they want."

When we reach Saratu's quarters, I stare out a window examining stars. I wonder if the planets rotating around them, if they even have planets orbiting them, experience the same adventures or imaginations found on Ki. Is there anything sentient and intelligent to breathe life into their systems—or are they simply frozen rocks, vast empty oceans, or molten spheres void of drama, stories, myths, and legends?

"Sam, you need to see this," Luca says.

I jerk my head back to *now*. "See what?"

Luca curls a finger for me to follow him as he ducks into a tiny room.

We walk a few short steps through a narrow hall, and I thrust my arms deeper into the blanket for warmth. That's when I feel something within the pocket of my nightwear and abruptly stop.

"Sam? What is it?"

"It's a buckeye," I say, and hold it up to him. "It's sprouting."

The veils are drawn back and two bangs echo through the monastery. A door leading to a tiny shrine is open, its light warm and inviting against the death and chaos outside. It's a small room with a single half arch running along the ceiling. A familiar sword hangs from a strap, attached to the highest point in the room. A light breeze from the open window causes the sword to slightly sway and spin. It is then I stop in my tracks. My heart ticks in my ears like a grandfather clock striking midnight when I see Camael, intact, standing in a corner, wearing the form in which he first found me—Cameron the Cop. He places an index finger to his lips and points. A single tear trickles down my cheek.

I pause behind the little girl and Reggie, who have their backs to me, my mouth agape. Long russet ringlets fall down the back of her saffron robe. They kneel before an altar of a Buddhist deity known as *White Tara*, goddess of wisdom and compassion. It is said that *Tara* has seven eyes—all-seeing—and often returns to Earth as a woman, to help humans reach enlightenment...an Emergent.

I quietly kneel beside them, looking up at the thangka above our heads. It is then I spot Bennie's bio-electromagnetic spider Cutie Pie creep behind the frame.

"I thought you were dead," I say to Reggie without looking at him.

"Typical," he leans over and whispers. "I find it cliché that the black guy always dies in the movies, don't you? I may have to phone a lawyer."

"Is that so?" I ask.

"You keep putting me through this shit and I might," he says. He pushes Bennie's tin of salve in front of me. "Thank you."

I slide the sprouting buckeye toward the little girl. She smiles widely with what looks like glee and tilts her head in my direction. She blinks at the buckeye with sage eyes, leans into me, and whispers, "Mum, did you know I can be in two places at once?"